INVISIBLE MAGIC
BOOK 1: ALEX NOZIAK

MARY BUCKHAM

AWARD WINNING AUTHOR

Cover and book design by
THE KILLION GROUP
www.thekilliongroupinc.com

DEDICATION

This book is dedicated to all the readers who have supported
me along the way.
Thank YOU!

ACKNOWLEDGEMENTS

A note of appreciation to P.J. Friel, Anne Norup and Laurel Wilczek for being early readers of this story. You guys rock! Thanks to Kim Killion for a cover I love and Jennifer Jakes for formatting the pages and patience beyond measure. A special thanks to Mimi Munk for copyediting, you are my Grammar Goddess. Also, a huge hug to Dianna Love for her support and lovely cover quote as well as eagle-eyed reading. You're a pearl beyond price. And, of course, thank you to my husband who keeps me sane—which is a full time job! Any mistakes or adjustments in detail for the purpose of fiction are entirely my own doing.

CHAPTER 1

First demon you summon, it's kind of scary. After a few hundred, it becomes just another job. Unfortunately I hadn't reached that point.

My name's Alex Noziak and I'm one of the five sorry-assed members of a team called the Invisible Recruits that are supposed to stand between the world's humans and the rising population of non-human bad guys. One of the team was here voluntarily, and it wasn't me. But that wasn't my biggest problem right this minute.

Wrestling with an echo-demon that looked mostly like green slime and a smattering of the living dead was.

I'm part shaman, part witch, not a card-carrying Wiccan but a blood-born witch, and one of my abilities was to summon others to me, both human and non-human, but only within a limited range. Sounds useful, but how many times do you really want to invite a Were, or vamp, or foul-mouthed dark angel to a party? Exactly, which was why that particular summoning spell was a little rusty. Okay, a truck that sits on the back forty for twenty years is rusty. I was in the what-the-hell-am-I-doing category.

Embracing magic was not a piece of cake, because it came at a cost. Always. My last summoning here at the IR (I for Invisible and R for Recruits) compound was coming back to bite me now. Sort of like an athlete who was a star performer one day but a dud the next. So now I was more witch-wanna-be who had to produce something, and fast, to keep my spot on the team.

A thought one of my team members actually voiced just about then. "You going to make this demon appear sometime in this millennium, Noziak?" Mandy Reyes snapped, standing kitty-corner from me across the training gym at our Maryland facility.

Mandy had hot Latin blood, a mouth like a stevedore, the patience of a gnat, and was one of the four non-voluntary members of the team. I wasn't sure what was being held over her head to work this gig, but I knew it couldn't be pleasant. I also knew her talent-she was a spirit walker. Which meant she could walk between the spirit world and the real world. Again, sounds cool, but the price for that specific ability was to be soulless. Which meant when you were on the spirit side, or when spirits crossed over or remained on our side, you were an empty vessel with a neon For Rent sign flashing. Any spirit looking for a new home, she was the perfect candidate.

Right now though roving spirits weren't our issue; a missing echo-demon was as four of us maneuvered in a gym that looked like an average high school holding cell. Nothing fancy for our group. Mandy and fellow team members Jaylene Smart and Kelly McAllister formed a triangle around an X-marked-the-spot circle. A circle that was outlined in salt for protection once I called forth the demon as training for taking one down in real life.

Our instructor, M.T. Stone, and our team leader, Vaughn Monroe, the only one of us not coerced into being an IR agent as far as we could tell, were watching this exercise from a room near the rafters. Smart people.

Not that an echo-demon was all that threatening; they were nuisances more than deadly as they had earned their names based on their willingness to make a lot of high-volume screams that could scare the willies out of people and echo in a person's mind long after the demon had departed. At least when the demons traveled alone they were manageable. In packs, they could turn really nasty, really quick.

The intention of this little training session was to make sure I knew what the hell I was doing, which I didn't. Get some practice in whipping demon butt before we left the safety of the compound. And learn to work as a team.

That last was the biggest challenge. None of the five IR members were even trained to fight *human* bad guys yet. We were just humans who had a little extra-extra to our genetic make-up which would make us freaks among humans, *if* the humans knew what we were. The four of us had spent most of our twenty-some years hiding our talents unless we really needed them, like I had when a rogue Were was about to kill my brother.

I had used a summoning spell. That was my first mistake. Second was summoning a death demon who made such a mess of the Were that I faced life in prison for murder. Try telling a lawyer or judge there were extenuating circumstances, like the victim was a Were and my brother was a shifter who was caught turning, which meant he was too vulnerable to defend himself. I was damned lucky I hadn't killed my brother along with the Were.

Yeah, so that's why I was here, sweat pouring down my face, my arms shaking from holding them straight before me for the last thirty minutes and my throat getting hoarse from repeating a summoning spell that wasn't working.

Instead of telling can't-you-do-more Mandy where to shove her comment, I was saved by Kelly. "Leave her be, Mandy. You can tell she's trying."

That was Kelly all over. Raised in the flat farm country of Iowa and a former kindergarten teacher, Kelly could make muggers melt with kindness. She was our team placater, the rah-rah cheerleader and the let's-all-play-nice playground monitor. She'd never said what had landed her here, but it was probably because she had sweet-talked someone to death. Nothing else made sense.

Kelly's ability was to disappear. Which sounds uber cool, but that too came with a price. She could remain truly invisible for only a few minutes at a time and when she reappeared she was blind for twice as long for every minute of invisibility. Which made her really vulnerable to attack if all the bad things were not vanquished. Another downside to her ability was that she wasn't very good with it, so that when she was frightened she could wink out of sight unintentionally.

But then who was I to talk about being proficient?

Kelly stood braced just to my right, and though I couldn't see her except out of the corner of my eye, I could feel her gripping a sword with a white-knuckle death grip. Echodemons hated metal, as did a lot of the non-humans, so this late afternoon's session was steel vs. demon blood.

If I ever called the freaking monster forth.

I glanced at the observation room window and caught M.T. Stone eyeing his watch. But what did he expect? We were barely three weeks into our regular training and only just started flexing our other abilities earlier this week. That was after one of our fellow recruits tried to kill me and wasn't too picky who else she took out at the same time. About the time, I wondered if prison might not have been the safer option.

Then we'd gone on one official mission, but that was mostly a babysitting session when Vaughn went up against the son of a Russian mob lord-a guy she had known in her previous life as a debutante. It wasn't a picnic, but it wasn't demon baiting either.

Talk about neophytes. Most of us rarely, if ever, voluntarily used our gifts in the world we came from and some, like Jaylene and Mandy, had skills that didn't directly translate into taking down anyone. Jaylene was a psychic, or had visions. A fat lot of good it did to hang out with visions when monsters were out for blood. Human blood. Even I could guess at what the future held in that situation.

M.T. Stone's voice broke over the loudspeaker making all of us jump. "This is a no show. We'll call it a night. Try again tomorrow."

"No," I shouted back. I'd been raised with four older brothers; I could hear M.T.'s tone if not his thoughts. Wimp. Lightweight. Poser. No one called a Noziak a loser and got away with it, even if it was my own inner voice. "Give me one more minute. Let me take this up a notch."

"You sure that's a good idea?" Jaylene asked.

"Yeah." Though I wasn't really.

I heard Mandy and Jaylene groan, which only helped me go deeper. I could do this. I would do this.

Here in this place and before the eyes of the unbelievers, come forth.
I call the creatures of the elements. The seekers of release who wish to walk amongst the humans.
I bid you to destroy the binds holding you in thrall.
Come. Prove yourselves.

Salty sweat seeped into my eyes. I bit my lip till I could taste blood.

Of course! There was no human blood. What an idiot I was. That was the missing piece.

"Jaylene, cut your finger and squeeze a few blood drops into the inner circle," I shouted, holding my pose. This was blood magic, second cousin to black magic, but just a smidge might help. White magic sure wasn't doing squat.

"No way am I cutting myself," came the bullet-fired retort. Jaylene might be six feet tall and built like an Amazon, with looks that could earn her a fortune as a model, but growing up alone on Chicago's south side had made her very wary of sticking her neck or a bloody finger out for anybody.

"I'll do it," Kelly offered and stepped forward.

"No." She'd probably cut a vein with her sword and then disappear on us before we could stop the bleeding. "I'll do it myself."

I dropped my arms, swiping one bare arm across my forehead to wipe the sweat as I reached with the other toward Kelly. "Put your sword out here."

She did as I asked even though the blade shook. It was wicked sharp, the better for demon killing, but instead of a paper cut I dug a pretty deep slash into my right finger. "Ouch."

I swear I could hear Mandy snicker so I shot her a glare, cupping my right hand with my left to make sure I didn't leave a trail of blood for the demon to escape the inner containment circle. Just in case my teammates were not quick enough, or skilled enough to kill him.

That was one of the sucky parts of being the one doing the summoning. I couldn't be holding a weapon of any kind, no matter how deadly the non-human being called. If this echo-demon found a way past the containment area, I was sorry out of luck. Except for my anathema dagger I had stashed against the nearest wall. Noziaks came to a rumble prepared to fight, but witches couldn't carry other weapons when using magic. Which made us very vulnerable.

Using magic with a physical weapon in hand—a gun, knife, staff—meant the magic was not being honored and it could back fire on the user.

It took a few steps to reach the crudely salted circle where the demon should appear, and only seconds to have a nice snack of fresh human blood drops scattered on the floor.

Man, a sliced finger could hurt. Sucking it as I returned to my spot I realized I was focusing on the minor pain to avoid the bigger issue. If the blood did its thing then I was about to break a promise made to my father years ago. He was a full-blooded shaman, a shifter, and a wise man in his own right. Plus he loved me to the depths of his soul. He rarely punished his children, especially me, the baby, but when he did it was serious.

"Great gifts are not given lightly, Alex," he'd said. "They come with great responsibility and consequences. Do you understand?"

I nodded my head like any fifteen-year-old who wanted to get out of immediate trouble for doing something wrong.

"Then you must promise never to use your abilities for harm of anyone or anything."

More head shaking on my part. Right then I'd have agreed to anything he'd asked. That's how much trouble I was in.

"Promise me as a Noziak."

My head had started to bob faster when he'd raised one calloused hand. "And the love you have for me."

That wasn't playing fair. Especially since, after my mother had left us when I was five, my dad had been my whole world.

"Will you promise this, Alex?"

What could I say? I nodded and meant it.

I sucked in my breath, ignoring the throbbing in my finger which I pressed tight against my thumb to make sure the blood flow was stopped. It was harder to push aside the tenseness in my gut, wondering if calling a demon to its death meant I was harming another? Or if my dad would forgive me if he ever found out, because I felt a shift in the air and I wasn't giving up now for anything.

CHAPTER 2

I ignored Kelly's breathing next to me, Mandy's scowl across from me, and Jaylene tightening both her hands along her sword's shaft. The late afternoon sunlight was streaming through clearstory windows around the gym, the hiss of kerosene lamps I'd set up for backup lighting mingling with the quiet. Demon baiting in the dark was suicidal.

My voice was calm and deep as I raised my hands and began the summoning chant once more:

Here in this place and before the eyes of the unbelievers, come forth.
I call the creatures of the elements. The seekers of release who wish to walk amongst the humans.
I bid you to destroy the binds holding you in thrall.
Come. Prove yourselves.

A faint wind brushed against my skin. A hot, dry wind, not from damp Maryland in March, but someplace far away. Smelling of sulfur and brine.

I squeezed my eyes shut and kept chanting, stretching my arms higher, deepening my voice, ignoring the frisson of warning along my skin.

There is a reason for being. Journey here. Now.
May your masters honor and bow before you. Sending you on your way.
You who laugh at the mortals. Come close.
Echo-demon I summon thee!

The wind picked up and I swore I could feel grit and sand abrading my skin. Kelly caught her breath. I kept my eyes closed.

We welcome you demon of the deep. Come play with us. Show us your might.

Demons did love a dare.

The lights in the room flickered then went out. My eyelids flew open. Fortunately the few kerosene lanterns stayed lit even as they cast long wavering shadows dancing across the room and deepening the darkness in all four corners.

Mandy was no longer scowling but sending wary glances over both shoulders. Jaylene faced where the danger was greatest, head-on, towards the circle. After her childhood, what was one lone demon?

Kelly's breathing came short and shallow. I feared she'd hyperventilate before I finished the summoning. But I couldn't stop now. The echo-demon was too close. I could feel its presence like sharp cat claws stepping paw-by-paw across my exposed arms. The tensing of my neck and shoulders. The knot tightening in my gut.

"Come on," I whispered. "Show your ugly face. Come forth and die."

Now! Echo-demon. Close nearby as day dissolves into night. Show us your—

The explosion ripped through the room, tossing me far enough backwards that I landed with a curse on my tailbone. Ten feet in front of me, Jaylene and Mandy held their positions. They were no longer waiting or wary. Legs braced, swords held high, muscles tensed. They were ready for bear.

Crap. Where was. . .Kelly had winked out. Only her sword shook in the flickering light. The late afternoon sky had clouded over, as if evil brought its own darkness.

And not one but three echo-demons swirled like a bad nightmare in the middle of the gym; twelve feet tall, brackish green in color, scales covering their bodies as they materialized into more corporeal shapes. First one, with three horns sprouting from his misshapen head, then the second, with a gaping mouth of shark-like teeth, and then the third, with a double-forked tail, each ending in a knobby spike.

Oh by the Great Spirits, what had I done?

CHAPTER 3

Kelly's sword splattered against the ground as the horned demon laughed. A rasping, high-pitched roar climbing the scales that could make a hardened soldier's blood curdle and be heard as far as Washington D.C.

What the heck were the four, or the three of us who were visible, to do now?

Not sit on our asses for sure. I pushed my hands to the floor to jump to my feet. Too late, I realized my mistake. I forgot my bleeding finger.

Even this far from the kerosene lights I could see the splayed imprint of the fingers of my right hand against the floorboard. A jagged outline of blood from my still bleeding finger clearly visible.

I'd just given the demons permission to break the containment circle.

"Watch out," I shouted, slamming forward, unarmed. "They're free."

Too late. The laughing one had already swooped toward Mandy who was whirling and slashing as if she'd been in sword fights all her life.

Jaylene swore and attacked the two demons still wavering in the circle.

Go Amazon!

I rushed toward Kelly's sword only to trip and fly, face first onto the floor beneath the nearest demon. The one with the snapping jaws who gaped down at me, looking as surprised as I was. At least I thought his expression was surprise and not, "oh-yippee-ki-yay—a snack."

I'd forgotten that just because I couldn't see Kelly didn't mean she wasn't there.

Idiot.

Dead idiot if I didn't do something.

Kelly's sword was out of my reach as I rolled away from a massive, clawed paw slamming the floorboards beside me. The two-tailed demon was no longer off guard and no longer immobilized.

But it would be, I thought, as I rolled onto my back, pulled my knees toward me, and thrust my feet out, hoping what I aimed for was a set of very large demon balls.

Being raised with brothers taught me where males were most vulnerable and not to hold back when in a brawl. Especially a life or death one.

A blood-curdling scream rattling my eardrums told me I'd guessed right.

Score one for Noziak.

The demon curled in on himself, not enough to be out of commission, but enough for me to clamber to my knees and slam a shoulder into the backside of the nearest other demon knee, the demon Jaylene battled.

It faltered, but that was all. My shoulder would be black and blue for a week.

Now I knew how David fighting Goliath felt. But at least he'd had a slingshot.

Two-tail monster was straightening, looking as pissed off as an echo-demon could. He released another bone-rattling scream and lunged toward me.

The only place for me to back away was deeper beneath the shark-toothed one Jaylene fought. But if I scuttled too far beneath it, I risked Jaylene slashing me. Not far enough and I could be smashed by one of two-tail's hammer tails or his reaching claws.

"Alex!" Kelly screamed my name from somewhere outside the circle as I saw a sword sliding across the floor my way. I just hoped Kelly wasn't attached to it.

I turned, curled, and lunged as if heading for home plate with a third out hanging in the balance.

My grab for the sword was clumsy, but I wasn't going for style points as I grabbed and thrust the slicing sword's edge toward the nearest green. It proved to be the leg of the two-tailed monster that wanted me. Bad.

"Take that. And that." Yeah, I sounded like a cartoon character, but if I could shout I could still breathe as I slashed right and left, aiming for tendons, or joints, or anything that would topple this monster. I fought from the floor and then my knees. The team's martial arts instructor was going to rake me over the coals for my sloppy control.

If I lived.

"Mandy," I heard Jaylene scream somewhere to my right. "Get up."

Not sounding good.

And all my slashing and hacking was like dismantling a California Redwood with a butter knife. Only this dude was yucky green and grinning as if it knew whatever I did was in vain.

Think, Noziak, think.

But with an echo-demon bearing down on me thinking was the last luxury I had.

I slammed the sword hard enough into the monster's foot to earn another roar and vibrations up my arm as the blade bit into floorboard beneath the beast.

Damn.

"Noziak, roll away," a voice shouted. Male. Must be Stone.

Thank God, the cavalry had arrived.

I didn't question but flipped into an awkward, wobbly roll taking me a few feet away from the heat of the battle. I hadn't even come to a full stop when I heard a hissing rat-a-tat-tat like a muted jackhammer.

What?

I scrambled to my knees, sword held at an angle in front of me, my arms shaky from muscle burn and saw the two-tailed echo-demon doing the rumba.

Wiping sweat out of my eyes. I could see it wasn't dancing as much as reacting to a warfare stun gun gripped in the hands of Stone, standing not five feet from it. The scent of burning demon flesh made me throw my arm across my nose, but it didn't help. Besides, I could see Jaylene needed backup with the two demons converging on Mandy.

Jaylene held the most threatening demon at bay as I rose to my feet and rushed forward to do a swoop and grab toward Mandy who cradled her good arm and was tottering on her feet. Of course a swoop and grab works best when the other person knows I'm coming, is capable of grabbing my arm back, and isn't freaked to the max. Instead I did a body tackle that splayed Mandy on the floor a good ten feet from the nearest monster. I jackknifed to my feet, hearing her cussing a string of Spanish I didn't want to know the meaning of.

"You're welcome," I shouted as I ran and slashed at the nearest demon, the shark-jawed one.

"Just hold them off," I panted at Jaylene, fighting almost shoulder to shoulder, which wasn't smart with swords, but we'd gone from smart to suicidal the second the demons had appeared. I'd be happy for survival.

"Stone coming." Hack.

"Stun gun." Hack. Hack.

"Hold on." Splat.

An arm bigger than my mid-section swatted my shoulder and sent me careening into the nearest wall, taking out a kerosene lantern on the way, and ending in a sprawl against wooden side boards.

The air whooshed out of me as the lantern winked, then sputtered out. I swear my bones rattled.

"What the . . ." I raised my head enough to see Stone had one demon down, but not dead, unless they could twitch indefinitely. Stone was tasering the horned one while Jaylene had taken over swiping at Jaws. But her strikes were wide and weakening.

Swords weren't cutting it. Pun intended as I scrambled for what would stop these things. For good.

A drop of blood slipped into my vision from a cut near my right eye. It stung like a banshee's bite but knocked some sense into me.

At last.

I'd summoned the demons. I should be able to send them back.

Optimum word being the word *should*.

I mentally apologized to my dad for the second vow I was breaking. Calling forth demons, of any kind, came at a cost. Sending them back did not eliminate the price the one who summoned them had to pay. This was not a child's game.

No kidding.

Besides I didn't know if I had enough left in me to do anything except flap my hands, and even that was in doubt.

I wavered to my feet, bending at the waist as cracked or broken ribs were not giving me much leeway.

Fine. I stretched my arms from there, no doubt looking more like a bowing supplicant than an all-powerful witch-shaman.

Inhaling as deep a breath as I could, I tried to ground myself in the moment, ignoring Jaylene and Stone fighting without me as I shouted the names of the four elemental kings.

Yod He Vau He, king of the east.
Adoni, king of the south.
Eheieh, king of the west.
Agla, king of the north, from whence all warriors abide.
Call back those who belong to you.

My voice wasn't loud enough. I sounded more like a wheezing lightweight. But if I didn't get this spell cast, Jaylene was going down. Then Stone. Then the rest of us.

I straightened a little more, gasping at the pain and pushing it to the side, ignoring my blurring vision.

I conjure thee O Circle of Power that beist a boundary between the realms of men and the realms of demon-kind.
Guardian and Protection I shall preserve and contain.
As I have called so shall I send.
Be gone!
Demons of the deep. Be gone!

I slid to my knees, every ounce of energy within me sucked dry. Except for one last call.

Be gone!

The power of three. With a loud crack as if something solid torn asunder shook the room, Jaylene staggered backwards. Mandy remained curled on the floor. And even Stone, the one amongst us with the most battle experience, swayed.

But I didn't care. Not then. Right then I was a hundred percent focused on the swirl of orange and red sweeping from what had been the middle of the containment circle. Only now it was a vacuum of power, a whirlwind spinning counter clockwise and inhaling the three demons as if they were fallen leaves.

Stone ducked. Jaylene fell to her knees, head bowed.

Kelly's voice shouted, "Take that you green baddies."

Baddies? Muggers and forgers were baddies. Echo-demons in mass? Oh, we'd passed baddies a long time ago.

The volcano of power whirled and twirled and then, poof, disappeared.

And silence reigned, broken only by the hiss of the remaining lanterns, heavy breathing by all of us, and a small whimper from someone. I couldn't even manage that.

Jaylene crawled toward where Mandy lay in a motionless fetal curl. Stone looked around as if not trusting the disappearance, or he was trying to figure out where Kelly was.

I just concentrated on my next shallow breath. It was all I could do. That and try not to let go and sink into the oblivion clawing at me.

Noziaks didn't faint.

Until Jaylene called out, her voice hard and guttural, "She's dead. You killed her."

Damn, what had I done?

Maybe, just this once a Noziak could black out.

CHAPTER 4

The following morning I was still asking myself what had I done wrong. But for different reasons.

I was flat on my back in one of those sterile hospital beds in the compound's infirmary. Morning light cantered through the side windows, making everything look more metallic and white than it was, if that were possible.

You know the uppity-ups expected a high-casualty rate when the fanciest, most well-equipped room I'd seen so far at the training ground was the hospital. No doubt this place saw a lot of action. I hadn't seen the morgue yet, so maybe that was even more state-of-the-art.

"You're an idiota, Noziak. You know that? A freaking pendejo."

And this was my punishment. A bed next to Mandy with no bars, no sound baffling, and no referee between us.

Jaylene had been wrong. Mandy hadn't died. Close, but not close enough. She might feel like death was still an option, but she was alive and kicking with her mouth, the only weapon still available to her. And man, was she using it.

A very small, very petty part of me wondered what it'd take to quiet a spirit walker? What kind of dispersing spell might work? Not for good, but long enough to have her shut up.

But it seems that it takes a lot more than an echo-demon attack to take out a Latina spirit walker.

My luck.

"Didn't the doctors tell you to keep a lid on it?" I snarled back, wishing I could turn on my side away from her, but the bandaged ribs, cracked not broken, and bruises along both shoulders made that move too painful to contemplate. And it was only last week that I'd regained use of my left hand, badly mauled by a Were-hyena the first week of training.

"Docs said I was lucky to be alive. No thanks to you."

"Weren't you the one busting my chops to get a little demon action?" I asked in my smarmiest, sugar-coated voice. The one my brothers would recognize meant walk warily around me. But Mandy was not one of my brothers, or my family, or even a friend.

Damn, I should have accepted the pain meds when they'd offered them earlier. But no, Noziaks didn't do painkillers.

"You are one dumbass bruja," Mandy continued as if she hadn't heard me. "And you're supposed to be our ace in the hole. More like ass in the hole. Our asses, your hole."

Okay, I got it. She had a busted arm, a fracture in her right leg, and a gash or two, or maybe more, but that didn't mean I had to lie here and take her crap. Not when I had enough crap of my own swirling through me.

Guilt. Regret. Anger.

Mandy was right. I'd nearly killed the whole squad in one training exercise. And I hadn't even told them it was a bloody miracle that the dispersal ritual had worked. Stone expected us to work together as a unit, dependent on each other for survival when we faced non-humans on assignment. What was going to happen when we hit the real world, with real demons and other monsters that made echo-demons look like pussycats?

My mind whirred through a litany of bad-ass non-humans and they were only the ones I knew about, no telling what other ghoulies walked the earth.

Maybe life in prison wasn't such a bad option. There all I'd have to worry about was staying alive. Here I had that to deal with while praying to the Great Spirits I didn't kill anyone else. Especially someone depending on me to protect them. What if it had been Kelly in that bed instead of smart-mouthed Mandy? The room would be quieter, but the guilt would be even worse. Or Kelly in the morgue because of me?

That was it. Let the IR team be minus a worthless witch-shaman. Let them find someone else to summon evil and battle it at the same time. I sucked at both abilities.

"I'm out of here," I mumbled, grabbing the bedsheets with a white-knuckled grip to yank me into a sitting position, one accompanied by a lot of grimaces and shallow breaths.

First stop: tell Ling Mai, head of this organization, that I was reneging on my earlier agreement. I was now opting for Door Number One. Life in prison for killing the rogue Were who'd attacked my brother.

Second stop: say goodbye to Kelly, the only one of the IR team members who would actually notice I wasn't around anymore. Vaughn, the team leader, might catch that I'd vamoosed, but I didn't want to hang around long enough to track her down.

Third stop: find a phone and call my dad before I was hauled off in cuffs.

Yup, sounded like a plan to me. Sweat had popped out on my forehead by the time my bare feet hit the coolness of the linoleum floor.

"What the hell do you think you're doing?" Mandy grumbled, turning her head in my direction.

She looked like hell, with green and blue bruises marring her face, her jaw swollen, and a killer of a black right eye. For once, I didn't feel like pointing out the bad news.

"I'm going back to where I belong," I managed between gritted teeth. Both feet were now on the floor, but I was standing only by my death grip on the bed and sweat soaked my cotton hospital gown.

"You're heading back to Podunk, nowhere Idaho?"

"It's Mud Lake." I shook my head. Big mistake as the ringing bells took up residence and my vision blurred. "And no, I'm goin' to prison."

Mandy actually whistled, one of those low, can't-believe-what-I'm-hearing sounds.

That made me crack a smile. Now I knew how to shut her up. Shock her into silence.

But she surprised me. Before I could do anything more than breathe Mandy was back chewing on me. "Ling Mai's under a lot of pressure to make the agency succeed."

"And I should care because?"

"She'll sacrifice any of us in a heartbeat if it makes the team stronger. Especially a screwed-up witch."

"Don't you get it? I'm making her job easier." I exhaled and shuffled forward.

"Ling Mai doesn't like to fail. You bail on her, there'll be a bigger cost than going back to wherever you came from."

Maybe, maybe not. If I bailed that might save face for Ling Mai. It wasn't like I was screwing up a mission and she had to scramble to hide the fact one of her agents couldn't cut it.

I glanced around the room, looking for where they'd stashed my clothes when the thud of footsteps marching down the hallway made me look up. Another painful move that had me sucking air. Who knew how much of a person's ribcage was attached to the rest of their body?

It was M.T. Stone, looking as gruff and dangerous as he was, even if he wasn't that much older than I was. He was the poster boy for what an assassin should look like: whipcord lean, muscles rippling beneath his black t-shirt, hair that dark shade between brown and black and cut short, so short an opponent wouldn't have anything to grab in hand-to-hand combat.

As if any opponent were stupid enough to even try. Stone had that edgy danger vibe that either said psychotic threat or lethal mercenary. I hadn't made up my mind which it was, even if Vaughn and he were now an item.

Our team leader must like walking on the wild side. Waking up next to Stone would be like waking up next to a hungry panther. Not an easy thing to do.

But no longer my problem. Vaughn was a big girl and could handle herself way better than her debutante image made you think.

And Stone? He'd always land on his feet, most likely with a dead body nearby.

But I was determined to say my goodbyes, pack what I could take to the Gray House, and head out as soon as I could move.

"What do you want?" I growled at Stone, not caring if I sounded snarly and pissed off. He wasn't my instructor anymore.

"Where you going?" he asked in that low-timbered, hint of a Southern charm voice, that left no doubt he was going to get answers.

"She's goin' to prison," Mandy piped up from the other bed. "Knew she was a lightweight. Goin' when the goin' gets tough."

If I could have swung round and bopped her one I would have. No Noziak was a lightweight unless they were dead, and I wasn't running away. No matter what it looked like.

"That true?" Stone asked, holding his ground, like a steel wall to walk through, rather than around.

"Yeah." I ducked my head. "I'm out of here."

He shrugged. Which stung. No pep talk, no convincing me I was wrong, just a roll of the shoulders that made me feel like an A-plus loser. That and it made me want to crawl back in the bed and pull the white sheets over my head.

"Better report to Ling Mai first," he said, as if my bailing were expected and not news. "She'll want to know."

Well screw him and his stick-up-the-backside attitude. Same with Mandy. This time tomorrow and they'd be so far behind me I'd forget their names in a week.

"Good." I straightened but couldn't stop a wince, which Stone caught but said nothing except narrowing his eyes. "I was heading to Ling Mai as soon as I found where my clothes were stashed."

I wasn't crawling to the director in a wispy hospital gown. Enough of me had been stripped already. My determination, my pride, my backbone. I'd salvage what I could, even if it killed me to wrestle into a pair of jeans and a t-shirt.

Stone marched over to a cupboard behind the open door, flung it open, grabbed a stack of clothes that stunk of sweat and echo-demon slime, tossed them on my bed and said, "I'll wait for you outside."

It was all I could do not to stick my tongue out at him as the door clicked shut behind his exit.

Supercilious prig.

Thirty minutes later I knew I was right about two things. Tussling into day old, stiff clothes was not a piece of cake, and left me sweating and bracing my legs to hold myself upright. And the second thing: I was more determined than ever to say goodbye to the Invisible Recruit agency and compound.

That's what I kept repeating to myself as I followed Stone's straight back gait over what must have been a mile of hallways until we reached Ling Mai's office in the main house. The compound had started life as a summer retreat for a wealthy DC mucky-muck back when rich houses meant tons of stone, rare woods, high ceilings, and a staff of servants to dust and clean the place.

My shuffling footsteps echoed on the wood floors as we came to Ling Mai's closed door and Stone stopped. He shot me an appraising glance, one that had his eyes narrowing again. "You're sure you're up to this?"

How many times did I have to repeat to myself that Noziaks were not lightweights? Though I could understand why Stone's basilisk-like face actually showed concern. Even if the expression was gone as fast as it'd appeared.

My skin was clammy with sweat, hair tendrils glued to my face though my waist-length hair was pulled back into a ragged braid. I was breathing heavily, if in short gasps, and was chewing my lip to keep from moaning. "I'm sure." I wished it hadn't come out like a wimpy whisper.

Stone straightened. "Fine. Your call." He knocked once then pushed the door open. "After you."

The man was not a half-wit. Facing Ling Mai with news she didn't want was only for fools or desperate idiots. I fell into both categories.

"Miss Noziak." Ling Mai nodded her regal head an inch as I shuffled into her office, a setting that matched her cosmopolitan background. Gold brocaded chairs, an ornate desk that was probably some fancy furniture style, Louis the XIV or something, a small Chinese altar very discreetly tucked into the feng shui power position, according to Jaylene.

Ling Mai was Director of the IR Agency, a gracious Amerasian woman of indeterminate age, but probably somewhere between thirty-five and late forties, killer looks, and a soul-deep poise, especially in times of crisis. Her self-assurance made me feel like I still carried the dirt of Mud Lake, Idaho on my boots.

She was the last person one would suspect of running a group of covert operatives tasked by the U.S. alphabet agencies to do the jobs they couldn't or wouldn't tackle. And only a few power brokers in those agencies knew about the recruits' additional abilities. The woo-woo factor. Most humans didn't know or believe in non-humans, but a rare few of the ones we had to interact with did. And less than a handful of those truly believed in our abilities. Bottom line, ninety-nine percent of those who knew about us didn't believe in what we could do and were just waiting for us to fail.

The one percent? They were the dangerous ones because they were the ones smart enough to know that non-humans and humans existed side by side. Knew and meant to retain the status quo between two worlds existing among each other. Humans did not want to know about non-humans. Funny thing was most non-humans felt the same way, happy to hide their abilities and talents to avoid witch hunts and wholesale slaughter.

We non-humans, the organized ones, governed ourselves using the Council of Seven. Seven of the most populous beings—shifters, demons, shamans, fae, mages, druids, and vampires—with one representative elected for a lifetime position. They held ultimate power among the law-abiding non-humans and the council's sole function was to keep the knowledge of non-humans from humans. Not an easy task but a necessary one.

I was so focused on thoughts of the council, the same council who let me be imprisoned for an unintentional killing I committed, that I almost missed Ling Mai's next words.

"Congratulations on the success of your summoning exercise," she said, setting down a Mont Blanc pen, a whisper of a smile shadowing her lips. "I knew you could live up to your promise."

I glanced at Stone to see if this was some kind of a joke. He kept his face blank, eyes forward, hands clasped behind his back at parade rest. He couldn't have shouted you're-on-your-own-Noziak any louder.

Fine. I was used to fighting my own battles. But I didn't really mean to blurt out my next words. "I just about killed the whole team. I wouldn't call that a success."

Ling Mai allowed one elegant brow to arch. "And yet you summoned a demon."

"Three," I mumbled under my breath.

"And you were able to send them away."

Barely.

"Did you expect any of this to be easy?"

I shrugged.

"Then don't behave like a disappointed child. You are undisciplined, only because you choose to be."

Ouch.

She continued, "To become proficient with any ability you must practice at all times. Without practice you are an empty vessel, of no use to anyone."

From what Ling Mai had told me when she recruited me, she was right. She'd said it'd be hard and there would be casualties. What I hadn't realized was I didn't care to be the one killing my fellow teammates, intentionally or not. It was clear as an Idaho blue sky that Ling Mai and I were on opposite sides of a great divide as to what was acceptable to get the job done.

She swept an elegant hand toward two chairs facing the desk. "Come closer and sit down."

"I'd rather stand," I said, squaring my shoulders and raising my chin. "I'm here to tell you I'm leaving."

There. That wasn't too hard.

"Oh." Ling Mai clasped her hands in front of her on the desk, the picture of calm control.

I wanted to slam fists to her pristine desk, shout, throw something, anything to break her serene expression.

Yeah, lady, you'll have to find another patsy to sacrifice for the greater good. Ling Mai's perceived good.

Instead of speaking to me she angled her head toward Stone. "You were aware of this decision?" she asked, as if Stone did my thinking for me.

"She told me in the infirmary."

"Did you tell her what has been happening?"

Damn, I hated it when people spoke as if I weren't in the room. "Tell me what?" I demanded, as if I cared. Not really since I was out of here.

"Please, Miss Noziak." Ling Mai pointed to the chairs again. This time I shuffled toward one and plopped into it. Easier than continuing to be bull-headed and risk toppling as my knees had begun to shake.

"Thank you. Now, Mr. Stone." Ling Mai managed more communication in a nod, a smile, and crease of her eyes than most drill sergeants were able to produce in a whole repertoire of barked orders.

Once Stone took his seat, more graciously than I had, Ling Mai reached for a lavender-colored folder on her desk. Who kept purple folders for important information? The woman was in a league of her own. She didn't open the folder but placed it beneath her clasped hands as if reading whatever was in it by osmosis.

"I'm afraid I have some disturbing news, Miss Noziak. News that I had planned to impart to the whole team later this morning, but which I'll share with you now."

Okay, I was as much a sucker for a secret as the next woman, but when I caught myself leaning forward in my chair, I pulled myself back.

No one said anything though. In the interest of prodding this show along I circled my fingers, the only thing on my body that didn't ache if I kept the movement slow and my arms flat against the chair's armrests. "So what's this news?"

"We are seeing a disturbing increase in the number of negative incidents involving non-humans and humans," she said, which wasn't really saying a whole lot.

I glanced at Stone but spoke to Ling Mai. "But there have always been human and non-human interactions. Most humans just don't realize what they are dealing with, and from what I know, most non-humans prefer to keep it that way."

This I knew firsthand. My father was a recognized Shoshone shaman, though few outside of the tribe were aware of his designation. And only one within the tribe, and no one in the general population except for his immediate family, knew he was also a shifter. He and my four brothers. I, being the only girl, bypassed the shifter gene and took after my mother, a full-blown Celtic witch. Which is where I got my green eyes and my propensity for spell casting, rusty as it was.

"Correct, Miss Noziak." Ling Mai nodded as if I'd answered an easy question on a pop quiz. "Humans and non-humans have existed side-by-side for centuries."

Yeah, I got it. Most humans were clueless about their non-human peers. The only way non-humans could protect themselves, even though they were by far the more dangerous species. Dangerous but they could still be killed by people who didn't like to share their world with anything other than themselves. From a non-human perspective most humans operated from a kill-first-then-ask-questions-afterwards position.

I think Ling Mai actually may have forgotten her control long enough to sigh. The woman must be seriously bothered. "Not all non-humans are dangerous, though there are enough races that can be a threat to humans if they decide to change the current status quo."

Obviously I'd hit my head harder than I'd realized as I stumbled through translating her words. Finally I spread my hands and asked, "Who's changing the status quo? And why?"

"Good questions and ones I'm afraid we don't have the answers for."

"Yet," Stone growled with a low-timbre sound that sent chills snaking down my back.

"But someone or something is?" I leaned forward in earnest now. "Are you sure?"

I wondered how much she knew about the Council of Seven? Not that blabbing about them was going to make me friends with that group. Just the opposite. One spoke of the council only if they were tired of living.

"The signs are pointing not only to an increase in agitation among the non-human population, but a possible union among non-human groups."

"What?" I glanced at granite-faced Stone before continuing. "You mean like Weres aligning with shifters? Or the fae joining forces with the pixies? Not likely."

"I'm afraid it's not only possible, but it's already begun." I heard a tremor of deep unease beneath Ling Mai's tone.

That was seriously bad news, if it was true.

"But most of the non-human populations are enemies. Going back centuries and beyond. What would cause them to play nicey-nicey together now?" I asked.

It was Stone who answered. "An organized bid for power. Someone or something has found a way to set aside differences for a unified goal. Something that's changed in the non-human world that's more a threat than exposure to humans."

"No freakin' way." I was sure this was a ploy to justify the existence, and thus the funding of the IR Agency. That was all.

I guess my look said what I was thinking as Ling Mai shook her head. "We are not fabricating these incidents," she said.

The lady could be seriously spooky.

"In fact, the agency was conceived knowing full well that this scenario was a very real possibility at some time."

Stone jumped in. "We didn't expect to see the signs this early. The signs and the speed at which the agitation is growing."

"Meaning what?" I ignored the worry swirling in my gut. I had lived among shifters and Weres. I knew how dangerous they could be if unleashed on humans. But the thought of Weres joining with vamps, fae, or demons chilled my blood.

"We're hearing of sightings worldwide," Stone said, angling forward, leaning his elbows on his knees and clasping his hands together. "But it's not that non-humans are coming forward to be seen, it's what they have been doing."

"Such as?"

Stone nodded toward the file on Ling Mai's desk. "A cadre of shifters and vamps broke into two Swiss banks a week ago."

"Stealing money?"

"Customer information," Ling Mai said, the two words hanging like an iron weight in the room.

Since I came from a background where scraping together and doing without was the norm, and becoming a beauty operator was a step up financially, I was confused. "Why a bank? Or banks?"

"Not just any bank, but banks that service some of the richest individuals and corporations in the world."

I shrugged.

"Information is power," Ling Mai said, "With the lists removed from just those two banks, a third of the world's most influential and powerful people can be identified and compromised if the details of their financial holdings, holdings which they work hard to hide, are revealed to their enemies or competitors."

"Okay. I can see where this isn't a great scenario," I offered, thinking the situation might suck for some mucky muck who wanted to hide his fortune, but other than that, so what?

"There have been several more incidents," Stone added. "A bio-research lab in Russia, which is one of the two locations where the remaining, live smallpox virus is stored, had a break-in yesterday."

"Which means?" Usually I wasn't this slow on the uptake but my head was ringing and the effort to just inhale my next breath was taking all of my concentration.

"Which means the virus can be replicated and used in germ warfare." Ling Mai looked at me closely.

"Against humans?"

She nodded. "Combine germ warfare with magic and the potential for disaster is multiplied."

That was an understatement. "Who was behind that event?"

"We only have information from the survivors but from initial reports fae and Weres joined forces to stage the break-in. It's hard to verify as most of the video cameras were destroyed," Stone answered. "Or wiped clean by magic."

"But these still sound like isolated events," I said, wanting to hide my head a little deeper in the sand, remembering Ling Mai's words when she'd first recruited me. There were three ways to deal with the world of non-humans: ignore them and hope they go away, fight them directly, or seek to understand them so should the time come when humans and non-humans became aware of one another officially, hard choices could be made from a solid understanding.

"The incidents could be isolated, but we've received intel from an operative deep undercover in a shifter colony in Europe that there are rumors circulating about one leader being the puppet master."

My oldest brother Van was stationed in Europe with NATO. Yeah, he was a shifter, but a lot of shifters and Weres worked for military organizations throughout the world. They could fit into the regimented hierarchy and structured environment easier than a lot of other career options.

"That sounds like pretty vague intel," I pointed out the obvious. "Any clue who the leader is? Or what species he is? Or even what he wants?"

Stone shot a quick glance at Ling Mai who angled her head as she answered me. "Unfortunately our undercover man disappeared before he was able to send details."

"Sucks for him," I whispered, knowing full well what wasn't said. Some stranger had most likely given his life for his country. That would be the good news. A quick death versus being held captive by non-humans to extract every thought from his head before killing him.

"Yeah, it does suck for him," Stone said, his voice suddenly gentle.

I glanced his way. With his military background, he, more than the rest of us, had to know what it meant to die far from home, with no blaze of glory or heroic flag waving. More often than not an unmarked grave, if there were enough pieces to gather together.

But none of this really had anything to do with me. My being here or not, given what a mess I was at being a functioning witch, would not change what happened to the missing agent, or the upcoming battle between humans and non-humans. In fact, my being out of the line of fire was probably the best thing that could happen to the rest of the team, given Ling Mai's acceptance of collateral damage.

"Not my problem," I said, straightening my shoulders and looking Ling Mai in her dark eyes. "Last thing anyone needs is a witch who can't control her abilities. Can you see what would have happened if those echo-demons had escaped the gym yesterday? More human casualties not less."

"I'm afraid you're wrong, Alex," Stone said, keeping his gaze focused on his clasped hands.

"Are you kidding? The size and power of those demons could have decimated dozens if not hundreds if they'd—"

"Not what I'm talking about," he interrupted.

"Then what?" I spread my hands before me. "I've already killed once. I don't want to use magic to take more lives, especially those of my teammates. My going or staying won't make a difference to anyone."

"You're wrong, Miss Noziak." Ling Mai shot me that even, calm gaze that gave me the willies. "It will matter to one in particular."

"Who?" I flung the word out like a dare, not liking being kept in the dark.

"Your brother," Stone said, his words so low I had to shift toward him to catch them.

"Which brother? Are you threatening one of them. . . " my words trailed off at his shaking his head.

Coldness started low in my belly and grew. I was proud though that I kept my voice steady as I started putting two and two together. "Which brother?"

Ling Mai answered. "The missing operative—"

"Van?" I whispered past a bone-dry throat.
Ling Mai nodded.

CHAPTER 5

There are some times in your life that you can clearly point to a before and an after. Before you enter school and after. Before you have sex for the first time and after. Before I heard Ling Mai's words and after.

I couldn't find anything to say. As if all thought had fled, all ability to speak, all ability to feel. Instead I focused on the mundane: the tick of a grandfather clock behind the closed hallway door, the subtle scent of Ling Mai's jasmine perfume, Stone's breathing in the chair next to me.

Inside I screamed until I was hoarse. Not Van. Please, please, please not Van. Tears acid-etched my eyes. But Noziaks didn't cry in public.

I swallowed past the lump clogging my throat. "When. . ."

"Two days ago," Stone answered.

"And no one told me?" Find a convenient punching bag. Stone was close, and he could take it.

"We were, right after the demon summoning."

"Which I screwed up and ended up in the infirmary." Crap times ten. I couldn't even point the finger at someone else. I raised my head, spearing Ling Mai with a tell-me-and-tell-me-straight look Noziaks' learned before they learned to crawl. "Is he alive?"

"From everything that we know," she replied, softening her words as if that would soften their blow.

I slammed to my feet, grabbing the edge of the chair to keep from toppling. Stone was right beside me, his left hand steadying me, his expression harsh, but not for me. "We're doing everything we can to find and bring him home," he said.

Did I believe him? Or trust him?

"I want...I want...oh, hell." I sank back into the chair, knowing full well I was the only one who really gave a damn if Van lived or died.

So if he was to be saved, I was his best bet.

"Where was he last sighted." I was already planning how I could get from Maryland to Europe.

But no one answered. I glanced at Stone, then Ling Mai, then back at Stone. I asked him, "What?"

Ling Mai answered. "You cannot leave the compound or the agency, Miss Noziak."

"Except for prison," said Stone,' voice brittle as ice.

I pressed back into my chair. Moments ago prison was exactly what I'd wanted. But now? Van needed help and I was jammed tighter than a bear in a badger's hole.

It was Ling Mai I faced. "You'd hold me to that agreement? Now?"

"Yes."

How could one word gut a person?

She continued, "This is not a personal decision, Miss Noziak; this is a pragmatic one. Our agreement was clear. A year as an IR agent or prison. You leave here and it will be to the PWCC."

Pocatello Women's Correctional Center. Yeah, I knew that, but knowing and wanting it, now, was a world apart.

"So you'd send me to prison rather than let me help Van. And what about him? If I choose PWCC?" My tone was bitter, scalding acid biting from deep inside me.

Stone shrugged, a wealth of words unspoken but needing no translation. If I bailed, Van died for sure. If I stayed? What then?

One small step away from prison and walking away from the only group that stood a chance going up against non-humans. And we sucked.

I scrubbed my face with both hands before I spoke again. "If I stay, is there anything we can do?" I raised my head then, knowing I looked as desperate as I sounded. "Anything?"

Ling Mai nodded and I'd have sold my soul for her, even as I loathed her with a hatred so deep it burned black within me. This woman didn't care about me, or Van, or anyone. Pragmatic my ass. She was a lethal bitch and she held my life hostage. My life and Van's.

Van wasn't just my older brother; he was my best friend. My protector. The one I could cry on when I missed the mother I barely knew. The one who would fight my battles for me until I got big enough and strong enough to fight my own. The one who explained to Dad why I was disappearing into a shadow world no one could speak about until my time was served. Or I died.

Van was my hero and I felt so damned useless sitting here, trapped but still safe even if I was banged up, but only because of my own failures as a witch.

Ling Mai cleared her throat. "We need what your brother knows. We also need your abilities."

Yeah, right.

Stone added, "We won't stop until we bring him home."

A smidge of unexpected compassion. I wanted to believe him, but my trust level was at an all-time low. But what choice did I have? Leave, knowing my actions doomed Van, or stay, and give him what small thread of hope I could.

"I'll stay," I said, the words a vow and an oath. I could be as cold as Ling Mai. As long as her goal was to save Van, I'd do whatever it took, use whoever I had to.

And if her goal changed? I'd cross that bridge when I got to it.

Right then and there I wondered how human Ling Mai was. She had all the attributes of a vampire: cold, calculating, and without remorse, no matter whose life was on the line. If she was human, she was a sociopath. Bad news was, she was also my best chance to save Van.

When I was sure my eyes were not tear-bright I lifted my head and asked, "What now?"

Ling Mai cut a glance at Stone before answering. "We do have a single person assignment for you at this time."

"Van?" Hope fluttered like a trapped hawk within my breast.

Stone shook his head. "You're in no physical condition to go up against the types holding him."

The hawk died. "But—"

"We'll be sending your teammates to turn over some rocks." His tone brooked no argument.

"Turn over rocks? That's pretty lame. We need mountains turned over, and now. If you won't do it I will."

"Relax." Stone raised one hand. "Just checking to see if demon-summoning Alex was on board or pussy-whipped Alex was still hanging around."

"Stick it where the sun doesn't shine," I snarled, earning a quick cant of Stone's lips. The man was a sadist.

It suddenly hit me, "Does my dad know?"

Damn, it'd kill him if he did. He probably knew something was up, being a shaman with great abilities, but he'd learned over the years not to over react to what he could see through his shamanic sight. There was seeing, and then there was knowing.

"He's been informed that your brother's missing but not the details surrounding the incident," Stone said. "Or the danger."

Thank the Great Spirits for that. I'd have to get ahold of Dad as soon as I could or he'd be knocking down the doors of the compound looking for me to find Van, even if he didn't know where I was. Dad was that good a shaman, and I didn't need that complication.

As for me? Whatever waste of time, for the good of the team assignment they stuck me on, didn't mean that was all I had to do. If I was out of prison, and alive, I could help Van.

Yup, Noziaks were bottom-line kind of thinkers and my bottom-line had become save Van. No matter what.

CHAPTER 6

Once Ling Mai and Stone believed that I was willing to toe the party line and be a good little, obedient IR recruit in training, or at least act like one, Stone left to round up the rest of the team. Those that were still ambulatory.

I took my sweet time moving from Ling Mai's office into what looked like a corporate boardroom. Not that we had all that many in Mud Lake, but once I'd been arrested for murder, I'd seen a number of these places while dealing with lawyers and judges and prosecutors out for blood.

The agency's boardroom was more upscale than any I'd seen in Idaho, but still focused on function, with a plasma screen console, comfy leather chairs so your butt felt better before it was hung out to dry, and enough hardwood to qualify as a museum of dead trees.

Ling Mai didn't chitchat with me. Not that she would normally, psychopaths didn't do small talk, but the woman was smart enough to know that I'd probably go for her jugular today.

It took a few minutes for the other recruits to shuffle in. Jaylene first, giving me a stink-eye look that bounced right off. After the morning I'd had, it'd take more than prissy glances to phase me.

Kelly came next looking like I felt, ripped apart but still walking. "Oh Alex, I'm so, so sorry," she said even before she was through the door. She walked right up to my chair as if heading for an execution.

"Sorry for what?" I asked, backtracking to remember what I'd missed.

"For. . ." She fluttered her hands. "You know. For disappearing on you. And everyone." She cast a wary eye at Jaylene.

I actually laughed. It was more bark than a happy sound, but I'd forgotten about the gym for a few moments. "Kelly, I was the one who called three bad-ass demons instead of one. I should be the one apologizing."

"Damn right," Jaylene snarled.

I flipped her off just as Vaughn walked into the room and caught the gesture. She rolled her eyes with a children-play-nice look that reduced Jaylene and me to playground brawlers.

How'd she and Ling Mai do that with just a look?

Kelly grabbed the chair nearest me, which I thought was very nice of her, given Jaylene had plopped herself down as far away as possible while still being in the same room. That could be my eau-du-demon-slime encrusted clothes reeking, or just her being her. Vaughn took a place opposite me but still within arm's length. Which let me know where I stood.

Kindergarten teacher Kelly wasn't pissed at me, wary but more guilty for her own falling short, so she wasn't busy casting stones. Team leader Vaughn was neutral, which fit her position and style. The lady might be a former debutante but she was also nine-tenths diplomat, a role her old man had held before he took over the CIA. Jaylene was definitely in the same camp as Mandy. The card carrying blame-Alex-for-screwing-up cadre.

And these ladies were the ones I was to trust with my life for the next eleven months. Lucky me.

But it wasn't the next year I was thinking about right then. It was how soon could I find Van and would this team help or hinder me? If they hindered, they'd be under my bus.

"Ladies." Ling Mai brought us to order. "In spite of the fact you have not yet finished your official training program, due to the success you had on your last mission we've been asked to complete two limited but important operations." Ling Mai's smile was tight and on the small side. She did emotion on the level Jaylene did, zilch to grudgingly.

"Non-human this time?" Jaylene asked, never one to shy away from plain speaking. If I didn't think she was such a PIA I could admire that about her. But not today.

Ling Mai's smile dimmed. "Yes and no."

"You want to explain that?" Jaylene pressed.

"Jaylene, you and Kelly along with Mr. Stone will be sent on a mission that will place you in contact with non-humans."

"Hurrah," Jaylene murmured under her breath. But I couldn't tell if it was sarcastic or not. Maybe echo-demon butt-kicking hadn't been enough for her. Next to me I noticed Kelly went very still.

Ling Mai continued in her precise, calm way. "At this time you'll be fact-finding only. There will be no interception or interaction with the non-humans if possible. Your training is lacking at this point and we have no intention of throwing you into a world where the threats are very real and very lethal."

Yeah, right, like that couldn't change in a heartbeat.

We could all read between the lines. We'd barely survived a controlled environment with echo-demons intentionally summoned. Going nose-to-nose with Weres and vamps was a whole different game. And no soothing words such as "you'll be fine," or "I'm sure you can take care of yourselves" would change that fact.

But damn it anyway. This was Van they were going after, what good was a bloody surveillance mission going to do? If he was being held by non-humans there had to be interaction with them to extract him.

Interaction my ass. I'd show them interaction. Get me anywhere near him and I'd interact until there wasn't a live body left, human or non-human.

I glanced beside me where Kelly folded her hands demurely in her lap, but I noted the white knuckles. That same tension knotted my muscles, still so sore I could barely sit.

"We'll have Stone with us though," Jaylene clarified, always watching out for number one, herself.

"Yes." Ling Mai angled her head. "But before we get to the recon assignment we have another mission that needs our attention."

No doubt Kelly could do the same rap-on-the-knuckles, pay-attention-class tone as the director. Eye and tone communication—I needed to get me some of that mojo.

Exhaustion was making me punch drunk, even though I hadn't been out of the infirmary bed that long. But pain and exhaustion weren't holding the images pounding through my head at bay. Van alone at the hands of monsters. Torture. A slow, painful death as the best option.

Let's move this meeting along so we could get to the part where I did something, as much as I could with banged-up ribs and a body full of bruises.

Was I ready to jump into more of this get-the-crap-beat-out-of-us-again so soon? For Van's sake? Yeah, in a heartbeat.

Ling Mai was already passing around a packet of op folders before returning to her desk and activating the HD 3-D visual screen in front of us.

Ready or not.

As the screen image materialized into a three-dimensional reality the folder stayed closed on my lap and my breath jammed in my throat.

Talk about a one–two punch. I even forgot about my ribs long enough to suck in a breath.

"Hum-a-hum-a," Jaylene whispered, followed by a low whistle. Even shy Kelly gave a yum-yum grin.

I simply stared, my mouth dry, my pulse not as steady as seconds ago.

The man on the screen looked like a cross between a Halleluiah prayer answered and one's best wet dream. Thick dark hair, killer sky-blue eyes, cheekbones that made my own Shoshone facial structure look flat.

Danger. Seduction. And trouble with a capital "T." Woman trouble.

"Who's the hunk?" Jaylene asked. "He fae? Or a fallen angel?"

That'd make sense, given his looks. Or a seduction demon. Had to be some otherness about this guy. No one looked that good.

"Not as far as we know," replied Ling Mai. "He's human. Or we believe he's human, but until someone who can identify a non-human gets intel the point is up for debate."

No freakin' way was he human.

Ling Mai added, "Name's Bran."

"Just Bran?" Kelly scanned her printed material. "No other name?"

"No." Ling Mai glanced at the image. "He was born with only one name, a power play between his biological parents. His mother a princess of one of the lesser royal houses of Europe, his father an Irish musician."

Royal house? Most of those had Vamp or demon blood for sure.

"Says here his old man was Colin Bran. He was the lead singer for the Bullets." Jaylene was reading her folder, too, as she continued to whistle long and low. A sound that made my hormones heat at the same time I was getting the chills. "Colin Bran's not a musician, he's a legend."

My folder still lay untouched, a dead weight in my lap.

Fatigue.

Liar.

I wanted to let the image speak, not the words. When was the last time a picture of a guy knocked me for a loop?

Never.

Maybe I needed to get out more often. Oh, wait, I was a prisoner of the agency, which didn't take kindly to its recruits wandering the streets for a booty call. Even if I wasn't that kind of a gal. But for a guy who looked like this, I might change my policy.

"Our subject was the uncalculated result of an indiscreet affair," Ling Mai said.

"The man's a bastard." Jaylene always called it like she saw it.

"Yes, and the only heir to the kingdom of San Morin and his father's sizable fortune. Both of which he has turned his back on."

"Why?" Kelly asked, echoing the surprise I felt. Who turned down wealth? A saint? Or a sinner?

"He's become quite wealthy and well-known in his own field. Haute couture."

"You mean he makes dresses?" Jaylene said the words lodged in my throat.

The man had to be as gay as a Parisian cross-dresser. I released an audible sigh. So much for wet dreams.

Ling Mai continued, "He's considered one of the world's up and coming fashion designers. The next Versace or Armani."

"What a waste," Jaylene muttered.

"On the contrary. No doubt one day Bran's name will be a household word. Right now he associates with the world's most elite and most-highly connected clientele and has an independent fortune."

"Some men have it all." Jaylene crossed her arms. "What does he have to do with our mission? He need a babysitter?"

Ling Mai folded her hands on the pristine surface of the boardroom table. "His group is the common thread behind a string of international thefts. Seemingly unrelated; art, antiquities, jewels, and lately, top-secret government information, including some paranormal intel that could be very dangerous, especially to us."

"Wait," I found my voice by focusing in on the business. "Don't thieves usually specialize in one commodity? Like jewels only?" I was ignoring the paranormal comment. One land mine at a time to diffuse.

"Yes, they do." Ling Mai turned her onyx-black gaze on me, reminding me of the Chinese witch I'd trained with as a child. A power glance quickly banked. One of these days I'd have to find out what Ling Mai really was. I shook off my train of thought and focused on what she had to say.

"The disparity in the types of burglaries is why it's been so difficult to link these incidents to a common denominator. Interpol has been tracking Bran and his traveling fashion shows for nearly a year now and in a number of major locations he's visited, within a week or two, a theft occurs."

"So our hunk is a common punk?" I asked, disappointed all over again. Gay and a criminal. That so sucked. And so much for my taste in men.

"That piece of the puzzle is still in dispute. In fact," Ling Mai glanced back at the screen. "Bran has been approached on several occasions about the missing items, and to prove his own innocence, has agreed to allow an undercover operative to travel with him in hopes of pinpointing exactly who within his organization, or connected to his organization, might be behind the thefts."

"Agreed?" Kelly asked, saving me the trouble. "As in volunteered to have someone checking him out?"

Ling Mai nodded. "He wasn't given much choice. From what I have heard he tolerates the situation, but as an astute businessman knows you must take the negative with the positive."

"But he still could be the porch climber?" Jaylene said, using a term I'd heard in prison for thief.

"Yes, there's still that possibility." Ling Mai smiled her enigmatic smile that raised more questions than it answered. "He's agreed to cooperate, but he's less than pleased with the situation."

I glanced at the face on the screen. Yeah, I could see that arrogance allowing law enforcement to travel with him while he kept on being a bad, bad boy right under their noses. A game within a game to someone like him.

It didn't take an experienced woman to realize this was *not* a man you would want to come up against. At least power to power, not body to body.

Poor Vaughn. With her background as an ambassador's daughter and being a world socialite, this op sounded right up her alley. Maybe she'd go undercover as his lover. Not a bad gig, if the man was straight, and Stone wasn't aware of what his cuddle-buddy was doing. None of the group knew what Vaughn's "other" talent was, but when you looked like a cover model and had wealth as a fallback position, being extra-endowed was just plain overkill.

"So when does Vaughn do this?" Kelly asked.

I relaxed my shoulders, my thoughts already on what I needed to do to free Van, with or without agency backing, and anxious to get onto what was my mission.

"Vaughn?" Ling Mai's eyes clouded before her smile deepened, reaching her eyes this time. "Oh, I see, but I'm afraid you have it wrong. Vaughn has something else to do. Infiltration of Bran's operation must happen immediately and does not require the full team's involvement. It should be a simple reconnoiter and report assignment and only one operative is needed. Besides, Bran insisted on choosing which team member he was willing to have on the inside."

Several of our gazes clashed. Since when did a suspect get to pick and choose who might take him down?

I cleared my throat. "So who's going up against this guy?"

Ling Mai's gaze speared me. "He chose you, Alex."

CHAPTER 7

Twenty minutes later, after Jaylene and Kelly had their assignment, the one I should be on, going after my brother, I was back in Ling Mai's office, so frustrated I could chew glass.

Someone had to talk some sense into the director. This wasn't just pairing the wrong talent with the wrong job, this was Van's life at stake.

I waved the op folder clenched one-handed in front of me, alone at last with the director. "This is not what I should be doing." Understatement. "I mean I can be a hairdresser, but that's not the problem. Van needs me. Some poof-guy doesn't need a witch to take him down."

"I don't understand?" Ling Mai sat still and contained behind her desk that cost more than my dad's farm, the perfect picture of controlled calm.

"I need to find and save Van." I huffed a breath, and held up a hand to forestall Ling Mai thinking I was only focused on my own needs. Which I was, but that wasn't my point. "Besides I do physical real well. Give me a mountain to scale, a building to jump off, a non-human to summon—" I glanced at the folder crumpling in my grip. "This is frou-frou stuff."

"Frou-frou?"

"Yes, you know what I mean. Girlie clothes and rich people hobnobbing with each other. Van is in—"

"You *are* a hairdresser. Is that not girlie?"

"No." I shook my head. "Well, in a way it is, but in a way it isn't. Hairdressers can wear jeans and be invisible. Vaughn is the best person for this mission. Not me. If we're going to take this op then give it to someone who can get the job done and done quickly. Jaylene could be a model for the clothes or Kelly could go in, do her disappearing act and get everything you need in a snap."

"You're wrong." Ling Mai's look told me I was getting nowhere. "In fact, you're the perfect person for this mission."

"Good grief, why?" Other than it would keep me out of her hair, and away from where Van was. Is that what was up? She didn't trust I could be a team player? Or was this to punish me for being a screw-up?

"You underestimate yourself, Alex." Ling Mai had dropped the Miss Noziak bit. Good news? Probably not. "True, the people Bran associates with are in a different social-economic sphere than you are used to."

Another understatement.

"But they are no different than you."

Oh, yes they are.

I leaned forward. "Look, I appreciate this vote of confidence." Or the sucking up, though it wasn't Ling Mai's style to suck up to anyone, especially a recruit. "I really do. But there's no way I can...I can mingle with people I can't even talk with. It's not like we can discuss pork prices or the best way to shear sheep." And no way could I chit-chat with Van's life on the line.

"I think you'll be surprised at how easily you'll fit in with Bran's group. Do not underestimate yourself."

"I'm not—"

"What is it you're really afraid of here, Miss Noziak?"

My shoulders snapped to attention. We were back to queen to peon, besides no Noziak was called a coward. "I'm not-—"

"Then what is it?"

I glanced up, as if reason hid in the ceiling plaster. Then decided to go for broke. "You're keeping me from helping Van. He needs me now. Don't do this to me. To him."

"So you think you are the only person capable of finding information on where they are keeping your brother?"

Why did the director have to sound like one of the Star Wars characters? Obi Wan Kenobi. Or maybe it was Yoda. So calm and reasonable when I wanted to scream.

"Yeah, I think I'm the best chance my brother has at living, and if he's alive he can give you the information you want." I flared my hands in front of me, sounding less than gracious and ignoring it. "You want me to go in to this other job, shake everyone's hands, waste my time, while my brother is being tortured and could be dying. There's no reason I'm the one being sent on this wild-goose chase. None."

"Even if the last theft tracked back to someone who attended one of Bran's events happens to be the bank robbery in Switzerland?" Ling Mai asked, her gaze level and clear.

That had my heart stopping and my breath backing up. "You mean this guy is tied to whomever, or whatever, has Van?"

Ling Mai leaned forward, just a hint, but enough to have me mimicking her move so I didn't miss a single vowel. "I'm saying there *may* be a connection. Bran travels the world. He has contacts in a lot of places. I believe it's more than likely that there is a link between the thefts, the people who took your brother, and Bran's group."

More than likely? Was that a bone tossed to me to gnaw on? Or was Ling Mai's gut instinct a solid lead? Could I afford to ignore either?

I sat back, my thoughts whirling. "So you're saying if I go check out this dressmaker, and find a connection between him—"

"Or someone he's in contact with."

"Yeah, yeah, or someone he's in contact with." I sucked in a deep breath, ignoring the whap of pain across my ribs, stilling my fears enough to make a hard choice here. "Doing this piece-of-fluff mission might actually help me find Van?"

"And if you do find a lead the agency will act on it, as much as is within our power."

Like I believed that for a heartbeat. Ling Mai took care of the agency and the agency had its own agenda. But even if Ling Mai was lying through her pearly white teeth, if I could find a link, or a hint of where Van was, then I'd be one step closer to saving him.

Ling Mai continued, "In the meantime we'll have Ms. Smart, Ms. McAllister, and Mr. Stone following through on what NATO has discovered about the possible whereabouts of your brother."

I held Ling Mai's gaze steadily with mine. There would be no doublespeak, no grey areas between us. "You're saying both operations stand us a better chance to find Van."

"You forget, Miss Noziak, that I am very interested in the information your brother knows about who is behind the increased agitation and unification actions among the non-humans. You want your brother safe. I want your brother safe for what he knows."

Pragmatism. I could deal with that. Especially my version of it, doing whatever it took to save Van.

"Fine." I staggered to my feet, biting back a whimper. No way could I betray that I was in worse shape than I looked. I didn't want to give Ling Mai any ammunition to stop my finding Van. "When do I start?"

She waved me back to my seat.

"You depart tomorrow for France."

Good, last I knew Van had been working somewhere in France or Germany. This op was sounding better and better.

"—but I shall not let you enter the tiger's den without assistance," Ling Mai continued as I scrambled to take a deep breath and catch up with what the director had been saying. "I recommend you take this along with you."

I leaned as far forward as my ribs allowed to see what she had pulled from her top desk drawer. Whatever it was had to be small, really small to fit in Ling Mai's dainty hands. Reaching forward, palm up, I waited for a weapon, or listening device, or some techno whiz gadget. Instead the director slipped a ring onto my palm.

"Seriously. . ." I turned the smooth yet plain silver band over and over, feeling an incised letter or symbol, like a misshapen R on the inside curve. I glanced up at Ling Mai. "Please tell me this has some powers, some abilities?"

"Of a kind." The director actually smiled, which under other circumstances might have been a positive sight. Right now all it did was disconcert me.

"The symbol marked on the silver is from the Elder Futhark runes," Ling Mai said.

"I need that in English." I understood runes; most witches used them in wardings, or to create protection circles, but this Fut-whatever was new to me.

"The symbol is a very old one. A very valuable one."

"Meaning?"

"Journey."

"Great." I stood, disappointed, with fatigue weighting my shoulders, pain tap dancing across every nerve ending. Pain and maybe a twinge of fear. "I don't mean to be dense here, Director, but I'm just a country girl. You're telling me that all I need to accomplish this mission is a ring with some writing on it?"

Ling Mai leaned back in her chair, and resting her elbows on the silk-covered wooden arms, she steepled her fingers before speaking. "There are many kinds of journeys we can travel, both external and internal, and the ring is a reminder of that." She nodded at where I had curled my hand around the piece of jewelry. "The ring is so much more, if you allow it to be. When you come within a twenty-foot radius of non-humans the ring will heat your skin and enhance your natural abilities, in your case to identify non-humans or to cast spells."

"This will alert me to the presence of non-humans?" Okay, that might come in handy. "How will I know which kind of non-human I'm dealing with?" That was the big issue. As a witch I was marginally more aware of the otherness of non-humans, more than say Kelly or Jaylene, but knowing I was coming up against a threatening non-human versus just another being who wanted to be ignored to get on with their lives, now that was a useful tool.

"At this time the ring can only help you identify non-humans, but not their specifics," Ling Mai said.

I snorted. I already knew there were non-humans out there. This piece of crap was as useful as going into any inner-city core and having a piece of jewelry tell me there were folks who carried a weapon on them.

Ling Main continued as if I'd spoken aloud, "The ring enhances what you already have."

"You mean if I had this on when I summoned three echo-demons instead of one I could have ended up with six?"

"I maintain that you have many more abilities than you are currently using, which is almost nil. Your challenge is to harness what you possess, focus on your intentions, and embrace what you are. You have abilities to hone."

Easy for her to say; last time I seriously accessed my magic abilities I killed a man. For witches magic could be light or dark. The more you used any kind of magic, the easier to cross that line into a dark magic user. It's what my father had warned me against, years ago. It's the road my mother had slipped down. And now Ling Mai expected me to jump wholeheartedly into being a witch.

All magic had a price.

"You were born to be a witch, Alex, do not throw that away out of fear."

She stood. This meeting was over, until she added, "Think of the ring as a connection to a larger good. Remember that you are of this agency, and that though you may travel alone, you need not be alone. You're part of a team. Choose to belong and you could be unstoppable."

I hurt too bad to buy into what the director was saying, but I did stop myself from rolling my eyes. Barely.

Cutting through all the woo-woo stuff I understood the bottom line. I'd signed on to do what needed to be done, when and wherever. Plus taking this mission meant I was going after Van, with or without Ling Mai's permission. I cracked my neck as I mumbled, "Fine, I'll wear the ring and do the mission."

"I always knew you would."

Yeah, right, which is why the director had resorted to blackmail and threats against Van. The agency was just one big happy family.

Bull. I'd agreed to do my job and I'd do it.

But that didn't mean I was going to like doing it.

On the other hand, maybe Vaughn would get freed up and before I knew it I'd be back doing something useful— something putting me closer to Van.

"I see you're already smiling," Ling Mai noted.

"Yeah." For now.

"The team is counting on you, Miss Noziak. Become the witch you were meant to be."

Now why'd she have to say that?

CHAPTER 8

As I exited Ling Mai's office I saw Stone leaning against the wall down the hallway. The hallway I had to pass to return to the infirmary or get to my room. I could be a chicken-shit and take the long way around to avoid him, but I doubted I had enough whomp left in me to make it.

So I squared my shoulders as if that didn't have me clamping down on my lip from the pain and started walking toward him. Two could play the we're-just-being-casual crap.

I gave him a jerky chin nod as I drew even with him but kept walking. Maybe he was waiting for Vaughn.

"Hold up," he snarled as I passed him.

Or maybe not.

I stopped, not graciously. If he had something to say to me he'd say it, one way or another.

"I'll walk you to your room," he said, as if getting an escort from the agency's main instructor was par for the course.

"I can find the dorm myself." I started walking.

His hand on my arm had me stopping short, sucking in an oath at the whiplash of pain his action had caused.

"You up to this?" he asked, surprising me. Stone wasn't known for being a warm and friendly kind of guy. First week of training when one of the other recruits, one who didn't make it, dared to bitch aloud about her sore muscles and bruises, Stone handed her a straw and told her to suck it up or leave. She left but not because she'd wanted to.

I turned to face him. This time I was the one snarling, "Say what you have to say." What was unsaid was I held little patience and less energy to take a lot of bull. But Stone was a smart guy. He could fill in between the lines.

"Look, I know you're concerned about your brother."

I raised my brows. "Ya think?"

"Don't go running off half-cocked here, Noziak. We're a team. Not a bunch of crazy cowboys."

"Never was a cowboy," I said, in spite of my Idaho roots.

"Cowboys and wild-ass Indians only get people killed and missions blown."

"I already told you, I wasn't a cow—"

"Don't play stupid with me." He gave me one of his get-it-or-get-out laser looks. "You go off the reservation and I'll be on you so fast your head will spin."

Now he was just pissing me off. "I may be half-blood Shoshone, but I've never lived on the rez. Not planning to start now."

"You're on my rez, and don't forget that. Play with the team or—"

"Or what?" I stepped into his space, so close I could read the fury in his irises. Or maybe it was an echo of my own mirrored there. "What'ya going to do to me, Stone? Force me to put my life on the line? Oh, wait, you've already done that. Will do it again. Smack me down till my ribs are cracked and every muscle screams? Nope, can't do that either because I'm already there. Threaten me? Been there, done that, didn't get a t-shirt."

"I can make sure no one in this agency lifts a finger to help your brother," he said, his tone so cold it froze the marrow in my bones. "And that includes you."

That quickly he won this smack down, because I had no doubt, no doubts what so ever, that he'd follow through on his words.

"You're a bastard, Stone."

"Been called worse."

Yeah, I bet and probably by his friends.

I took a step back, shaking my head, wishing I could place a gnarly black hex on him. My daddy taught me better than that. But damn it was hard.

Before I lived up to Stone's low brow expectation of me I shrugged off his arm and started walking again.

"Walk the line, Noziak, or pay the price."

His voice followed me down the hall.

CHAPTER 9

In the bright morning sun the Chateau du Parc looked like any typical fairytale castle built in the eighteenth century in the south of France. Not that I had a whole heck of a lot of experience with fairytale castles. Or fairytales. Or white knights or any of that crap. Though I had already faced a few dragons—of the human kind. Ogres, too, and a couple of witches. High school in Mud Lake had been brutal and that was before I realized how many non-humans lived among humans.

I shook my head and glanced around, seeing a white stone facade covered with English ivy mirrored in a reflecting pool, one turret tower, identical windows echoing each other across the front.

What the hell was I doing here?

I stood rooted on the grassy verge facing the ten-bedroom pile of stone, my knees trembling. Jet lag or indecision? Or both? A dozen sleek, very expensive vehicles angled around the drive—Peugeots, Rolls-Royces, a vintage Lamborghini. My brothers would be in car-envy heaven.

I jammed the thought of Van away. I had to in order to focus on the business at hand. The sooner I found a connection between the people in that chateau and Van, the sooner I'd find him.

I glanced around, wondering what I did now. The scent of lavender mingled with the high-pitched squeal of peacocks.

"Damn it, Ling Mai, I hope you know what you're doing," I mumbled, shaking my head, which reminded me that flying commercial wreaked havoc on a beat-up body. But I was here, looking for a lead, any lead on Van. Oh, yeah, and taking down a foo-foo dress designer.

He chose you.

Meant nothing. I was not here to play footsie with some guy. No doubt he'd chosen me because he thought I'd be a push over, but if he had he'd underestimated me.

Focus on the business at hand. Send healing thoughts Van's way and pray for a bloody miracle that he was found quickly and alive. On second thought, no blood wanted.

Straightening shoulders crumbling with exhaustion, I stepped forward, one suitcase firmly in hand, one bright silver hairdresser's valise carrying the tools of my trade clutched in the other. My calling card meant to get me through the front door and into the haute couture world of single-name Bran. I ignored the pain still banding my rib cage. Doctor said a few more weeks and I'd barely notice.

How did Ling Mai make this mission sound so reasonable back in Maryland? Logical even. My undercover role was to be one of three hairdressers to the small cadre of models who showcased Bran's designs to select, very wealthy, and very connected women in exclusive locales around the world. The chateau was one example. Only thirty-five minutes from Paris, in the heart of Bordeaux country, the building slept seventeen, and could host twice that many across its nine hectares of land. Heck, that was barely twenty-two acres. No way could someone farm for a living on twenty-two acres.

"This is *so* not Idaho."

Front door or back? Arrive like a guest or an employee? My instructions were simple. Report to Franco, who handled the day-to-day details of staging fashion shows, a new one in a new location every few days, or find Dominique St. Clair, pronounced like *sand clarhair*, cousin of Bran and CEO of Bran Inc.

Unfortunately neither person was in sight. No one was. It was just me and the peacocks. No doubt these people had some security around, but if they were, they were discreet.

"Don't give me any grief." I nodded to the nearest bird. "I know a few spells that can have you plucked and stuffed for a meal in the blink of an eye."

"You."

The shout startled me, as did the slim-built man rushing toward me, haircut soldier-straight, Caesar-style, and dyed bulls-eye, blood red. Rings lined both ears; his casual pink polo shirt was iron-creased. I didn't even know anyone who owned an iron.

I glanced around, making sure I was alone before asking, "You talking to me?"

"No, the peacocks, dahling." The words huffed. "What took you so long?"

Now I noticed two burley security guards shadowing him. He waved them off as I mumbled, "Long flight."

"Spare me your excuses and get moving. I can't have you standing around all day gawking." He scanned me from head to toes, very quick, very professional, and very dismissive. "Love the hair. Is it real or an extension? Doesn't matter. With those cheeks and your dusky coloring, very exotic. You'll look stunning in the emeralds and oranges. Hurry. You're late already. Chop. Chop."

His accent was a blend of cockney, French, and something else I couldn't quite place. He accompanied his Gatling-gun delivery with clapping hands, then pivoted and sashayed toward the rear of the house before I could answer or ask any questions.

As if I could even form any. So I tightened my grip on my luggage and followed. Not that the man gave me another option.

"There." He pointed toward a shadowed door. "Through the kitchen. Second bedroom on the right. Your first gown is all laid out. Let's hope you're not too bony for it."

He almost disappeared before I stopped him, showing restraint by only using my voice and not a smack of palm to his head or jaw. "I'm not a model."

He paused, his nose pinched.

"I'm the new hairdresser." I raised my silver tote, and my brows, in explanation. "I'm to report to Franco."

"I'm Franco." He elongated the syllables in his name until they rolled several times, but he still didn't look convinced.

"I do hair." Great. Here three minutes and I was already reduced to sounding like an idiot. "At least that's what I'm supposed to be doing."

"Well." He fisted hands on hips that made mine look positively round and fluttered his head. "No one tells me anything. 'Keep it sharp, Franco,' 'We need more energy, Franco,' 'Bring in a new girl, Franco,' but do you think they'd tell me anything? Noooooooooo. Last to know."

"I'm sure the young woman commiserates with you, Franco, but now is not the time."

The dark, measured voice came from behind us and had me bracing. Not a normal reaction.

I was glad I had held myself still when the man stepped from behind me onto a grassy walkway bordering trimmed shrub hedges.

Bran.

Man, oh man, his picture did *not* do him justice. He looked a lot like the soccer star, David Beckham, with that height and those broad shoulders, and that same rough-edged hardness. A deep-set slant to his eyes had me wanting to step backwards.

And then there was the way his casual jacket hung on him. No wonder he was making a name for himself in fashion. If his clothes offered even a hint of the power he possessed, they'd make a woman feel unstoppable.

"You know I can *not* work under these circumstances," Franco's voice rose in pitch.

"Of course you can, you have so far." Bran kept his gaze even and steady on mine. Enigmatic, yet inviting me to tease the over-pompous Franco. Tempting.

I caught myself biting my lower lip. Smiling at the majordomo's expense was probably not the best way to ingratiate myself on the first day on the job.

"Hi." I swallowed as I set my suitcase down to extend a sweating palm, stealing a quick glance at my ring. The device was tingling, warm but not as much as I'd expect. So did this tingle mean a preternatural or was it simply my nerves on hyper-drive? "I'm Alex Noziak. The new hairdresser."

"Bran." His grip was steady and strong. He exuded sexy, but I doubted he could help himself. Not with the way his dark-blue eyes looked at a woman as if she were the only other human on the planet. Then he stepped closer. An intimidation move? Most likely. But I wasn't about to give an inch, even if it meant rubbing thigh to thigh with him.

Oops. Bad image.

"Noziak?" he murmured, an aged bourbon over ice sound, sending a frisson of electricity down my spine. "An unusual name."

"My father's."

He continued to imprison my hand, which I didn't like because touching his skin was volatile, as if I were plunging my hand into a hot circuit and holding on.

I swallowed deeper and added, "It's Shoshone."

Franco gave me a blank look.

"You know, Native American. Indian?"

"Explains the hair and bone structure." The slight man shook his head. "Shame. Exotic always sells."

Bran spoke again, "And Alex is a man's name, no?"

"Yeah," I said, "but I'm not."

"I see."

Holy crap, even talking to him was like dancing among landmines.

I snatched my hand back, and tightened my smile. Point to Bran. Ten seconds and he'd gotten under my skin. Not a good sign. Nor was the fact I couldn't learn more about him other than he was clearly hiding something. But what?

Blocking Bran out, like that would be possible, I shot Franco a quick glance, "If you tell me where to set up my equipment and let me know what you want, I'll get started."

Yeah, it was kind of running away but a smart fighter knew when retreat made strategic sense.

"Wait." Bran's voice stopped me and had Franco stepping away. Far enough to give Bran and I a semblance of privacy. Or he was smarter than I was.

I stood my ground as silence, broken only by the high-pitched screams of peacocks, swirled around me. Bran simply stood there, his dark eyes shadowed, secrets hidden in their depths.

"If you don't mind, it's been a long flight and I'd like to get settled," I uttered, when he made no move to speak.

"This is *my* business," he said, his tone no longer inviting—a whispered threat, curling the hairs along the nape of my neck. "Do not forget that."

"Why should I?" I'd played with bullies before. They didn't scare me. As long as I didn't get lost in the darkness of those eyes.

"You report to me here."

"Sorry, no can do." I kept my tone light and flippant, smothering the urge to tell him where he could take his demands and shove them. "I have my own orders."

"I'll not let you destroy my business."

"Then stay out of my way and let me do my job." Each word came evenly spaced as I curled my fingers tighter around my suitcase handles. Threats tended to piss me off.

"Oh, Mr. Franco," I called, putting an end to any response by Bran. "I'm ready to get set up."

Franco looked shrewdly between his boss and me before shrugging. "Fine. Follow me."

I did, aware that turning my back on Bran wasn't easy. And then I stopped in my tracks, glancing over my shoulder. He stood where I'd left him, his eyes hooded, his stance so still it looked like he wasn't breathing. Maybe he wasn't.

That's when the heat from my ring kicked in. But ring or no ring I had just realized what he was.

Warlock. Yin to yang.

Enemy to witches.

CHAPTER 10

Bran, the man in charge, a freakin' warlock. I should have known this assignment wasn't going to be a cakewalk.

He said nothing more as I walked away from him. Score one for me. Maybe anger was the way to deal with him. Keep him at a distance. And boy would that be necessary, especially until I was able to determine what kind of warlock he was, and if he recognized me as witch-born.

That would not be good as witches and warlocks made oil and water seem compatible. We had not always been blood enemies, but more times than not we played on opposite sides, no matter what. It was as if we were separate halves of a whole and always worked better against one another rather than together.

At the least he could neutralize my magic abilities, such as they were, but more common was to usurp them for his own use. Think of walking zombies, which explained the cold shiver down my back as I followed Franco's scuttling form.

I rolled tense shoulders, ignoring what that did to my ribs, and focused on my first objective, which was to infiltrate the corps of models and attendant personnel: seamstresses, assistants, stage crews, the works. Tackling the High-and-Mighty could wait a bit. Not long but a bit. Until I got my feet under me. Or hell froze over.

One challenge at a time. I'd tried to tell Ling Mai that being a hairdresser was one thing, being a fashion hairdresser was a whole other profession. It was the difference between being a professional mechanic and a Jiffy Lube serviceman.

The first focused on big issues and survived by their reputation; the latter ran clients in and ran them out, bada-bing, bada-boom.

But Ling Mai had only smiled, nodded her head, and given me twelve hours to prepare and pack. Hardly enough time for me to tuck my own hair into a no-nonsense French braid and grab some clean clothes. Now I wished I'd dressed a little spiffier, less jeans and washed cotton shirt and more sissy. Like Vaughn, or even Kelly. They should be doing this girlie thing, not me.

I followed Franco through a doorway made for much shorter people, aware his hips swayed more than mine, and stepped into a blue-and-white-tiled kitchen. I opened my senses for warding spells but caught none. Interesting. Either warlock Bran felt very secure in protecting his own without any magic insurance or he guarded only what really mattered to him.

Crossing stone floors we emerged into a short hallway from which I caught a quick glimpse of the main entryway with a grand staircase and a hundred thousand dollar chandelier.

So not my world.

Franco flipped his hand to the right. "Through there is the billiard room and library. To the left the dining room." He eyed me. "For the guests." He enunciated each word in case I didn't catch his drift.

I did, tightening my hand on my silver valise, aware my fingers were sweating and not because of the heat. I could sense ley lines running beneath the old house, like faint breezes whispering against my skin. When in need they could be tapped into like a backup generator for magic use. But they could be unpredictable, so working around them always meant being extra aware. As if I needed a reminder with X-factor Bran around.

"Back here is our en suite. Wardrobe and assembly are staged from here. The first show is in." Franco glanced at a fancy gold Swiss watch, as I shifted my focus from magic and danger to the more mundane. "One hour. The models are waiting for you. Suzette is your assistant; she will get you anything you need. But do not be a little piggy, you are here to work, not play. The chateau is off limits to you except on business. Remember that."

Franco no doubt was a very lonely man, or half-man, with his lack of personal skills.

"You do understand?" He blocked a closed doorway to the room beyond, waiting for my answer.

"I understand perfectly." *You twit.*

"Then chop chop."

He opened the door to utter chaos.

CHAPTER 11

Six hours later I wanted to curse Ling Mai, wring Mister Chop-Chop's neck, and have nothing whatever to do with fashion, or skeletal models, or high-strung, nervous women again. Give me a cold beer, a bar full of testosterone, and five minutes off my feet. Or even a deep breath—my ribs were killing me.

Instead one of the models burst through the door, the top of her diaphanous gown already around her naked waist, steely-eyed and demanding a cigarette. Which was taboo. Franco would set her on fire before he'd let one of the gowns be soiled by cigarette smoke, or lipstick, or, God forbid, hair products.

I'd already learned that the hard way. Do not gel a model *before* she slips on a gown, only afterwards, when she had less than ten seconds before racing away on stiletto heels. Made me want to whip out a few spells to make my job easier. But only a fool used magic for personal gain, even in small ways.

The actual promenading didn't take place on a runway as I expected. Here at the chateau I learned the dozen models strutted and strolled amongst guests lounging poolside, or sitting at intimate cafe-style tables set near the vine-draped arbor. A quartet played Mozart and Bach, while local wines, cheeses, and pate were served.

Not in the three bedroom-headquarters allotted to model prep. Here we were lucky to get a swig of bottled water. No food. When I made the mistake and asked for a bite, having

slept through dinner and breakfast on the plane, Franco raised
his hands in sheer horror.

"The clothes," he shrieked.

I quickly caught on that any faux pas created the cry, "The
clothes," whereas all other crises were announced by "Chop.
Chop." or "Girls" stretched into seventeen syllables with
accompanying eye rolling and heavy sighs.

Within an hour I'd crossed Franco off my list of likely
suspects, even though my ring, and my upbringing, identified
him as non-human. A shifter I guessed, though I doubted he
was any higher on the food chain than a rabbit or gerbil.
Within two hours he was off the suspect list altogether. No
man could plan and execute such a variety of thefts when a
dangling thread sent him into a tizzy.

Sheesh!

After one emotional outburst, caused by my taking
seconds too long to curl hair, one of the longtime models
leaned close to me and stage-whispered, "It's his time of
month."

"I heard that Collette," Franco huffed. "You'd be better
served closing your mouth; too much bread passes those lips
as is."

"Should I torch him?" I clutched my heated curling iron
tighter, aware if I dug deep enough, and tapped into the ley
lines, I could turn the iron into a sweet flamethrower.

"I'd give you twenty francs," came Collette's quick
response.

"I'll give you fifty," said a woman called Jade. "But only
if I can watch."

In spite of jet lag, being a fish out of water and already
being overworked, I smiled. Female bonding. Nothing like
male bashing to make it happen. Not much of a male but at
least something to rally around. Maybe Mister Chop-Chop
was going to come in handy after all; if he didn't drive me
over the edge first.

Between style changes, meeting and remembering a dozen
models, and at least that many accompanying assistants'
names, several who warmed my ring, alerting me to their

non-human status, I had little time to do anything except crimp, curl, mousse, and gel. There wasn't a second to spare.

So much for intel gathering, though some news could be snatched. As the models changed they'd often let slip some interesting gossip about the elite clientele.

"The Prime Minister's wife is eyeing the apricot number. She'd look like the Chelsea flower show in it."

"Was that the bank financier's wife by the arbor?"

"No, that's his mistress. His wife is near the poolside. She's the sexy one. The mistress has been with him a good twenty years and looks it, poor woman."

"I hear Mademoiselle Robichard is involved with that scientist who's in trouble with the ECE Council. Obviously crime does pay."

Ling Mai might be surprised to know how many people could be aware of potential targets among the clients; some who would be staying the three days the show was in residence, others who came and went, joining the shows at different locations as it moved around.

It seemed blackmail made more sense than theft though. Maybe both were happening and only one issue had come to light.

I would report my theories later. If the day ever ended.

Which I was beginning to doubt would happen when the room grew suddenly still. Like an aviary aware of a predator in its midst, all fluttering, talking, and movement stopped.

I glanced up into cold, blue eyes. Bran.

"My office, front room," he said, then paused, as if he'd thought of something and added, "When you're done, of course." Then he walked away.

No hello. Small talk. Go to hell. He appeared and disappeared like gray smoke on a winter's morn. Yup, a warlock through and through.

The models and assistants eyed me warily until Collette broke the silence. "Not good when the new girl gets called on the carpet first day."

Great. Ling Mai hadn't factored for the possibility of my not being good enough as a hairdresser.

"Ouch," the girl whose hair I was crimping jerked beneath my hands.

"Sorry."

Another bad sign.

Now the minutes flew past until Franco bounced into the room announcing, "That's it girls. Could have been better, but we always have tomorrow."

"He says that every day," Collette whispered, grabbing for her purse and a cigarette.

Franco ignored her. "Tomorrow. First light. Staff meeting in the library. New girl, chop, chop, mustn't keep Bran waiting."

Could I kill Franco before I was fired?

Not in front of a dozen witnesses looking at me as if I were on my way to the guillotine. Either that or something else. Raised surrounded by Dad and only older brothers. I often missed the nuances of women's nonverbal communication. Like now. For all I comprehended the women could be expecting a train wreck where I'd disappear in the fallout, or envious of me having one-on-one time with the big guy.

If they only knew. Warlocks were an iffy bunch. Arrogant. Egotistical. Selfish. These were the common denominators among them, but their powers could vary depending on what type of warlock they were. Some were sorcerers, others mentors, though I doubted Bran fell into that category. Some sought power, others pleasure; with Bran's looks I could believe that. The one thing I did know about warlocks was the fact their very name came from the old Scottish meaning oath breaker or traitor. That said it all.

Wiping damp palms along travel-wrinkled jeans, I glanced quickly at my suitcases. I hadn't yet been shown to sleeping quarters. Another bad sign? On the other hand having both cases handy gave me a second to snag one of the techno-whiz thingies I'd been handed to use. Technology was so not my thing, but some of the spy toys we got to play with were uber-cool. When they worked.

I warded my suitcase as I zipped it closed. A simple spell and as natural as breathing. What was mine stayed mine.

That was different than using magic for gain, but in this place I expected even a simple spell to backfire.

Since when had I become such a pessimist? From what Ling Mai had said, big shot warlock had no choice but to keep me. My presence kept Interpol from shutting down his operation on a flimsy pretense while they investigated.

So either hunk-of-the-year played friendly, or I blew the whistle. Or he cast a spell over me, which I couldn't counter and I became his patsy as he continued to do whatever the hell he was doing.

Too bad the knowledge didn't help unknot my stomach as I knocked on the closed office door.

"Come in." Even behind thick wood his voice sounded deep and magnetic.

Pull it together. He's just a warlock. With a sexy accent. And killer looks. And a royal pedigree. And a fortune.

So there might be a few intimidation factors.

But I carried an anathema dagger, more a sweet, lethal knife than a jabbing stick, tucked against my ankle and the power to shut him down.

There, I'd just evened the playing field.

Yeah, right. A witch needed all her wits about her to play in the same league as warlocks.

Good, I loved a challenge.

I shoved the door harder than I meant, then lunged to catch it. So much for professional first impressions. He looked up from a desk, no less powerful sitting down and across the room, than up front and inches from my face.

Distance. Think distance.

He silently released a sheaf of papers he'd been reading. "Close the door. We must talk."

Why did that sound like something a principal would utter? Right before the ax fell. Probably because one or two had, back in my wild days. They also showed the same intense, controlled determination Bran's face now showed.

Plus my ring was tingling, but on low-voltage, as if it couldn't make up its mind how much of a non-human Bran was, or how much of a threat.

I had the answer to that already. A big one.

I smiled between tight lips as I closed the door and stepped forward, but only one small step, opening my senses to determine if there was a warding in the room.

Nada. But then he could have taken it down given I was coming.

I steeled my voice to a casualness I didn't feel. "I'm here, so talk."

"There's been a development."

Van? My heart slammed to the floor. *Don't let him be dead. Please.*

But Bran wouldn't know of my connection to Van, or why I was here, seeking information on my brother. So I sucked in a tight breath and found myself still bracing for Bran's next words.

"I have contacted your superiors. You have to leave."

CHAPTER 12

Why did I have to leave? Van or something else?

"Is there a problem?" I asked with a lump the size of a fist in my throat. "Something other than you don't want me poking in your business?"

Push the fight to his ground. First playground rule of warfare and I had no doubt I was on the front line of a battle.

I felt a wave a magic wash against me. A compulsion spell followed by, "It's better for you to leave. Trust me on this."

Not in this life, big guy. He didn't get to jerk me around. I was here, to stay, until I found what I'd been sent to find and maybe a little more. But something had happened to make him change his decision to allow me access to his fiefdom. I raised my hand, pushing against his compulsion as one would push against a stiff breeze.

Questions jackknifed through me, but before I could voice any of them the door slammed open, right into my backside.

"Oh, sorry," a stunning woman said in a foo-foo fancy French accent, her tone implying just the opposite. "I did not realize you were with someone."

She spoke directly to Bran, completely ignoring me standing there, one hand massaging a sizable bruise on my shoulder, my ring kicking into overdrive, heating enough to make me want to wave my hand to cool it off. A scent of cinnamon and something else wafted around her, but I was too busy focusing on her to pay attention, that and being aware the compulsion spell had lifted.

Damn, I'd almost forgotten about her.

Well, bite me!

I recognized her from the ops pictures, but again even three-dimensional imaging didn't do this woman justice. She was everything I once dreamed of becoming when I was a little girl: beautiful, poised, totally pulled together in that no-wrinkle, no hair-out-of-place kind of way fashion models achieved in magazine photos. The honey and amber highlights in her hair alone would take a fortune to keep up.

This woman looked like she would never have made a social guffaw, never have done anything with less than total assurance and style. Plus she had that take-me-to-bed French accent.

I hated her on sight, even if she was non-human and thus had extra elements we mere humans didn't possess.

Bran's voice broke through my checking out his cousin. "You needed something, Dominique?"

The tone bordered on brusque, or frustrated; yet their body language screamed that there was a great deal of familiarity between them. But how familiar? This was Europe and a much more cosmopolitan world. Were kissing cousins acceptable in this world? As if that should be my first thought.

More to the point, did Dominique know about my mission? And if she did would I-don't-want-you-here Bran share that intel with me?

In my mind, though, the one thing I knew for sure was that I was odd one out in the room.

Dominique raised one perfectly arched eyebrow and shot me a who-dragged-this-in glare though she still spoke only to Bran.

"Well, if you're busy I can always come back later." Then, before Bran could answer, Dominique waved one exquisitely manicured hand toward me. "And you must be?"

The gum on your shoe.

Pissing contests were not in the mission plan.

"Alex Noziak," I replied, extending my hand.

Leave it to Ms. Nose-in-the-Air to ignore my gesture.

Fine, too bad I didn't scent magic on her. Power, yes, but not magic.

Interesting. This woman was clearly not all human. But what was the otherness? Fae? Selkie? Some type of an elemental? Why hadn't I spent more time studying the folklore books Kelly always kept handy? And why didn't the IR Agency have a tool that could actually identify the type of preternatural? So not helping in this situation.

I let my hand fall to my side and brushed it against my jeans. Note to self, contact Kelly soon and push her to dig deeper into who or what Dominique St. Clair might be; as well as check the IR contacts to see what kind of warlock Bran was.

Dominique glanced at Bran, clearly trying to place me, the interloper.

Bran ran a hand through his thick, jet hair. "Alex is our new—" he looked at me for a second as if searching for the proper word. "Hairdresser. She arrived today."

"Oh."

What a wealth of dismissal could be contained in one small word.

Dominique's lips tightened, her smile slightly more jaded as she slid her attention away from me and focused it totally on Bran. "We really must finalize the last three cities and the contract with Papadolapas is waiting."

I'd been shut out by a pro.

Bran cast me a wary look by glancing around Dominique's stance, not an easy feat as the woman strategically dominated the room front and center.

"Alex, we'll discuss our business later."

Yeah, right. Contracts always trumped dismissal. On the other hand, if we were to talk later, it meant I was still here for now. Bran just handed me some time, which I planned on putting to good use.

Dominique verbally pounced on Bran's words. "What business?"

"I was wondering where I got a bite to eat," I lied, but only partially as I slid myself forward to be closer to Bran's desk.

"The help *always* eats in the kitchen."

Ouch. Between her and Mr. Chop-Chop, I wouldn't have much of an ego left.

"Thanks, I appreciate that." My tone was neutral, my emotions anything but, as I slid my fingers along the carved lip of the massive desk and left a small, almost invisible calling card. I could have cast a quick seeking spell, but with Bran being a warlock I didn't want to alert him that I was invading his private space, and warlocks were damned good at sensing other magic being used. I was hoping he didn't possess that ability when it came to traditional listening devices.

I didn't even glance toward him as I left the room.

Even before I was down the hallway and headed toward a safe location where I could eavesdrop, I jammed the listening device into my ear and hooked an iPod to my belt in case anyone wondered why I was concentrating so intently.

Thank heavens it was free time and I didn't have to return to the crowded staging room and a dozen chattering models. I avoided the kitchen where the hired help were already eating and escaped through the front door, marching down the crushed shell driveway as if I belonged.

It took less than ten seconds to hear Bran's rich voice coming through loud and clear, and the tone indicated he wasn't happy.

"That wasn't called for," he said. "We're already down two personnel; no need to make it three."

"Bran, darling," Dominique's voice oozed appeasement. "You know models and assistants and. . ." she paused, then continued; I could imagine her waving one manicured hand toward the door. "And people who fuss with hair."

"She's a professional, Dom, a hairdresser."

"Whatever." Dominique's tone tightened. "They're easily replaced."

She actually sounded like Ling Mai for a moment. Lose an agent, find a new one, no big deal.

Dominique continued, "You shouldn't be bothered with such trifles. You know I handle those pesky details so you can focus on what you do so well."

Oh, that held a wealth of unstated meaning. What was it, besides clothes, that Bran did so well? That question moved to the top of my to-find-out list.

There was silence. Not a comfortable one. The sound of someone moving in the room. Bran probably. Doing what? Creating space from his cousin or giving him time to think? "You mean designing."

He sounded weary, as if carrying something heavy. I hadn't heard this side of him yet.

"Yes, designing," Dominique continued, adding, "And finessing the clientele, who I do believe even now are waiting for your appearance."

"You make me sound like a gigolo."

I could hear her give him an air kiss that actually sounded dismissive. "Do be a dear and put in an appearance. These women always buy more when they associate your clothes with you."

He took that crap from her? I'd heard of warlocks enthralled by other beings more powerful than themselves, but had thought that was an urban myth.

Bran spoke again, "And if I want them to buy the clothes based on the design, the textures, the care and attention I put into every piece? Is that too much to ask?"

Okay, so maybe all was not well in paradise. There was a sharpness to Bran's words that would have had me backing up a step, or raising a quick deflection spell to defend myself. So if he was bespelled he wasn't hiding it in his tone. What the heck was going on around here?

Dominique's tone sharpened. "These women are cows. They must be led to water, or hay or whatever they feed cows."

"Now I'm cow fodder?" Bran replied.

"Don't take this so personally, darling. This is simply business. You trust my business sense, do you not?"

"Yes."

"Then do as I ask."

More silence. A weighted one. I used my fingers to press the listening device deeper into my ear, my breath held, to see what he would do. Tiger in the den—managed by his cousin or ready to snap?

"Go on now," she shooed. "Make nice."

I could hear movement. Waited.

When his voice came it sounded resigned and far away. Probably near the door. "I'm thinking of canceling future trunk shows. I think we have enough name recognition to do just Milan and New York once a year."

Take that manipulating bitch! I wanted to high five him, especially as I could hear her struggle to reign in temper beneath her words.

"But we have contracts, commitments."

"We'll discuss it later," he said, then the door opened and closed, not with a bang but with controlled silence.

Interesting? It was obvious that the cousins worked as a team, but not all was easy between them. I knew I butted heads with my brothers, still did now, but no matter how much we goaded or pushed at one another, there was always caring beneath our words. I wasn't hearing that between Bran and Dominique. So what did that mean? Familial dysfunction or something more?

I was just ready to remove the earpiece and return to the house, assuming the fireworks were over, when I heard Dominique's voice again. Loud and clear and sharp enough to snip through metal.

"St. Clair here."

So Dominique hadn't left Bran's office. Must be a phone call as I couldn't hear any other voices enter the room and the phone must have been on vibrate as there'd been no telltale ring.

"There were complications," she said, with barely schooled composure in her voice. I wonder what she meant?

A pause, as if she hesitated or was listening. "Nothing I can't handle. We proceed as planned."

Back to business tone.

"Explain?" she snapped the word.

Crap, what I wouldn't give to hear the other end of the conversation.

"But we've had—" A sudden silence, followed by Dominique speaking in a different tone. One more conciliatory. Or afraid. "What kind of test?"

I wondered if the agency could tap Dominique's cell phone? Something was going down here and I wasn't getting enough intel.

"I need lead time to make plans, you know that."

Crap. Crap. Crap. What test? What plans? Was this about the thefts? Or something else?

More silence until she asked sweetly, too sweetly, "What kind of problem?"

I found myself bracing against the danger beneath Dominique's voice. Then she asked, "Who?"

Followed by a mirthless laugh. "What do you mean he's not cooperating? He's trained to resist but all beings can be broken, even shifters."

Van? Could she mean Van?

My heart kick-started as my breath stalled.

"They'll never find him," she said. "I'll make sure they don't."

Then she swore. One short, pithy phrase I'd heard a thousand times except this time it made my blood freeze.

The door to the room opened and closed.

Then nothing.

CHAPTER 13

"Of course she didn't mention Van by name, but I know that's who Dominique was talking about," I repeated in the secure call I made to Mandy, my stuck-in-a-hospital-bed-because-I-put-her-there handler on this mission. After Dominique's call, I skipped eating to make a quick check-in to the IR headquarters, feeling the situation had taken a dramatic turn. While at the same time all I had were bits and pieces of what that turn meant, and who was the driving force.

I stood far enough from the house to have a measure of privacy, keeping my voice low just in case. "It was the tone of what she said."

"Yeah, right, that's going to go over big in a report to Stone and Ling Mai," Mandy replied, "The witch has a hunch."

It so was a good thing there was a whole Atlantic Ocean between us right then.

I snarled, "Would it be too much to ask to get a trace on Dominique's phone?"

"Get me the number and I'll pass it along."

"Would you like me to borrow the cell and send it to you, too?" My tone was so saccharine sweet I'm surprised Mandy didn't go into diabetic shock.

"No, that's okay. Just the number," came her whiplash response, just as syrupy and insincere.

And Stone wanted us to work as a team. Bull pucky.

I held my phone away from my ear, not sure if strangling it was going to help my tension level at all.

"Listen, Chiquita," I enunciated every syllable. "If you can't handle being my go-between, I can send a request direct to Ling Mai and ask for someone a little more competent. Like say the janitor?"

"Keep in mind, witch, who sees Ling Mai every day before you start huffing threats around."

Damn and double damn, she was right. She was there, with Ling Mai's ear, and I was here, isolated and vulnerable.

On the other hand, I had a very good memory and I would not be in France forever.

It took every ounce of control I had to keep my voice level as I repeated. "Have someone get that phone tapped. The number should be available from your end."

"Yeah, work, work, work." Mandy released a huge sigh before shifting the conversation, "You met hubba-hubba hunk guy yet?"

Bran.

"Yup." Tread warily around Mandy, no telling how she could translate the least hint of hesitation on my part. Hesitation or caution.

"And?"

I glanced around, only a small cluster of ladies sipping wine near the pool, peacocks mingled amongst them. "He's a warlock of some kind, but I need to know what kind."

"I thought witches could tell that kind of crap?"

This assignment was getting harder and harder by the second.

"Fine, I'm not getting enough intel to determine what that means." Except for it being bad news for a witch, but no way was I telling Mandy that tidbit. "Any way I can get some other clue as to what Bran is or isn't?"

"How the hell are we supposed to know here. You're the one on site, with all the fancy woo-woo abilities. Can't you cast a spell or something?"

In spite of Ling Mai's direct orders to practice my magic at every chance I got, she had no idea how volatile magic was, or how easy it was to slide down to the dark side of it. A simple warding spell here, a summoning spell there and pretty soon you were using magic for all the wrong reasons.

But there was another issue. "Last thing I want to do is alert Bran to my abilities. That's like giving him a green light to usurp them if he's that kind of a warlock."

Mandy laughed, as if she enjoyed my being in the hot seat. "I'd think that stirring him up, up close and personal like would be a perk."

"Bran's about as friendly as a polecat in heat."

"Oh." I could have sworn Mandy snorted, but her voice was level as she asked, "You want me to report that verbatim to Ling Mai?"

Not in this life. "Let's just say he's aloof, very controlled, and better looking in real life."

I so did not say that last part. Not aloud.

"Poor girl." Mandy obviously wasn't feeling my pain. Oh yeah, this gig was a barrel of laughs. "Hang in there, witch, it's only your first day."

From Mandy it was meant as a bitch-slap, and it stung.

"Any specifics Ling Mai wants ferreted out? Besides what I've already found?" I asked, back on task, and already second-guessing myself.

"We have a list of models etcetera but you're to get fingerprints from everyone in the group to cross reference against what Interpol gave us."

Sure, nothing like a small task. A dozen sets of fingerprints, taken surreptitiously, while living and working in utter mayhem—piece of cake.

"Ah, Mandy, you know of any non-humans who can be beautiful, ice cold, and lethal?" There was something about Dominique St. Clair.

"Figure it out yourself, witch. That's what you're there for."

Damn she was a PIA. "Let me rephrase. If I get you some specifics about a non-human's attributes you think you could be bothered to dig up some info that will help me identify her? If she was a run of the mill non-human I'd have pegged her by now." Which was stretching the truth, but no way was I giving Mandy any more ammunition to shoot me down.

"Who is it?" she asked, though I doubt she realized how much curiosity she revealed in her tone. "Bran's cousin—"

"That Dominique woman?"

As if Bran had a dozen cousins hanging around. "That'd be the one. Something not a hundred percent about her. I got a hit off my ring but fat lot of good that does." I glanced around, making sure no one had walked up anywhere near me. "Anything I can do to make her show her true colors?"

"Have you tried pissing her off? You should be good at that," came Mandy's not-so-helpful advice.

On second thought, that might not be a bad idea. Dangerous, but a sure fire way to find out. Most non-humans, like humans, showed their truest personalities while under duress.

"Alex?" Mandy's voice poked me.

"What?"

"You know that was a joke," she sounded unsure, like I'd felt when unleashing three echo-demons instead of one.

"Joke or not, it might work."

"I don't think that's a good idea." Mandy's tone made the hairs on the back of my neck stand up.

"Why not?"

"Didn't you listen to any of Fassbinder's lectures?"

Mandy was talking about the IR instructor tasked with teaching our so-called team what was known, and not known, about the creatures walking among humans; heavy emphasis on the unknown. Growing up in a household of shifters I had more experience than the rest of the group with non-human contact, but let's face it, Mud Lake, Idaho wasn't a hot bed of non-human activity. Shifters, the periodic Weres, a vamp or two that wandered by on the way to Seattle, but not a lot else. I saw a pixie once, but it was suffering from dementia so I don't think it counted as a good example of how all pixies acted.

I shook my head, as if Mandy could see me. "Fraulein Fassbinder has that stupid lisp on top of her German accent and every other phrase out of her mouth was, 'We think but don't know for sure.'"

Mandy released a sigh on the other end of the connection. At last there might be something we agreed on. "There was that, but Fassbinder knows her mythology."

"Fine, so if I screw up things go wrong," I admitted, mentally bitch-slapping myself for telling Mandy too much. "Just give me the condensed version of why I shouldn't poke at a potential fae, or fallen angel, or whatever the heck St. Clair is?"

"Because most "others" only reveal themselves when they feel threatened."

Wasn't that the point? I might be wiped out, but I wasn't dumb. "As in when they turn dangerous."

"And deadly."

Well crap, there was that. "Why don't I just ask her what she is, would that help?" I asked, my turn at a snide joke.

"You do that."

And just like that Mandy took all my fun away.

"Fine. Anything else I should know in the meantime?" I asked, only partially tongue in cheek.

"No." She paused, then added, "You do know that Bran being a warlock makes this a whole new ball game."

As if I hadn't already figured that out, but damn, I didn't want Mandy to realize it so quickly either. The agency knew that witches were vulnerable to warlocks and as soon as Ling Mai got the report she'd pull me out so fast my head would levitate. Time to shift Mandy's attention.

"Look, Mandy," I paused. A Noziak asking for help didn't come easy, even if the request was half ploy. A Noziak asking for help from Mandy might be a very bad idea. She could hang me out to flutter in the wind, or screw up my request, which could put me in more danger, not less.

"Yeah?"

I fingered the ring Ling Mai had given me. Its coolness seemed to help as did hearing Ling Mai's voice saying, "Remember, you're part of a team and you have abilities to hone. Do so and you could be unstoppable."

"You need something?" Mandy prodded, for once not sounding snippy.

"Yeah." I released a sigh. "With St. Clair's phone conversation, I'm thinking I need more backup here."

This time it was Mandy who went silent, no doubt in shock because I'd even asked. Heck, I was in shock.

"I'll tell Ling Mai, but you know she'll yank you out. You've already screwed the mission just by being an incompetent witch, now you're asking for help?" came the withering response. So much for a hell, yes, we'll cover your six.

Best to act as if I were a lone witch, which I was until I got yanked from the mission. The clock was ticking.

"I'll get the prints to you as soon as I can find a means," I said. "Out."

I didn't return to the staging room inside the chateau immediately, though. Instead I stood looking beyond the lavender fields, a row of poplar trees framing the fading cerulean sky. I scanned the house, mellow golden in the early evening twilight. A quick glance picked out Bran standing amongst a flock of French matrons. His shoulders looked rigid, but that could be a trick of the light.

Was he involved with Van's disappearance? If so why allow an agent in his midst to poke around? Unless he figured a measly hairdresser from a small agency was no threat at all. What was that expression? Keep your friends close but your enemies closer. And by keeping me on a tight leash within his sphere of power he no doubt thought he could neutralize any damage to him.

"Think again, big guy," I whispered aloud. "Think again."

If Big-Shot, single-name warlock Bran thought he was safe, he was wrong. And if Miss-I'm-Too-Good-For-You cousin believed the same thing, she was wrong, too.

Very wrong.

I didn't want to be here, but I was; and right now I was probably the only chance of finding out what the hell this group was up to. And I'd better do it quick, before I was ordered out. Like I was planning on following those orders. The second I left this Bran bunch, Van's life expectancy plummeted.

No matter who was involved, or what they were involved in, or who I had to take down in the process, I was staying, with or more likely without my team's backing.

Hone your abilities.

Maybe Ling Mai was giving me more than a pep talk. Start with small spells and work my way up. Do no harm to others and I should be okay. With hope.

One last glance at Bran and I headed toward the house. First things first. Find some grub. Even peons were allowed to eat.

Then I'd get to work. The sooner I found the puppet master and thief, the sooner I could focus one hundred percent on finding Van. So help any of these people if they were involved in that.

I loved it when life was black and white.

CHAPTER 14

I clenched my frosting pick and wondered if it'd be rude to jab it up a certain prancing man's backside? Poor form, no doubt.

"Chop chop, ladies, time's a wasting."

Oh, it was so tempting.

"New girl. Jade needs more oomph with her bangs."

I was not a miracle worker. I couldn't manufacture bangs where there were none to begin with. Not in seventeen seconds.

"You want me to cut some from back here?" I fisted my hand in a hank of hair along Jade's neck. "And glue them on her forehead?" I asked sweetly. Too sweetly. My brothers would know to tap dance around me with that tone. Mr. Chop-Chop was about to learn.

He spread his hands like a flock of pigeons taking flight. "It's your job, not mine. Must I do everything around here?" He flounced off before I could respond—or use the frosting pick.

A shame.

"The man is clueless," Collette murmured behind me, changing into a frothy gown of diaphanous pink and orange. A color combo I'd never consider going together, but on the dark-haired woman it looked sharp and sassy.

As I spritzed Jade's hair, sans bangs, I asked, "Is he always this . . ."

"Big a pain in the ass?"

"Impossible?"

"Cruising for a bruising?"

I laughed. "Yeah, that about sums it up." I handed Jade a jar of gel, making sure I handled only the top and bottom as I passed it to the model. "Can you hold this?"

Jade nodded, planting a full set of prints around the container. "He wasn't always this bad," she offered to a series of head shakings and groans. "No, I mean it. Four months ago, when he started out, he was actually kind of shy."

Interesting. Not the shy part, I didn't believe that for a moment, but the fact the man hadn't been with the group long. Since the thefts had gone on for at least a year, that let Chop-Chop off the hook.

Too bad, I'd have loved to use cuffs on the guy and not in a sexy, let's-have-some-fun way.

I nudged the conversation in the direction I wanted it to move. "Hasn't the show been on the road for some time? I figured everyone's been with the group since they began. You all seem very comfortable with each other."

"What you're really saying is we're all as crazy as fruitcakes and rubbing off on each other." Collette grinned. While changing, or with the models, the woman's Liverpool accent came through loud and strong. Amongst the guests, the model spoke what sounded like charm-school French in a demure whisper.

I eyed the woman's half-empty water bottle; glass, not plastic. Two down, a good ten or more to go.

"So how many have been here since the show started?" I asked, winding a coil of Jade's hair around my index finger. Chop-Chop might not get bangs, but he'd get his volume.

Collette glanced around. "I've been here since the start. Actually worked with Bran when he was still at Brighton, doing his one-a-days."

"One-a-days?"

"Yeah. You rent a hall. Gather a core group of models. Promote like hell and hope a couple of nabobs will hear about it and take a risk."

"Sounds iffy." I curled another ringlet, securing it above the last one, not wanting to think of Bran scraping and struggling, daring all on a near-impossible dream. Not that the average warlock ever struggled, not in their genetic make-up. So why did he not use the dark powers most warlocks had access to in the blink of an eye? Was there more to him than I'd first noticed?

It was safer to think of him as in control of his world, on top and assured. Not that I wanted to think of him at all. He was a mission. That was all.

"Those early years were iffy." Collette shimmied into a dark red silk sheath that made my mouth water. "Man's a bloody genius, though, and a frigging hard worker. Would have been easy to bitch and moan about the way his family treated him, but he never did. Not even when they tried to stab him in the back."

"In what way?"

Intel, not interest.

In a pig's ear.

"Early days he could have used a bit of endorsement, if you know what I mean. But that harpy of a mother of his did just the opposite. Poison, sheer poison, her spreading lies and rumors. His old man simply turned his back. Bloody pikers the two of 'em."

"Didn't seem to hurt him much," I said. "I mean, look where he's at now."

"All by his own blood and sweat it is." Collette looked around the crowded room, her voice low against the chatter of the other models. "And he never forgets who helped him either. Man's a bloody saint if you ask me."

Warlock turned saint? Not likely. And definitely not the man who told me to take a hike yesterday. I'd avoided him since then so he hadn't had a second chance to tell me to leave. Could he have cast a blood spell for success? Very powerful stuff, but I'd believe that sooner than I'd believe he didn't call on any of his magic to get where he was today.

I casually asked, "What do you mean he's a saint?"

"Two years ago, Suzette's mother died sudden like. Man had her flown back home in the middle of a show, by private jet, and all the funeral arrangements taken care of. He that don't have a lot of family, he knows they matter."

I glanced toward the assistant Suzette, who nodded her bobbed head, eyes all but invisible beneath her bangs. A different image of Bran was appearing; one warring with my instincts to label him as strictly bad news.

Collette continued, "Then when Pamela had that boyfriend who was no good. Kept slapping her around. Well one night Bran went and paid the wanker a visit. No problems after that."

I wondered what spell Bran had used? A disappearing one? Or a mind-wipe one. They were harder, requiring much more magic, and very tricky. Not that I'd ever done one. They were black magic and I didn't touch the stuff. But I bet Bran did. Still?

"The man went in person?" This didn't sound like the aloof, hands-off guy I'd butted heads with yesterday.

"Sure did. Never said a word, but Pamela saw Bran, didn't you, Pammy?"

A willowy blond who looked as ethereal as air popped her head out of the neck of an organza blue cloud of a dress. "Sure enough. That man's all right in my book."

"Interesting." I nodded for Jade to move away. The woman glanced at herself in the standing mirror.

"Oh, I like this. A bit of all right. You go, hairdresser."

Take that Chop-Chop.

As if summoned, the slight man bounced into the room, his face wreathed in smiles, his hair poker-straight. "Ladies, attention, ladies." He clapped his hands as if we were scattered over a football field instead of in a ten-by-ten foot room. "I have an announcement to make."

I wanted him to get on with it, but the man had his own sense of timing. He waited until all voices subsided before waving in a woman standing directly behind him. "Girls, pay attention."

Jade's bubble gum popped.

"This is Sasha. Our new model." Franco beamed, though the smile held a hint of tightness. "Sasha, this is Team Bran. Girls, be nice to her."

No one said a word. I glanced around. Tension bloomed, but I couldn't pinpoint the why or where it came from. Of course "Team Bran" would ruffle any sane person.

I cast a look at the new woman. Striking enough in an angular way. Long-legged, dark-skinned, gaunt look around the eyes. Was it professional jealously from the regulars? Or Franco treating them like half-brain peons? Or something else?

The woman looked as uncomfortable as a jackass introduced into a herd of thoroughbreds. But her look dared anyone to say a word.

My ring started to heat and I looked closer, but couldn't see a lot. Fae, maybe? There were as many different kinds of fae as there were shifters and warlocks, but one thing they all had in common was the ability to hold glamour well. Which could explain her looks and her stillness.

"Now, girls," Franco barged ahead, either not sensing the unease or aware, but blatantly ignoring it. My money was on the latter. The guy could give lessons to a steamroller. "Sasha has done mostly runway work. I expect you all to help her transition into the way we do business here. Now chop, chop. We have a show to put on."

The man hopped away, but not before I caught a very un-Franco like glance at Sasha—one filled with wariness. But it happened so fast, I couldn't be sure if I saw or imagined it.

Suzette stepped up to direct the woman to a corner of the already cramped room and conversations started buzzing around us once again.

I sidled over to where Collette stood, her eyes sharp on the new model.

"What's the problem?" I asked, keeping my voice low and pushing the acquaintance a little too fast, but then time was something I didn't have to waste.

Collette cast me a speculative look before shrugging, her voice a husky murmur when she spoke, "If that woman's a model, then I'm a hairdresser."I glanced back at Sasha: long legs, nice enough figure, stunningly angular face. What was Collette seeing that I missed?

"I don't get it," I admitted. "Why do you think she's not a pro?"

"The way she walks. The way she holds her head. No calluses on her feet in those sandals. There's a hundred small signs."

Go figure.

"From what I heard, Franco needs a model," I pushed, hoping the half-guess was mostly true. "You think he's desperate enough that he's willing to go with someone without much experience?"

"Doesn't make sense." Collette shook her head. "He could have a dozen girls here by the end of the day by using Bran's name. Women want to work for him as he treats them like people not cattle."

I didn't mention that benevolence didn't extend to hairdressers, but asked instead, "Maybe Franco's doing a favor for a friend?"

"And risking his own job? The minute Dragon Lady finds out Frankie-O hired a dud, the man's toast."

I didn't have to work hard to figure out who Dragon Lady was. Dominique St. Clair. Interesting. Bran was a saint, but his cousin, far from it.

"Oh, well, luv, not my problem," Collette sighed. "I'll give the bugger a chance and wish her luck."

I nodded before coming to a decision and crossing to greet the new model, my hand extended. "Hi, I'm Alex, the hairdresser. Well, one of the hairdressers."

The woman glanced at my outstretched hand as if it contained typhoid germs. She said nothing.

I let my hand drop. I'd have to track down Vaughn and ask her if they greeted each other differently in the hoity-toity world, as my track record was now zero for zero with the handshaking approach.

Lord, I hoped that didn't mean I'd have to start hugging people. Or air-kissing? Yuck! Just my luck.

"I wanted to say welcome." I cleared my throat, noting the other woman's look was very direct and very guarded. "I'm new here, too, so I don't know much, but thought you'd like to know you're not alone."

"Thanks." The word was said in an insipid whisper.

So much for winning friends and influencing people.

"Fine." I wiped my hand across my smock, aware nerves had dampened my palms. "I'll see you around."

As if sharing small prep spaces, eating meals together in the employee-designated zone, and sleeping like college kids dorm-like in two small bedrooms gave us any other option.

The better for my task. I snatched a discarded ceramic mug Suzette had used earlier. Three sets of fingerprints down. At this rate I might get most of the crew by the end of the day.

Things were looking up.

CHAPTER 15

Things were going to hell in a hand-basket.

"Report." The message scrolled across the laptop window.

The agent typed carefully. At any time someone could enter the library, though it was the least visited of the rooms in the chateau.

"Insertion completed successfully."

"Any suspicions?"

A few shrewd glances. A smirk. The new girl watching very carefully. "No."

"Any new data?"

"New body on site. Staff."

"Details."

"Alex Noziak. American. Native-American ancestry. Hairdresser."

"Who brought her in?"

Hadn't determined that. "Best guess—Bran."

"Doesn't St. Clair handle new employees?"

"Usually, yes."

"Get a set of her prints."

"Will do."

"Anything else?"

How could one describe the intangible? The increasing tension. Wariness where weeks ago there was little. The sharper tone uttered more often. Nothing concrete, everything nebulous. Stress probably, but it could be something else entirely.

"Nothing else to report."

"Next check in?"

"Moving tonight. Monte Carlo. Hotel de Paris. Next day, the Annaliesse. Yacht. Owner—Andrea Liveras. "

"The tycoon?"

"Yes."

"How's he involved?"

"Not sure yet. Will report from there if possible."

"Get data on the new American."

"Will do."

The communication was complete.

CHAPTER 16

I stepped out on the rooftop terrace, the evening stars beginning to twinkle in the darkening sky. It'd been another long day, filled with people. Eight prints down though, so it'd been good.

I still hadn't heard from the agency. Was I really so completely expendable? No orders to pull out and no news on any backup. Cut the agency's losses and find a new witch to train? It's what I'd do and Ling Mai and I were very much alike in that way, bottom line kind of people. But as long as I was out of prison, I was here and I could push to learn what was going on. That and find a connection to Van.

On my own or not I still needed to find out what, Bran and his cousin knew about Van. That would determine my next moves.

All in all it'd been a good day. Except for the tension. Something had happened when the Sasha woman appeared. Less unrestrained talk. More wariness. Less give and take amongst the behind- the-scenes people. A shift in perception that I couldn't put my finger on.

But then it was hard to analyze and think with people always swarming around. It was everything I could do to keep from rubbing up and bumping into everyone all day and no way was there time or space to practice magic.

"You are undisciplined only because you choose to be."

Ling Mai's words echoed inside me. Damn, I hated how she made me doubt myself even more. Or maybe she just picked at an open wound. What did she know about using magic? About the backlash. I'd been very lucky I hadn't killed my brother when I'd killed the rogue Were trying to take him out. And the backlash? I'd say prison counted. Both prison and being a disposable IR agent.

I shook my head to clear it from negative thoughts. This end of the chateau was relatively quiet now, most of the guests and models mingled around the pool area, lit up by a hundred intimate candles. Wine flowed freely as did appetizers prepared by the chateau's gourmet chef. I had to give the man credit, he made one mean sauce over duck. Even the peons got to taste some in the back kitchen. No doubt Dominique would be appalled.

With a sigh I moved across the flat roof, square and bordered by a stone railing, soaking in the blessed near-silence. Too late I noted I wasn't alone.

Bran.

Double damn. I recognized his silhouette even in the deepening gloam and before my ring warmed my skin like a faint tingle. Could it protect me against his dark magic? Or against him? It'd have to be one doozy of a protection emblem to do either.

He'd been facing away, his gaze over the Bordeaux landscape, but the minute I appeared he pivoted as if he sensed my presence, though I wore soft-soled shoes. He looked very much alone. A warlock with the weight of the world on his shoulders. I had a few issues to discuss with him, but now didn't seem the time. The night closed us off. It created a false intimacy. A dangerous awareness.

"I'm sorry to intrude," I said, planning on turning and leaving. "I didn't know you were here."

"Stay." His one word stopped me. Or maybe it was the tone. A dark, compelling sound laced with a French accent. It was as intoxicating as the lavender-laden scents brushing the air. A scent that also smelled ocean fresh.

Think with your head, not your hormones. This isn't a tryst. It's business. And he isn't a lover.

Yet.

Damn, I so did *not* think that.

So why did my hands get clammy? My pulse kick up? I could barely see the man in the deepening twilight and I was acting like the first time I'd sneaked out to meet Billy Wilder. And look where that'd gotten me. Grounded for a week, never ending jibes from all four of my brothers to this day. And one hell of a first kiss.

Okay, nix the last thought.

Business. Focus on the business.

"You want to talk?" I said, glad my voice sounded level. Calm.

Okay, I could do this.

"As I said before, you must leave."

Been there, said that, still wasn't going to make me leave. Not with Van's life on the line.

"Not your call." I was pleased my tone was even.

"You have no idea what you're dealing with."

"Then tell me." I stepped forward. A dare, but dangerous as it put me that much closer to him. Besides why the hell did he care?

Back to task.

"Little witches who play out of their league can be badly burned," he said, his voice deeper, lower, a cross between threat and caress, the tone at odds with the words. "Little witches who leave listening devices where they don't belong are especially vulnerable."

He held out his palm and I noticed the small bug I'd planted under his desk earlier.

Caught. He knew what I was as I knew what he was. But there were degrees of knowing.

I shook my head, trying to clear it. So now he knew I wasn't beyond checking him out as a suspect.

Deal with one issue at a time. But before I could he asked, "Do your superiors know what you are?"

"Not your concern."

He tilted his head. "It can be my concern if I reveal to them what I know about you."

"I don't respond well to threats." I stepped close enough my voice wouldn't carry. "Especially from arrogant warlocks."

He smiled, his teeth a gleam in the darkness.

I was near enough to smell his very sexy cologne and the heat of his skin beneath it. No cinnamon here as there'd been in his office; something more elemental, more primordial.

Mistake.

He paused, then asked, "Are you willing to die?"

"Not if I have a choice," I answered truthfully, surprised that I spoke so freely to him. What was wrong with me?

He said something in a tongue I didn't recognize. I didn't hear it as much as feel it, wrapping around me, lulling me, soothing.

A spell? Would he be so bold?

In a heartbeat.

He stepped closer, hands now jammed in his pockets, his shoulders loose. So why did I feel threatened?

"What are you doing?" I asked, my voice hoarse, my legs weighted to the rooftop as if they grew there.

Not good. What had Ling Mai called this place? The tiger's den. And Bran was the tiger. I fingered my ring, twirling it slowly, each revolution like hearing a song sung far off and faint. Touching the ring was like having a crossing guard stop sign flashed before me. It could shout STOP, but didn't indicate if a Mini Cooper or a semi-truck was bearing down on me. And it sure as heck wasn't making it easy not to get caught in the web Bran was weaving.

Van. Think Van.

I squared my shoulders and shook my head. "If you have nothing new, it's been a long day and I understand we're leaving early in the morning for the next location."

I summoned every ounce of energy I had to whisper the words. There was tired and there was stupid. Stupid could get me killed.

"Yes." He didn't move, but I sensed a change. "I mean what I said."

I too easily recalled his words. "About my leaving?"

"It's still true."

"*You* asked specifically for me."

They weren't the words I'd meant to utter.

"My wanting you to leave is not personal."

Like hell, it wasn't. I came, he saw, not that I wasn't good enough. Sounded personal to me.

"I won't get in your way as long as you don't block mine." There, I *could* do this.

He waved his hand. Not spell casting, but as if breaking his own train of thoughts. Not a Franco gesture, but the movement of a man searching for different words than he'd originally meant to use. "Are you willing to face the risks of remaining?"

He smiled in the darkness, bringing my attention to the shape of his lips. *Dangerous territory.* I could handle him better butting heads, thinking of him as a dangerous warlock.

"Yes." I flexed my fingers against my jeans, aware they had been clenched. "I'm here to do a job. The sooner I can finish it the sooner I can leave."

Two polite strangers, dancing around one another.

Just when I thought I had my racing pulse under control he stepped even closer. So close there was little but shadows between us.

Beware the darkness, there be dragons and warlocks.

I remained rooted to the spot. Training? Not likely, especially as it couldn't explain the breathless free-fall my stomach took. I told myself the sensation was because I feared his powers as a warlock, which I did, but that wasn't all.

He reached toward me, his sculpted face all angles and slashes in the moon-tinged darkness, his lips curled in a sexy half-smile. His fingers ever so lightly touched my collar. Touched and lingered.

"It is off," he said.

My collar or my sanity? Or both?

I said nothing as his fingers paused, sucking away the remainder of my breath. His nostrils flared, the skin of his face tightened. Arousal? It couldn't be. This was the world-famous Bran and I was meant to be invisible.

He wasn't even touching my skin, for cripe's sake. Get a grip on it. He was a warlock.

He wasn't my ally, or even my real employer. There'd be no emotions between us. Not even those between casual acquaintances. If he were behind Van's disappearance, I'd take him down. No matter how sexy his smile, or how dark his scent on the night air.

Until I could prove otherwise he was the enemy and it was vital I remember that.

"You are frightened?" His words lingered as his fingers had, which now thankfully had been removed.

I shook my head as no response seeped past my desert-dry throat.

"Yet you tremble."

That snapped my spine straight. I wasn't a giddy schoolgirl; I was an operative. Best to remember it.

"Nonsense." I stepped back, curling my arms around my upper body. He was right, I was trembling, but it'd be a cold day in Vegas before I'd admit it. "It's been a long couple of days and I'm still dealing with jet lag."

"Are you?" Now the tone mocked. Or was I mocking myself?

"Yes. I don't like to fly." Truth was I didn't like to free-fall. He remained standing there, close enough I watched the increase in his breathing, could almost hear his heart pound louder.

"I'm the hairdresser," I spoke to him but also to myself. Setting the record straight. Wanting to end the crazy tension lacing between us. "It's best we both remember that."

"Are you afraid of me, little witch?"

"No." On some levels it was the truth. But on others—best not to go there. He wasn't just any man and I wasn't just any woman. Keep thinking warlock to witch. Keep my guard up.

"You are sure?" The man was like a waterfall, relentless, determined in his own way. But wanting what? To confuse me? He was doing a damned fine job of that. Distract me? Yup, doing that, too. But making me lose sight of why I was here; he wasn't going to win on that level.

"Good night," I said, with more force than I intended, stepping farther away, breaking the invisible spell between us.

"I shall see you tomorrow?"

"Most likely, since I *am* staying." Bring it home, Alex. Make it clear. "Until my task is complete."

His head snapped as if I'd slapped him. His tone tightened. "I understand. But it is not over between us."

Another threat? Or something else?

I was here to do a job, and the sooner I did it the sooner I could find Van.

"Good night," I repeated.

"Bonne nuit."

Damn, even the simple phrases packed a wallop when he spoke them. No doubt it was the accent. It had to be the accent.

I crossed the rooftop, pausing as I reached the stairs leading below to glance once over my shoulder.

Bran remained where he'd been. Only he was no longer looking out across the chateau's grounds.

He was watching me.

I brushed at the sudden goosebumps crawling up my arms and headed downstairs.

CHAPTER 17

When I reached the bottom of the stairs leading from the roof I realized I was breathing hard, as if I'd run a fast race and barely escaped with my skin.

Ridiculous.

A quick glance down the hallway reassured me I was alone yet I'd only taken a few steps when a nearby door opened. Suzette poked her head out of the room, looking in both directions, obviously as focused as I was on not being seen. Unfortunately neither of us were going to get what we wanted.

"Good evening," I said, as her gaze zeroed in on me. She wasn't tall, a good four or five inches shorter than I was, and had a slender build, a nervous manner, as if easily spooked. Her bobbed dark hair and wide glasses made her look like a kitten waiting to be pounced on.

Her eyes widened, as if she'd been caught doing something, but her voice was a conspiratorial whisper as she stepped out of the room and closed the door behind her. "Good, I was hoping I could speak to you," she said, surprising the heck out of me.

"Why?"

She leaned closer, as if her words might carry far even though she was speaking so low. She glanced in the direction I'd just left, a hesitant smile tugging at her lips. "I don't mean to intrude," she said.

"Intrude on what?" I didn't do nuances well. After a verbal battle with Bran on the rooftop and a very long day all I wanted was to escape to my bed. I could practice witchcraft tomorrow if I could find a private few moments. Ling Mai be damned for now.

Suzette glanced down the hallway again, shirking one shoulder in the direction of the stairs I'd just descended. "It's not my business, but I thought it'd be kinder to tell you."

I was tempted to grab her shoulders and shake the words from her, but kicking the helpless wasn't my way.

"Tell me what? I'm really tired and not firing on all pistons."

Her brows tightened as if I were talking Greek, then she ducked her head, making the dim hall lights spark off her glasses. Her voice carried an accent that wasn't familiar to me though she spoke impeccable English. "You're new and may not realize how he operates."

Now I was glancing toward the stairs. "As in Bran?"

"Yes." She fluttered her hands as if I had shouted the words. "He's a good man, deep down, I think. And he can be kind. . ."

I waved her on, leaning closer, more tempted than ever to rattle whatever she had to say out of her. "What should I know about him?"

"He plays favorites," she said it with a rush of air as if she revealed a deep dark secret.

That was it? Favorites?

Her brow raised, as if willing me to translate what she was saying so she didn't have to say it herself.

I latched onto the quickest explanation. "You mean he has affairs with the hired help?"

She jerked her head as if I'd goosed her. "I wouldn't call them affairs." Her nose scrunched as if smelling skunk. If my ring wasn't stone cold, meaning she was all human I'd think she might be a Wererat or Weremouse with her small tells. "He means nothing by them. But. . ."

"But it's easy for the women involved to think he does," I said, watching and not surprised to see her shoulders relax, her expression smooth. I'd come to the right conclusion without her having to betray her employer.

Lucky me.

"As I said, he's mostly a good man but it's so easy to see girls get hurt. Thinking he means more than he does. And then. . ."

This drifting off with sentences half said was driving me batty, but I kept my voice neutral and even offered a tired smile as I finished the last part. "And then there are hurt feelings. Maybe a scene or two. People losing their jobs—"

"Oh, he never fires them."

I bet he didn't. I bet he left that up to Dragon Lady.

"But they leave," I clarified. Another list of possible suspects—jilted lovers with an agenda. They'd know how the shows worked, where they were being held and how to get behind the scenes.

"Best for all," Suzette murmured, bringing me back to the present, her gaze skittering away.

"So you're warning me to be careful around him?" I'd figured that out myself already.

"Yes." She glanced at me, her look pleading. "I knew you'd understand. It'd be so lovely to have you stay for a while. You're nice."

Boy, had she pegged me wrong, but telling her would be doing that kitten-kicking thing. Besides, she'd tried to do me a favor here. I patted her shoulder, new best buddies. "Thanks, Suzette, I appreciate the advice."

She smiled, a relieved sigh following it before she nodded and headed down the hallway, stopping at the end to turn and offer a small wave.

Yup, new best buddies. Which could work out great. Having the assistant as my conduit could give me behind the scenes intel. Sweet.

And as for Bran, now his actions on the roof made sense. If you can't get rid of the problem, seduce her, and keep her focused on what *he* intended, not what *I* intended.

Made perfect sense. Hurt like a mule kick but it made sense.

I started walking in the direction that Suzette had gone, but when I reached the turn at the end of the hallway I heard a noise and looked behind me. For a second I thought it was nothing, but just in case I cast a simple cloaking spell, pulling shadows a little deeper around me. It wouldn't help if someone came up close but could let me see the length of the hallway without being clearly seen in return.

Take that Ling Mai—there were some spells I could do easily, especially the white magic ones.

I waited a few seconds and bingo, there was movement at the opposite end of the hall, near the roof stairway.

Sasha, the new girl, stepped stealthily from shadow, through the dim light, and disappeared up the stairs, heading to the roof.

Right behind her came a large, buff-colored poodle with fluffy hair that would take a full-time stylist. Funny, I hadn't noticed a dog at the chateau before this, but it looked like something one of the clients would bring along. Another way to stand out to Bran.

Who was being a very busy boy tonight. A tryst? Or something else?

Would he sweet talk Sasha like he'd tried with me? Or— and just like I put what I'd heard on the rooftop with what I knew of non-humans and I knew what type of warlock Bran was.

A word wizard.

Hot damn. I'd heard of them before, but they were rare, so rare a lot of witches thought they were an urban myth. Word wizards could manipulate language, use the sound of their voices to get what they wanted. The stronger ones, and I held no doubt Bran was one, could actually have humans work against their own best interests, if the word spell was potent enough. Savonarola, the Italian Dominican friar had been a word wizard type of warlock—so had the Russian mystic, Grigori Rasputin and Hitler. Some said Churchill might have had a spark of word wizard blood flowing through his veins, too.

No wonder I'd been so rattled speaking to Bran. What could he convince an innocent human to do? Or a smitten woman?

Time to stop being either and start treating him like the threat he was.

CHAPTER 18

Cars revved along the stone streets of Monte Carlo, flower sellers hustled with fishmongers and a brisk-scented ocean spray blew off the Mediterranean. A scent that reminded me of Bran. A sensory bombardment bordering on overload, especially combined with two hard-pressed days of fashion shows from the Hotel de Paris.

I'd stayed out of Bran's way since the rooftop, and surprisingly he'd kept away from me. Two wary adversaries circling one another. Either that or he was too busy with nose-in-the-air Sasha who did not play nice in the sandbox with the other models and kept herself to herself. And that wasn't jealousy speaking. That was a professional assessment of the increasing tension.

The troupe was shifting to a new venue; one that had the hair on the back of my neck standing up straight. We were heading to a luxury yacht and I wanted to go running in the opposite direction.

Instead I softly groaned. Even mention such a la-de-dah statement to my brothers and I'd never hear the end of it. From the Curl Up and Dye Salon to the Hotel de Paris—I'd come a long way in a short time; Mud Lake to Monaco. Who'd have thought it?

Which could explain the fish-out-of-water sensation slapping against me. That and the fact I still hadn't heard from the IR agency. Intentionally?

My nerves warred with my thoughts. Would they contact me if they found news about Van? Truth was I didn't trust my team yet. I didn't trust them to watch out for me and I didn't trust them to work as hard to find and free Van as I would. Problem was I had a real team before I'd ever come to the IR agency—my family, and hanging out doing my hairdresser thing was not getting me closer to helping Team Noziak. That and expecting to be pulled and sent straight to prison if I screwed up, no passing Go and collecting anything, had my nerves razor tight. No way could I help Van from behind bars.

Ling Mai was a pro at playing her cards close to her vest.

With a quick prayer to Ayami, my shaman spirit mentor, for the rash act I was about to commit, I edged away from the crowd of models and assistants standing near the quay waiting their turn to be ferried to the foo-foo yacht in the harbor, our next design venue. Monte Carlo was glitzy and exotic and even more fairytale like than the chateau, but the yacht was said to put the town to shame.

Either way I was out of my comfort zone. Plus it'd mean I'd be isolated physically, and over water. Water meant it was harder to access ley lines for back up magic, plus warding spells didn't work well without being able to ground to earth.

So working on a yacht, no matter how big it was, felt like stepping into a big box with my powers seriously compromised. The powers I was trying to fine tune and practice but rarely got a moment alone. No wonder my hackles were up.

I paused near an older fisherman, leaning against a stack of plastic crates, my ring alerting me to his otherness. A selkie was my best guess. Mostly harmless if left alone.

I'd been on my mission less than a week, but even a slow learner could comprehend this wasn't going as I'd hoped— no quick in and out gig. Which brought its own set of frustrations. Were Bran and troupe involved with Van's disappearance? What clues was I missing? When was I going to get yanked? And the biggest question: how long could I remain ineffectual with my brother's life at risk?

I wasn't the only one who appeared to be walking on nails. I couldn't put my finger on the cause or causes of the models' unease. The new model Sasha? Who barely spoke, much less mingled with anyone else? Franco Chop-Chop with his frenzied dictation and changing hair colors? His short Caesar now dazzled lava-color with highlights of apricot. It almost required sunglasses to look at him. And then there was Bran, who I should be treating as just another suspect.

Too bad it wasn't working that well. I'd caught his gaze on me time and time again. A gaze that made my stomach clench and my breath back up.

Magic casting? Possibly? He was a word wizard, but that didn't mean he didn't have other talents. I could use white magic and then there was my other ability. The one I'd promised my dad I'd never access. Because when I did, things went from bad to worse, really worse. Which is why I was an Invisible Recruit versus locked away in prison for manslaughter.

Magic could backfire in so many ways and I was living proof of that.

Or maybe Bran's actions, or lack of interaction with me, was simply my imagination?

But I had to keep moving forward as if I didn't know that Bran was a powerful warlock and his cousin Dominique St. Clair was something "else." It didn't take my ring to see that she was planning something. What she was I didn't know, and my breaking into her office at the last two venues was a no-go based on how public the venues were. All day and most of the night people traipsed through the chateau and hotel and sleeping with a dozen other people didn't make for easy disappearing and reappearing. Talk about a mess.

I still had three sets of fingerprints to collect, including the new girl's. Two days ago the model had caught me slipping another girl's water bottle into the overlarge backpack I used. A stupid mistake on my part, but nothing had been said, only brows raised.

"They getting to you, luv?"

I snapped back to the present and glanced up to see Collette leaning against a low stone wall, taking a drag on a cigarette like it'd be her last.

"They?" I glanced in the direction of the quay. "Oh, you mean the rest of the group?"

"Like living back in boarding school, not that I did boarding school mind you, but criminy, these women never shut up."

Or leave a person alone. But maybe I could use that. Build a local network of backup help, even if they didn't know what I was doing or why. As it was Suzette had inadvertently helped me by being a font of local gossip, so maybe it was time to buddy up more to Collette.

I grinned, propping my butt on the wall next to her—a chance for a little more probing. "So feeling sardine-style jam packed is not just me?"

"Nah, luv, it's why I smoke these things." Collette stabbed the air with her Turkish cigarette. "Gives me an excuse to get away a bit, if you know what I mean. I grew up with sisters, three of them, and between them and my mum, my old man high-tailed it to the pub every night just for a pint and a bit of privacy. Surprised we didn't drive him around the bend."

"I grew up with brothers." I sighed, missing them terribly. Well, maybe not all of them, not like I was missing Van, but just the camaraderie of focused, task-driven, intelligent kindred spirits. I was so solo here and flying in the dark.

"Brothers? You don't say. Any of them look like you? I mean the coloring and the height? You're a looker, you know. Surprised Frankie-O didn't get you to be the replacement girl instead of that twit he brought in. Did you see the way she paired gold Tiffany cuffs with the magenta Escada fur hat? It was too gauche. Everyone knows silver would have been better, much, much better."

Yeah, as if I knew what a magenta Escada fur hat was. I grinned again before focusing on business. "I thought Sasha was doing all right." It was an outright lie. The woman had rubbed nearly everyone wrong except Franco, but maybe they were twins separated at birth. Or maybe it was Bran's protection as long as Sasha and he were enjoying whatever they had going on.

"Give me a break." Collette chortled. "The woman's a flub. Can't walk, can't talk."

"I thought you were supposed to just model the clothes."

"Oh, no, dear, you've got to get out of the back rooms more and see what's happening. Early in the day just strutting is okay, the clients don't seem to be chatty then. But after the liquor starts flowing they start asking all sorts of questions and we're supposed to be friendly-like."

"What kind of questions? About the clothes?"

"Sometimes." Collette took another drag. "A lot about Bran. What's he like? Who he's dating? The dirt."

"And he doesn't mind?"

"Sure he minds, but he also knows that's business, so he puts up with it. Most days."

"Then what?" My mind tumbled with the options for payback a pissed off warlock could extract.

"He needs to break away the same as the rest of us. Only it's harder for him cuz he's the reason so many of these women come personally to the shows and buy big."

Suzette's words came back to me. Of course he was the reason. A few word spells cast and they'd be snapping up clothes right and left. And doing more? Like stealing for him? Kidnapping people? It wasn't too far a stretch.

It usually took time to fully cast a word spell. Cast it so strongly that the victim would be ensnared even away from the warlock. The female clients weren't here very long, but then a lot of them would be easy prey. Maybe it didn't take that long with the most susceptible, but hell, he had enough women stuck right with him 24/7.

But did that sound like Bran?

A tiger trapped in a gilded cage. I glanced over my shoulder at the yacht floating gently in the harbor. The boat was huge, especially when compared to the casually drifting sailboats and scuttling power boats wafting past it.

Part of me actually felt sorry for him. How long had he been doing this? Was the pressure getting to him? From his tone in the office with his cousin, I'd say that was a big yes.

Wait, that wasn't my issue, unless it impacted the mission. The man was an adult, and an adult warlock at that, with more going for him than the average male. Last thing he needed was my sympathy.

Get my head on straight. Now.

"It must take a lot of money to host these events in these kind of locations." I kept my tone casual, trawling for some insights as to who would want to steal and why. Two reasons came to mind. Money or power. Intel easily translated into power, but money was the more direct reason.

Collette glanced toward the yacht. "I hear that place alone goes for a hundred thousand a week."

"A week? To sleep on a boat?" I coughed out the words. I could buy my dad's pig farm ten times over for that.

"It's not a boat, dearie, it's a yacht." Collette dragged out the word to take the sting out of her correction. "And that don't include the fancy guys doing the ferrying back and forth and any of the extras. Extra servers. Extra booze. Extra everything."

"That's a fortune." Here was a reason to steal and steal big. Cripes, with that kind of money I could help Dad—

"Big funds to you and me, that's a fortune, but those dresses Bran designs start at six figures and go up. And some of these ladies, after a day in Bran's company, they'll buy a dozen of 'em."

"For dresses?" My theory tying Bran, or his cousin, into needing money as an excuse to steal was disappearing like mist in the morn; but I was reluctant to give it up. Greed made so much sense for thefts. Unless the thefts meant something else? Was Bran the one behind the rumors of a single creature that wanted to unite the non-humans? Warlocks were known for their egos and I'd already seen his in action.

Collette stubbed the butt of her cigarette out beneath her sandaled heel. "Not that I don't think Bran's clothes aren't worth it, but blimey, I could get me a nice flat in Notting Hill for what some of these ladies dole out in a day. You coming, luv?"

"In a minute." I waited until the other woman walked off before I bit my lip, squared my shoulders, and did what I'd wandered over here to do. I speed-dialed Mandy; who answered on the third ring.

CHAPTER 19

"Anything to report?" Mandy asked, right on task, no how the hell are you doing or chitchat. No Ling Mai wants to talk to you either.

"No, but I'll be going on board the yacht for the next two days and may not find the privacy to check in. Any news on Van—"

"No. Jaylene's still in Paris. Kelly's backing her up. If they find something they'll tell those who need to know—"

In other words, suck it up and quit whining

"Got it." Wouldn't I love to use a quick rash spell or maybe a human-to-newt transformation spell? Who was she to smack me for asking? I didn't need that message being shoved down my throat.

"There is another option." Mandy held out an olive branch. So why was I guessing I wasn't going to like what she had to say?

I waited until a noisy Vespa putted past to push in the direction I wanted. "For backup?"

"Possibly," she paused, then rushed ahead as if countering my objections before I even had any. "Not from the agency."

Of course not. Which meant I was still persona non grata.

Mandy continued as if my silence meant I was listening. "This could be a temporary Band-Aid but at least you wouldn't be alone and—"

"Who?"

"We could ask help from Interpol. They—"

"No."

"But you haven't—"

I waited until I heard her deep intake of breath on the other end of the line.

"We call in Interpol and it's admitting we can't handle the job. Ling Mai is so not going to go for that." Plus Ling Mai would point the finger at me as not being up to snuff and poof, I'd be out of the agency, heading to prison, and Van would be on his own. And to think just days ago leaving the IR group was *my* agenda.

"I just thought—"

Yeah, right. Two strikes and I'd be axed. That would suit Mandy to a T.

"Forget it, I've got things under control." So maybe I had a smidge of my dad's stubbornness, but damnit, no way was I going to give Ling Mai an excuse to pull me because I wasn't up for the job. No freakin' way.

Asking for outside help sounded like a desperation move. Ling Mai's whole focus had been on the team working with complete independence. If other organizations were called in to save our fannies how could any of the others trust us?

I eyed the boat nearing the quay to snag the last load of us, and talked fast, "Any more info on St. Clair?"

"No. Not yet."

Some days it didn't pay to get out of bed.

"Fine. I've got to go," I said, tightening my shoulders. There was one more stop I wanted to make before getting on any floating boat.

"I'm sure you'll be fine on the yacht," Mandy sniped, as if something bad could happen on a luxury yacht with three dozen people around. But it made sense, too. Yeah, I was isolated with at least three non-humans, Bran, his cousin, and Sasha, but how likely was something to happen in a small, cramped space filled with very wealthy and very public people?

Which reminded me. "Do you know how deep they've run financials on Bran?"

"As in his net worth?"

"No, deeper than that. Underground money problems? Does the guy have a gambling issue?" He was a risk-taker, oh, yeah; but I wasn't sure about being a gambler. "Or does he support a dozen illegitimate children around the world?" *Or lovers.* That sounded more than plausible, but did I want that answer? "Or is he having cash flow issues? These venues are not cheap."

Most likely scenario, but would it be enough to risk getting caught as a common thief? On our previous operation Ling Mai had run a thorough background search on all the players, but it never hurt to ask again. There had to be a big reason for someone to take the kind of risks they were taking with these thefts.

For Bran's reputation, the publicity alone could make it worth it, in a world where publicity, good or bad, sold product.

"It looks like at one time Interpol went into that line quite a bit, but found nothing."

Crapola. Good news? Or bad?

"Check again, just in case." I eyed the launch approaching, white against choppy waves.

"More problems?" Mandy asked in her sweet-coated sarcastic way.

Don't be a whiner. I've been in a chateau, a hotel fit for kings and now a luxury yacht, and I'm acting like a frustrated two-year old.

It wasn't the hairdressing part. *That* I could do with my eyes closed. It was the lack of solid leads and pussyfooting around in a world so far from my Idaho-plain background. That and not getting one step closer to finding Van.

"No. Nothing. You got anything else for me?" I figured I had two minutes max before I had to cut contact.

"One of those sets of prints you sent came back belonging to a woman with an assault and battery record and working under a false name."

Yes, finally, now I was getting somewhere. "Who?"

"Name she's currently using is Collette Henderson."

CHAPTER 20

I had to scramble to accomplish the last errand I wanted to run before boarding the launch, which was smaller and wobblier than I had imagined. Magic issues aside I didn't have a lot of experience with boats and nerves stretched too tight weren't helping.

"You sick, girl?" Franco asked, his tone taking me to task.

"No." Not yet.

"You look like hell," came his snappish response.

Bite me, punk! But knowing getting snippy with him would haunt me I squeezed my lips shut and grimaced. Which was easy to do. Maybe I was sea sick, or only too aware of what lived in deep watery depths. Mer people, selkies, hyllas, the list went on and on. I may have grown up in landlocked Idaho, but I'd read my fairytales as a kid and knew water held as many threats as dark forests or isolated castles.

Good thing the trip from shore to ship lasted less than fifteen minutes, which was about fourteen minutes too long for my taste. Before I scrambled up the gangplank or whatever they called the ladder thingy near the back of the boat, I touched the items I'd picked up right before I boarded the ferry. A silver necklace with a cross and two small, but still workable, silver earrings also in the form of crosses.

Yeah, I looked like a repentant sinner, but a lot of non-humans disliked silver even more than iron, so I felt marginally safer.

At least I did before I reached the top of the ladder, one hand clutching my hairdressing valise, which made it problematic to clamber up anything. My ribs strained against the awkward action which meant I was breathing in short, shallow breaths as I reached the last rung. Above me a hand appeared topside to help me from ladder to deck. I grabbed it rather than risk a dunking in the sea, only to realize as I was tugged forward, that it was Bran doing the heave-hoeing instead of some helpful deckhand.

I stumbled, blaming my clumsiness on my carrying case and not on my surprise, or the fact that he was close, way too close for my comfort. He steadied me which only made things worse as it meant his hands bracketed my shoulders, my face practically buried in his chest; and a very nice, very broad chest it was.

"Warding off threats?" he murmured, scrambling my brain even more as he raised a finger to brush against my necklace, the touch feather light but very intimate.

Of course he'd notice what I was wearing, not that my silver was burning *his* fingers.

I stepped back a few inches, as any more distance and I'd topple backwards off the boat.

"Next time I'll get the version that keeps pesky warlocks at bay," I whisper-snarled, wanting out of the awkward closeness, but it wasn't easy to step around him. He blocked the way toward an open door which I assumed led inside the yacht. So I forced the issue. "That way?" I shrugged a shoulder in the direction I wanted to go. Right then I might even have considered heading back down the ladder, anything to move away from him.

The curl of his lips told me he knew exactly what I was thinking as he held his stance and me, making sure I knew who was in control here.

It wasn't me.

Then he stepped aside, but only enough that I was forced to brush past him.

Bully.

I'd only taken a step forward when he leaned in, so close I could feel his breath against my ear as he whispered, "Beware, little witch. There be dragons in these waters."

Great. Just great. My own thoughts circling back to mimic me.

I wanted to stick my tongue out at him but the half-moon canter of his lips dared me to do just that, so instead I straightened my shoulders and stepped forward.

Last glance out of the corner of my eye was of his face, but he no longer showed a mocking expression. No, he looked worried.

CHAPTER 21

Dominique glanced around the twelve-hundred-square-foot bedroom and grimaced. Not bad for a yacht, but she wanted more.

"Patience," she hummed as she waved her private maid away. At least Liveras got that part right, each of the twenty-some guests were also provided their own crew-member to serve them. Several of the crew looked quite yummy. Maybe later.

Her cell phone buzzing interrupted some pleasant planning.

"Dominique here," she answered.

"You've erred again." The distorted echoing voice was like scratching a chalkboard.

That quickly her plans disappeared, as did the warm anticipation.

"What do you mean?" Everything was already underway for the next test. What more did they want?

"You have a second informant on your staff."

"An informant?" That was ridiculous. But there were two new girls. Both strangers. Both not hired by her. Could they both be infiltrators? "Who is it?" *And more importantly, how did the voice find out before she did?*

A knock on her door had her jumping. She cupped the phone speaker. "Just a minute," she called out.

"Who's there?" came the voice on the other end of the line.

"I don't know. I'll take care of them in a moment. Who's the leak? One of the new women?"

"Yes."

She knew it. The minute she shifted her attention, it got screwed up.

"Both—?"

But the line went dead.

Merde. She had to fix everything personally.

The knock sounded again. Schooling her features to a calmness she didn't feel she crossed to the doorway, opening it with a smile. "Yes?"

Her smile deepened when she saw who it was. She might have a new impostor in her midst, but she also had her own insiders. It was time to change the test. Move it up a bit.

"Come in, we must talk."

CHAPTER 22

"New girl, you're all thumbs today. Pull it together."

I glanced over at Franco. He was right, but that didn't make it any easier to swallow.

"If you can't do the job—"

"Lighten up Frankie-O. The poor thing can't get anything done with you breathing down her neck," Collette shouted from where she changed in full view of the room.

"Does it look like I'm talking to you?" came Franco's acerbic reply.

"No, and you wouldn't." Collette thrust a finger toward Franco. "Because you're a twit, not an idiot, and you know I'll clobber you if you push."

"Well, I—"

"Thanks, Collette, but he's right." I had to stop the war before it accelerated. I looked at a stunned Franco, fisted hands on his bony hips covered in lime-green cargo pants. "I'll try harder."

"That's the attitude I want to see around here, less lip and more zip." He grinned, then realized he'd taken the thunder out of his own earlier words. "See that you do."

He was gone before he caught sight of the other finger Collette gave him.

I did a last tease to Pamela's indigo-through-chocolate bangs, finishing the sex-kitten look before calling, "Next?"

It was the new woman—Sasha—who shimmied over and sat down before me.

"What number are you wearing?" I asked, wondering what to hand the woman while I had her trapped.

"The woodgrain Shibori chiffon."

"Could you say that in layman's terms?"

Sasha's voice reeked of ennui. "The kimono. Golds. Pleated, quilted, and dyed silk."

For love of the Spirits. Growing up in jeans, and owning less than half a dozen dresses in my whole life, I sure liked a few of Bran's designs too much. Lucky Sasha to get to wear one of them.

"I'm going to keep your hair simple then." I eyed the woman as I'd caught Franco eying the clothes. "A sleek side-part chignon."

"Whatever."

Or I could make the woman look like Bride of Frankenstein and have neck pains all day.

I picked up a jar of gel and held it toward her. "Could you hold this for me for a moment?"

The woman looked at it then nodded to a nightstand next to us. "Put it there."

Oh, yeah, Bride of Frankenstein was sounding better and better all the time.

"Fine." I set the jar down, reminding myself I loved a challenge, even an obnoxious one.

Before I could formulate Plan B, though, the assistant called my name.

I looked at Suzette, who was everything a good assistant needed to be: quiet, efficient, ruthlessly competent, and nearly invisible, even as she smiled at me and gave a shrug of her shoulders. She stood less than five feet tall, but made a good ally here on the yacht. Ling Mai should nab her for the agency, she was a natural for not attracting attention.

"Yeah?" I asked.

"Mademoiselle St. Clair would like to see you later. In her private rooms."

Ugh. Dragon Lady in close quarters. The day just kept getting better and better. But maybe I could get more intel on what she was or what she was up to.

"What time and where exactly?"

"When the last models are done. Her suite is in the fore of the lower level, across from Bran's."

Yeah, like I'd know where Bran slept.

So do not go there with the images. I was thinking business. His personal space would be the best chance to discover secrets. Like me, I doubt he was able to use many warding spells on this boat. There were too many people in and out of every room, except for this evening when all staff and guests were to be off the premises. Bran had ordered some down time for everyone. And if Dragon Lady wanted to see me all the better for being on board and doing some snooping.

"Thanks, Suzette, I'll be there." I returned my focus to Sasha's hair, surprised when the other woman spoke.

"You know Dominique well?"

So the brat could play nice? Or wanted something? But what?

"No, I don't know her at all." Nor did I want to, but I swallowed those words.

"But she's asking you to her private rooms?"

Probably wanted to can me, but I wasn't going to voice that thought either. Besides, she'd need to stand in line. "I'm sure she has to run all the business issues out of her private suite."

"Oh, that makes sense. I haven't been to the fore of the yacht."

Nice and chatty all of a sudden, I noted, slicking some firming gel along the nape of Sasha's head. But who was I to pass up a gift when given. "No, neither have I. In fact I'm not even sure I know where the fore part of the boat is."

"In the front. Down the set of stairs marked private." Sasha stiffened beneath my hands, then relaxed.

Slipped up there, lady. For someone seemingly in the dark about where the most private of rooms were, she'd answered far too quickly. Especially since we hadn't been on the yacht more than a few hours. A few very long hours where I'd done nothing but work, and work some more, ticking off the minutes without word on my fate or Van's.

Sasha added, "I'm sure you can find a steward or crew member to direct you."

"Good idea." I finished smoothing the model's hair. I'd have to wait till later to get the fingerprints. "There, that should do you. Next."

As if I'd gouged her with a curling iron, Sasha bolted.

More and more interesting, but there was no time to consider the nuances as the next model was already waiting.

Later, much later, after I put away the last of my products, I glanced at my battered, bought in fifth-grade watch that still worked just fine for me and remembered I was supposed to report to Dominique.

I tugged off my smock, and wondered if I should change before facing the woman. Not that I had a suit of armor on hand—the only thing that sounded remotely appropriate. On the other hand I did have another one of those nifty listening devices. I should have thought about that earlier and bugged Dominique's room before this.

I shook off my nerves as I tightened and released my hands several times. After all, what could the woman possibly do to me?

CHAPTER 23

Walking through hushed carpeted hallways, on a boat for land's sake, it was the calm hour after the day's "official" work was completed. It seemed eerily quiet after being used to the evening's "unofficial" work beginning about now. Some nights formal dinners were given. Other nights held more of a party atmosphere, often lasting till dawn's light. Except tonight there would be no work, which made the boat more deserted and spooky.

If I could get some solid intel to deliver to Ling Mai she might not nix me.

Right. Who'd want to retain a half witch/half shaman who botched all but the simplest spells and threatened to screw up my first, and only, solo mission. Ling Mai wasn't running a halfway house for other-tainted women. Her attitude was produce or prison.

Focus on the job.

After Collette's earlier words, I realized there was probably more business, and more information exchanged in the night hours than during the day's events. Something my role as support staff kept me isolated. No one invited the hairdresser to mingle with the guests.

At least not yet. And if I was lucky, I could get what I came for without wading into that world too deeply.

With only two false turns, I reached the fore compartment area, mentally cursing boat lingo that made no sense. Why couldn't the crew just say left instead of port? Who made up this stuff anyway?

Focus. Keep your mind on the mission and the next step.

Don't waste an opportunity to try and figure out exactly what species Dominique was and squeeze some useful intel out of Dragon Lady, no matter what her agenda. Yeah, right, like Dominique would want to socialize with the hired help enough to spill any clues; but I could always hope.

Maybe Bran then? That should be as easy as keeping a match lit in a snowstorm. *Start with a simple, hey, I need to pry into even more of your life?*

Or maybe—*want a date, warlock?*

Like that would ever happen.

I'd figure out the approach later, as in when I found my backbone and could keep my stupid thought process on track. Think Van. He needed my attention and my help. Nothing else mattered.

I paused, aware of the listening device in my sweaty palm, as I raised my hand to knock on the teak door of Dominique's room. That's when I heard the voices on the other side. Voices thundering in an argument.

Bran was one of them. Funny how I could pinpoint his voice first. The other? It sounded like Dominique, but not the cool, controlled woman I'd met last week. This woman was pissed.

"What do you mean? I have *always* handled operations. Now you're hiring this person here, letting Franco hire over there, are you crazy?"

"It's nothing, Dom. We needed help, you've been busy. Enough."

"No, it's not enough. Have I not made you?"

Silence.

I lowered my hand: partly out of duty, there was more to learn from eavesdropping than not, partly because of the tone of both the voices—Dominique's frenzied anger and Bran's lower and deeper tone, as inflexible as forged metal. I'd hate to go up against that voice, but Dominique didn't seem to mind.

Did she know what Bran was? Tweaking a warlock was not a smart idea. But maybe she felt family ties kept her safe. I'd never felt fear around my shifter brothers, well, except for that one time, but that didn't mean I treated other shifters as if they were pussycats and teddy bears.

"I don't know what's gotten into you." It was Bran's voice again but colder. I shivered in the hallway as he continued. "But the new women stay."

"They stay if I say they stay," Dragon Lady snarled.

"No, Dom, it's my company, or are you forgetting that?"

Ouch.

"I'm forgetting nothing. Not all the effort I've put into making you what you are. Not the fact I sided with you against the family."

"Don't go there, Dom."

"Why? Because you don't want to hear the truth? I'm what made you and now you think you can handle operations without me? Think again. You're nothing without me."

The woman wasn't pulling any punches. I was flinching and I had the door between her and me. In fact, I was thinking it might be safer if I slunk away, except I was here to learn what I could. Hiding someplace safe wasn't going to help Van.

"You're upset. Not thinking rationally. I'm doing everything in my power to protect you."

Now what did he mean by that?

Dom didn't answer as Bran added, "We'll talk later."

Too late I realized Bran was directly opposite me on the other side of the door. The same door that swung open—right in my face just as I raised my fist as if ready to rat a tat-tat.

I staggered back as Bran slammed against me, a wall of enraged muscle and heat. He grabbed my upper arms in a steel grip, hard enough to leave bruises. His emotions swirled around me. Anger. Betrayal. A sadness so deep it felt bottomless.

I hadn't crossed paths with him much since arriving on the boat, too wary to trust the vibes between us. In a flash, that changed.

One second I was an interloper, now I was caught in the vortex of a volcano. A hot, angry, barely controlled volcano with a name—Bran—staring down at me, his nostrils flared, the skin of his face taut, his body strained against mine, chest-to-chest, thigh-to-thigh. If I could breathe, I would, but not while he glared down at me, and I wasn't a small woman.

I doubted he even saw me until I managed to clear my closed throat. "I . . .I have a meeting with Dominique."

I'm not the target.

The haze in his blue, blue eyes shifted, cleared a bit. His grip released. I barely caught myself from falling backwards. But I was thankful. Touching him was too much, like brushing up against uncontrolled heat lightning: emotions—fear, concern, anger, and yes, lust.

He shuddered, the movement of a man hanging onto his control by a thread.

Being raised around brothers with tempers, I recognized the symptoms. Being raised around shifters with tempers made me extra wary. I gingerly altered my stance, the instinctual response of a smart animal in the path of an enraged predator.

Bran said nothing. Not that I expected him to, in fact I wanted just the opposite. From the scrap of conversation I'd just overheard it was patently clear that I was one of the women under discussion. My presence, and the fact I hadn't been hired by Dominique, had precipitated the argument, and it was a doozy. I knew why Bran had no choice but to have me on staff, but it was obvious he wasn't sharing the info with the closest person in his world—his cousin.

That answered at least one question; he was holding my operation as a tightly-guarded secret. But that also raised another. Why didn't he trust his cousin? He said he was protecting her. Who from? From me?

That sounded more like what I'd heard about Bran, but it also made him more of a loner and isolated than I'd originally thought. A man with everything, and nothing, estranged from the one person he had history with, denied him even as his world was under attack.

That split realization made my heart ache.

I raised one hand, an automatic gesture of comfort at odds with the man before me. But one didn't pet a wounded lion, or pat a leashed tiger on the paw.

His eyes narrowed and I stayed my hand, swallowing deeply and letting it slide slowly back to my side.

I did possess some semblance of self-preservation. Not much, but a little.

He stepped around me, disappearing into the room directly opposite, taking all the air in the hallway with him.

Get a grip.

I jerked my gaze back from his door, closed not loudly but silently, a move speaking of control. But I hadn't come to see Bran; I'd come to talk with Dominique.

Who even now waited beyond her open door.

Oh, well, when in doubt, fake it.

I stepped toward the door and cleared my throat, which after touching Bran was needed. I spoke to Dominique's back. A very rigid back sheathed in a business-like silk suit of blood red. It fit the woman like second skin. "Hello? I can come back later if now's a bad time."

Understatement.

When no answer came, I stepped farther into the room, aware of two things. The first, my ring was burning my skin as if just branded, and second, moving forward now might reveal what Dominique was as well as how she might be involved in the thefts. Damn, I wanted to blame them on her and get the hell out of here. "You asked for me?"

So this was how Daniel felt, edging into the lion's den; only Dominique was not a lion, not when she turned around in a very sinewy, very precise motion. She was more a snake. Smooth, calculated, and deadly. A cobra or viper, not a common rattler like I'd faced as a youngster in the sagebrush-and-sand landscape of my childhood.

If I hadn't just heard the argument and felt the fury coursing through Bran, I'd never have known the woman before me had just sliced and diced another with her words. Dangerous in her own way, Dominique was all poise, smiling even, though it was a cold smile, and well-trained. All my senses screamed wariness for this was a non-human.

"Oh, I didn't realize you were there," she purred.

I didn't believe her for a nanosecond. My neck muscles locked so tight they ached as I kept my attention one hundred percent on the threat in front of me.

"Come in, please." Dominique waved to the center of the room. "And close the door behind you."

Walking into a closed room with a predator was stupid and my daddy hadn't raised stupid. But if I missed out in the grace and poise genes, I received double the tenacious and foolhardy ones; both helped me step forward, clicking the door shut behind me.

"You wanted to see me?" I asked, aware of the quiver beneath my words as the other woman remained silent. Silent but very much aware, as her gaze, calculating and shrewd, sized me up.

One on one? In mud wrestling or street-fighting I could take her no problem. If I figured out what she was. But I doubted this woman ever got that kind of dirty.

Stop looking with your eyes, Ms. Noziak, Fraulein Fassbinder had lisped, look with all of your senses to determine what you are facing. They expect you to see what they want you to see, but you must be smarter than they are.

So what was I seeing? Or not seeing. The air smelled of cinnamon and. . . sandalwood. Thick with the scent, under-layered with seething emotions. And, when I glanced at Dominique obliquely were her eyes rimmed in green? Yeah, a thick freaky green glow outlined her dark brown eyes. And her skin? Did it slip a little? As if she were having a hard time keeping it in place? Or was fighting to keep from morphing?

Please, Jude the Apostle, patron saint of desperate cases and lost causes, make Dominique a benign creature. Not that she looked benign at all.

My gut screamed warning signals, as were the fine hairs on the back of my neck. Walk warily around this one, very, very warily, no matter how calm and reasonable her tone.

"I just thought we should talk." Dominique crossed to a side table displaying cut-glass decanters. I was happy that her move created a few more feet of space between us while still leaving me closer to the door. "Get to know each other a little better."

What game was she playing?

"Do you want my resume?" I asked, not trying to be stupid, then wanting to kick myself as I watched the woman's hands clutch the crystal stopper too tightly.

Smooth. Try for placating instead of confrontational next time.

"Oh, nothing so worthless." An empty glass was raised. I shook my head in the negative, so she continued. "I'm sure there's so much more to you than words on a page."

What the heck did that mean? This was not the kind of woman to get chummy with the hired help. Had she discovered something about my mission? Not from Bran, if that argument was a clue, but could he have slipped up somewhere and exposed me as an agent?

Not good.

Never one for the slow pussyfoot approach, I asked, "So what is it you want to know about me?"

One perfectly groomed dark brow shifted upward, but Dominique took a slow, measured drink of amber liquid before asking. "Why here? Are you not a long way from Montana or wherever it is you come from?"

The wrong home state told me two things. One, that the woman had done some fact checking of her own, and two, that the error was probably an intentional dig. This wasn't a woman who let details slide.

"I'm from Idaho, not Montana, and why not here? Travel. Exotic locations. Good pay and great scenery. It's a perfect job."

"I think you are not a stupid woman, Miss Noziak."

Backhanded compliment, delivered with just the right amount of bite. Slick job and very snake-like.

"Is there something in particular you want from me, Ms. St. Clair?" *Other than blood.* But then two could play bared-fangs, as long as Dominique stayed in her human form. If she shifted I was out of here. The simple wards I kept about my person, amethyst and amber, would never stop her, or even slow her down. They'd probably give her a quick buzz and enrage her. So vamoosing was a good plan, if I lived to get out. I lowered my voice, even as I pushed back, "Or are we on a fishing expedition?"

Keep the tone quiet. Not subservient, because I couldn't do that, but fangs retracted.

The idiom had the woman's eyes narrowing. "I do not *fish*. I run this company, and as such, you answer to me."

Now we were getting somewhere.

"I understand that." I spread my hands in a supplicating manner. "Are you unhappy with my work?"

"It is adequate."

Rousing endorsement.

"Then have I done something else to displease you?"

"I am being, how do you Americans say it?—proactive, this is all."

And if I believed that I didn't deserve to be an agent. Something was driving this woman enough to pitch her hissy fit with Bran and call me on the carpet. But what? Something had happened to trigger this sudden interrogation.

Once, when I was about seven, my brother Van and I stumbled across a mama black bear with two little cubs. Me, being too young to know better, lunged toward the cute furry animals, but Van had grabbed my arm so hard I'd squeaked. I didn't have to listen to his words because I felt his fear, even though he wasn't showing any. Just the opposite, he was all calm control. We'd backed, slowly and carefully, away from that encounter and right now I felt that same holy terror dancing along my nerves.

I spoke with intention, purposely keeping my hands loose at my sides. "You will tell me if there's something I should be doing, or not doing?"

"Yes, this is one of my many duties."

Right, micromanaging I got, but taking the time to chase around the bush with a hairdresser? What was the point?

Dominique lowered her gaze to her diamond-studded wristwatch then glanced up quickly. Her tone changed, from tight to something less rigid, maybe even buoyant, as if she'd scored a point while I was unaware of what the game was I played.

"I think we understand each other, Miss Noziak; you may leave now."

Understand what? Would I lose my position if I pointed out that just the opposite was true? This useless conversation only muddied the waters. Something had happened here and I hated being in the dark.

"That's all?"

"Yes." She paused. "Except you can tell me which models are still on the yacht?"

Since I'd just left the staging room and knew most of the models were still prepping to leave I rattled off the half-dozen names I knew.

Dominique's eyes were now solid brown, her skin looked very human and the waft of cinnamon and sandalwood was a faint tease. So whatever had threatened her seemed to have dissipated. But what? And why? And how?

Stone trained us as newbie agents that sometimes retreats were necessary. This seemed to be one of those times, even if I hadn't even placed the listening device.

"Oh, Miss Noziak?"

My hand on the cool brass doorknob, I rounded at Dominique's words but held my tongue.

"Would you mind finding the new model and sending her to me?"

"Sasha?"

"Yes, I believe that's her name."

Did I look like a messenger? On second thought, I was interested in seeing what Sasha's reaction to a summons might be. So what if it meant missing the next boat back to the hotel for staff in town? In an hour I could catch the last one.

"Fine." I nodded, my smile plastered on tight but it was there. "It may take a bit for me to track her down, but I'll give her the message."

"Oh, just as soon as you can. I'll be here for some time." Dominique smiled.

Definitely snake-like.

CHAPTER 24

I had no intention of being Dominique's lap dog, but her wanting Sasha gave me an excuse not only to stay on the yacht after hours, it gave me an excuse to snoop around. A win-win for me.

Leaving Dominique's room I stepped across the room to press an ear against Bran's door. No sounds came from inside so I knocked. Nada. The hallway was empty, that tingle-up-your-spine-spooky kind of empty.

I already had accepted the constant noise surrounding me, people all around, guests as well as models, the sounds of the staff going about their business, even the lap of water against the hull. But as I stood in the shadowed hallway it were as if all the turbulence had evaporated. Or the ship held its breath.

Get a grip, Noziak. Find Sasha. Give her the message. Grab the last boat to shore. Get a way to break into that safe.

Easy peasey.

So why did I stand there, across from Dominique's room, as if waiting for something to happen. A sudden near-silent click had me look to the left, down the hallway where I caught Bran's wide shoulders stepping out of a room. He was closing the door behind him before he headed away from me.

I released the breath I didn't realize I'd been holding. That could have been awkward, explaining why I was hanging around his and Dominique's rooms. Now what? Follow him? Or avoid him for the time being?

Scaredy-cat? Or smart woman. Give him enough time to calm down from his scene with Dominique before I confronted him with some demands of my own. Demands I was still finalizing based on one priority. I wasn't finding Van by pussy footing around Bran, powerful mage or not.

So first steps first. Find Sasha. As I turned to head in the opposite direction Bran had disappeared in, I nearly tripped over a mid-sized dog. Not just any dog but the one I'd seen at the chateau a few days ago, the buff-colored poodle.

Odd. What was it doing here? The guests weren't on board so it couldn't belong to them and no staff member had enough privacy to hide such an animal. Maybe Dominique kept one for show. It looked like that kind of dog, all poofed and fancied. Not a farm animal kept for protection or herding.

The poodle paused for a second, gave me a what-the-hell glance, then continued on its way as if it owned the boat. Which it might for all I knew.

With a shrug I headed in the direction the dog had come from, ignoring the goosebumps crawling up my arms as I crept along the shadowed hallways. Wouldn't Mandy and Jaylene have a field day with the witch who was scared of her own shadow.

Good thing they weren't around, but the thought of them put some starch in my backbone.

Twenty minutes later I wondered if I'd been played for a fool. We were on a bloody boat; where could Sasha be?

"Ask Frankie-O," Collette suggested when I bumped into her heading to the last ferry boat. "He was looking for her a bit ago. Must have found her by now."

Great. Two of us were searching for the same person. Just my luck he'd have already found her, and both of them were headed to the launch.

"How long till the boat leaves for shore?" I asked Collette.

"You have thirty minutes, luv, then you're stuck here for the night."

Why did that thought give me the shivers? As if Collette read my mind, or my expression, she added, "You want me to send the ferry bloke to pick you up if you miss the next trip?"

"Nah," I waved her off. "Thirty minutes is plenty of time." I hoped. But how big of a boat was this? It was beginning to feel like something from Alice in Wonderland as I opened one door after another, all empty.

Fifteen minutes more and still no Sasha or Franco. Could they have taken a private water-taxi back to shore for some reason?

A quick check with the launch crew nixed that idea, though it seemed Sasha had made arrangements for an earlier trip to shore, but never showed.

Now I was down to ten minutes before the last launch left.

Stop by Dominique's and tell her I was sorry out of luck or keep searching?

There really was no reason for me to continue looking so I headed to Dominique's room again. I'd just stepped into the hallway near her suite when I smelled it. Not it but them— the two men with crossed arms standing outside Dominique's door. I didn't need my ring to tell me they were non-humans, my nose did. And these weren't the regular security detail. They were new.

Growing up with shifter brothers had trained me to a shifter's scent, even in human form. Think wet dog, sweat, and anger all rolled into one eau du shifter. Most shifters carried a residual chip on their shoulders for a lot of reasons: being the strongest in a world where they couldn't show their might or just for being different. My brothers never believed I could smell them; after all the ability to smell keenly was one of their gifts, but I could. At least shifters. No other non-humans, except vampires. They had that whole undead whiff about them.

Just about the time I was making up my mind to turn and leave, the two goon guards glanced in my direction. A very creepy move that had them both swiveling their necks my way at the exact same time, as if pulled by puppet strings. Their bodies remained motionless but poised, as if ready to launch, which had my neck hairs standing straight on end.

But why? I wasn't a threat to them. I wasn't a threat to anyone, except for the small throwing anathema attached to my right ankle. But these guys were big enough, easily over six feet tall, and broad enough, that steroid kind of pumping weights bulk, that I should barely register on their radar. Sort of like a mosquito threatening a pair of hungry lions.

So why the tightening of their facial muscles and the rocking forward on their feet?

Maybe I was being paranoid. So I gave them a tight smile that felt like it would crack my face, a small hey, hi-ya wave and a chin nod. *No harm here guys.* Then I took a step backwards. Not even a big step, more I've-changed-my-mind step to let them know I wasn't even going to cross into their territory.

That should have been enough.

Yeah, I could have turned my back on them and acted as if I were just a lost, dumb chick, but there was no way I was going to give my back to these two. Which was probably a smart thing as they stepped forward.

"She the one?" one of them mumbled to the other.

"Yeah."

They both took a step toward me.

I took off, scrambling up the stairs I'd just exited, the hounds of hell pounding after me.

I had no idea what kinds of shifters they were, but it didn't really matter. All shifters were faster, meaner, and more dangerous than I was. If I had ten to twenty minutes, I might manage a containment spell or create a protection circle for me, but they were right on my ass on a boat that suddenly seemed way too small.

Up the stairs, out on the deck, skidding to the right. Where were other people when you needed them? Franco? The crew? Somebody?

These guys wouldn't take out others would they? Who knew? Maybe a crewman or kitchen staff, but not somebody who'd be missed. Like Bran.

But I didn't want to take the chance, or miscalculate, and bring a threat barreling down on him. Or any innocent.

Wait a minute. Why was I worried about a warlock? He could take care of himself.

My first instinct, to run to anywhere there might be more people, the safety in numbers instinct, was quickly tossed. I had no idea where there were people, except for Bran and

Dominique, and my gut told me Dragon Lady was most likely behind this whole mess. And I didn't want the ferry crew put in danger.

Next option? Weapons. Where?

Shifters were like vamps, damn good fighters and almost impossible to kill. Except something sharp to the heart or capable of lopping off a head. My ankle anathema wasn't going to do either. If I got close enough to use it with a shifter I was already dead.

So where? Where? Sweet Jesus they were gaining on me. Whipping around a corner I leaped over a doorway and almost took a header down some stairs. Hurdling over steps, another corner, duck in a door, and I skidded to a stop.

The kitchen, or galley, or whatever they called it on the yacht.

Good. Knives. Plus the lingering smell could mask my own for a few seconds. Nothing would hide the sound of my pounding heart from a shifter so there wasn't a point in trying for a cloaking spell. No time to do anything except run or fight.

I glanced around the metal contained room, shrouded in half-light and empty as a church with free drinks at the nearest pub.

Knife? Where were the damn knives?

There. A row of them along a magnetic strip. I grabbed the longest, sharpest two, much better than my anathema for defense and paused, listening for the goons.

"They want her alive," one voice said, just outside the galley door. "Don't forget."

A laugh that sent shivers through me answered. "Alive doesn't mean I can't have some fun first."

In your dreams a-hole. Or my nightmare. But now I understood why they hadn't shifted yet. In human form, it was a lot easier for them to snatch me without too much damage.

I looked around. Two exits. The one nearest where the shifters were, and a door at the other end of the rectangular room.

Door number two it was. No idea where it went, but it gave me a few more feet between my new fiends and me.

What then?

I'd figure that out when I got to it.

I crept along as silently as I could, feeling each breath I chugged, sounding like air bellows wheezing and each step I took rocking the boat. But I kept going. Incremental movement forward.

I was almost there. Almost, when two things happened at once.

Suzette stepped through the door in front of me and I heard a bellow behind me, "Got her!"

CHAPTER 25

Time squeezed to a stop. Suzette poised in front of me, one foot inside the door, one out, her mouth a round O of surprise, her eyebrows arched. Behind me, enough growls and oaths to wake the dead.

Which we'd be if we didn't escape.

Then I caught the direction of Suzette's gaze. She wasn't stunned by the goons bearing down on us; she was staring at the knives white-knuckle gripped in my hands. As if I was the threat.

"Come on." I leapt toward her, half-shoving, half- pulling her out the door. "Run!"

I had to give her credit. Except for a small stumble that cost us a second we didn't have, she followed my lead, through the dining room, into one of the main staterooms, shadowing me like a good little new best friend. Not that she had a choice as I clutched her wrist with a steel-banded grip, the knife hilt I clutched biting into her.

We didn't have enough time and nowhere to go.

Nowhere safe.

Then I spied an oversized lounge chair. All I cared about was it was big, big enough Suzette could ditch behind it.

"There." I pushed her toward it, managing not to slice her in the process. "Hide there."

"But—" her gaze danced in the direction mine did, waiting for the threat thudding down the hallway toward us.

"Hide." I wanted to scream, but that'd take breath I didn't have. "They'll follow me. When the coast is clear, circle back to find help. Go to Bran."

"But—"

"Don't have time. Hide. Now."

I didn't blame her. Hiding felt like being a sitting duck, but no time to explain as I vaulted toward an outside door. I hated abandoning her, but it gave her the best chance to survive. For one of us to survive.

If I was going to die here I damned well wanted to take down Dominique with me and the only way to do that was to alert Bran to what happened. Then it was up to him to connect the dots back to his cousin.

Why I trusted him in that second didn't make sense. But I did trust him. Not with my life, but with Suzette's, and with doing the right thing.

I hoped I was correct.

As I catapulted toward the door, I shouted like a girlie-girl, "Help. Save us."

My brothers would have wondered what the hell I was doing.

Buying time for Suzette.

I didn't even glance behind me to see if she followed my directions.

If the goons weren't following me, they didn't deserve to catch me.

The chill of the ocean air slapped me. Cold on my heated skin; waves smacking the lower decks a good two floors beneath me. I was in the front of the boat, or the foredeck. A few deck chairs, but nothing to obscure the view in front of me with a wall of glass to my back.

Great. Only my knives as weapons, which meant closer fighting than I wanted.

What was even worse was that the two goons had split up. One coming from the door I'd exited and the other from the opposite door, which is why they hadn't been on my tail. A classic pincher movement with me the idiot in the middle.

A protection ward wasn't going to keep them away from me, not without glyphs drawn on the deck to back it up. A propulsion spell might push one of them away for a moment or so, but not for long and not very far. Besides I'd need to drop my knives and anathema dagger to make any magic work. That whole no physical weapons while using magic problem.

So what now?

I bluff.

"You guys don't know who you're messing with," I lied, brandishing the knives I held as if I chopped up shifters on a daily basis. "I thought shifters were smarter than that."

The fact I knew what they were had them pausing, casting a quick glance at one another, then me.

"That's right," I taunted, each word made husky as I gasped. Racing around a yacht was not good for cracked ribs. "Didn't think I knew what you were. But I do. Which means I also know how to kill you."

"Big talk, girlie," one said, tucking his head between beefy shoulders. His voice was the one who'd said I was to be taken alive. The brains of the two of them, which wasn't saying much.

"Oh, I know more than you think." I shuffled backwards, until my back touched the cold metal of the rail. Nowhere to go from here but over. Which gave me an idea. "In fact." I stepped one leg on the other side of the lower rail, which gave me just enough space to duck through. "Your bosses won't be too happy if I jumped and left you two with no prize to return with."

"Whoa, now girlie," Brains shouted as the other guy scuttled forward. Just enough that I shifted to make good on my threat.

"Back, Gurn," Brains growled at his partner. "All the way back. Now."

Gurn looked like he was debating with himself, or considering insubordination. Most shifters believed strongly in obeying a hierarchical order. But not all, especially if they owed no allegiance to each other, and I was counting that these two lobos might fall in that last category. Divide and conquer. Or buy a few seconds for me to come up with another plan.

Then Gurn started shifting: bones cracking, skin tearing, a long, vicious snout replacing his face. Guess he didn't like my threat.

Brains pulled out a 9mm pistol with a silencer, raised it, and shot Gurn in the head.

Poof. Splat.

Gurn dropped like a mighty tree, his brain matter scattered over the deck.

Not exactly what I'd planned, but the odds had just improved for me.

"There, girlie," Brains soothed, obviously having no love lost for his partner as he barely batted an eye at the dead shifter at his feet. "It's just you and me and I don't mean you no harm."

"Except that whole kidnap thing," I pointed out, me and my big mouth as I cast a quick glance at the black water below me. Could I survive the jump? And then what? The lights of Monte Carlo were in the far distance, too far to swim with beaten ribs and not a lot of stamina as a swimmer. But I might be able to make it to a nearby boat. If I could find one.

"Nabbing you is just a job. Nothing personal," Brains reassured, taking a step closer.

I tightened my grip on the rail even as I swallowed. "Seems damned personal to me."

"Come on, girlie, I took out Gurn for ya."

"You're all heart."

He shuffled another step closer, his grin feral, his muscles tensed, so tensed I expected him to shift any second. Strong emotions tended to force many shifters into their non-human selves.

"Oh, no you don't," I countered, pulling my other leg over the rail so now I was standing on the far side of it, the cool metal the only thing anchoring me to the boat. I dropped one of the knives so I could hold on tighter but clutched the other knife as if my life depended on it. Which it did.

Brains jackknifed to a sudden stop. And even took a step backwards. "Don't do anything you'll regret," he said, raising one hand, the one without the gun. "Let's talk this out. I'm sure we can work somethin' out."

"Yeah, right." Not. But maybe this was exactly what I needed. Here was someone who might know something about who was behind the thefts or Van's disappearance.

"Who sent you?" I asked. After all, what did I have to lose? Other than my life. "Was it Bran?"

"Nah, he don't have anything to do wit' this."

I was assuming "this" meant the whole kidnapping thing. But was Bran involved in the thefts? Or Van's disappearance?

As long as Brains was willing to talk, or give himself enough time to figure out how *not* to lose the prize—me—I could keep going. If nothing else I was getting a few minutes to catch my breath before I hit the water. "So who are you working for?"

"You should know." He sounded confused, as if trying to figure out if I was pulling his tail, something only an idiot did literally, or metaphorically, to any shifter. "You know what we are."

"I do." Time to push. "I just want to see if what I know jives with what you know." Play the whole, we're-on-the-same-side approach. A long shot.

"Oh." So Brains wasn't the brightest crayon in the box. Not unusual for certain kinds of shifters who relied on brawn to survive in both human and non-human form. He leaned his upper body forward, as if it were just the two of us chatting but best to keep his voice low.

I mimicked his movement, even as I felt the rail grow slick beneath my sweaty palm. "So who is it?" I whispered in a conspiratorial voice. Just us pals shooting the breeze.

"We call 'em Seekers. What 'bout you?"

What the hell was a Seeker? Or Seekers? "The same." I gave him a chin nod before adding, "Sid your contact with them?" I pulled a name out of the ether, sort of like when I was twelve and blaming Brian Frick for the baseball through old man Gunderson's window when there wasn't really a Frick kid around.

That confused look again on Brains face. "Nah, Vaverek. Who's Sid?"

Who was Vaverek?

I waved my knife hand, blowing off his question. "Vaverek is higher on the food chain than Sid, that's for sure." When in doubt, flatter the ego. Nine times out of ten it worked.

From Brains' smarmy smile, I'd struck the right note.

"So Vaverek still working out of Monte Carlo? I heard he'd transferred to Paris," I said. Please, please, please give me a solid lead.

"Nah, he's usually in Paris, but he's meeting us in D.C. for the end of the tour," Brains replied, a hint of hesitation in his voice. "You really know him?"

"Sure I do. Or know of him, which is the next best thing." Bullshit.

Brains' expression tightened. I think I'd just run out of time. "What's Vaverek look like then?" he said.

"Never met him personally. Like I told you, I work mostly with Sid."

"Tall? Blond? Stupid looking?" Brains asked, stepping closer. I didn't have to be a witch to hear the trap. Whoever this Vaverek was I bet donuts to dollars he wasn't anything like what Brains described. Or maybe just one out of the three.

Time was up. I glanced once at the water, counting the seconds before Brains lunged.

"I knew it," Brains snarled, "You don't know squat."

I knew when it was time to leave the party.

CHAPTER 26

I squatted lower, in order to launch myself in a dive. Was there enough room to clear the boat? Could I hit the water cleanly?

If the fall didn't kill me I stood a chance.

But I'd underestimated the speed of Brains. Just as I went to let go a clawed hand speared my arm.

My choked off scream was instinctual.

"No, you don't," Brains snarled. "They want you."

He pulled and tossed me in one smooth arc over the rail away from the water, up in the air and smash into the windows of the front stateroom. My breath whooshed out as I slid in a heap onto the deck.

Damn that hurt. My cracked ribs now felt splintered, stabbing into my lungs.

No breath.

Fat lot of good my silver necklace did for protection.

Brains loomed before me, wide-legged stance, hands on his hips, his face shadowed. His laugh, though, told me all I needed to know. He thought he'd won. That I was out for the count.

Almost, but never count a Noziak as down if they can still inhale. Even in small pants. I'd lost the knives but still had the anathema dagger against my ankle so I wasn't even sure I could use magic. Only one way to find out.

Sucking in as deep a breath as possible I started a chant. "*Musca. Moveō. Volō.*"

Brains' laugh deepened.

A breeze stirred.

"Volō. Volō. Volō. Rumpō."

The breeze picked up tempo. Not enough.

Brains stepped forward.

I thrust one hand in front of me. All theatrics as my other hand clutched my ribs. I mentally screamed as I crunched myself straighter to deepen my voice. *"Musca. Volō. Rumpō."*

He paused, glancing to both sides. "Whatja doin?"

My voice grew louder, but there were only the two of us to hear. *"Volō. Rumpō."*

This time he staggered backwards.

My point.

I crawled to my knees, focusing one hundred percent on him. *"Medius. Damnum. Rumpō."*

The spell wavered, threatening to break, but then so was I. At this point something was better than nothing.

Brains struggled, as if against a wall of air. I braced one palm on the cool deck and shouted as loud as I could. *"Damnum. Rumpō."*

That was it. It was all I had.

My arms gave out and I crumpled, face forward on the deck, but not before I heard a curse. Something sticky coated my fingers and I gagged at the coppery smell. Blood, fresh blood. I'd landed in the widening pool of Gurn's blood.

Ugh.

I shifted my head, watching Brains' massive boots shuffle then slide. But not toward me. Away from me. The propulsion spell was working.

Finally.

The rail would catch him so I wasn't safe. Not by a long shot. I was buying myself a few minutes to come up with Plan B, that was all. Maybe this silly ring I wore could magnify my abilities.

I raised my head and spat the last words I had. *"Damnum absque injuria."*

Loss without injury. Even as I wanted injury, big time— Brains' injury, to guarantee my safety.

Then I heard his scream.

I jerked my head to look up, catching his arms wind-milling, his back against the rail.

The spell wasn't that strong. I wasn't that strong. So what. . .?

He shouted, then toppled backwards. I watched, powerless to help as if in slow motion he hung suspended before he winked out of sight.

His voice echoed before being swallowed by a splash.

I crooked one elbow to see if I were imagining things. No Brains. No nothing. Not even the sounds of struggle in the water.

A lot of shifters couldn't swim. Their body mass ratio made them too heavy to float easily. But no way had I. . .and then I looked around me. Gurn's blood.

Of course. A spell aided by blood and the power of my ring. Ling Mai had said it'd increase my power. I'd crossed that line between magic and black magic. Didn't mean to. Didn't want to.

Didn't matter.

I sagged, every ounce of energy spent and closed my eyes. In a second I'd figure out what to do next. But not now.

Now I felt the effort of my fight. Air washed around me, kissing my skin, but lessening with each breath I took. My heartbeat slowed, like a clock winding slowly down: Thump. Thump. Thump.

Is this what it felt like to die?

Very quiet. Very slowly.

For a second I struggled, but only for a second. Too much effort.

This was peaceful.

I could no longer feel fingers or toes. The breeze had gone away.

Or maybe it was me.

Thump. Thump. Then darkness.

CHAPTER 27

The darkness wasn't bad. Not like I expected; a shadowy play of light and darkness. In the distance I could see a shape moving toward me, a rough outline. A woman?

"Grams?" my voice cracked, as if I hadn't spoken for a long, long time.

"Go back," she said, sounding much like my father's mother, though her face looked different as she neared. Worried. Disappointed. "Van needs you. Go back."

But I didn't want to. This was easier. Lying here. The pain gone. Everything gone. Worry, fear, struggle.

"Come back." The voice had changed, grown deeper, angrier.

Not Grams.

I sensed someone standing over me. The pain slid back into my body. The thud of my heart echoed in my ears.

Thump. Thump. The pounding weak, but there.

"You won't leave." A direct order. But whose? Oh, please, not yet. Not another shifter.

A touch to my shoulder and a mumbled oath. A familiar voice. That familiar, pissed off voice.

I peeled open my eyes, squinting against the darkness. But I didn't need clear light to know who was now kneeling beside me.

"Bran?"

"You're wearing a protective ward," he snarled, ignoring my question. His hands hot against my skin, calling forth the pain screaming through me.

"You're hurting—"

"Enough. Can't hold onto you."

Yes, sir, your Royal Mageness. I would have shaken my head but couldn't muster enough power.

"Suzette?" I asked through dry lips. Even half-dead I had my own agenda and it wasn't letting Bran through my warding.

"She's fine," he answered, poking me some more, but even a weak ward was like sticking your hand in an electrical socket. So what was he doing? Trying to finish what Brains and Gurn had started? Killing me and tossing my body after Brains?

Next time I'd create a stronger ward. One strong enough to keep shifters off me, that much was clear.

The pain eased, from a headlock grip to able to breathe through it in small pants.

Then I remembered who else was at risk on this damned floating casket. Sasha. Had to find her.

"You seen Sasha?" I mumbled, my voice shaky.

"Forget the model. Remove all your wards," he repeated, as if talking to a recalcitrant child.

"Not safe," I managed. So much more I could say. I don't trust you. I trust no one, but especially not you. But those took coherent thoughts and I was losing the fight with the pain.

He leaned closer, his voice weaving around me, seductive for what it promised—safety, a release from distress, a willingness to share the burden. "I'm a healer," he whispered. "Remove the warding so I can help."

Believe or not?

"You have internal damage." His voice sounded less gentle, more insistent. "I can't help you if you won't let me."

I hesitated. Words were his weapons. Was he promising what I wanted most to get me to let my guard down?

"I swear on all you hold dear, I only seek to heal you here and now."

He must be able to read minds, too. But a mage's word was a sacred bond.

I sucked in a breath, praying to the spirit guardian of my shamanic ancestors that it wouldn't be my last, and released the last ward.

CHAPTER 28

I lay there on the cold deck, shifter blood congealing next to me, the salty scent of ocean wind brushing my skin. I wasn't giving up or giving in. I was trusting, which was much harder than dying had been.

And if Bran screwed with me I'd return from the afterlife and do the same to him.

"Hold still," he murmured, as if I had a choice.

I don't know what I expected. A shock maybe. A jolt. Something, anything except the wave of warmth covering me; toasty, comforting warmth, like a hug only better.

Bran murmured some words. Not Latin. Not spell casting. Something else. Something older, more primordial. I could have floated in that cocoon of heat and sound forever.

Then he touched me again. Feather light but demanding at the same time. His hands spanned my ribcage and a spark of fear lit within me.

"Shh, I'm only helping."

So he said, but how easy would it be for him to crush. Easier than to mend.

What came next was as if a weight lifted, slowly but surely. Air seeped back into my lungs. Lungs that felt as if they were slowly being pumped full.

Never had a breath tasted so sweet.

"You've made a real mess, little witch," he said, as if talking to himself. "Lucky I came when I did. I'm good, but if you'd been dead for much longer . . ."

I whispered through dry lips. "Noziaks are very hard to kill."

"Looked like you gave it your best attempt."

I wanted to tell him where he could take his opinions but he shushed me. "Focus on healing. I need your help here."

What was I supposed to do?

"Visualize your bones knitting," he said, as if listening to my thoughts.

I snorted instead.

"Either trust me or do not."

Fine, if he was going to make me sound like an ungrateful baby. I squeezed my eyes shut tight, then followed the pressure of his hands, his fingers, across the ribs, one at a time, light pressure. Sometimes I sucked in air when the pain spiked, but mostly I centered my thoughts on what rib bones looked like, their shape, their texture. I saw them as one of those skeletal teaching aids in hospitals, no flesh, no organs, just the white bones.

"Feeling better?" he asked after a bit and I realized I'd drifted away.

How long had I been gone? Long enough that the sharpness of the pain had ebbed. I was back to the cracked rib stage I'd been in before I'd been tossed by Brains.

I squirmed, starting to sit up when Bran pushed me back down. "Not so fast. I'm not done."

"I don't need—"

"You need what I say you need. These ribs have been recently injured and not fully healed. What did you do?"

My exhale warned him that I'd tolerate his being bossy and pushy but only so far. "I messed with a trio of echo-demons."

Okay, so his whistle helped massage my ego a bit.

"You win?" he asked, his hands now moving from my ribs to my arms.

"I'm here, aren't I?"

He actually chuckled, which created a different kind of warmth coursing through me. One I had no reason to feel.

I squirmed again, pushing his hands away. "That's enough. We're done here."

He raised both hands palm up before me. "You want to still hurt, so be it."

That's not what I wanted. It was more what I didn't want—to be so near a pool of congealing blood with a far too sexy and too dangerous warlock rubbing his hands all over me. But no way was I going to say that last part.

Nor was I ready to deal with how powerful a warlock he really was, bringing someone back from the dead. That scared me, on many levels. If one didn't mess with magic without ramifications what did it mean to cheat death?

"Here." I shivered, then thrust a trembling hand out. "Help me up."

He did, not with a hard jerk but a very gentle tug that allowed me to gain my feet and only waver a bit. I braced my legs, only too aware that every movement was one I would not be taking if it weren't for Bran's intervention.

I grabbed a moment to look around, struggling to find a sense of normalcy, focusing on the small details because I couldn't grapple with the bigger issue. The whole dead-but-not-dead one in particular. "Where's Gurn?" I asked, noticing first what was missing. "His body was right there." I pointed to a spot on the bloody deck to my left.

"A friend of yours?" Bran stood too close to me. Either worried that I'd topple and he'd have to re-do all his work, or not trusting me not to cast a spell in his direction. What kind of spell? An undo-whatever-the-hell-he'd-just-done spell?

Back to the normal. "No, Gurn wasn't a friend. He was the second shifter after me."

"Why after you?"

His voice sounded strange, but I wasn't sure why. If it was because he was surprised there were two or expecting more, I didn't know. Or maybe he was drained from snatching me from the dead. Either way I stepped back, so I could point at the stain and give myself space between us. "Yes, two. Gurn was shot by his partner and his body was right there."

"And what happened to the partner?"

I nodded toward the rail. "He stumbled back."

"Toppled over?"

I nodded, still surprised that the propulsion spell had that much power, even with blood magic. And had Bran used black magic to jumpstart my heart? Oh, hell, I hadn't even thought of that.

I glanced at Bran, not seeing his features all that clearly but clear enough to see the furrow of his brows.

Focus on the shifter, not the fear.

"Mostly Brains slipped in Gurn's blood." I glanced at the front of my sweatshirt and jeans, glad they weren't plastered with blood. I wiped what was on my hands along my jeans. Yuck. "Like what's on me."

"How hard did you hit your head?" Bran asked, as if I was making everything up.

"Don't believe me, but there were two and they planned on kidnapping me." This I could talk about, even get pissy about.

"Why? Two shifters need their own hairstylist?"

Smart ass. When he put it that way though it didn't make any sense. Who knew why they wanted me? To get me away from Dominique? Or was something going to happen and they didn't want me asking questions? Or just being around. New girl on the block.

Which reminded me. Sasha. If someone wanted me could they also want her?

I turned to stagger back to the interior of the boat.

"Where are you going?" Bran asked, right at my side.

"To find Sasha."

To get my world back on an even basis.

He paused then followed me, which was fine because the sooner I could find Sasha the sooner I could make sure she was okay. The fact I'd been attacked made me worry about her safety. If she was all right I could leave. I'd had it with boats and too many questions. Way too many about what Bran had done and what price I'd have to pay for it.

And damned if he wasn't right, about how I'd feel. I hurt as if I'd been the punching bag for a couple of shifters. I should have let him finish fixing me the way he'd done to my ribs.

He caught up with me as I stepped into the stateroom.

"Why are you looking for Sasha?" he asked, his voice suddenly wary.

Oh, yeah, I'd forgotten the whole Bran and Sasha together thing. I glanced at him over my shoulder. "Don't worry, I'm not out to hurt your squeeze. I just want to make sure she's okay."

He was right on top of me as I left the stateroom. It was empty which meant Suzette was okay. Gone, but then I didn't blame her, she looked easily spooked. Most people were from attacking shifters. Go figure.

Bran grabbed my arm, not rough but he managed to pull me to a stop which caused me to suck in an oath.

He look bothered, then added, "Tell me what you want with Sasha. And what do you mean by squeeze?"

I stared at him, my brows drawing down. "You know, romantic interest, girlfriend, temporary bed partner."

He actually looked like I'd gob-smacked him. He could revive corpses but get stopped by a comment? "She is not—"

The suave, urbane Bran actually sounded like he was stuttering.

"Doesn't matter," I cut him off, knowing if I didn't find Sasha soon I was going to crash into a heap and I didn't want that. Especially in front of Bran.

I was about say something else, when I spied Franco beetling down a far passageway.

"Got ya." I stiff-legged it to catch up to him, which sounds way faster than I was moving, hailing him when I got close enough not to shout. "Franco. Wait a minute."

He stopped as if jerked by invisible strings; only when he saw who it was did some of the tension seep from his shoulders. His tone was sharp as ever though as he said, "You are a disaster. A total disaster." He stretched his hands wide to make the point of how total he meant.

So bite me. If only he knew all of it.

Then I remembered. I had Gurn's blood smeared on my hands and parts of my clothes. I must have hit my head pretty hard after all to go running after Sasha looking as I did, or maybe it was that dying thing.

"What have you been doing?" Franco asked, his eyes wide, his skin pale.

"Working on an outfit for Halloween, what do you think I've been doing?" We were wasting time here chatting. My gut screamed, *Find Sasha now!*

Franco shot a glance between me and Bran. "Seriously? Halloween?"

"No," I bit back. You idiot. "I'll tell you everything later." Or as much as I was willing to share, which wasn't much. "As long as we can find Sasha."

He tsked, tsked with a wag of one finger. "You should be off the yacht by now. Staff is not to be seen here at all tonight."

That's right. I'd forgotten about that. It explained why I couldn't find anybody on board, but it raised another niggling question. Why tonight?

Later. One problem at a time. "I'm trying to get off the boat," I said, in my most patient tone, which wasn't so patient about then, as Bran joined me, earning only a quirked brow from Franco. I cleared my throat to get Chop-Chop's attention. "I've been looking for Sasha."

"Why?"

The question slapped like a wet cloth on bare skin.

"Dominique wants to see her."

"Oh, she won't be happy that you haven't found her and are still hanging around."

Too bad this wasn't kindergarten show-and-tell, like the time I'd tried to talk my brother Jake into going as my pet wolf.

I flattened my palms out before me. I was not the enemy here. Maybe I should start wearing a pin stating that fact if the men around here kept biting my head off. "Collette said you were looking for Sasha. I thought if you've found her, you could let me know where I can, too. Nothing more."

He eyed me for a moment, as if hunting for a hidden agenda, then shook his head before speaking to both Bran and me. "I can't find her." He sounded worried, genuinely worried. "I've checked everywhere I can think of."

I found I wanted to wipe the worry off his face. The man was a prick, but right now he was a concerned prick.

"If you've looked in all the logical places Sasha should be, it's time to check the rest." I pointed toward the front of the boat. "I'll check those rooms." I didn't add the word, "again," even though I thought it. "And you check the other direction. The last boat is long gone, but I can call a water taxi after I get cleaned up."

Franco glanced in the direction I pointed, at the community rooms, which included a Roman bath, a personal spa, and a training gym. Yacht life had all the benefits. "Maybe we should check these first together," he said, "before we bother Dominique whose room is down that hall."

As if I didn't know that already. In fact the community rooms were behind the door I'd seen Bran exit earlier that evening. Was it only a little over an hour ago? Felt like so much longer.

Franco's advice also let me know he was as cowed by Dragon Lady as the rest of the staff. Interesting.

"Okay." I wasn't a fool, I wanted to keep my head, and my job, too. "Let's go. Spa first."

We found Sasha in the second room we searched, the Roman bath. Whorls of steam circled the air, making it both hard to see and breathe the minute we opened the plate glass door. Which made no sense, as the bath should have been empty.

But it wasn't.

I stumbled over an outstretched arm, causing me to slam down hard on my knees on the mosaic-tiled floor.

That's when I recognized Sasha, reclining back against the tub edge, one hand thrown out, her head against the rim, her throat cleanly sliced from one side to the other.

"Bloody, hell," Franco whispered in the mist above my head, his tone as thin as the air. "She's dead."

CHAPTER 29

What was it about death that slowed time? Elongated each moment as if the ritual of passing suspended the laws of physics?

Bran had said nothing at first, but I sensed him right behind me, a solid wall. Obstacle? Barrier? Or protection.

Could he do for Sasha what he had done for me? How to get rid of Franco to ask?

I could hear Franco suck in a breath like a land-locked fish, while I rose to my feet and stood there, trying to read the crime scene as if I'd seen one before. Wait, I had. In fact, I had created my second one back on the foredeck. At least there were no bodies for the cops to find there. Could I get the blood cleaned off of me and the deck before the now inevitable law enforcement arrived?

When I got back to the agency compound I was going to pitch a hissy fit if we were sent out again being so ill equipped to deal with being attacked, fighting non-humans and dealing with brutal murder.

As if Ling Mai gave a flying fart what I thought.

Bran broke the silence. "Franco, you find Dominique. Tell her what's happened here. She'll know what to do."

My brain cells kicked into hyper drive. Leave it to a warlock to take charge, but then Bran was looking out for his interests, which also meant Dominique's interests and that could be a conflict.

"And if she doesn't, you call the police. Secure the launch boat first, so no one leaves the yacht before all are accounted for," I added, not trusting that Dragon Lady would make sure a killer was apprehended. Or that she wasn't the killer herself.

My tone must have alerted Bran that our tentative truce was over as he gave Franco a short nod before the other man scuttled off, taking one last hard look at me before he did.

Not the time to wonder at that glance as I knelt on the tiles near Sasha, not that I wanted to get closer to that cold, still body.

"Can you help her?" I asked, adding, "Like you helped me?"

I glanced over my shoulder to see him shake his head. "No. Too much time has passed and even if I could, I'd used everything up helping you."

Damn. I turned back to Sasha, mentally asking her forgiveness.

"Does your cousin know who to contact here in port?" I asked, more to keep both of us focused on the mundane and not the girl before us.

"She'll call the Gendarmerie Maritime." His voice sounded ice cold and matter of fact. "They'll contact the Sûreté."

That's right. This was his world. I couldn't order a meal, but he could snap his fingers and know whom to contact in any situation. Must be nice.

I stood again, which wasn't that easy knowing there was nothing I could do for Sasha. It left a bitter taste in my mouth.

"Are you all right?" Bran spoke right behind me, his strong hands cupping my shoulders and turning me toward him.

He'd surprised me. The touch and the tone of his voice. I'd expected more anger; after all this death was not removed from his immediate world, neither was the threat of it. But instead all I sensed from him was concern. For me? Why?

I kept my gaze averted as I managed a response through a clogged throat. "Of course—"

"There's no of course." His tone now slashed with exasperation, as if I'd poked a sore spot with a torch. This I could deal with, even as he continued, "I want you out of here. You should not be seeing this."

I inched backwards, forcing his arms to drop, placing steel beneath my tone. Two adversaries once again. "This *is* my job."

"It is not right."

"There is no right, no wrong. *It* just is."

That reached him, his lips tightening as his gaze shifted to survey the scene.

"What do you know about this?" he asked, his tone now clipped and distant. I looked, but noticed no change in eye color from him, no pulling a mage mantle across him, no whisper of magic swirling. Whatever Bran was right then, he wasn't acting like a warlock. Right now he was simply a very focused, very determined male.

Good. I needed the wall of professionalism between us. I'd barely begun to grapple with the fact he could restore life but clearly with restrictions.

"It's murder." I swallowed and looked at the lovely body lying so still yet relaxed. "Suicides don't slit their own throats like this. An easy enough process for someone to quietly walk in from behind, grab her hair and pull her head back. Plus there's no knife within sight, not to say it's not around the scene somewhere." I didn't want to disturb anything looking for it. Or step nearer all that blood again. I'd reached my limit of wallowing in blood this evening.

"How long do you think she's been dead?" he asked, though clearly knowing there had been a time delay between death and our arrival.

"Less than an hour," I lied, then added, "but not much longer by the texture of the blood congealing, though I'm no expert."

"Convenient that we all three found her together."

I glanced at him over my shoulder again, at the tightness of his expression, the tension riding his muscles. "Meaning?"

"At least that part isn't complicated."

I now understood. If I'd found Sasha on my own, I'd have become an immediate suspect. Which I'd been meant to do, having been sent specifically to look for her.

The group was small enough, and close-knit enough, to mean that as long as I was suspected of murdering one of their own, my effectiveness as a covert operative seeking information was canceled.

Whoever set up this scenario was brilliant and calculating. Dominique?

Yup, just up her ally. But why take out a lowly hairdresser—unless she realized I wasn't just an employee. I glanced again at Bran, at the strain bracketing his eyes, the cant to his full lips. Was he up to hearing my suspicions? Suspicions founded on what? Gut reactions toward a woman I hated at first sight.

Maybe I needed a little more concrete info before I rocked what was left of his world. Or before I accused him of being in this area of the yacht himself a little under an hour ago.

Damn and triple damn, this was getting complicated.

"If I were you," I offered, giving him action instead of answers. "I'd get the purser to block off this area of the yacht ASAP and maybe have someone you trust keep any people still remaining on board separated as much as possible from one another. The law will want to interview them."

"Dominique will not like this." Bran's gaze remained focused on the dead woman.

"Like it or not, the killer is someone on this boat unless someone has recently left on one of the shuttles back to shore." He glanced up then and I noted the bleakness, the shock being held tightly in check, as if he'd wrestled his anger into submission not that long ago. But then he'd been able to do something to change the outcome. I had lived, Sasha had died, and there wasn't any changing that.

I hadn't been an agent that long myself. But I understood the hard reality-slap of violence too well and too recently: images of Gurn's brains splattered across the deck, of the other shifter right before he fell, the scream, splash, and then silence slammed into my thoughts.

I swallowed bile. This wasn't time to deal with a flashback. Not with a dead woman at my feet.

I quieted my voice, for both our sakes. "This is going to be hard on everyone, the innocent and the guilty. You have a small window for damage control before the law arrives and takes over. I'd use that time wisely if I were you. Do whatever PR stuff you need to do to give your spin on this before it hits the news from some rag journalist listening to the police scanners or with a cousin on the Monte Carlo force."

"You've done this before." He looked at me then, really looked at me as if seeing me for the first time.

"Let's just say I understand law enforcement mentality. They have their agenda and you have yours. In places they'll merge."

"To find a killer."

"Exactly. But everyone has something to hide." My fingers clenched as if seeking grounding before I continued, "Some information you'll feel the police don't need to know, or you might feel has no bearing on the investigation. But the law will want to know about it anyway."

He made a noise, as if in protest, but I shook my head and shut him out. I knew firsthand what it meant to be a suspect in a murder inquiry and no amount of it'll-be-all-right coddling was going to sugarcoat the process.

"It's just the way things are. A man in your position should have contacts, acquaintances, friends. Call them. Now. Before you lose the opportunity. A murder can unravel a lot of lives. There can be a number of victims, not just the dead."

"This sounds very cold and heartless."

"It is." I nodded, clutching at the shreds of my control now. "We're losing time here."

"I will do as you suggest." He didn't look happy about it, then speared me with an icy glance. "You work in an ugly world."

I couldn't have drawn the line between us any more clearly. His world was on one side, creating beauty, mingling with the movers and shakers across the globe; mine was on another, the ugly reality of death and mingling with cops and body baggers. And that was without the whole warlock versus witch element.

As if I hadn't known there was a huge gap from the beginning.

"You're wasting time," I said, there being no need to address his comment.

"And what about her?" He looked at Sasha.

"She's no longer your problem. Finding her killer is." *Before he or she destroys the rest of your carefully constructed world.*

He nodded once but paused, as if fighting an internal battle. I had wanted to offer comfort, some soft words but found that none would come. Just as well, ours was not that kind of relationship.

I turned back to look at Sasha when I felt Bran's hand hit my back. I stumbled then took a dive into the sauna, coming up dripping and swearing.

"What the—" I sputtered.

"The blood," he said, standing there on the pool rim. "No one will notice the blood on you or your clothes now."

As if they won't wonder why I went swimming in my clothes.

Then he left. Leaving me standing in the pool, aware there was more than blood on my clothes that I'd have to explain. There was blood on the foredeck, the fact Franco had seen me smeared with blood, and my police record as a killer.

Oh, yeah, the nightmare had only begun.

CHAPTER 30

Once I crawled out of the pool I was thankful for two things. The first, I wasn't carrying my phone so there might be a small window to collect it and send a message to the team, and two, Bran was right, the shifter's blood was off of me, or what I could see of me, which meant I wouldn't be arrested immediately.

I was still drying off when the purser-cum-onboard-lackey arrived, sticking his head in the door and blanching. I clutched the towel and pushed him out then joined him in the hallway, squelching as I walked.

"No one gets in this room until the authorities arrive. No one, you understand?"

"Oui, mademoiselle."

"Not even Bran or Dominique."

If the man looked pale before he looked worse now.

"Oui." His agreement sounded a lot less assured, too.

Not that I blamed the poor guy. I didn't figure he ran across a lot of dead guests on his watch.

But I didn't have time to worry about him. I had to get somewhere I could send a text message. The minute the law arrived, and I was identified as discovering the body, I'd lose my phone and any way to communicate with the agency. This mission had just turned deadly up close and personal, and Ling Mai and the team needed to know. Maybe this would get them off their asses. Either that or I was more on my own than I'd ever thought possible.

By returning to the staging stateroom where I'd left my locked and warded valise I achieved my first goal—accessing my cell. I whipped it out, shocked to find a few bars of reception. Punching in a quick text message to Mandy, I hit the send button.

New model murdered. I found body. Advise.

I'd left off the whole P.S. Oh, and I died, but don't worry, I'm alive now bit. They'd yank me in a heartbeat for having a mental breakdown.

I hadn't brought dry, clean clothes along so I rubbed myself a bit more with the towel before discarding it. For now, I was stuck looking as if I'd taken a shower with my clothes on as I heard a put-put-put alongside the boat. A quick glance out the port window and I spied an official looking boat pulling up to the launch dock. The Gendarmerie Maritime, the officials who handled suspicious deaths in coastal French waters, hadn't wasted any time. One more clue that Bran's world was not mine. Men like him received immediate attention. Someone else might have waited longer for the law to arrive.

Of course lights and sirens weren't flashing. Bran must have worked very fast to keep the approach low-key and confidential.

That approach would no doubt extend to the manner in which the gendarmes handled Bran's core staff.

Would that approach also be given toward a lowly hairdresser who had a lot to hide once Bran was out of sight?

I was about to find out.

Dawn had just slipped over the horizon when a commotion outside Bran's stateroom arrested my attention. Bran entered his room as the rose-yellow dawn exploded into bright sunlight beyond the open balcony doors. My getting into his safe had been a bust. The man cast one great warding spell. So I was on to Plan B—find a way to circulate outside of the back room. Which led to Plan C— link Dominique to the attack on me, the brutal murder of Sasha, and the guy who might be holding Van.

I shied away from examining how I knew it was Bran as his door opened before I looked. We'd avoided each other for hours, ever since finding Sasha's body in the spa. Now there would be no avoiding him and my reaction to him.

Keep it professional. Please let me keep it professional. Not personal. So don't go down that road.

"You?" He stopped just inside the door, looking as constrained as I felt and as wary.

"The purser is looking for a place to stash me." I tripped over my rush of words, trying to reassure and explain all in the same breath. Last thing I needed was for him to disappear before I could ask a few key questions. "I'll be out of here soon."

When the silence grew between us I jammed my hands in the pocket of my jeans, rubbing my ring and asked, "How is . . .how are . . .?" Oh, hell, I didn't even know what to ask.

There. That was professional. Not.

A cynical and exhausted smile tugged the corner of his lips. He'd been up all night, too. "Today's show has been cancelled. I've been on the phone with our guests most of the night. Some claim prostration, traumatized as only twittering, senseless women can be. Others are ghouls, calculating how much press coverage they can expect from almost being at the scene of a crime."

Maybe the smile was more than cynical. Or was it the tone of his voice? This was not a man who suffered fools well.

"And you?" I asked, breaking my own rule so quickly it was a surprise I didn't get whiplash. I was so treading on personal grounds. "How are you doing?"

He crossed to the king-size bed and sat on the edge, weariness etching his posture. He raked one hand through thick, already tousled hair before spearing me with a glance even bleaker than the one I'd seen on him in the Roman bath hours ago. What surprised me was that he allowed how on edge he was to show.

"How am I?" he repeated, more to himself than me, his voice tugging at me. "A woman under my protection had her throat brutally slashed with no apparent motivation. I have a yacht full of law enforcement officers, because they know a killer is somewhere on the boat. My name—" he paused, then spoke again in a tighter, lower voice. "My name, already under investigation for robberies, is now linked with a murder. How do you think I am?"

Yeah, the edge sliced razor-sharp. But I needed him now. I needed him in control and focused and determined. He was my only potential ally on this ship. The only person who knew my true role and the only person who could help me get the answers I was determined to get.

So no matter how much I ached to empathize, or soothe, which really wasn't my nature anyway, there was no time for it. Any moment Dominique could slam through his door with her own agenda. Later I could find time to talk to him about his very unique gift, but for now I'd keep focused on Sasha.

"Have you talked with Dominique?" My voice was more get-with-the-program intense than I intended, but it worked.

He glanced up, his gaze icy. "Of course, I have. She handled a lot of the most hysterical of the women and the press releases."

"Anything else?"

"What does it matter to you?"

This was not personal, this was business.

I stepped closer, though approaching the leashed fierceness straight-on took years of training as a sibling-sister amongst bigger, badder, meaner brothers. "It matters because there's only one person who knew, for sure, I'd be looking for Sasha and most likely find her. That Franco and you were there, too, was a fluke, nothing more."

He didn't respond, which was fine because I stumbled against one of the questions that had been bothering me since last night. "Why were you there?" I asked, blaming exhaustion for not wondering before this.

He glanced up, his eyes devil dark. "Why was I where?"

"On the foredeck. How did you find me?" How did you revive me?

His shoulders relaxed as mine tightened. There was something I was missing here. Something he thought I was going to discover. His body language betrayed him.

He shrugged, "Does it matter?"

"It does to me."

His glance was razor sharp, more warlock than human. "I wanted some fresh air."

"So you just happened to walk to the foredeck?" Think, Noziak, what was he not saying?

"Yes," he bit out, jerking to his feet. "I took a walk. I found you. I . . . I healed you. Would you rather I'd have left you to die?"

I hesitated. Was now the time to ask at what cost was his healing? I already knew one price; he could not help Sasha. Which brought me back around to what was niggling at me.

The dead shifter. That was it. Bran had to have seen the dead shifter. I had no idea how long I'd been dead on deck but it was long enough for someone to dispose of a dead body. Someone strong enough, like a warlock, could have tipped Gurn into the sea. But why?

"Did you get rid of the man's body?" I asked, stepping back, feeling as if I were shadow boxing, trying to figure out the details.

"If I say yes, will you stop hounding me?"

Not really a yes, but not a no either. I figured I'd pushed him as much as I could.

"Nothing makes sense," I murmured, scrubbing my hands across my face.

"I'm not the enemy here, Alex," Bran's voice washed against me.

I glanced at him as he continued, "If I were *your* enemy you'd be at some Monte Carlo police station facing a murder charge right now."

Still was a strong possibility of that happening, given the direction of the questions they'd asked me earlier. Or the fact I had a criminal record. But why hadn't the police made a bigger issue out of my wet clothes? Franco had to have told them I had blood all over me

One step at a time.

I looked at Bran, really looked at him before crossing to a chair opposite him and slipping into it. It wasn't lost on either of us that the chair was as far away from him as I could get and still be in the same room.

"Why are you afraid of me?" This was Bran, the multimillionaire who'd created his own empire, talking now. One step accomplished. I had his full attention. A Taser on stun would have had less power. Bran was not an easy man to be around in the best of times; in my limited experience most powerful, self-made men weren't. Warlocks fell into the same category. And now I had to tell him that the person he trusted most in the world might be working against his best interests.

Not fun.

"I need to tell you something you won't want to hear," I said, my voice shaky with fatigue. Maybe I should put off this conversation, not that it would ever get easy. I was asking him to do what I was not willing to do, abandon family. I was here because of Van, and with that thought front and center I steeled myself to push forward. "We need to talk about Dominique."

"Talk about her why?" His voice sounded constrained.

"Her possible involvement in events."

"You don't know my cousin."

"True." I didn't know him either, so taking him as a temporary ally right now might make all my other mistakes pale by comparison, but I needed answers. I looked at him, my hands loose on my knees, my voice flat. "What I do know is that Sasha's murder changes the thefts happening around this show." I watched him flinch, but plowed ahead. "Those thefts were externally directed. Someone using the cover of your tour locations to line their pockets. But Sasha's death was the result of one of two things. Possibly both."

"Go on," he said at last without raising his head.

Small progress that he didn't shut me off totally. I inhaled and braced myself. "The first is that Sasha stumbled onto information she shouldn't have and was killed to keep her quiet."

"She'd been with the staff less than a week."

"But it's still a possibility."

Small, baby steps.

"And the second issue?"

"The second issue is personal." I steeled myself, twirling my ring on my finger like a weapon. "Someone wants to destroy you."

He raised his head and stared at me as if I'd just sprouted horns and a forked tail. Ironic given he was the only warlock in the room, and angry warlocks had often been described through history as the devil's own.

"Don't be ridiculous." He stood, a powerful, controlled move as he thrust hands deep into the pockets of his linen pants. He paced, but with each step measured and held tightly in check. This was not a person to be prodded into anything—especially a theory at odds with his world view.

I kept my gaze averted, not to avoid him, but to give him some room to digest what I'd laid before him. Breaking a granite shell took time, and Bran was all granite.

"I trust the people around me." He scowled at me, his tone making it clear I was an outsider threatening his world. Fair enough, my response would probably have been the same. "They are not just my employees, they are my friends. My family."

Then this guy obviously didn't have a lot of luck with family.

"Look." It was time for damage control, but there was no avoiding the truth. "I could be wrong about this being personal." My gut told me I wasn't.

"You are."

"Fine." I raised my hands. *No harm, no foul.* "So we focus on the first issue. Sasha knew something, or saw something she shouldn't have."

"And none of that has anything to do with the staff or Dom." His words were angry, his eyes desperate. "So keep her out of this."

That had me sucking in air and curling my fists. Noziaks didn't back down when things got ugly. We plowed ahead.

Besides, keeping out was not my call. If the cinnamon scented Prima Donna was involved, it'd come out sooner or later. With hope before there were any more casualties.

I tried a different tack. "That still leaves a number of guests and your staff to look at closer. My gut tells me staff is

where we should look in more depth, but there's no telling if
Sasha knew one of your guests previously and her past
caught up with her here. From what I've been able to see
some of these women arrive at several of your events in a
year. So we can't eliminate guests totally at this point."

"Is that all?" He didn't even look at me.

"No, but having two shifters running free on the same
yacht can't be a coincidence. Something is going on here."

There, I gave him a little wiggle room, but no way was I
going to avoid what the facts spelled out for me. First thing
law enforcement had to have done before they contacted the
IR agency as a what-the-hell last option was cross-reference
guests with thefts. The fact no names surfaced must have
been clarified with Bran before I came on board.

"I agree." He now stood right next to me and stared me
down. "But you're saying that Sasha's death could have had
nothing to do with her being one of my models."

I was afraid he'd clutch that very teeny, tiny straw too
quickly.

"There's a scant chance." I backpedaled, accepting that
just because I'd jump first and rethink things after the fact,
not everyone acted under that principle.

"Then we must discover if Sasha knew one of the guests."
At least he sounded like a man stepping away from the edge
and not toward it. "What next?"

Great. I'd gotten myself out on this limb, it was time to
continue holding on for dear life—or jump.

"Next?" I said, averting my gaze again, flexing fingers
that had become rigid fists before I stepped in the direction
I'd hoped to avoid. "It's time I move out of the back room. I
can investigate only so far when I have access to half the
people involved. And I need your help to do that."

He went still, his whole body taut, his eyes carefully
banked, his gaze shuttered. Warlock under threat.

Not quite the response I'd wanted. Why did I feel I'd just
propositioned him?

Maybe all I'd sensed between us was only my imagination
anyway. There was no spark zipping between us—no crazy,

illogical attraction that blurred the edges of professionalism and made thinking difficult. All one-sided.

That was good news; it was better to lose my mind than my professionalism. So why did it hurt like a horse's kick? Damn, I hated feeling like a fool.

I slowly rose to my feet and stood there, in the center of his room, waiting for him to throw me out on my ear. Not a sensation I was inclined to tolerate for long.

I sighed outloud to break the strained silence. So what if my voice came out a little too breathless. "I just need a way to move among your guests as freely as I now move among your staff, that's all."

"Is it?" His husky voice deepened, enough to give me a chill of goosebumps dancing down my arms. Fatigue. It had to be fatigue. Or the whole dead-undead thing messing with me. Again.

"Exactly what are you asking?"

My words stuttered, not nonchalant as I'd intended. But then again I was caught and held in that predator stare of his, the one that could make a grown woman weep, or beg, and I wasn't sure which side of the fence I wanted to sit on.

He stepped closer. I held my ground.

"You tell me exactly what it is you want." His words vibrated like the thrum of a powerful engine held in check. "What do you want from me?"

A touch? More? All of you? Where was this coming from? I didn't lose my head over gorgeous, sexy, dangerous warlocks. Okay, I didn't run across all that many.

Mine fields. Dangerous, dangerous mine fields. Remember, I'm an agent here, not a woman. Don't listen to my hormones' knee-jerk response, to my heart pounding harder, my muscles clenching, the hot, tingling warmth starting from my core and racing outwards.

Fatigue, damn it, that's all.

"Guests," I stuttered again and grasped for brain cells that had fled the minute his scent reached me. The second he neared enough to touch, if either of us reached out. "I want guests."

His smile taunted. Promised. Seduced. His lips curled in a secret, wicked smile. So maybe he was more than a word-weaver and heal-from-the-dead mage. Right now he was the king of seduction.

"Guests?" The single word feathered like a whisper, a caress across raw nerve endings. "You're sure?"

"Of course I'm sure."

"Have you heard of the *acies acendo adamo*?"

He'd thrown me for a loop, which was not the first time this evening. "I don't know what you're talking about." Though the language was familiar, Latin, the meaning was obscure. Could it be a spell?

His gaze bore down on me. "The portent is very old. Lost in the mists of time."

"What portent?" I clenched my hands, bracing myself.

"Between a powerful warlock and the even more powerful witch who would bring him to his knees and start the time of change. The time of loss."

What were we talking about? And why did it make me want to lash out? Or weep?

"You don't know your history?" he asked, with a quirk to his brow.

History be damned. It wasn't as if I got exposed to a lot of Latin, or witch lore in Mud Lake.

"Let down your wards again, little witch, and you'll find the meaning to the portent."

A quick rat-a-tat at the door saved me. We both started, glancing toward the door, avoiding each other's gaze.

Dominique cruised into the room without waiting for an invite, her hand clutching a newspaper, her gaze immediately riveted on me. "What are you doing here?"

The words shot like an angry accusation more than a question.

"Waiting for a room."

"Why do you need a room?" Dominique's gaze slashed to Bran's and her voice shot up in volume. "She's not staying on the yacht."

"She is."

"But is that wise?"

"She found the body, Dom. The gendarmes insist she stay." Bran gave a deep sigh as he added. "She didn't kill Sasha."

"Says who?"

Whoa, Dragon Lady. No one calls me a killer. Not to my face.

I stepped forward, my fists balled. "Says me." I ached to ask a dozen unspoken questions. *Where were you between the time I left your room and found Sasha? The spa was only down the hallway from your suite. Plenty of time to nip in and nip out.*

Dominique released a snarl of outrage. She glanced at Bran. "She can't talk to me in that tone. It's insubordinate."

Like she was playing nice and I was the playground bully?

I noted Dragon Lady hadn't actually denied her implication that I was a killer, but she sure played the helpless female card well and Bran was sucking it up. No wonder he and I butted heads if he went for the damsel in distress type.

"Ladies." He stepped between us. "It's been a very long night. Nothing will be served by taking shots at each other."

Oh, but it sure could clarify a few key points. A quick glance at Dominique confirmed my hunch that the other woman would have liked the chance to get a few licks in, too, but was willing to bide her time. Her smile was serpentine, her eyes pinpoints of calculation, with that suspicious green rim to them.

A quick glance at my ring wasn't necessary to know my preternatural alert device was red-hot against my skin. Good, a wakeup call. Focus on the mission.

But Dominique's voice was the real piece de resistance—from controlling woman-of-power to sulky-and-little-girl-helpless. I wanted to gag, but Bran didn't bat an eyelash. What kind of world did he live in where women were so manipulative, flashing from hot to cold depending on what they wanted? Give me a good knock-'em-out fight any day to this crap.

"Bran, dear, it's been dreadful with all these…these law people dashing about." Dominique shot me a telling glance indicating exactly who was at the root of the crisis. But I didn't stick my tongue out, tempting as it was. "I'm almost prostrate."

I held back a snort, barely. I doubted Dominique was ever prostrated a day in her life, and now she was devastated over the death of someone she barely knew? Give me a break.

Bran countered. "What do you need?"

A good bitch slap? I bit my tongue. Vaughn would have been proud of me. Jaylene, on the other hand, would have been in Dominique's face straightening out the wilted flower and I'd have paid good money to have watched.

"I'm afraid there's worse news." Dominique gave a dramatic pause. The stage lost a consummate actress in this one.

"What?" Bran asked, his tone wearier than moments ago. *Yeah, what was worse than murder?*

Dominique grinned at me behind Bran's back—a quick, sharp jab before tipping her chin up.

But it wasn't her attitude as much as her words that had me seeing red.

"It's her." Dominique pointed right at me as if there were a lot of other females in the room. "She's been arrested for murder once before."

Busted.

CHAPTER 31

Bran stood near the doorway, his hands thrust in his pockets, his face unreadable but tense. Dom flounced out of the room after dropping her bomb. Smart move, no need to clean up the blood. My blood.

"Is that true?" he asked.

"Yes." I glanced at my curled fists, aware it was none of his business, also aware of the sharpness of my tone. I managed to blink back the dampness stinging my eyes before sharing, "My past has nothing to do with this."

Did his expression change or was it a play of shadows? He shifted, looking as if he wanted to speak but couldn't find the words. At least I wasn't the only one.

But he'd never been at a loss before. Why now? Did he expect me to lash out and kill him, too?

"I'm sorry." His gaze rested on mine. "For this situation and your involvement in it."

I didn't need nor want his pity. Not that I expected either but that thought helped steel my shoulders and my tone. "This involvement is my job."

He flinched. "Having your personal reputation smeared publically is part of your job?"

"Not usually." I shrugged, as if I dealt with this kind of crap daily. That was me—uber James Bond spy with no emotions. As if. I hadn't been this tongue-tied with a guy since grade school; but I hadn't expected this lack of response to Dom's news from him. "As long as your cousin doesn't broadcast my past to everyone this will be over soon."

"Will it?"

Were we talking about my reputation or his now? Mine in shreds was one thing; his in shreds destroyed his world. One he'd carefully and methodically created. Was that why he seemed so on edge?

Maybe one day Vaughn could give me some lessons in diplomacy because they would come in handy in these sort of awkward, tight moments. Tiptoeing around an issue wasn't my style.

"Is there another problem?" I asked point blank.

His gaze shifted then returned, if anything more intense. "I've been thinking about what you said."

I scrubbed one hand across my face. When? Before death or after—before he discovered I'd killed someone or after? Or was he about to explain his cryptic Latin phrase?

"I'm speaking about moving you beyond the back room."

"Oh." That quickly my mouth dropped open, my hands re-curled and my mind went blank. Not a good thing for an operative, even one operating on no sleep and adrenaline.

"That's all you have to say? Oh?" The sudden tilt of his lips did it, broke through to me in a cold wash of reality. He hadn't suggested anything, and here I was acting like a clueless ninny.

Pull it together, Alex.

"Fine." I cleared my throat. "What do you have in mind?"

The skin across his cheeks tightened as his breath quickened.

I wasn't imaging his reaction. Was I? Or my own?

The clenching in my thigh muscles returned, as did the freefall sensation in my stomach.

"Bran?" My use of his name sounded shaky, tasted strange on my tongue. It was harder to remain witch to warlock with his name wrapping around me. "If we're going to work together, it's business—all business."

One dark brow angled as he faced me, his whole body on tense alert. When he shook his head, as if waking from a strange dream, I knew it'd be all right. For now.

"Of course," he replied. "Business only."

There was nothing "of course" about it; but stepping back from the precipice once was about all I could handle now. And he hadn't brought up the portent. That was good.

"Any ideas?" I said, "I could go along as your hairdresser—"

"You'll be my date."

"Date?" Pulling the single word out was like stepping away from hot tar. "No one will believe I'm your date. You and I are from different universes. No one would believe you'd—"

"It's done." He made as if to walk away. "When we get to the Maldives, first evening will be a gathering of guests. The first show after. . ." He waved his hand to indicate the zoo beyond the open door. "You'll be with me."

If we got to the Maldives, a big "if" given an open police investigation and that they now knew about my past. I had no doubt Dom was sharing it even now.

"Wait." This was *so* not going to plan. My plan.

He glanced at me, his look withdrawn. He might have worked himself up to a position of power, but I bet he possessed that king-to-peasant look in the cradle. Or it was a warlock thing. No wonder they had such a reputation.

Gulping a ragged breath, I unclenched sweaty palms and wiggled them. "It won't work." I took a deep breath and continued. "I'm a pretzel-and-beer kind of gal, you're a—" I waved one hand before me.

"A?"

"A champagne-and-caviar kind of guy. No one's going to believe we'd be an item. I think we've got to find a different way to work this."

Damn it, but we were short on time.

"You're going as my date. Deal with it." There were husky undertones here, male-to-female vibes that were screwing with my concentration.

"No way am I going to be accepted as your date. And if I'm not, I'll be even more shut out than I am now. I need to find out how these thefts and this death have been set up. See how the marks are selected. Connect the dots."

"Do not fight me on this, little witch. Trust that I know my world as you know yours."

He eyed me, not as he had earlier, but with a critical look I'd seen Franco use before sending the models out to strut and sell their wares.

"You will have no worries," he said at last. "I'll have a consultant meet with you."

It wasn't a consultation I needed; it was a miracle.

"But—"

"I was forced to trust you earlier. Now you must trust me."

Yeah, right. Not a fair move: not his words, not his look— one that rattled me to my core. Not my immediate response. What could you say to a man who asked for your trust? And spoke without heat but with understanding? The man did *not* play fair at all.

I swallowed and nodded, no words would come.

"And what of your cousin?" I asked, clutching at straws. "If she tells everyone about—"

"She won't. I'll make sure she won't."

I believed him.

"Good," he said it gently, a devious means of scaling my defenses. "I'll send the consultant to you as soon as it can be arranged. We do not have much time. For now, get some rest; you are tired."

He left, which was a good thing. I needed some adjustment time, major adjustment time. I needed to get my head back on straight and my hormones under control. There was absolutely nothing between Bran and myself except a mission.

Now, if I repeated it about a million times, it might sink in.

Maybe.

CHAPTER 32

I woke from a short power nap as a knock sounded at my door later that day. I'd finally been stashed in the purser's room as a temporary means of keeping me handy for the ongoing investigation. Which meant every hour on the hour some French gendarme knocked on my door, asked the same questions they'd already asked, gave me the stink eye, and then left. They'd make a great alarm clock service.

But they hadn't pushed too hard about my previous record, which surprised me. On the other hand maybe my text message to the agency had gotten through and Ling Mai was covering my back. Like I'd believe that. If Ling Mai had brushed my record under the mat it was because I'd then owe her a favor and a big one. Plus I'd have to keep her happy. Talk about a lose-lose scenario.

At a second knock, louder this time, I yanked open my door to find Franco.

So maybe I wasn't awake but was having a nightmare instead.

"You look like hell. Again," he greeted me, brushing past me in a cloud of musky cologne. The same scent Collette often used. Go figure. "Close the door. No one else is coming in."

Great, just what I needed, a large dose of snippiness.

I left the door ajar, mostly out of spite. There was little traffic in this section of the boat, so little reason to worry about being overheard.

Then I got a good look at Franco and bit back the short reply on the tip of my tongue. The man was hurting. One could read it in the fan of lines around his eyes, in the tightness of his shoulders; different people dealt with shock and grief in different ways. Obviously Franco's method was to up his irritation level and let it spill over.

"What do you want?" I asked, with just enough snarl to earn a grin from him.

"Why, dahling, surely you've heard?"

Alarm bells sounded.

I kept my tone level, with effort. "Heard what?"

"I'm your new consultant. Ta-dah."

I'd kill Bran.

"Why, dahling." Franco twirled once around my very small room. "You are looking less than pleased. Not a good look for you by the way. It brings little frown lines between your brows. Very aging."

"I don't need you—"

"Oh, but you do, Sacagawea, you so do."

"My name isn't—"

"Tut tut, dahling, more frown lines. This will not do at all." He placed two fingers beneath his chin and tilted his head, looking at me critically. "Bran told me we have two days and a long plane ride. The man is such an optimist."

I'd kill Bran slowly, very slowly, right after I took out—

"Chop, chop, luv. Lots to do."

"Look, Frank." My words, or my tone, or both, earned a moue of disdain. "I'm not your pet project. Find me a dress and call it good. I don't want you here. You don't want to be here. We're even."

"Oh, but we're not." He shook his head. "I'm not doing this for *you* but for Bran. He needs me. He asked me to come and, viola, *I* am here."

His Supreme Mageness was going to suffer. But that wasn't the point. I was not going to become Franco's pet project no matter what Bran thought I needed. Torture was not my thing and the steady gleam in Franco's eyes left no doubt he was enjoying my annoyance.

I glanced at my ring. A slight buzz indicating preternatural warning. More like a preternatural skin rash. Too bad I couldn't use that as an excuse to bust the PIA.

"*I* don't need you here." Okay, so I was lying again, but one had to draw the line somewhere. I spoke around a tight, a very tight jaw. I was juggling enough issues without having to deal with this drag-queen-on-Prozac. "In fact, I'm pretty sure this arrangement won't work at all. So pick out the dresses and, viola." I spread my hands in a mimicking gesture, then lowered my voice. "We'll be done."

"Dresses? Bran does not create dresses, he creates masterpieces."

Oh, great, now I'd set Franco off.

"One pulls dresses from the rack at mall stores," he continued, looking as if he were sucking lemons. "Bran does not *do* dresses."

"Fine. Get me—"

"No." Franco made a chopping movement. "I do it all or you look like the savage amongst the roses. There is no inbetween."

Damn and double damn. Give me a gun and a few bad guys over this any day. And savage? He didn't have a clue how savage I could be, but he might find out. Real soon.

On the other hand, I had a mission to complete and Chop-Chop here was the quickest way to get where I wanted to go.

"We do this my way then," I snapped.

"We shall see."

"There's no negotiations about it, buster. My way or the highway. Understand?"

"I understand you have deep, volatile emotions, but you hide them, or so you think. It is the way with savages. I have read a book, so I know this."

I stepped up beside him, fisted my hands in his pink silk shirt and tugged him off his feet until he dangled an inch above the floor. "Here's a lesson you won't get from a book. Call me a savage once more and there'll be nothing left of you to put back together. Are we clear?"

"Problems?"

Franco and I both looked toward the door.

Bran lounged there as if he belonged, a half-smile playing about his lips.

"Doesn't anybody knock around here?" I growled.

"Not if the door is open."

Crap, my own fault.

Bran entered and closed the door behind him. "I think you'd better release him. His color no longer looks good with the fuchsia of his shirt."

I let go, smiling when Franco stumbled then righted, glaring at me. If Bran hadn't been in the room the little man probably would have said *neener, neener* to me. Instead he shook himself like a wet dog and miffed, "Well, I never—" He looked at Bran. "Speak to her; she will not listen to me."

"She'll do what needs to be done," came Bran's steely reply.

"My way—"

"Alex," Bran said with that tone that said there was only one answer. Fine. He was right, but that didn't mean I had to like it.

I glared at Franco and Franco glared back, before straightening his shirt. Keeping my gaze on Franco, I said, "I'm sure we understand each other perfectly now, don't we, Frank?"

"Yes." He narrowed his eyes, but I'd tackled bigger challenges than pip-squeak here and I was sure he knew it, even as he announced, "I shall do as Bran asks. A complete transformation. Face. Body. Clothes. The works!"

I growled but Bran stepped closer, all serious now. "Good, because we'll have to work fast. We have bigger problems to deal with."

"Like what?" I asked, beginning to feel like a general fighting on too many fronts.

"They've found the knife used to kill Sasha."

"Where?" Franco's voice sounded harsh; his expression matched it.

"In your room, Franco."

CHAPTER 33

Dominique swatted at a pesky fly, inhaling deeply. At the prices they were paying for these staterooms one would think flies would not be allowed. She punched in the familiar numbers, pleased her hand remained steady.

"Yes," the voice answered without preamble.

"I've done what you wanted," she said. "The model is dead."

"I know. But your execution was sloppy."

Dominique's tone hardened. "The potential infiltration has been neutralized. I handled it quickly and efficiently. Some mess is to be expected, but I have everything under control."

"Do you?"

The space of several heartbeats galloped past, but Dominique was not a minion. Never had been and she would not stoop to that level now.

"I said I've taken care of the problem and I have." No need to mention the other issue that cropped up. One down, one left to handle. Would her life never be sane?

"There still remains the American."

She inhaled and enunciated every word. "One death can be justified; two would only cause more problems." If those idiots had done the job they'd been hired for all of this would be finished by now. But no, she had to handle every detail. "Don't worry, the remaining one is very busy with damage control and will not cause problems. I'll see to it."

"And if she does?"

"Then I'll take care of it." Dominique twisted a strand of hair then stilled her hand. No need to lose control now, the hard part was already done. Murder was a messy business.

Time to turn the tables and be the one making demands.

"Is the next phase ready?"

"All is set."

"Good."

"There have been no changes to the itinerary?"

She shook her head, even though the mechanical sounding voice could not see her. "No. Adjustments have been made in the time frames, but we're on schedule for the Maldives and Miami after that."

"And then Washington D. C.?"

"Yes, as planned."

"Then we are ready. You will not be contacted by us until you reach Miami. Make sure there are no more mistakes."

She tightened her grip on her cell phone, sure the inconsequential piece of plastic would splinter, but she kept her tone even and calm as she answered, "There have been no mistakes on my part thus far. It will continue to be so."

Her only answer was a dial tone.

With a curse she threw the phone across the stateroom.

CHAPTER 34

I glanced at Franco, his mouth an open "O" at Bran's announcement, still echoing in the stillness of the room. The first few seconds were always a dead giveaway as to guilt or innocence, because very few people could pale on command.

"This is not possible," Franco's words tumbled as he shook his head. He was stunned, but there was something else flashing through his eyes. Wariness? Confusion? The look came and went so fast I couldn't put my finger on it before he whispered, "How? Where? When?"

Bran shot me a focused glance before responding to Franco. "The gendarmes are searching your room now. I expect they will find you shortly and request your presence for more questioning."

The process all sounded so civilized, but that wasn't the reality of a murder investigation. The sour taste of fear, the relentless questions battering at a person, the seconds of time Franco would need to account for, explaining away the unexplainable.

"He's not to blame." I hadn't realized I spoke aloud until both men looked at me.

Bran's gaze would have frozen hell. "Explain."

Fine line to walk. Franco couldn't know who I really was or how I came by my knowledge, but neither could I let an innocent man take the rap for a ruthless killer.

"It's simple." I thrust my hands into the front pockets of my jeans, aware of my ring rubbing the denim. "We came across Franco a good five to seven minutes before we found Sasha. During that whole time he was in our sight."

"And this means?" Franco threw his hands in the air. "Sasha could have been dead hours."

"Not possible." I shook my head, risking my mission, with the truth. "Her blood had barely started to congeal. Which means she was killed probably less than fifteen minutes before we found her and the police surgeons will determine that."

"And you know this how?" Wariness coated Franco's words as Bran stood silent, his gaze anchored on me. Yeah, I'd told him something different when we'd first discovered Sasha's body, but there was a reason. I wanted to see if he mentioned his being in the area prior to the murder, but he'd said nothing. Why?

He continued to pin me with his glare. Smart man, not wanting to help me dig my own grave.

"My father's a pig farmer. We slaughtered animals on the farm so I have seen death, and blood, before. Besides, you had no blood on you and you were wearing white. As you saw, there was blood everywhere. It's called blood spatter. You'd have been covered in blood if you killed her."

"A pig farm?" Bran kept his tone enigmatic. Nice trick if you could do it. I liked the fact my being a murderer didn't faze him but my being a pig farmer's daughter surprised him. Go figure.

"Yes, a pig farm." Temper tightened my spine. "Not glamorous but it taught me a few facts of life." Like how to deal with arrogant, in-charge men and warlocks. "Franco didn't kill Sasha."

"I *know* I didn't kill her," the small man said, all the normal bluster leeched from his tone.

"I'll have lawyers meet you in Monte Carlo." Bran was back to his authoritarian voice.

"You believe me then?" Franco asked.

"Of course I do." Bran glanced at me. "Besides you have a witness who backs up the improbability of you being a killer. Two including me."

"But you see the problem?" I said, thinking through the repercussions of the knife.

"Besides my being accused of something I didn't do?" Franco's voice almost reached his normal high-pitch-with-attitude tone.

"Besides that." I speared Bran with a steady look. "It means someone is setting Franco up. Someone on the yacht, who would have access to his room. The killer. Or they had help." I so didn't want to think about the possibility of more than one killer running around, especially as I focused on why was Franco being set up and not just me?

Easy. I had no room. But I did have my hairdresser's valise. A knife could have been slipped into it easily enough except for the protection wardings. Finally being a witch was paying off.

I had spoken no names, but read in Bran's lips that he understood I meant Dominique and he didn't like the implications.

He spoke to Franco. "We'll make sure you're not detained for long." A knock at the door made him add, "Don't worry."

Franco shook his head dog-style as if adjusting the short spike of red-blond hair made him taller. "I shall be vindicated."

The gendarmes who appeared at my door took Franco away without incident, which meant Franco would be treated better than if there'd been a row. I waited until he was gone before I circled around Bran.

"What aren't you saying?" I demanded, tired of tap-dancing around in the dark.

"You know all that I know." This was not a seducer's tone, but a businessman's, one whose toleration level was nil. "All that it's safe for you to know."

"Don't play dumb with me." I kept my voice low and steady. I might not be a multimillionaire, but that didn't mean I took crap either. "Something is going on with Franco that has nothing to do with a weapon being planted in his room."

"Are you always this suspicious?"

"I am when I'm being led a merry chase."

"And by merry chase you mean?"

"Don't do this, Bran. I'm on your side." Unless he was behind what was happening. "If you're not honest with me, I can't help."

Tell me. Tell me about coming out of the spa room door. Trust me.

"Is this the way you help?" His tone took on a sharp edge. "You accuse my cousin of involvement with no proof. A woman is dead, and now a man I know is innocent has been arrested."

"He's only been detained for questioning."

"And I should be happy about this?"

"It means that in spite of the weapon they don't believe Franco killed Sasha any more than I do. If they did, they'd have him wrapped up tight." I stepped away. Was I wrong about my suspicions? That there was something else going on here?

I walked toward the porthole window, seeing only undulating turquoise blue sky from its circle then turned and speared him with a don't-mess-with-me look.

He stood there like a pirate—dark, dangerous, and totally off limits and just as frustrated with me as I was with him.

So I pushed. "I saw you." When he said nothing I added. "I saw you leave the community rooms."

"When?" He bit the word out. I noticed he'd avoided the question with a question of his own.

"Shortly after your argument with Dominique." Which we both knew put him outside the window of time of the killing. If Sasha was killed shortly before we found her, then she wasn't dead when I saw Bran leave the area. But it still begged the question why had he been there and why hadn't he explained that fact.

"Are you now accusing *me* of killing her?" he asked, a bleakness around his eyes even though his voice was all angry warlock, which meant it whipped like a live wire.

"No." Idiot. "I'm saying you were there. Why?"

"Am I not allowed to move about on the yacht that I'm paying for?"

He was still avoiding the question. And was now the best time to push? He didn't kill Sasha. I threw my hands up. "Fine. This is your life—"

"You're right. This is *my* life. *My* business. Not yours. You have no idea what you are involved in and yet you keep racing ahead into trouble. With no idea how much trouble."

His thunderous look shut me out; asking for help was not easy for him. One thing we both had in common.

So why did it hurt? I was a professional, here to help. But from the first look at his image on a screen in Ling Mai's office a little over a week ago I'd not been impartial about this man.

My problem. Not his.

"Alex." His tone had softened, no longer ready to zap me to a nether world.

I was getting sappy if his saying my name made me quiver.

He continued. "What's happening with Franco has nothing to do with you."

His tone asked for exactly what I was asking for from him—trust. He was hiding something from me and telling me to look the other way.

But it wasn't my job to trust nor really in my nature.

So we were at an impasse; neither willing to really trust the other, yet both compelled to try anyway. What a mess. But I wasn't here to clean up this particular mess; I was here with a specific job to do. Find out who was behind the thefts and now a murder. And my own agenda, find Van.

I anchored my voice to a calmness absent from my emotions. "What's the status of the rest of your tour?" I asked, my back ramrod straight, my hands curled at my side.

"Alex, I—"

I waved him off with a look and one hand.

He didn't get it both ways. Either we were partners in a lopsided way, or. we weren't, and I wasn't going to let the entreaty of his tone, or his look, intense and focused, to sway me.

"Is the rest of the tour on or not?"

He nodded once, his mouth a flat line. "It's on."

This was not a man who liked being thwarted.

Poor warlock, neither did I.

"Will there be any business conducted here on the yacht before we leave?" I asked.

"No."

"Good." One less issue to deal with. I could still move among the models and staff, even with sharp and wary gazes darting my direction, but I didn't have to start the charade of moving in Bran's world. "When will we leave for our next destination?" I asked.

"I already have my lawyers working to allow us to depart."

"And with Franco's detention, have they indicated a time frame?"

"Tomorrow unless there are more complications."

This whole mission was a complication, but then he could afford the kinds of lawyers who'd let the tour move along.

We spoke as two strangers: short, clipped, impartial. Except there was more. Hurt. On both our parts. Uncalled for, unexpected, and definitely unwanted.

"When is the next social gathering scheduled?" I reminded myself the sooner I found a thief and killer, the sooner I'd be out of Bran's life, and vice a versa.

"The evening on the second day we arrive at Kurra Huras. We'll be ferried to the island the first evening."

"Then I'll be present." As his date, though I couldn't get those words out.

I was casting my lot, willing to enter his world to catch a killer. I'd better catch the bastard, because I was so not looking forward to rubbing shoulders with the rich and bored for long.

"Alex—" He stepped forward, raising a hand as if to touch me.

I wasn't going to let him get to me that way. His touch would unfocus me from my job. I accepted that fact on a woman's level, rejected it as a professional.

I stepped back, keeping my gaze even. "In the meantime I'll pursue my inquiries."

Ones you'll not be privy to, and that will definitely include your cousin.

"You'll be my date on Kurra Huras?" he asked, as if expecting more argument.

"Yes." There weren't a lot of options to take the course of least resistance on this one. As long as it didn't come back to bite me on the butt. "I'll play hairdresser by day, escort by night. I'm sure you'll be able to explain my presence so it doesn't raise concerns."

I'd love to see just how he did that with his cousin, not that the thought wasn't petty and small.

"I'll take care of it."

Tension lay heavy and immobile in the room. It took everything I possessed not to flinch as I held his gaze, his eyes smoldering blue embers, his face chiseled stone. He was not pleased, but then I wasn't either.

Checkmate.

I was much more an arm-wrestling kind of gal; and maybe that was the problem. I wasn't part of his world—an aberration, forced on him. Not friend. Possible enemy, in spite of the sparks between us. Sparks that only complicated the already very troubled tour.

He left without another word.

Only then did I start breathing again.

CHAPTER 35

"So how's life in paradise?" Kelly asked, sounding like she stood in the next room instead of separated by the Indian Ocean, the closest she could be inserted to the Maldives without arousing suspicions.

"Damn, it's good to hear your voice instead of you-know who," I said.

"Mandy means well," Kelly soothed.

"Said the rattler before she strikes."

Kelly snorted on the other end of the line then sobered quickly. "I'm so sorry we couldn't find more about Van."

That was the bad news. The team had hit a stone wall, which is why it was more important than ever for me to find out who this Vaverek guy was and see if he led me to Van. The shifter on the yacht was associated with Vaverek. The shifter was also standing guard outside Dominique's door. So in my book Dominique, or someone on this tour, was associated with Vaverek, who was tied in with Van's disappearance. It was a thin thread but the only one I had left.

"You tried your best," I offered, knowing it wasn't enough. Every hour Van was held hostage was an hour more of pain or an hour closer to death. Either option unacceptable, so cooling my heels in a tropical paradise sucked.

I groaned aloud. Was there anywhere else on earth as idyllic as the coral island I stood on? The brilliant blue of the Indian Ocean lapped at platinum sand beaches, a humid breeze whispered the thatched roofs of the private bungalows, the soft spray of an outdoor shower rained in the background.

I leaned on the rail of a private sun deck of one of the water villas built over the smooth glass of the ocean, the air scented with jasmine and sea salt. Bran had given me one of the exclusive accommodations, when other staff members were put up in the nice, but not as idyllic, beach bungalows. Way to paint a target on my back. The message the staff received loud and clear was if you got suspected of killing someone you earned a promotion.

Wait till they found out exactly what that promotion entailed. The big test came tonight and already my stomach was a wreck.

"You there, Alex?" Kelly's voice jerked me back to the present with a thunk.

I replied, tongue in cheek. "I was thinking there was a serpent in paradise."

Still was. And maybe more than one.

"Any leads?" Kelly's tone turned serious.

"Nada. Franco is very subdued, which should be a good thing."

"But?"

"It's so un-Franco like it's making everyone jumpy. He didn't snap once today." I watched a seagull float high overhead, white against the turquoise sky. "You hear anything from the Monte Carlo police on his status?"

"Still a person of interest."

"Which means they're not buying him as chief suspect. Good for them. Any intel back on the murder weapon?"

"No prints. Only Sasha's blood on the blade. One of the knives from the galley on the yacht."

"Which means a big fat zero. Anyone could have had access to it and wiped it clean." Heck, I'd grabbed two of them myself.

"Yup."

"Give me some good news." I heard the frustration in my own voice. But between Franco being downright morose, Bran with a stick up his butt, and me having to keep an eye on Dominique plus the rest of the staff, I was juggling a lot of balls. Any one of which might crash down on me at any time.

"Did you find any information on the green-rimmed eyed, cinnamon smelling creature?"

"A little but not a lot."

"Right now I'll take anything."

There was a pause before Kelly spoke again, sounding as if she were reading off a document. "Looks like we're dealing with a Grimple."

"Say that again?"

Kelly spelled it out for me then said, "Like wimple—"

"Or pimple?" I asked, finding a smile for the first time in days.

I heard Kelly choke back a laugh. "Yeah, that could work, too."

"So tell me more?" I prodded.

"I went to the source."

"Fraulein Fassbinder?"

"Yup, but she didn't have all that much either. It appears that the cinnamon and sandalwood scent is the strongest indicator of a Grimple. The rimming of the eyes could be intense blue, green, or even red, depending on the emotions felt by the creature."

"And the skin slippage?"

"Fraulein Fassbinder seemed to think that might be morphing more than slippage."

"Morphing into what?"

"That's the problem," Kelly sounded apologetic. "Since Grimples are very rare, and have legendary control over their emotions, there are not many descriptions available as to what they look like in their non-human form."

I bet it was snake-like, but held that thought to see what else Kel knew. I didn't have tons of time before Franco was supposed to show up to "prep" me for tonight.

"Anything else I need to know?" I asked.

"Though rare, the Grimple are considered extremely dangerous. One of the reasons why there's not many first-person accounts of what they look like. Fraulein Fassbinder is very envious that you might be dealing with one in person. She asks that you keep detailed notes on your observations and if the individual morphs into her full Grimple state, try and get some photos. That is . . ."

My stomach dropped. "Meaning that when a Grimple changes they are not a lot of survivors."

"You got it."

This mission was getting suckier and suckier by the moment. "Did Fraulein Fassbinder have any ideas how to minimize or neutralize a Grimple?"

I assumed I'd need to know how to neutralize more than minimize, but good to know as much as I could.

"Fassbinder indicated that fire and water wouldn't work."

"I was thinking more along bullets or knives." That was the problem dealing with creatures most people thought of from myths and fairytales, the dark kind and not the happily-ever-after ones. There wasn't a lot of mention about using contemporary weapons to stop them. Plenty of mention of scimitars, mortuary swords, and pikes, but they were not easy to slip into a purse or hide in a shoulder holster.

"I'll continue to dig," Kelly said. "But Fraulein Fassbinder says since these creatures are so rare, you may become our leading authority on the subject."

Lucky me.

"According to the Fraulein, a Grimple is an aberration of a Sith, mixing a preternatural genetic background with a demonic one."

"That explains a lot." I had no doubt about Dominique as a demon.

"Tell me, does Bran ever smell like ocean air? When not around the ocean?" Kelly asked.

"Now that you mentioned it, he does. Not salty or briny, just—"

"That scent of primordial fresh air."

"Yeah, how'd you know?"

"The Fraulein mentioned that warlocks have an affinity with the oceans of the world."

"So is she saying Bran is dangerous or not?" I asked, not wanting the answer.

"All warlocks are dangerous."

Like I didn't already know that. At least I'd sensed it; I hadn't actually seen Bran zap anyone or whip out a powerful spell. Yet.

"I do have good news," Kelly added, as if she knew I stood in the middle of a mind whirlpool.

Thank heavens, leave it to the perpetually sunny kindergarten teacher to find some silver lining.

"Jaylene did one of her tarot readings and pulled a special card for you."

"Knowing Jaylene, what doom and gloom am I going to have to deal with now?"

"I think it may mean good news. She pulled the magician card."

"Speak in English." I swallowed, only too aware the magician card was also called the mage card. Mage meaning warlock. I tightened my hand on the railing. "And?"

Kelly slipped into her teacher lecturing mode. "Jaylene said the magician means someone skillful and self-confident. A powerful magus with a strong sense of his own infinite power."

Now why did that sound exactly like Bran?

Kelly continued, "The magician calls on all powers; all the possibilities are laid out, all the directions a fool can take. He calls forth the sword of intellect and communication, the fiery wand of passions and ambition, the overflowing chalice of love and emotions, the solid pentacle of work, possessions, and body."

Did Kelly have any idea how her words were making things worse, not better?

"Cut to the chase, Kel, I've got to leave in a sec."

"Jaylene says beware the magician and you should be safe."

I didn't have the heart to tell Kelly that avoiding a particular mage was impossible.

"Okay, will try my hardest," I lied, adding, "Ling Mai know you're spreading Jaylene's predictions?"

"Only the decent ones."

"Good. Here I was afraid of a daily tarot reading." I glanced over my shoulder, aware of the sun creeping toward the horizon. Tonight would be my first night outed as Bran's date; as if anyone was going to believe that. But that wasn't my problem, mixing and mingling was.

As if reading my thoughts, Kelly asked, "You up for tonight's op?"

Good phrasing. For Vaughn this would be a piece of cake; for me, anything but with small talk and pleasantries with a bunch of strangers I was trying to pump for intel. Stepping into Bran's world was worse than stepping into a pit of vipers, but for the sake of the mission, I'd do this, acid eating my stomach every minute.

"Ling Mai's going to owe me for this one." I meant every word of it.

"You have clothes to wear?"

"Bran sent a message that an outfit was on its way." Coward didn't tell me in person.

Not that he should; he was a busy man.

Great, now I was making excuses for him.

I shook my head, clearing thoughts. "Have you heard anything more on Sasha's death?" I asked, back on track.

"No. They should have a blood analysis in a few more days."

Days? Just what I wanted, more tiptoeing while waiting for a killer to strike again. I didn't think Sasha's death was an isolated event. The model either knew something, or someone wanted the girl out of the way. But why? And was I next on the to-die list?

"That's it? Tell me Sasha had some big dark secret in her background that could explain her death and that it had nothing to do with the thefts."

Kelly's silence sent my stomach plummeting.

"What is it?" I demanded, keeping my voice low. "What have you found out about her?"

"We haven't confirmed anything yet."

"What haven't you confirmed?"

Kelly cleared her throat. "There's a possibility Sasha was a member of a new investigative branch of Interpol."

CHAPTER 36

"Interpol?" I waited for my heart rate to slow as I pressed against the verandah rail. "But I thought I was sent in because Interpol found nothing."

"You were and they didn't," Kelly replied.

"So why is an Interpol agent here, or was here?"

"I said possible Interpol. She was undercover and breaking their cover, even when dead, is not easy. Besides, Interpol normally doesn't handle undercover assignments. It's not in their mandate."

Undercover but not invisible. Collette spotted Sasha as an impostor the first day. I should have listened to the warning. So who else had also made her? Was that why Sasha was killed?

"What do you mean by a new investigative branch?" I asked, my mind whirling with the implications, but at least it kept me from focusing on Bran, and what he did or didn't know about Sasha. "Like us? Going after you know who?"

"Can't get enough specifics to know for sure."

A sigh escaped me. "But if Sasha was Interpol, I'd think they'd be all over this tour."

"On some levels it doesn't make sense, but on others it raises some serious issues."

"Such as?" I braced myself.

"They don't trust us to get the job done."

Well, duh! I could live with that. It wouldn't be the first time another government agency doubted the viability of a team of agents without years of law enforcement background. Vaughn's own father, the director of the CIA, had been a major stumbling block not that long ago and the IR agency was so new on the block we were unheard of by a lot of the big name organizations.

Kelly continued, "Another option is Interpol *is* involved with the tour, but not obvious."

"Another agent inserted?"

"It's a possibility. Then there's the chance they know something more about the thefts, something that bumped this to a higher priority status and they were compelled to take action."

"And they're not sharing that intel with Ling Mai?"

"Exactly, which means they're using her, or more specifically you, on one level, while keeping us in the dark. Believe me, Ling Mai's looking into that aspect as we speak."

Good. Maybe something would start to go right. So far the mission had been a bust and I was no closer to who, or what was behind the original thefts.

"Have you made any progress on searching individual rooms?" Kelly asked.

"Not so far. With everyone on high alert, I haven't had an opportunity. But I'm planning on going in tonight."

"After your date?"

Date, my foot. "Yeah. I'm planning on leaving the function early so I'll get to a few rooms before people return."

"I don't like this," Kelly admitted. "You watch your back."

"Believe me, I will." But against whom? Dominique? That was a given. Bran—I couldn't ignore the fact he might be involved on some level, even if only to protect someone else, like his cousin or a staff member he treated like the family he never had. I knew he was hiding something, just not what. Who else? Collette with her background? Or could Collette be an Interpol agent?

"Kel, did you or Mandy find anything else from the fingerprints I gathered?" Had it only been days ago? "Mandy started to tell me about one of the models, Collette, but didn't go into a lot of details. All I know is she had a criminal record."

So did I, which is why I hadn't followed up on the information until now. My bad.

I listened to the ping-ping-ping of keys being pecked before Kelly came back on the line. "That's right. Criminal record. Plea bargained away years ago when she was going under the name Connie Backus."

"What type of charge?"

"Fencing stolen goods."

Crud. Collette just zipped to the very suspicious list.

"Anything else?" I didn't really want to hear more.

"Yeah, we're having trouble with your Franco's fingerprints."

So not my Franco. "What kind of trouble?"

"Ling Mai's pushing for a deeper check on him; something popped up that grabbed her attention. And then there's one other staff member that's requiring a deeper background check. Beyond what Interpol shared."

That didn't sound good. Not that I expected Interpol to hand us everything, but enough to get their dirty work done.

"Who—"

"Suzette."

A knock on the door had me looking up.

"The assistant?" I asked, lowering my voice as I eyed the door.

"Yeah. Nothing major but some inconsistencies with her background."

Great. The list of possible suspects was growing not declining.

"Gotta go, Kel, someone's here."

"You play it safe."

"Always do." Well, not always. Okay, maybe not most of the time, but that wasn't the point.

"Check in tomorrow. Same time."

"If possible." The knock came again. "Bye."

I knotted my bathrobe tighter before crossing to spy through the peephole.

Franco. With a plastic covered dress bag and a small Asian woman at his side.

I opened the door tentatively, hoping I could snatch the dress and close the door in one quick move.

No such luck.

Franco barreled through like a Japanese bullet train, tugging the small woman in his draft. "At last. We do not have all night. Teena, there."

The woman beetled in with what looked like a bulky card table in her hands. She crossed to the center of the room and proceeded to flip locks and twist knobs.

"What's going on?" I eyed the growing contraption that emerged like a praying mantis from a cocoon.

"We have less than an hour." Franco sounded his normal domineering, snippy self. "Quick. Undress."

That had me rearing back. "Not in your wildest dreams."

"Tsk, tsk." He shook his head, and spread the plastic parcel he'd held across my bed. "Don't be difficult or a prude. We are here to get you ready."

"For what?"

"Tonight of course, silly woman."

The man was so cruising for a bruising.

"All I need for tonight is a dress." I flattened one hand on Franco's chest and pushed. "Thanks for bringing it. Goodbye."

"Not so fast." Franco braked against my shove and puffed up like a cocky rooster. "You have two choices. The ayurvedic oil rub or a Javanese Lulur wrap with sandalwood, ginger, and tropical flowers."

"Since I have no idea what you're talking about I choose neither."

He sidestepped my hand, tsked, tsked again and spoke to the Asian woman. "Teena, we'll go with the oil rub and a neck and upper body massage."

I glanced at the woman, now smiling and standing near a table covered in white cotton towels. "I'm not—"

"Oh, yes, you are." Franco stepped forward. "Think of me as your doctor."

I backed up in disbelief. "Not in a zillion years."

"Fine, then as your mentor," he said.

My get-real glance bounced off him. "I don't need a mentor."

"You do if you are going to blend into Bran's world."

"He said that to you—"

"Of course not." Franco sighed. "He indicated he was escorting you this evening. The man assumes you can handle the shark pool he swims in daily, but I know better."

"Know what?"

"That you have vulnerabilities." He gave me a steady look I didn't care for at all. That and the 'v' word.

Good grief, I was on a mission, not getting ready for my wedding day.

"Forget it, Frank. I only need a dress, nothing else. I can hold my own."

"I'm your ally here." His voice sounded calmer than I'd ever heard it before. "I don't know why Bran is escorting you, though I have my suspicions with that look in his eyes; but that is not my business. I will not let you leave this room until you look your best. After all, my reputation is at stake here, too. Besides, I owe you."

"For what?"

"For believing in me when it would have been far easier to keep silent."

I brushed his answer aside. "You're innocent."

"That's not my point. A different woman would have held her tongue, not become involved, but you didn't. I will not forget that." He pointed to Teena. "Now we must get moving."

"Tell me why I have to do the lulu-what-ever-it's-called thing?"

"Because you will have no friends tonight once you leave this room. The ayurvedic rub will be your shield, protect you against your enemies, or those who wish you harm."

I assumed he included Bran in his comment of no friends.

Franco continued, "You must be on the attack, your defenses in place, all your weapons ready."

"You make it sound like I'm going into battle. I thought it was a social gathering."

"See." He flared his hands. "This is why you need me. You will be the object of speculation, envy, and yes, even hatred, especially after I'm done prepping you. Women do not play fair. They are more cunning, vicious, and dangerous than any male adversary."

And here I thought having been raised with only brothers had given me such a warped view at times.

"You know women well." I shrugged, aware I'd always found it far easier to deal with men than women. At least most men, one arrogant, complicated, tempting dress-designer warlock being the exception.

"Yes. It's my job to know and understand women, and I am good at it."

No ego there.

He clapped his hands. "Now chop, chop. I shall turn my back."

"How grand of you."

"Yes. I make this one exception as we are short on time. Some miracles take longer than others to create."

As he spun about, crossed his arms, and tapped one foot like a bandmaster, I released a trapped breath. He wasn't going to leave or concede. And on one small point he was right. I had little time. Better to bite my tongue and get through the next thirty minutes, then I could dress and would be on my own. But I wasn't going to take my eye off of Franco for one minute. Not until Kelly confirmed his fingerprints.

Twenty minutes later I heard my own languid sigh, and had to force my eyelids to stay open. Teena was a miracle worker, loosening muscles I didn't even know were clenched rigid, rubbing oil into my skin in slow, methodical movements. If the mission didn't dictate that I get up, get dressed, and attend the function with Bran, I could have spent all evening just being pampered.

"See, I told you it would be worthwhile." Franco's voice sounded positively smug, but right then even that didn't bother me. Another miracle.

So he was right about this part—didn't mean I had to buy his gloom-and-doom analysis of what awaited me at the gathering.

By the time Teena wiped away any excess oil, folded her cot, and disappeared and I had shimmied into a dress the color of Bran's eyes, a deep, deep midnight blue, I was ready to face the evening.

Until I glanced in the full-length mirror.

"You are magnifique." Franco came up behind me, looking peacock proud.

"It's not me." The words escaped before I could call them back. The dress, spread on the bed had looked simple and uncomplicated, but the shape was deceptive. On me it molded like a lover's embrace, hugging curves I didn't know I possessed, draping in a shower of silk, darkening my skin tones and bringing out the inky blackness of my hair.

"You must wear your hair down and loose," Franco said, eyeing me with an appraising look.

"I'm the hairdresser here," I snapped back. But was I? I didn't look anything like the person who curled and moussed all day. The woman before me was exotic and sensual. The neckline exposed cleavage and the cut of the dress, voluptuous curves. The thigh-high slit along my right side made my legs look miles long. My skin gleamed golden from the oil and the pampering. And Franco was right, down, my hair added to the wanton sexuality.

My brothers would never believe I was their little sister. My dad would have me under lock and key. And Bran? Not that his opinion mattered; but, damn him, it did.

"You like?" Franco asked.

"It will do." Even my voice sounded husky and dark.

"I knew that dress was right. It is as if Bran designed it with you in mind." Franco fluttered around me, smoothing here, fluffing my hair. "It will bring out the animal in him."

Yeah, right. So why did the words have my stomach muscles clenching even tighter.

A knock on the door interrupted my totally unprofessional thoughts. Thank heavens.

Franco preened while I shooed away second thoughts. "Think mission. Think mission," I whispered, running my hands down the silk beads along the waist.

"So how does she look?" Franco crowed in the doorway.

I turned, slowly, my attention only on Bran, a dark silhouette behind the smaller man.

I so could believe he was more fallen angel than warlock right then, with a share of a demon's pull.

Time stilled. The lap of the water beneath the bungalow measuring the beat of my pulse. The humid tropical air wrapping around me, did nothing to erase the goosebumps along my arms. Bran's gaze lasered in on mine. Potent and intimate. Burning and consuming. The mission was forgotten. Franco was forgotten. Only the two of us existed. Nothing more.

Until Franco cleared his throat. "Well, did I not say the blue would be best for her?"

"Yes." Bran's voice sounded as strangled as my pulse.

Franco's gaze ricocheted between the two of us. A smug smile skittered across his lips before he cleared his throat again. "Well, then, I'd—"

"Goodbye, Franco." Bran still did not move, did not even look at Franco.

"But, I'm not finished. There's still—"

"Goodbye, Franco."

I smiled—not at Franco's indecision, nor the situation. But at Bran. Mine was a woman's smile when the heat of a man's look seared me.

"Then I shall be off," Franco's words trailed away as neither Bran nor I moved.

Time eased past, slow and tense.

Bran broke the impasse. "Either we go now or we don't leave this room for two days."

CHAPTER 37

Bran's words were plain enough, and oh so tempting. Impossible but tempting. I exhaled a slow, shallow breath of air, calming jittery nerves.

He was a warlock; I was a witch. He was part of my mission; I was an operative.

Yup, a definite no go.

Dredging up the snippets of common sense and professionalism I still possessed, I shook my head, fighting through the lassitude in my limbs even as my thoughts called me a fool.

I grabbed a beaded purse matching the dress and straightened my shoulders. "Let's go then."

Bran said nothing, which was just as well. One word, one murmur, and I'd forget all my best intentions, the mission, and the million other reasons why an Idaho farm girl did not get involved with a man like him.

He walked slightly behind me on the crushed rock path, beneath an inverted bowl of stars. The breeze whispered palm fronds as we approached the twinkling lights outlining the outdoor infinity pool, crowded now with mingling guests and heated by the hot licks of a salsa band.

I paused. Once I stepped into the circle of light there'd be no going back.

Bran drew even with me, slipping his arm through mine. The skin of his hands warmed my bare arms. His voice was no longer raw but still intimate. "I did not know you feared anything."

"I'm not afraid." Just crowds of strangers in fancy clothes who've been groomed with impeccable manners since the cradle. No pig farmers in this group.

"Yet you tremble."

So maybe one of his gifts was to read emotions, too.

His words from a French rooftop came back to haunt me. I'd trembled then too when he touched me and he'd called me frightened. Tonight I couldn't afford to be afraid, no matter how far out of my element I was.

"It's this dress of yours." I fought to keep my tone light and casual. *Pretend you're Vaughn. She could do this with her eyes closed.* "It exposes far too much skin."

His predator's grin in the darkness alerted me to my slip. A demon angel grin.

"I know." He brushed his lips close to my ear, scrambling my brain cells. "We can still return to the bungalow."

Too easy an escape on too many levels.

"Not an option." I wished for more force behind my words.

"So be it." He leaned forward and skimmed a kiss across my bare shoulder; an intimate brand marking me all the way to my soul. "But remember, I did offer."

As if I'd ever forget. And the kiss. That was not fair, not fair at all.

Mission, think mission. Hard to do when it was a challenge to think at all.

Fortunately I didn't have to move forward on my own volition, the arrival of Dominique did it for me.

The elegant woman dressed in a pale apricot chiffon design of Bran's that made her look as if she floated on air, crossed from beside the pool and stepped into the shadows, no doubt recognizing Bran even in the darkness.

"There you are," she said in her best hostess voice, snubbing me as if I didn't exist. "I thought you were ignoring us this evening. And so many guests wanting to speak with you."

I bet. This venue was jam-packed; nothing like a murder to bring out the ghouls.

Guests occupied over one hundred private bungalows and villas reserved for the show and more had been taken; that made a lot of people wanting a piece of him.

Dominique stepped closer, then froze when she recognized me.

"What are you doing here?" The hostess voice had disappeared.

"She's with me." Bran's tone gave me courage. Not that I needed it. Well, maybe just a little. Okay, a lot.

"She's what?" Dominique's gaze snapped to Bran's. "You can't—"

"I can and am." He stepped around his cousin. "Don't make a fuss, Dom. It's unbecoming."

Take that serpent woman. You grumpy Grimple.

I stepped forward on my own, holding my head high and ignoring Dominique totally. Payback would come no doubt, but later. For now I had other battles to fight.

Most of the people around the pool were women. Maldivian waiters wove in and out of their tight groupings, offering fluted champagne glasses, sparkling golden in the subdued light.

My ring heated. I was surprised it wasn't searing my skin from the inside out. Who'd have thought so many of the rich and spoiled were also non-human, or enough non-human to register on Ling Mai's device. On the other hand, combine ruthlessness with longer than average human life spans and it made sense.

You will have no friends tonight.

Franco's words echoed in my awareness as I watched the guests' expressions shift, distorted by the shimmer of the twinkling lights discreetly nestled in bushes and trees and the flicker of a dozen torches.

Collette caught my eye and gave me a wicked wink and thumbs up. Other models were more veiled, less obvious in their responses, as if not sure who I was, or what I was doing here. The guests were not as discreet. Some women frowned, especially as Bran shifted his arm from my arm to my waist. A move that startled me. The heat of his hand along the bare skin of my back molten, screaming possession.

"Mister Bran," a woman purred, licking her lips as she approached. "Is this one of yours?"

The woman's gaze skipped over me as if I were a piece of meat.

"The gown is mine." Bran pressed his hand more firmly along my back. "But Alex is an original."

"Oh." The woman looked confused, then shot me a pointed glance, addressing me when she spoke again. "But didn't I see your picture in the news?"

"Yes." I smiled, offering no other answer. I hadn't been identified as a suspect, just one who found a body. I caught Bran stifling a small smile while the woman glanced between the two of us.

"But, I—" The woman paused, then took a deep drink from a near-empty glass she clutched in her ringed fingers. "Obviously, when Dominique told us—"

"Told you what?" Bran asked.

I admired the fact the woman didn't melt away beneath his tone.

"Nothing, I must have misunderstood."

Wise woman.

When she disappeared, I leaned toward Bran. "I can't do my job if you scare everyone away."

"That is not my problem."

What was it about perfectly reasonable, mature men that made them sulky boys at times?

I stepped away from him, glancing over my shoulder. He'd done his part, bringing me to the party, now it was up to me to maximize the opportunity. "I'll see you around."

His scowl was all for me this time, making him even more dark and intimidating. Less man and more warlock. But the night was easier to handle when I didn't have him pulsing emotions through me.

No friends, only enemies.

How very astute Franco was. But I hadn't come to make friends or find allies, nor to linger in the spell of Bran's presence. I'd come to listen and learn and it was time to start.

An hour later I had a whole new respect for Vaughn and Vaughn's world. Meeting and mingling sounded far easier than it was, especially around women who saw me as either the competition or the usurper; both roles placed me beyond the pale.

Once, when I'd moved from grade school to middle school, I'd experienced the same sensation: the pointed looks, the not-so-subtle jabs, the conversations cut short as I approached. I was not only the sister of four really hot but very choosy brothers, I was also the daughter of a man who raised pigs. So on the one hand girls wanted to use me to get closer to my brothers and on the other hand they wanted to despise me for my dad's livelihood.

Van offered to knock a few heads together for me. I adored him for offering, but turned him down flat, deciding to use my own strategy. Franco was right about this, too. Women didn't fight fair, so to win with them, one had to play their games—only better.

"You came with Bran?" a woman who looked like a stick insect asked. Her tone implied the concept was inconceivable.

"Yes." Then before the woman could turn the knife of her comment, I said. "And he mentioned you."

"Me?" Her brows slanted in a dramatic V.

"Yes. He indicated how well you wore your clothes."

"He did?" Gone was the sharp edge of the woman's tone, replaced by intrigue. "Did he say anything else?"

"He mentioned your coloring."

"Oh, my." The woman nervously patted lacquer-red helmet hair. "Was that a problem?"

"Not at all." I stepped closer. "In fact he was impressed with how dramatic your coloring is, and how well the green sheath you are wearing looks on you."

The woman beamed, and I had a new friend for life. The fact this woman was non-human, according to my ring, probably a vampire, didn't matter. She no longer viewed me as prey, of any kind, but as a useful tool, and one rarely attacked their tools.

Within twenty minutes I'd learned more than I ever thought possible about the lives, lovers, spouses, and businesses of a dozen women. One was an Italian parliament member; a shifter, another married to an oil tycoon. She was human. Two were daughters of a Saudi Arabian royal family and were some species I couldn't identify but certainly not human, and a French film star who appeared to have slept with most of the Council of the European Union. She was clearly a succubus.

I was closer to understanding how easy it was to find potential marks to steal from, and growing more and more surprised by the minute that there hadn't been more thefts or attempts at blackmail.

I shamelessly used Bran's name, reassuring myself that it was only right as he'd win too in increased sales from his adoring fans.

Every once in a while I'd catch him staring at me as I made sure I remained as far from his immediate orbit as possible. His scowl remained firmly in place, deepening only if I gave him a small hand wave or smile.

After one such smile on my part Dominique slithered up beside me, her scent of cinnamon and sandalwood strong.

"I think you'd better leave now," she said, her voice pitched for my ears only, her smile looking charming to anyone at a distance.

"But I'm enjoying myself and the night is young." I realized it was too dark to clearly see Dominique's eyes turning green-rimmed, but I had no doubt they were. The woman oozed anger.

"Too bad. All little girls belong safe in their beds before. . ." Dominique let the words slip way.

"Before?" I didn't do veiled threats well. Maybe, as long as I remained within the circle of others, now was a good time to punch the buttons and see how far a Grimple, if that's what Dominique was, would go. "Are you warning me?"

"Stay away from Bran."

"He's a grown man. I'm sure he's capable of making his own decisions."

"Don't play with me, hairdresser. I could squash you in a heartbeat."

Do or die moment. "Is that what you did to Sasha?"

Dominique's features tightened before she looked away and took a deep breath. Her skin shifted but only a smidge before she wrestled her emotions under control.

"You're a fool. You may be of interest to Bran tonight, but you won't be the first pretty face or the last. You mean nothing to him. Do not confuse lust with anything else."

Good advice—too bad I had already come to the same conclusion.

But Dominique wasn't finished. "I know him much, much better than you ever will."

No denying that either.

"He likes his toys. Lots of toys. But toys can be broken when they are tossed away." Dominique gave me a full, false smile before sipping her champagne. "Sasha was a pretty play thing once, too."

Dominique walked away smiling as I grappled with the parting shot.

I'd brushed the Bran and Sasha link under the rug. He hadn't clarified what their relationship had been, but that didn't mean I could ignore what I'd seen with my own eyes. My job wasn't to protect him, it was to find a thief and killer. Bran and Sasha? Was that why he'd gone to the spa area that night? A tryst?

The implications slammed like a full body tackle. If Sasha was Interpol, could she have been investigating Bran directly and not his staff? Is that what had bumped up Interpol's interest in the thefts? Bran's involvement? Why was it I kept circling back to the idea he was involved?

"Did she snub you?" Bran's voice washed against me.

I whirled, surprised to be looking straight into those deep blue eyes of his. How had he sneaked up on me?

"Alex?" he repeated, his voice taking on that warm intimacy that undid me. "Alex, are you all right?"

"Of course I am. Why shouldn't I be?" I held the hand with my glass especially still so it wouldn't shake.

"You looked suddenly pale. I wanted to make sure you were feeling all right."

"I'm fine." Shattered. Disillusioned. Out of my depth. So very disappointed and totally blindsided. "I'm perfectly fine."

So my voice sounded a little sharp and my posture stood a little too brittle. So what?

The tightening of his eyes told me he wasn't buying my reassurances. He stepped forward, placing one hand on my shoulder.

I shrugged his hand off, my smile frozen as I stepped back. Time to regroup. Besides, I had a mini-mission to complete tonight—searching rooms. "Look, maybe I'm a little tired. I'd better be going."

"I'll walk you back."

"No." He looked like he wanted to say something but I cut him off before he could. "I mean, I'll be all right. You have guests to see to here."

He nodded, the movement jerky for him, his gaze still watching mine intently. "I'll check on you later then."

"No." How many times did I have to say it to him? Given his looks, his position, his power, he probably didn't hear the word "no" often and thus didn't recognize it. Is that what happened to Sasha? She thwarted him and he retaliated and it got out of hand?

"Alex?"

"I plan to go straight to bed when I get to the villa. And sleep." Liar. Liar. "So there's no point in stopping by later. I won't be awake."

"So be it." His words said he would give me space, his expression indicated he wasn't happy with my reasons and didn't believe them for a moment. But that wasn't my problem. My problem was in walking away as if there were nothing more pressing than a headache or fatigue bothering me.

"You're sure you're all right?"

"I will be." As soon as I got away from him and focused on doing my job.

"I'll see you tomorrow."

"No doubt." Unless I contacted Kelly and my teammate was able to dig up any history between Bran and Sasha. Any whiff of involvement. My stomach knotted. If *anything* turned up, then he jumped to the top of the suspect list— again. "Good night."

I didn't wait for his reply but fled into the night.

Not a coward, I told myself, walking as fast as the skin-tight dress allowed along the deserted path, nearing my quiet bungalow. A wise strategic retreat especially in light of my need to search as many rooms as possible before the party broke up.

Lost in my plan for the best place to start my hunt, I didn't see the dark shadow step from behind a bush.

CHAPTER 38

Heart pounding a rumba, I shifted on the crushed stone path, flowed into fight mode, legs braced and at an angle, shoulder forward, hands raised, before I even registered who stepped around the heavily scented bush.

"Cripes, Suzette, you scared me to death." My breath escaped with a whoosh, even as adrenaline spiked through me. I hadn't seen much of Suzette since the night of the shifter attack, but then I hadn't expected to. The girl was smart and it didn't take a brainiac to figure out hanging around me could be dangerous to one's health.

The owlish assistant raised her hands in mock surrender. "Were you going to hurt me?"

"Of course I wasn't." I dropped my hands and willed adrenaline-psyched muscles to relax. "You just scared me that's all."

"But wasn't that a martial arts move?"

"A modified one." I shook my head, mentally regrouping. "What are you doing out here?"

"I dropped off a schedule change for tomorrow at your villa."

"That's nice." The surprise in my voice caused Suzette to open her eyes wider, but I was thinking about the protection spell I'd left on my door handle, glad I hadn't made it strong enough to hurt anyone, just give them a start.

The woman shrugged. "How do you know martial arts moves?"

The last thing I wanted was the rumor spreading that I was more than a hairdresser.

"You've got to be kidding." My laugh was forced, but the other woman didn't know that. "I'm an American female. My father wouldn't even consider letting me move to the city without passing a defensive course for women. Besides, I had brothers I had to learn to hold my own against."

Suzette didn't look totally convinced, but all I wanted was the seed of doubt in her mind.

This time she was the one who changed the subject as she lowered her gaze and kicked a pebble with one ballet pump shod foot. "I meant to thank you," she mumbled, "for the other night. I was so scared."

"So was I," I admitted, waiting for my heart rate to settle.

"But you didn't hide." Suzette glanced up at me, pushing her glasses up her nose. "I'd like to be able to do that. Fight back I mean."

"Well, I didn't really fight back." No need to tell her I got pounded. Which reminded me, I'd meant to ask her where she'd disappeared to. "Ah, Suzette, about the other night—"

"Is everything all right here?" Bran interrupted from behind me and every muscle on me clenched. So much for relaxing.

"Everything's fine." I let an edge slide into my voice, as it was obvious the man didn't take subtle hints well.

"Suzette." He nodded at the young woman, now standing with her jaw open. "It is late for you to be wandering alone."

"Yes, sir. I'm heading to my bungalow, sir." Suzette sounded nervous. Not that Bran didn't make a lot of folks sound that way.

"Do you need an escort?"

Yes, say yes, Suzette.

"No. It's not far."

Rats. Besides she wasn't telling the truth. Her bungalow was on the other side of the party area.

"Then good night."

What was good about it?

I couldn't think about why Suzette would tell Bran an outright lie as I scrambled to figure out why he'd been following me. I held my ground until the other woman disappeared into the inky darkness before I turned to face him. "What are you doing here?"

"Making sure you arrived back at your room safely."

"It's right there." I shrugged toward the isolated room, now shrouded in darkness. "So you can go back to your guests now."

"They can wait."

He stepped closer and all the air on the island disappeared.

I wasn't going to back down. Wasn't going to step away. Or show that I was anything except calm, cool, and controlled.

Yeah, right.

He said nothing: just pushed into my space, dwarfing me with his size, his scent wrapping around me like an embrace.

The only good news was he didn't look like he was any happier than I was about the tension crackling between us. His eyes were narrowed, the skin along his jaw tight, even the pulse at the vee of his neck pounded.

How could I even consider being involved with a warlock? Yet it was hard to remember that as I stared into those eyes.

But it was his gaze on my lips that vaporized all the moistness in my mouth, while liquefying the muscles of my legs.

"Don't," I whispered, not sure if it was meant for him or myself. Adrenaline still surged through my system, making me heady. An excuse?

It didn't really matter. It was too late for words.

I was an agent, but I was a woman, too, and it was as a woman that I rose on my toes, ever so slightly, pressing against him. A meeting of equals here, a man wanting to taste one woman, and me wanting it just as badly.

My lips whispered across his first. Gossamer strokes, almost not there, afraid to want too much, too quick. Skin to skin touch could overwhelm me, but I ignored the warning signs.

He raised one hand to cup my chin, lingering ever so softly, so gently. Not threatening. Not something I could slap away, if I could move.

His thumb brushed against my jaw, then my lower lip, as if memorizing the curve. My eyelids fluttered. I swallowed, but held my ground, locking my knees so my legs wouldn't buckle. His touch let me know he was just as conflicted, just as aroused and fighting it just as hard.

He leaned forward. My hands ached to wrap around his back, to stroke through the thickness of his hair.

His hand shifted, from face to neck, angling my head with the strength of his fingers. I wanted this as much as he did.

He growled, deep in his throat, a tormented sound reaching me on a gut level.

My hands slipped upward then—waist to back to neck, using fabric as a small buffer between us. The hunger pounded. Demanded. His lips now swallowed mine. Taste no longer enough. Possession. Passion. Completion. The emotions—his and mine—roared through me.

His tongue met mine, thrust to thrust, mimicking what our bodies ached to complete. His fingers tangled in my hair, my breasts flattened across the planes of his chest, thighs rubbing against thighs.

Somewhere nearby a bungalow door slammed shut, an explosion of sound through the near-silent night.

The intrusion of awareness slapped against me, bullet like. I froze. His hands continued roaming across the open exposure of my back, his kisses just as deep, just as drugging but the spell was shattered.

He sensed my change and raised his deeply-lidded, burning gaze to sear mine, inches away. How easy to fall beneath their spell; to forget, even for moments, who we were and why I in particular was here.

"No," he murmured, reading my indecision, his hands tightening against mine. "No, do not pull away."

I shifted palms to the front of his chest but didn't push. Not yet. Not while my body still craved, my fogged brain fought to sort reason from madness. Dominique's words earlier. *He likes toys. Lots of toys.* Bran's look in the bungalow all hot and hungry. My duty to the IR team to find a thief and now a killer. And more than that, to find Van. All roiled and rioted with jangled nerves and throbbing heartbeat.

"A mistake," I whispered, placing inches between us, struggling still to find logic where there was none.

"Don't." His growl took me by surprise until I realized he was in no better shape than I was.

Then reason seemed to catch up with him. His hands dropped to his sides and he stepped back, breaking skin contact. Thank the Spirits. Cool night air rushed between us, sending a chill tap dancing up my spine.

But the coolness wasn't enough. The thrum of the ocean against the nearby shore didn't help. Its urgent crash mimicking my pounding pulse, clashing needs.

"It's late." My words mocked the tension between us, sounding false and hollow.

Stay away. If he's in the wrong, you'll have to take him down. He may be the enemy. And if Dominique is the enemy, I will be the one to take down someone Bran loves.

The hot light in his eyes cooled. His posture grew rigid, defensive—angry at me or angry at himself, I couldn't tell. Not that it mattered. We'd both crossed the line from professional to mindless; but both had too much to lose to take this further.

"I will watch until you enter your bungalow safely." He spoke with the cold tone of master to staff; only the square set of his shoulders, the clenched force of his hands betrayed him.

I found the power to move, to step away. One jerky movement after the other, propelling me in one direction when my body hungered to remain right where I was.

The mission had to come first. I was here for no other reason. Van's life depended on it. My first solo ops and I wasn't going to let hormones cause me to fail.

I didn't bother saying good night. My mouth was so dry I wasn't sure the words would come anyway. Without pausing I keyed my locked door and stepped into the dark room. I waited in the shadows, letting its cool mantle slow my pulse until the crunch of Bran's shoes faded away against the crushed stone walkway.

Only then did I flick on the light and discover someone had tossed my room.

CHAPTER 39

From the poolside bar, Dominique watched Bran return to the party and silently cursed him. He could blow everything. She was too close to success to let him destroy it all now. A few more days were all she needed.

Making small talk she crossed to where he stood, tense and brooding, scaring off most of the guests by his scowl alone.

"These women are here to see and talk with you," she murmured, when she drew near, standing close enough so only he would hear. "It does your business no good when you let your personal issues intrude on your professional responsibilities."

"Professional responsibilities be dammed," he spat the words.

Not a good sign.

"Bran." She rested a hand on his arm, leaning closer. "You've been under a lot of strain lately."

He glared at her, but no longer looked as if he wanted to take her head off.

She kept her tone soothing. "Maybe after the tour is finished you should take some time off. Plan on relaxing."

"And the business?" His tone sounded bitter.

"I'm sure it'll be fine for a month or two. In fact, your being absent for a bit would add to your allure. Between the publicity we've received this last week—"

"Is that all a woman's life means to you? Publicity?"

Several nearby guests raised their heads at his tone.

"Of course it doesn't." She forced a smile and waited until the women moved away. "But neither am I going to act like I'm mourning the death of a total stranger."

"She was our employee."

"As are the two other employees still on the staff who may be involved in her death."

He speared her with a piercing look, his features dark and harsh in the flickering torchlight. "Who are you accusing, Dom?"

She hadn't meant to go this far, but he was the one ruining everything. Everything she'd worked so hard to create and she wasn't about to let that happen. She glanced around once, sipped on her mineral water and lowered her voice even more. "Surely you don't think it's a coincidence that it was the new girl who found the model's body?"

"I was there too, Dom. Does that mean I'm involved in the death?"

"Don't be ridiculous. She no doubt pulled you in to use you as an alibi."

"And what about the weapon in Franco's room? Did the two of them kill her?"

She shrugged. "One killed the girl. One hid the evidence before the gendarmes arrived on board. They both alibi each other. You must admit it's very suspicious."

"And the motivation?"

"Why does there have to be motivation?" She shook her head. "The hairdresser could have been jealous. Sasha was very beautiful. The American was not happy that there might be a new interest on your part. The two women had a fight. Who knows? A senseless act and yet you keep those two around, frightening the other staff, frightening me."

When he made no response, she tried a different tactic.

"You know she's a pig farmer's daughter?"

"Who?"

"Your hairdresser, of course." She'd played this role a thousand times—concerned benefactress showering favors. She'd get through to him. "And a convicted murderer."

That made him go still. Just as she expected.

"I did a little research on her, to protect us all," she continued, when he made to interrupt. "Quite the sad tale. Her mother abandoned her father. Then less than a year ago she killed a total stranger."

"Then why is she here now and not in prison?"

"I don't have all the details, Bran." Just enough. "You know how those Americans are, so many criminals, such bleeding hearts."

He cut his glance to the distance, as if mulling over her words.

Time to bring the point home. "And you know what they say?"

"What?" he bit out the single word.

"Once a killer, always a killer." She shook her head, schooling her features to be concerned. "Come on, Bran. You know she's not *our* kind of people."

He lowered his brows. Maybe time to back off, just a bit. She glanced at her nails as she slid home her knife. "Besides, all of us are at risk as long as she remains. My life could be next."

At one time that would have been all she had to say to have him doing her will. Bran was a brilliant, complicated man in many ways. In others, he reacted predictably. She was his true family, his only family. A threat to her was even greater than a threat to him. She'd learned this when they were still children. At one time she thought he may have wanted more, seen her as a man sees a woman, but not Bran. There was too much honor and pride in him to risk his heart and his soul in the same place. This pride, this need for family, would be his downfall.

Yet tonight his smile was cynical, his stance tense. Maybe she'd underestimated the hairdresser. The little minx had avoided one trap already, now it seemed she was enchanting him.

That would never do.

"What are you thinking?" she asked him, when his silence lengthened between them—lengthened and grew taut.

"I'm thinking it might be a good idea to end the tour now. Cancel Florida and the rest."

"You're not serious?" Her voice rose, even as her smile remained frozen in place.

"I'm perfectly serious. With the tour over, no one else is at risk. I don't want any more lives on the line until Sasha's killer is found." His dark eyes held steady on her face; which meant he did not see the control it took for her to hold onto her glass.

"Don't be a fool—"

"Only a fool would continue to do the same thing and expect different results." He glanced away, at the milling crowds, the brittle laughter, the champagne-induced gaiety.

He was going to ruin everything if she didn't stop him. Just a few more days. Miami and then D.C. The tour had to make it to D.C. and Bran with it.

"Do you know how many millions we'd lose?" She wanted to scream but instead entreated. "We've placed deposits on hotels and venues. Paid for advertising, contracted with musicians and photographers. Just think about the lost sales, the women who've arranged to attend events. It'd be a nightmare to cancel."

"Yet you yourself say publicity is good. Read the headlines now—unexpected cancellation to the Bran tour. The press would eat it up."

He couldn't; he didn't really think she'd let him cancel. "Bran, come to your senses."

"For the first time in months, maybe I am. The clothes will sell without this." He waved his hand to indicate the total strangers feted at his expense. "We can reinvent the business. Stop the insanity of a new location every few days and concentrate on what we started—creating a solid reputation for the Bran brand and not me." He looked at her then, the weariness and exhaustion of the last moments replaced with a new light. "I mean it, Dom. It's time to make some changes. Have a life, for both of us. What do you say?"

She swallowed. It was too late to turn back now. Way too late.

"You will not do anything hasty?" She laid a palm along his sleeve. "Not without talking to me?" She had to stop him.

"I've always talked with you, Dom." His voice sounded flat. "Though I wonder if you always hear me."

"Of course, I do. You're tired, darling." Maybe that was all it was. He needed to get laid. She would send someone from the spa to give him a massage with benefits. Any woman would jump at the opportunity. Or maybe he'd prefer that heiress to the Italian automaker he'd been with last year? Or that French singer? There had to be someone, or even more than one she could strategically position in front of Bran immediately. Keep him occupied for the next few days. The hairdresser wouldn't do at all. She was a disaster and would be dealt with and soon. All Dominique needed was Bran to keep the tour going until Washington D.C., one stop after Florida. That was all.

"Why don't you head to bed," she said, already reaching into her Bottega Veneta purse. "We'll talk again tomorrow."

He brushed his lips against her cheek before disappearing. No good night, nothing. There certainly was something bothering him, something other than that woman.

"Is everything all right?" The frighteningly gay man who organized the models materialized at her side. Franco. Why Bran could not have cut his losses and gotten rid of him in Monte Carlo when he had a perfectly good excuse to do so amazed her.

"Of course everything is fine." She sipped her water, then punched in the number for the spa on her cell phone. "Why shouldn't it be?"

"Bran seemed distracted tonight," he paused, then added cattily, "Especially after the hairdresser left."

Had he stressed the word hairdresser? The man really was insufferable. "You are imagining things."

"Am I?"

"Bran has had his flings before. This new piece of ass is nothing."

Dominique would make sure she was nothing.

CHAPTER 40

Who had broken into my room and why? How had they gotten past the wards? Someone with magic then, or immune to magic. Did someone suspect something, or was there something else going on? The search hadn't been done by a professional. Too careless, as I glanced at the placement of my hairdresser's valise, the angle of an open drawer, the placement of my phone on a bureau. All had been shifted.

Maybe they wanted me to know they'd been there; that they could whip through wards like butter.

I stepped over the schedule change that Suzette had slipped under my door. At least the assistant hadn't lied about why she was on this area of the island.

I could scratch Bran off my suspect list for this, too. He'd been within my sight the whole time I'd been at the party. But Dominique? Dominique had appeared and disappeared. Could a Grimple waltz through a ward? Would Dragon Lady stoop to rifling through someone's personal belongings?

In a heartbeat.

But why?

I jammed down all the questions scrambling through me in order to take action. Action could get me some answers; stewing only created more stewing. I donned what Kelly called our bad girl wear. Black. Not New York City black, but stealth black—long-sleeved, close to the skin, covering as much of one's body as possible. A quick braiding of my hair and I was ready to do a little reconnoitering of my own.

I rinsed the scent of perfume from me with a washcloth, not enough time for a shower as guests would be leaving the party soon. But perfume was a telltale sign in closed rooms and something not present in mine when I'd returned. Maybe my visitor was not a total amateur, or simply someone who didn't wear scent. Most of the models wore perfume on a regular basis, and so did Dominique. The thousand-dollar-an-ounce variety. Vaughn no doubt would know the name whereas I only noted the smell earlier at the pool. The one that obscured her cinnamon and sandalwood scent.

So maybe Dragon Lady wasn't my intruder?

Rats. That would have made life simpler.

But then the moment I'd become an Invisible Recruit I'd turned my back on any hint of a simple life.

"Show time," I whispered, stepping from my room into the shadowed night. No telling when the party would break up. Which room first?

Dragon Lady's.

Keeping off the crushed shell walkway for silence, and pausing every few steps to make sure I was alone, I crept through the warm, moist night, my muscles tensed, my senses alert, pumping adrenaline making everything sharp. Every whisper of a palm frond became a potential threat, every echo from the party matching my beating heart.

I'd left off face-darkening makeup; that would take too much explaining if I were caught. But if someone saw me I'd still be hard pressed to explain what I was up to.

I angled across the beach to Dominique's villa, larger and set slightly apart from the others and right over the ocean. Bran's right next door. Second on the list.

Coward. I justified my priority order by the fact I'd given his stateroom on the yacht a quick review; but he'd barely arrived and might have anticipated my move there. Here he wouldn't.

I'd search his quarters. It was my job. Especially after Dominique's not-so-subtle hint about him and Sasha. There was something very personal about invading someone's bedroom. A violation by someone not invited in. I knew; it was what I felt right now about my room.

The doors to the villa were still key activated versus card activated, which worked to my advantage. That and the fact that the locks were as primitive as the setting. The bobby pin I'd jammed in my hair for just such a situation came in handy if my release spell didn't work. Which it did. There was something innately comforting in using one of the tools-of-my-witch-trade to breach Dragon Lady's lair.

Less than a minute and I was in. Another thirty seconds and I'd adjusted the hands-free climber's headlamp I'd brought along. It beamed a pulse of red light and I kept it focused downward, creating less chance of detection. The red also kept my night vision intact, one more plus.

A quick review of desk and bureau showed nothing out of the ordinary. The room was as spotless and organized as Dominique.

What did I expect, a file marked "Next score"?

I did a quick search of Dominique's designer wardrobe, looking for papers stashed where they shouldn't be. The same organization appeared with her shoes—sorted by color and style to boot.

Nothing. No clue, no hint, no X marked the spot.

But I knew she was involved.

I stood in the middle of the room, scanning every possible hiding place I might have missed when I spotted Dominique's Prada bag. Not the one she used every day, but a backup one I'd noticed once or twice.

This time I removed every item and laid them on the bureau top. Nothing one wouldn't expect from any woman executive's bag. Lipstick. Key ring. A plain phone.

"What do we have here?"

I picked the last item up. This was not the phone I'd noticed her using: designer chic, small, and sophisticated. This one was of more interest because of its ordinariness. Dominique did not do ordinary.

Why a woman would carry two phones?

A throwaway?

I clicked the generic phone open and turned it on. No numbers in the phone book section.

More and more interesting.

Who used a phone and kept no numbers in it?

A quick punch in to call history revealed only one number for both last incoming call and last outgoing call. A number without a country code but with an area code.

I memorized the ten digits.

Who knew what it meant, but so far it'd been the only anomaly in Dominique's room, and what little training I'd had the one thing that stuck was to look for anomalies.

Just as I crammed the last item into the Prada bag I heard the sound of shoes on the crushed shell walkway outside the room. They were walking fast.

Crud.

I slipped the bag back on the desk. My options were limited. The interior bathroom trapped me. That left the exterior balcony above the ocean waves.

Balcony.

Shark bonding beat facing Dominique any day.

CHAPTER 41

I slid the glass door closed behind me and flattened myself against the thatched wall of the villa even as the room's lights blazed on.

Of all the rotten—

If Dominique opened her balcony door, I was a goner.

Whispering a quick cloaking spell that wouldn't hide me for long if she came out on the deck I pressed myself against the wall.

Only one option. Swinging one leg, then the other, I lowered myself slowly and quietly from the balcony railing into the ocean waves below. The scent of briny salt surrounded me, the moon looking like a gigantic spotlight overhead. The high tide pushed and pulled as I clung to the rails, slapping seaweed against my legs. At least I hoped it was seaweed and not a jellyfish. Or something worse.

I didn't dare swim off too soon in case Dominique stepped out onto the balcony. Dragon Lady would certainly spot in seconds a body swimming away.

Instead, I submerged myself until only my fingers and head were above water, then slid beneath the deck, grabbing on to small gaps in the wood planking with the tips of my fingers.

I braced as best I could as the balcony door glided open and footsteps clicked onto the decking.

Crap.

I caged my breath in my lungs, fearful Dominique would pick up the sound above the wash of waves against both shore and pilings. The water wasn't cold, but the awkward hold stiffened my muscles and cramped my fingers. Plus the second I'd submerged myself the cloaking spell was ruined.

The tell-tale musical sound of cell phone numbers being punched reached my ears.

"Dominique St. Clair here."

Maybe a clue at last.

"I asked for a young woman to be at my cousin Bran's villa this evening."

What the—?

"I'd like to make that two."

What for?

"Yes, that's correct. Massage *and* amenities."

What kind of—

"Yes, I understand perfectly. The women will be amply rewarded. For *all* services provided."

That bitch.

Silently, I scissored my legs, heavy against the pull of the tide, to keep afloat while I waited and steamed. My fingers ached, my waterlogged clothes dragged me down, using up precious energy but I clung on.

Dominique the pimp. And Bran? His request or his cousin being thoughtful? Were these the toys Dragon Lady mentioned earlier?

Think professional, not personal. Yeah, right. Dragon Lady was taking the gloves off, but then, so could I.

The rising tide scraped my head against the underside of the balcony deck. A few more minutes and I'd have to make a choice; let go and see if I could swim far enough underwater before I had to come up for air, and hope to hell Dominique had either gone back inside or wasn't looking in my direction. Or—

Drowning wasn't a good second option.

Gulping in more and more seawater, I made my decision.

Two breaths and—

The shoes moved. Forward once, as if leaning on the railing, then back.

The door slid shut.

Peeling cramped fingers from the deck, I sucked in a quick breath and let go. I slipped beneath the water, kicking off into the dark sea, repeating the ten-digit sequence of numbers from the phone I'd found.

One way or another Dragon Lady was going down.

CHAPTER 42

"Well there you are, Pocahontas. Sleep well last night?" Franco strutted onto one of the resort's empty patios, spread out with a breakfast buffet. Just what I needed with my eggs and ham, a large dose of cynicism.

"Eat glass, Frank." I reached for a cup of coffee, large and black and wondered if any food would stay down. I so didn't need chipper and cynical first thing in the morning. I needed a return call from Kelly about the break in and phone number. I needed answers. Lots of answers. "Besides I told you not to call me—"

"You said Sacagawea. I distinctly remember that. Your exact words were—"

"Go away, Frank." I kept my voice pitched low though the closest guests to us were at the far side of the open-air room.

"And here I thought you'd be all starry-eyed and moony this morning with the way Bran was looking at you all evening. Yum. Yum."

"Get a life." I brushed past the man, wishing I had sunglasses. He was dressed in hot pink for God's sake, at six-fifteen in the morning. It was unnatural.

"I take it then you did not hear about the argument." Franco's plucked brows arched coyly. "The one between Bran and Dominique."

I paused. *Think mission.* I was there to get intel, and if Bran had a major row with his cousin and business partner it was important to find out as much about it as possible.

Yeah right.

Okay, so there might be a very tiny personal interest, too. But I wasn't asking for that reason; nor was I going to mention midnight masseuses. A woman had to have her pride.

"What argument?" I returned to Franco's side and plopped a pastry on my plate, feigning indifference—the quickest way to get Franco to spill his guts.

I was right. Barely a second ticked past before he gave a piqued humph. "Well, after you left so quickly, and trust me it was noted." He arranged three slices of mango artistically on his glass plate. "And then Bran left—"

He paused dramatically, as if inviting confidences but he was asking the wrong person.

"The argument, Frank. Spit it out or you'll be wearing that fruit."

"Well, the least you could do is let me have a little fun. Especially with such juicy tidbits to share."

Franco moved to a nearby table and I followed, reminding myself I was trailing in his wake only for the sake of answers. After sliding into a chair Franco tugged his shirtsleeves into place, then glanced around and lowered his voice. "When Bran returned, awfully fast, some said, and very put out—"

"The argument?"

"Oh, all right." He notched his chin at an angle. It was all I could do not to clip it. I planted myself in the chair opposite him, ignoring my plate of food.

"Well, Dominique met Bran and they started talking."

"They're cousins and business partners. They talk every day."

"Not with Bran looking like thunder, a very good look for him, by the way. Very testosterone and hunky."

I'd agree, but I wasn't going there.

"Anyway." Franco inhaled deeply as he arranged a strawberry next to his mango. It was a freaking piece of fruit. No way should it take three minutes to line up on a plate. I bit back a groan.

"It was obvious Bran was not happy about something and Dominique was yammering at him."

"Yammering?"

"Yes, you know, visualize one of those pneumatic nail drivers with painted nails and peach lipstick."

Good description of Dominique.

My stomach was already knotting. I slid my plate away on the table, the pastry barely touched. Nothing was going to sit well this morning. "What was the argument about?"

"Some said you." The knots tightened.

"But then it escalated."

"Into what?"

"Rumors are," Franco lowered his voice like a conspiratorial schoolgirl. "He wants to cancel the rest of the tour."

"Why?" How was I going to find a thief, and a killer, if all the suspects dispersed? Canceling the tour would be a disaster. The thief/killer would go to ground and there'd be no justice for anyone. Especially Sasha. And that didn't even count my sole lead to what had happened to Van.

Franco eyed me closely. "Seems Bran feels there's not enough security for his staff. Too many unanswered questions about Sasha. There are even rumors about indiscretions happening after some of Bran's earlier shows."

Only Franco could describe thefts as indiscretions. He continued, "Interesting don't you think?"

I ignored his question. "Can Bran cancel the tour?"

"He's the boss, he can do anything he wants."

"But wouldn't it cost an arm and a leg?"

"Yes." Franco brushed an invisible speck of dust from his sleeve. "But he's loaded. Besides, I don't think he's ever done this for the money."

"Then why?" Franco cocked his head, like a bird eyeing a worm. "Acknowledgement. Name recognition would be my guess. He has a lot to prove to the *tres-mal* family who rejected him. But Bran would never put his own interests above the people who depend on him. He's very protective that way. Some say too protective."

Fallen angel leaning toward the dark side if pushed too far.

Bran's name was being destroyed; and I was part of the juggernaut making that happen, especially if he was involved in the thefts in any way.

I set down my coffee, not needing any more acid in my stomach.

"Look, I've got a question." I wasn't sure if I should go down this path or not.

Franco angled a brow. "I'll answer yours, if you'll answer mine."

I held back a snort. "Fine. But nothing personal."

"You're so not fun." The man had the audacity to flap his wrist at me. Lord, it was going to be a long day.

"Tell me if Bran had anything going on with Sasha?" There, I'd asked, and if anybody would be aware of the gossip it'd be Franco.

"You mean our Sasha? New girl Sasha?"

I noted he spoke as if she were still alive. Not uncommon when faced with sudden, brutal death.

"Yes. That Sasha. Do you know if at any time they had a fling, or a relationship, or even knew each other very well?"

"Don't be preposterous." He sounded adamant, which stunned me. "Why? What have you heard?"

"Is that your question?"

"Don't be impertinent, of course it isn't. Did you hear something about Sasha and Bran together?"

"Yes." He leaned closer, his eyes shining, if wary. "Come, come, tell Uncle Franco all."

As if. But for the sake of the mission, I'd do even this. Gossip, so not my thing. Pulling up echo-demons en masse was sounding easier and easier every day.

"I heard she was a party girl and that Bran and she might have had a relationship, but it soured."

"And you believed that?" He laughed out loud, then sobered. "Let me guess, Dominique?"

"Does it matter?"

He shook his head as if disappointed in a favored pupil. "Of course it matters. Gossip is only as good as its source, and Dominique has been making the most outrageous innuendoes for days now."

"About what?"

"Everyone, sweet cheeks, including yourself. Bran and Sasha. That wouldn't happen in a million years."

"Why?"

"Because, dumplings, he's had eyes only for you since you joined. So do not tell me you haven't noticed."

When I was five my mother walked out of the house one day and never came back. Even now I could recall the shell-shocked feeling I'd experienced when my dad had sat me down and told me not to ask for my momma again. She wouldn't be coming home. The news was like a slam on hard-packed earth from a great height. Franco's words produced the same effect.

"You didn't know." Franco leaned closer, his eyes saucer-sized now. "How deliciously droll. No wonder the man has been practically foaming at the mouth. I don't think he's used to being frustrated. And by a hairdresser. Oh, this is too, too—"

"Shut up, Frank." I'd deal with his revelation later. *We were acting our roles, that's all.* "Tell me about Dominique's other innuendoes."

"Oh, well, there was a juicy one about you being a serial killer."

So Dominique was the one who had shared my background. No surprise there.

Franco pressed two fingers together in a gesture I associated with the Boy Scouts. Until now. "So, is it true?"

"Get real," I snorted, the easier to distract Franco.

"Too bad, that was so juicy." He shook his head then added, "Then she announced you were gay."

"As in happy?" Good thing I wasn't drinking my coffee or I'd have snorted it all over the table.

Franco moued his lips, "Of course you being gay all went up in smoke when you arrived with Bran last night. No one who saw the two of you together could have any doubts which side of the fence you favor."

I so was not having this conversation.

I responded dryly. "Anything else Dominique is saying?"

"Let's see." He pressed a finger along his jaw as if he had to think very carefully. "You're gay. I'm not. You, and I, or both of us killed poor, poor Sasha. Bran is being blackmailed by you."

I nearly fell off my chair. "What?"

"Her justification as to why you'd be with him last night. I thought it was a very inventive spur of the moment excuse."

"Yeah, creative points to Dominique." The woman was working way too hard to discredit me. Was my cover blown? Franco's voice slid into seriousness. "Don't let her fool you, sweet cheeks. The woman would make a barracuda seem tame in comparison. And she does not care for you."

"Tell me something I don't know."

"You should be careful with her. Bran can control her to a certain extent, but even he is clueless to how very cunning and very ruthless she is. The woman should have been born with balls. Steel ones. Some say she was."

"Thanks, I'll remember that." As if I wasn't aware of Dominique's ruthlessness and ambition every second I'd been on the tour.

"My turn now." Franco looked so delighted, I expected he'd start clapping his hands any moment. Then I'd have to slap him.

"Fine." So my tone wasn't gracious, sue me. "Nothing personal though."

"Have it your way. Did you sleep with him?"

"What?"

He popped a bite of mango in his mouth. "You heard—"

"That's damn personal in my book."

"Then you need a different book. Besides—" He glanced around though the buffet was still deserted. "I have money riding on this."

"Money riding on what?"

"Whether you did the deed with Bran." He sighed dramatically. "There's been a pool going for over a week now. Given how fast he returned last night, the fact his clothes were hardly mussed and the scowl on his face, I'd say I'm still in the running with a resounding no."

I pushed my chair away from the table. "Get a life."

"Oh, but darling, why should I when those lives around me are so much messier."

Little did he know.

I walked away, leaving him waving a fork after me and shouting, "It's all right. Hold out for as long as you can. I have fifty bucks riding on it."

His bet and my job.

CHAPTER 43

"Jaylene, is that you? Where's Kel?" I asked once back in the privacy of my bungalow, feeling as if I'd eaten a boatload of jumping shrimp for breakfast. Nerves? Anger? Frustration? All combined. I wanted answers, enough Ms. Play by the Rules.

"And it's nice to talk to you, too. Nice to know I've been missed. Nice to—"

Sheesh. Everyone had an agenda.

"Sorry," I mumbled, "too focused on the situation." And getting Van back alive. My tone said get over it even as I sucked in a deep breath, remembering Stone's words. Be a team player. I stared from my verandah across the empty bowl of blue ocean and sky and released a sigh as I chewed my lip. A scene as surreal as my earlier conversation with Franco.

"So how's the hunk who makes dresses?"

Leave it to Jaylene not to tap dance around the exact topic I didn't want to talk about.

"He's fine." Lord, that sounded lame even as I snapped the answer.

"You sleep with him yet?"

What was it with everyone asking about my sex life? Hadn't anyone ever heard of privacy?

"I'm not here to sleep with him. I'm here to investigate him."

Jaylene's throaty laughter rumbled through the line. "Nothing saying you can't investigate him up close and personal."

"And compromise the investigation?"

"Whoa, girlfriend. I'm not saying marry the dude. I'm saying have some fun if it presents itself."

"Well, it won't."

"What? Present itself or be fun?"

I rolled my eyes since no one could see me, then cleared a jam in my throat. "Can we move along? Any news on those numbers I called in last night? Or on the murder investigation?"

"Got some news on the killing of your model. Which is why I'm here with Kelly. I just brought her the intel in person." I curled my fingers around the verandah railing as Jaylene's tone turned serious. "I don't have all the scientific lingo, but the bottom line is she was found with a very unusual, synthetic, and previously unknown drug in her system."

"What kind of drug?"

"Not your street-variety kind that's for sure. Definitely high-price designer. Seems it's experimental so the chemist dudes are still trying to put all their geek heads together to pin it down."

"Is it a poison?"

"Nah. More like a combination date rape meets Prozac kind of thing. This is some serious bad news. A user wouldn't be aware she'd taken the shit and would have no memory of it later. She'd just feel very, very good with some vague memories that wouldn't seem real."

"Like Rohypnol?" I asked, adding up the implications like an accountant at tax season.

"Yeah, only this stuff appears to have an interesting side effect. It makes a person open to suggestion."

"Like hypnosis?"

"Yup, just like that."

I whistled. "So if someone was slipped this stuff, you're saying they could do something against their will and have no knowledge about it?"

"I'm not saying it. The scientists guys are. They think it was designed to be a Prozac knockoff and then someone figured out this side effect. Fassbinder has her own theories that Ling Mai is following up with."

"Like what?"

"Like it's been enhanced with a preternatural venom. Regular science dudes are never going to pinpoint that."

"Is this what Interpol stumbled on to? Someone's using this drug to force people to steal for them?" I asked, the tumblers clicking at last. This threw the whole investigation a curve ball. This was more than human to human bad stuff, there was clearly a non-human element at work. Which could explain why this mysterious Vaverek might be in the game.

"Interpol or the scientists or anybody know if the victims have all been human?" Not that it'd be an easy thing to find out without sending someone with the agency ring to meet each victim in person.

"No way to find out. Ling Mai is working with Interpol on getting more intel on this drug, but it looks like the drug is driving the thefts."

"But no clue as to who's administering it?"

"You got it, girl. All we know is that someone in that traveling circus you're with is possibly slipping it to select clients. Then the dupes perform the thefts without an idea they were involved."

Ingenious. And nasty, really nasty. I released another frustrated breath. "So what happened to Sasha? I can't believe someone would sit there and let their throat get slit without fighting back."

"They would if they're under the suggestion that something else is happening, or about to happen. Far as that poor girl knew she was going to get a neck massage or somethin'. She didn't fight what she didn't see coming."

"Holy crud."

"Ditto." Jaylene shouted something to Kelly in the background before saying. "So, given the crap you're dealing with, I'm going to be meeting up with you as soon as I can be inserted. We can get a good cover story down by Miami. Vaughn's joining us there too, but as a guest."

Two days away. Unless Bran cancelled the tour. Which he couldn't be allowed to do. No tour, the trail for the drug could go underground. As well as any intel on Van.

"You still there?" Jaylene asked.

"Yeah, I'm here." Grappling with all the implications. "Anybody have any idea of what this drug looks like? Pill or liquid form? How long it takes to act? If someone has to have a certain predisposition to it?"

"Whoa, girlfriend. They're stoked that they got as much info as they have about this. Seems it disappears from the system relatively quickly. They found it in the dead model because Ling Mai had the French cops rush the autopsy."

"Someone has figured out how to execute the perfect crime." I shook my head, amazed how simple, and how complicated the set up was. The mastermind never was present at the actual crime scenes, so no fingers pointing in their direction. And how did they find who the next potential victim would be? "This is slicker than cow slobber."

"Whatever. Not how I'd—" Jaylene snorted. "Anyway, this stuff ever gets to the market, no telling where it can lead."

"So Bran's tour is a testing ground. Someone's been using his clients as guinea pigs."

"Could be your hunk guy himself. I'd say that kind of power could be pretty addictive. Better than sewing dresses."

How far would a warlock go to make his name?

"He doesn't sew dresses." But he did have some issues with his reputation; and being the force behind this new drug could be a heady rush for a guy who valued being acknowledged.

"From theft to murder," Jaylene said. "I'd say that's about as cold and calculating as one could get."

But that didn't sound like Bran. At least not the Bran I'd gotten to know. Arrogant. Difficult. Complicated. All of those and more but not cold. Not the guy who made sure one of his employees traveled to a family funeral and had it paid for or made sure that another employee stepped away from an abusive relationship.

On the other hand, that could all be smoke and mirrors. Maybe Jaylene was right? I should have sex with the guy and get him out of my system so I could focus on the mission.

But what if he was as addictive as this new drug?

So who else could be administering the drug? That was the million dollar question. Dominique? Oh, yeah, that'd be an easy stretch of the imagination, the woman liked control. Control and power. Plus she had easy access to all the guests. But was she acting alone? And then there were still the unknowns. Franco's background check still was unclear. Collette with her early years of crime? And who had searched my room last night and why?

Franco was right; some lives were just a mess.

"Any news on Van?" I asked, expecting a no but unable not to ask anyway.

"Other than he was seen in the company of one of those two shifters you described as attacking you on the yacht. There's a connection Alex, we just can't put all the pieces together. But we will."

I nodded as if she could see me, but it was a lackluster movement. Every day with no news made bad news inevitable. "So you're coming on board the tour?" I repeated, loathe to lose the connection just yet.

"Soon as I can."

Good news. This was no longer a reconnoiter and report mission. It'd just blown up.

I went back to an earlier thought. "Any info on that phone number I gave Kelly last night?"

"She's working on it." Jaylene paused, then added. "Ling Mai's had all of us stretched pretty thin the last week, but it's still no excuse to leave you with your ass showing."

How apt. "I've had the operation under control." Most of it, anyway, but I did appreciate the recognition, especially coming from Jaylene who was more a bitch-slap- some-sense-into-you kind of gal than the warm and friendly pat on the back type.

"The team will be with you as soon as we can," she said. "Meantime, watch your back."

"Trust me, that's on my game plan." Along with a few other options.

I shivered beneath the strong rays of the tropical sun. I hadn't survived four brothers and the initial IR training to fall victim to some chemistry.

The team was coming. Good news.

Bad news—someone was playing for keeps, and wouldn't balk at getting rid of any obstacle—including a hairdresser.

CHAPTER 44

"You look like hell," Jaylene was standing on the patio of my poolside room at the Brasserie Lounge in Miami's fabled Delano Hotel, a soft ocean breeze kissing our skins, the pulsing beat of Afro Celtic music pouring out of the nearby lounge. The lounge totally commandeered this evening specifically for Bran's models and his guests. One of them a killer.

I stepped away from the door jamb I'd been leaning against. "Good, I feel like hell, too."

Juggling waiting for the team to get on board, my duties as a hairdresser, and the landmine of a difficult warlock would wipe out anyone.

"I can take over this op for you from here on in," Jaylene kept her voice low, if intense. "You can get some recovery time."

"Not likely."

"Girlfriend." Jaylene pulled herself up to her six-foot height and glared down at me. "So you haven't found anything concrete yet. So what? No need to beat yourself up."

I shoved useless hands against my dress. Who wore clothes without pockets anyway. "Sasha's dead. There are no leads, no concrete anything to nail this bastard. No news about Van. I'd say that's a big failure in anyone's book."

"Ever think you're looking at this the wrong way?" Jaylene had the street smarts to look away from me when she called me an idiot.

I snorted, in spite of the fact it took effort to do so, energy that was hard to come by.

Jaylene rolled her eyes and stepped closer. "Damn, you're stubborn. You ever think you've rattled someone's cage? That you're forcing them into rash actions? That Sasha's death means someone is running scared?"

"So now my actions led to an innocent woman's death?"

"She was an operative. You didn't kill her."

I shrugged, trying to release some of my tension. "Right now I'm pissed. This is personal, it's not just about stopping a thief and killer."

"Ling Mai hears you and you'll get yanked faster than a bungee jumper's cord. Personal doesn't belong on a mission." Jaylene whistled as she glanced toward the club starting to buzz with nightlife. Half-naked men. Barely there dresses on women. Tanned, taut flesh all around. Beautiful people playing hard. "But then what Ling Mai doesn't know isn't going to hurt her. You got a plan or just going to go in and knock some heads around?"

"Sounds good to me."

"Sounds like the way Montana Alex would approach the problem."

I shot Jaylene an exasperated frown. "I'm from Idaho, and I don't know what you're talking about."

"Sure you do. Shoot first and ask questions later. A fight isn't a good fight unless there's blood and broken bones. Isn't that what they taught you on the farm with those brothers of yours?"

"You don't know what you're talking about." I did know, but that wasn't the point. Finding who wanted me taken out was.

"Living with bruiser brothers isn't that far from living on the streets." Jaylene stepped closer. "And I know streets. I also know what it's like to doubt yourself."

"Every time I've turned around on this op I've screwed up." Bile rose in my throat.

"That's a bunch of crap."

"I haven't found who's behind the thefts or pushing the drug. Sasha's dead. Van's still gone. Reads like screw-up in my book."

"Honey, you're sounding like a broken record. *We* failed, not you."

That had me cranking up my spine. My op—my responsibility. "No—"

"We're a team and we weren't close enough to watch your back, even when all the flags and whistles were going off."

"I—"

"Shut up and listen, girlfriend. I'm only going to say this once. You came in to a reconnoiter and report mission. That mission changed the minute that model girl died and those shifters came after you. Where were we? Scattered all over the globe. She was killed, right under your nose, and we still couldn't get close enough to protect you. Sure, mistakes were made, but you can't claim them all."

I shook my head, feeling as light and disjointed as my body. I'd resisted this, being part of the IR team, in spite of Stone's threats to the counter. I didn't expect anyone to cover my six. I was the one who just about killed us all with the trio of echo-demons, so how could I trust Jaylene's words? "I should have—"

"Lordy, Lord, it's a good thing you're looking like death warmed over even in that killer dress or I'd have to slap you." Scowling, Jaylene leaned forward and waved one inch-long acrylic talon in my face. "Now listen. You *are* one of us, even if you damn near killed Mandy. But you are the one who got rid of those green demons. Then you go right back into battle, all banged up, without a whimper. You make Wonder Woman look like a wimp. So you don't go telling me *you* failed. You held on longer than any of us could have and never once asked to be pulled or demanded backup when you should have. Last I checked you're only human, or mostly." Jaylene snorted. "Not that you'd admit it. So lighten up."

I shook my head again, my eyes stinging, my gut wrung dry. Here everything I'd been doing was for Van's sake and

Jaylene was making me sound like some rah-rah IR poster child. If only she knew.

"I so am right, Alex Noziak," Jaylene said in that no-other-option way of hers. "You're just not smart enough to realize that fact. I don't want you going off and doing something stupid before you get your head on straight. Farm, or ranch, or whatever the hell you call it, those rules don't apply here."

"I'm not—"

"Oh, yes you are, girlfriend, else you wouldn't be figuring you had to do this on your own. You could wait for Vaughn to get her skinny ass here and have us go in as a team."

"But I'm the one with the cover in place."

"Circumstances have changed. I'm the new model; that should count for something. And it'll take Vaughn less than five minutes to have this whole crew thinking she's something special." Jaylene crossed her arms and wagged her head. "So why don't you sashay over to that boyfriend of yours and—" She glanced over to where Bran was standing inside the bar.

"He's not my boyfriend."

"You are just clueless all over the place."

"Thanks for the vote of confidence." I brushed my hair back, wearing it straight again. Killer straight.

Jaylene was right. Emotions could get us all killed. Now was not the time to focus on what wasn't working but to shift tactics. My team was behind me one hundred percent now. New territory. New rules. Time to play this game my way.

"Earth to Alex." Jaylene nudged me with her shoulder. "Speak to me, girlfriend. Tell me the plan."

I gulped a deep breath of ocean air. Noziaks did not let Grimples stop them from going in fighting, but I was more than a Mud Lake Noziak. I was a witch whose skills might be rusty, but I did have them—time to bring them to bear. I was an IR Agent and it was time to start thinking like one.

I glanced at the crowded lounge. "Everyone involved is inside that room, so that's where I need to be."

"Agreed."

Finally, something right.

Jaylene adjusted her leather and silk bustier. "My guess is best target to push is the Ice Princess or the Gay Guy."

"You mean Dominique or Franco?" Dominique, no problem. But Franco? As much as I loathed the prick, there was still something rock solid about the guy.

Jaylene mused aloud. "I so would not want to meet that woman in a dark alley. And as for pip-squeak in need of steroids, he watches everyone a little too carefully."

"But you just met both of them this afternoon."

Jaylene swept out all ten of her ringed fingers in an imperial gesture. "Girlfriend, you do not survive on the streets long if you don't quickly size up the opposition."

Good point.

Jaylene grinned. "Thing is, this is still your op."

"But I—"

"You say the 'f' as in failed word and I'm out of here." Jaylene didn't even glance my way.

I tugged my own dress, another Bran creation that hugged like mother love. "Time to go on the offensive," I said, staring at the lounge. "Rattle cages. Do the unexpected."

"You go, girl."

A glimmer of a smile broke through; rattling Dominique sounded straight up my alley. Franco, too.

"Don't forget hunk man either," Jaylene said. "Way I'm looking at the players, he's the linchpin everything hangs on. Don't know how or why, but you can't take him out of the equation. Not yet."

My stomach knotted. Rattling Bran could backfire. Problem was, any rattling of him stood to shake me, too.

Jaylene grinned, her teeth stark in the deepening evening light. "Got any ideas, girlfriend? 'Cause if you don't, step aside and let me have a go at him."

I bit back the immediate primordial and jungle-deep response. Jealousy was as foreign to me as catfights among women and backstabbing tattling. But I was learning; the last two weeks had been an education. Time to put my newly acquired knowledge to use.

"Don't worry," I said to Jaylene, thinking of a dress Franco had shown me earlier. A no-holds, momma-keep-your-boys-at-home kind of dress, "I know exactly how to rattle his cage."

"Thought you might."

Armor for battle. Just thinking about it got my adrenaline pumping in a positive way. I was getting surprisingly good at this fancy dress thing. "No time like the present to get started."

"You go, girlfriend."

CHAPTER 45

Two hours later, I spotted Vaughn standing near Jaylene at the bar that snaked along one side of the lounge. Playing by my new game plan I rumbaed closer to Bran and whispered a kiss across his jaw as I murmured, "Be right back."

The look he gave me raised the room's temperature from too warm to steaming. My plan was working. Instead of denying what had been simmering between us since our first meeting I was using the chemistry to rattle his warlock cage.

I hadn't expected that seeing him all hot and bothered, knowing I was in total control, would give me such a rush of power. Oh, yeah, I could handle this just fine. No wonder women liked the dress-to-the-nines thing.

"You look hot," Vaughn laughed as I shimmied closer. The music was loud enough that the three of us could talk without being overheard, as I stood close to Jaylene and left Vaughn appearing to be just a stranger nearby. "Sexy, watch-out-Bran, scorching kind of hot."

I smiled, a real one and a first in days, catching a quick image of myself in the Venetian glass mirrors bracketing the bar. I felt sexy hot. Yards of chiffon caged in gold lame and edged in a slick of sequins. I looked like a cross between Queen Cleopatra and a smoky seductress. "New game plan. Operation Cage Rattling."

"Bran may never recover."

"That's the plan." I shifted the subject. "Speaking of plans, you should have seen Dominique's look when I complimented her on her dress. Thought she was going to choke."

Vaughn glanced at Jaylene. "I'm not sure we're going to get our old Alex back after this op."

"Not sure we want her back." Jaylene raised her martini glass. "Here's to the new Alex. Butt-kicking-in-a-dress kind of Alex."

My grin widened. Having the team—or some of them—in place was good. Kind of like knowing my big brothers were around to watch my back though better—less sweat and more eye makeup kind of better. Together I'd get the info I needed to find out who, or what, held Van. And once I did, nothing was going to stop me from freeing him.

"Before you get too focused on your agenda, not that I'd blame you, Vaughn has good news for us." Jaylene raised a pointed nail at our team leader. "Which you can share at any time."

"You know that phone number you found in the Maldives?" Vaughn asked.

"The one on the second phone in Dragon Lady's room?"

"That's the one. It's a throwaway phone."

"Figured that—no registered owner."

"Right, but Kelly's been able to get the Feds involved and get a triangulation on the signal. The phone's been used only once here in Miami, but the connection was just long enough to pin down a general location, within a building nothing more."

My heart pounded faster. "And?"

"The call came from within the hotel here. We couldn't figure out which floor, but someone is definitely inside this place."

I was hoping for something more concrete. "That could mean the caller could either be a total stranger, unknown to us or on the tour. Why would someone call Dragon Lady on an untraceable phone if they saw her every day?"

Vaughn shook her head. "Your guess is as good as ours."

"There's more." Jaylene raised her martini glass. "Mandy put a tag on Dominique's phone after you asked for it, so while the good guys were getting the location of the second phone they also managed to pick up a secondary conversation from Dominique's end that indicates she's connected with the thefts."

"So she is involved!" I almost gave Jaylene a high-five right there at the bar.

"Looks like your witchy instinct was spot on," came her response.

"I knew it. I so knew it. Anything worthwhile?"

Vaughn and Jaylene grinned in unison, but Vaughn was the one who answered. "Whatever is happening is going to go down in Washington D.C."

"Our next stop on the tour?"

"That's right." Vaughn's face lit up like a lottery jackpot winner. "Last stop on the tour, day after tomorrow. It's show time."

CHAPTER 46

After speaking to Vaughn and Jaylene, I didn't return directly to Bran on the dance floor. Too many thoughts whirling through my head. Van. Washington D.C. Bran. Always Bran. How was he going to take the news of Dominique's involvement? How much did he already know? Was he using me or was there really something between us? Man to woman, not warlock to witch.

I stepped outside the crowded, loud bar area to the dark night surrounding the bottom-lit pool, the water still and quiet, the underwater classical music pumped through the pool switched off. Bran had told me the name of the designer who created the vanishing-edge design where the chairs appeared to sit in the water and not around it. Just one more of our differences. Bran knew designers by name; I couldn't give a rip. All I cared about right then was the fact the area was empty, the sounds of the bar music were muted here, like the thrum of a distant heartbeat.

I had barely taken a deep breath when Bran spoke from behind me, his voice as deep and intoxicating as the tropical air.

"You disappeared?"

Ever since the Maldives I'd been uber aware of him. How like him to ask about where I'd been, even if the patient-to-doctor tone meant we kept each other at arm's length. "Just needed some air."

He slipped his hands over my shoulders, anchoring me in place, forcing me to be aware of their weight, their texture against my bare skin. Without words he pulled me back toward him until his body heat encircled mine, his hands slipping down to curl around my waist, his chin resting against my head.

The first time since the Maldives he'd treated me as a woman and not an employee under his watch.

So easy to simply forget here—surrounded by him. And why shouldn't I? He wasn't a thief even if he might be hiding one. Besides, I sensed him untwisting some, and I wasn't about to snatch that away from him too soon. We'd both been in knots for too long.

"I worry about you," he whispered along my hair. "I don't want you out of my sight."

Ditto, but for different reasons.

I shifted, turning myself until I could gaze up at him, his face angled and stark in the shadows. His voice sounded harsh, wrenched from him.

"Bran, I never meant what's between us—"

He laid a finger upon my lips. "Meant or not, there is an us. Wanted or not. Feeling held at arm's length by you doesn't sit well, even if you are a powerful witch and don't need me."

So I wasn't alone. He'd been as impacted as I had, willing to voice the words I tripped over even in my thoughts.

Too bad though. Day after tomorrow I'd be walking away from him, leaving his world so alien to my own. I'd come to do a job, one that was nearing completion with the outcome still unclear. He would be hurt, a pain I would help inflict if what we'd discovered so far about Dominique turned out to be true. And I still had not discovered her connection to Van's disappearance. Once I did, all gloves would be off.

When had life become so complicated?

"Bran, there's no sense—"

"Sense never had anything to do with us." He paused, then added. "*Acies acendo adamo.*"

That phrase again. What did it mean?

But the time for thinking was past as he lowered his mouth, covering mine, silencing my protests. I expected heat from him. Fire and power and passion. And passion was there, but buried deep, layered beneath the care, the gentleness.

His lips brushed against mine, coaxing rather than devouring. Asking instead of demanding. So non-warlock I was stunned.

I stepped closer, wrapped within his arms, wrapped within him.

This was no longer cage rattling but inevitability. Consequences could be weighed and measured tomorrow; tonight I simply wanted. I was an agent, but I was also a woman. I was a witch who knew better than to fall for a warlock. I was too far gone to weigh the consequences. Tonight I made my choice.

I was the one who deepened the kiss. Opening my mouth to him, tasting and teasing him with my tongue, with my hands in his hair, with my body sliding along his. I didn't care if he was warlock or demon; I just wanted him, all of him.

His groan met my sigh. When he raised his head, I was steadied only by the force of his arms cradling me.

"You're sure?"

I simply nodded.

"Your room or mine." His words were not a question, though choice still lay in the balance.

"Doesn't matter." I cast my lot.

His grin was the first true one I'd ever seen from him.

He snagged my hand when a voice hailed us from the lounge.

"Bran?"

"Later, Dom."

"But I need—"

"I said later." He didn't glance back, but I did. Rage tightened Dominique's features, rage and fear.

"You're with me tonight," Bran tugged me along, his voice raw with need. "Only with me."

"No problem," I lied, but I'd deal with that later, too. Tonight there was only one agenda. The one between a man and a woman.

We reached Bran's room first. The penthouse, of course, the man did style well. His fingers shook as he key-coded his door, the awkwardness another first.

It was good to know I wasn't the only one with nerves.

We slipped into darkness; a huge space, though I saw little as he ignored the lights.

Fine by me.

He scooped me into his arms as if I'd escape otherwise and stepped to the bed, releasing me only to slide along his length to the floor.

"At last," he whispered, using his hands to memorize my face, the sweep of my neck, the cup of my head.

I let him explore, savoring his touch, his attention to detail, my responsiveness. My knees quaked, my blood pounded, my heart stuttered.

His hands brushed the strap of my gown, a tremble in the motion.

"Be careful of the dress," I smiled against his shirt in the darkness. "It costs a fortune."

Instead of answering he clenched his fist in the silk and ripped.

The dress shredded.

He stilled my intake of breath with a kiss. Another kiss followed, a whisper along my cheek. "The dress was in my way."

"Obviously." I swallowed more words, exposed to the coolness of air conditioning, to the hunger in his eyes. Lightness and gentleness were gone—replaced by raw need. I read his urgency in the tautness of his skin, the flare of his nostrils.

My own breath hitched and held.

"Come here." He stood only inches away but asked for more. For me to make the first move. Toward him. To accept what he was asking. Even here there was still choice. Still a chance to hold back.

Instead I smiled and closed the gap, my hands raised to wrap around him, the scrape of his clothes rough against my bare skin.

"I'm here," I whispered. There was no need for more.

His hands curled around my neck, stroked the length of my spine, cupped the curve of my butt as his mouth claimed mine.

Here was the fire, the heat, the controlled passion unleashed.

I was caught in the vortex of a volcano. A warlock volcano.

My hands clawed at his clothes, desperate to touch. He shucked shirt and pants in a rough, raw move, tumbling us both back on the bed at the same time.

Time flattened. Bodies heated. Neither of us could get enough. Enough touch. Enough taste. Enough connection.

"Please." It was my whisper coaxing him.

He raised above me, stark in the weak light cast from undraped windows. He paused only long enough for protection before he thrust. Hard. Fast. Deep.

Yet I wanted more. I met him, thrust for thrust, skin slickened between us, breathing harsh, nails digging into flesh.

More, I had to have more.

I rose off the bed, taking him deeper, matching his want, slipping over the edge first, my cry echoing through the room, his joining mine.

I closed my eyes and savored.

CHAPTER 47

We lay there, breaths slowing, arms and legs tangled, my hair washed across his damp skin. The thrum of Miami's South Beach traffic pulsed beyond the windows far below. The chill of the air conditioning had me burrowing closer to his heat.

He tugged the bed cover across my shoulders.

"We could get under the sheets," he said, his voice low and satiated.

"Too much energy." I kissed his chest, tickling my lips with his dark hair.

"Yeah, got to save our strength." I heard the smile in his voice. I raised my head just enough to see the curve of his lips. Those sinful, sweetly seductive lips. "You've got plans for something?"

"Yeah." He grinned. "Figure it'll take at least three days."

That quick reality slammed into me. Time. A very limited quantity between us, though he didn't know how limited. Washington D.C. was day after tomorrow.

I already ached, aware of the only possible ending between us, just around the corner.

I laid my head back against his chest.

"I lost you," he said the words as statement more than question. "Something I need to know about?"

Not yet. I wanted a little more time before the outside world intruded and forced us apart.

"Franco's going to be pissed over that ruined dress."My ploy worked. He laughed. A slow rumble in his chest until he curled his hands around my shoulders and tumbled me beneath him once again.

"Then we'd better make sure you suck up to Franco's boss."

I returned his grin. "Oh, sucking is now involved?"

"Among other things."

My answer was lost in his kiss.

CHAPTER 48

"You look relaxed." Jaylene raised arched brows at me late the next morning. "Must have been a mighty fine night."

"You've got a gutter mind." I reached for the coffee carafe in the dining room, aware no others stood near.

"Oh, yeah, baby, I do." Jaylene's speculative expression deepened. "And a very active imagination. Was he as good as —"

"Get a life." I brushed past her.

"Thought so." Jaylene sipped her own coffee, leaving a bright red lipstick ring on the cup's edge as she followed me to a window table. A quick glance reassured both of us no parabolic mikes could be used from any nearby building.

But before we could talk, Franco joined us.

"My, my, you two look cozy," he fluttered, a little edgier than usual. Which said a lot.

I ignored him and spoke to Jaylene. "You'll get used to Frank here. He's an acquired taste."

"Sort of like beets?" she asked with a shiver, eyeing Franco over the edge of her cup. "Never have gotten used to beets."

"All I'm saying." Franco slipped into the chair beside me, jostling my arm and spilling coffee with his move. "Is you two seem to have become fast friends awfully quick. Very buddy buddy."

"We have very common interests," I mumbled, wiping coffee from my jeans. "Like surviving nosy tour managers who butt in where they're not wanted."

"You're wounding me." Franco placed a hand over his heart but made no move to leave. "Seriously, ladies, I need your help."

I choked on a sip of coffee. "You want what?"

"I'm worried." He glanced around him before speaking. "Have you seen Dominique today? Ghastly, simply ghastly. I'm afraid the poor woman is losing her control." He eyed me. "And we do know the woman personifies control."

I set my cup down before asking "And what do you want us to do?"

"Well." He leaned closer. "You two, being the new girls, might notice what others are missing."

"Such as?"

"You know, you might see someone who doesn't look like they belong. Who might be bothering Dominique."

"Are you saying you think someone's threatening her?" Jaylene asked, her face betraying only mild curiosity.

"I don't know what the problem is." Franco released a dramatic sigh. "But I do know an unhappy Dominique makes an unhappy group."

"Maybe it's PMS?" Jaylene offered.

"Pahleeze," Franco's response was accompanied by a dramatic eye roll. "I'm around enough women daily to know the difference between hormones and...and—"

"And?" I asked, my lips twitching, realizing I might even miss Franco.

"And something else." His tone became very serious. "I don't like the way she's behaving, that's all. Not one bit and tomorrow we arrive in D.C."

My shoulders tensed. "And that has significance because?"

"Dahling, you must have heard. The gala reception? Kennedy Center. Everyone who's anyone."

"We've had receptions at every stop we've made."

"Don't be dense, poppet. Those were small potatoes."

"Enlighten me," I said. "I'm a pig farmer's daughter, not a potato farmer's."

"So you haven't heard?" Franco glanced between both of us. "But then you might not, word only just arrived hours ago."

"Spell the words out here, Frank." At this rate Washington D.C. would be two cities behind us before we received any news.

"Well," Franco lowered his voice. "Bran will be given an award. For creativity in the arts. Very posh affair at the Kennedy Center."

"Bully for him," Jaylene said drolly.

"Oh, but it's a very great honor. Only three people will be presented with the award." He looked at us both. "Dahlings, *everyone* who is anyone will be there, must I repeat that."

More schmoozing and cruising. "That's nice," I said.

"Well, I'd think associating with the First Lady would be a bit more than nice."

I caught Jaylene's narrowing of her eyes, before she steeled her voice to a calm tone. "The First Lady—what does she have to do with anything?"

"She's the one who's going to present the award to Bran."

CHAPTER 49

That evening the Blue Door Restaurant was ultra high-society. Only moments ago heads bobbled as some rapper with a non-Idaho guy name—Puffy, Baby, Booboo—floated through the entryway. Bran and I were tucked away in a private alcove so I could ignore him to study the menu. There wasn't a decent hamburger or sausage dog anywhere on the menu filled with fancy French words and unfamiliar ingredients. Plus no prices. Who didn't put price tags on their menus?

"You're too quiet." Bran regarded me across the crisp linen tablecloth, his hands stroking a crystal stemware glass, its dark, red liquid reflecting candlelight. The same hands that stroked me last night. Same sensuous movement. Same intoxicating spell cast. One more minute and I'd start begging.

I clenched my hands in my lap instead.

"Alex?" Bran prodded. "You want to tell me what's upsetting you?"

I leaned forward, sucking in a deep breath. *Now or never.* "What do you know about this award function in D.C.?"

"You've heard about that?" He cast his gaze down. Embarrassed or hiding something? "The whole affair is of no importance to me." He fingered the glass stem tighter. "I'd temporarily forgotten."

"You can't afford to forget. There's too much at risk to have meetings with major dignitaries slip under the radar. It's important and it's business."

"What do you want to know?"

"Who set it up?"

He shrugged. "Dom—she handles these types of affairs."

Bingo. "And how long has your cousin known about the arrangements?"

The lines bracketing his eyes tightened before he replied, "Far as I know the award concept had been presented as a possibility months ago. Yesterday Dom told me the arrangements had been finalized. Why?"

"We don't know for sure."

"We? You mean your agency?"

"Of course."

His lips quirked into a cynical smile. "And how much does your agency know about us?"

My stomach took a dive. "What kind of question is that?"

"An honest one." His voice deepened, his face looking dark and enigmatic in the flickering light, more demon than warlock now. "So, tell me Alex, was last night about us or about business?"

I reached for my own wine, swigging it as if water. "Last night had nothing to do with the agency."

"You sure?"

"That's a cheap slam."

This conversation was not going as planned. I was the one meant to call the shots, not get blasted by them. Warlocks always had to have the last say, it was a part of their need to control.

"Is the question so outrageous to ask?" He leaned back in his chair, the buzz of conversations around us contrasting with the pocket of strained silence between us. "I'm curious where we stand?"

"Can we get back to business?" I released a sigh when the waiter interrupted my next words. A steaming bowl of fist-sized shrimp and tempura-fried leeks in a pomegranate sauce was slid before me.

The dish smelled divine. Too bad my appetite had flatlined.

Bran nodded the waiter off, ignoring his own Maine lobster as he asked. "Will you be attending the award ceremony with me?"

Better question was would it serve the mission or would my part in the mission be finished by then?

"I don't know, it all depends," I answered truthfully, my throat raw.

"Let me rephrase." He leaned forward. "Regardless of any *business* between us, will you be attending the event with me?"

"Don't be ridiculous." The exasperated words escaped before I could tamp them down. At the flare of his nostrils, I added, "I won't need to be circulating in that crowd. Not as your date."

"So our being together *does* all come down to business." He sounded hurt, but that couldn't be. He knew the score from the beginning. We'd had sex, that's all.

"I don't know why you're upset." My fork remained on the table, my hands wadded together in my lap. "Why are you acting like this?"

"Acting? Who's acting here?"

"I don't know—"

"*Acies acendo adamo,*" he murmured, his ice cold voice chilling me.

Fine, two could play the emotion game. Only my emotion raged hot. My father warned me about my temper, but Dad was far away and this arrogant warlock was pissing me off. "Don't you spout your dead languages at me. I'm tired of pussyfooting around you and cousin dearest."

He spoke volumes with a quirked brow.

I lowered my voice and leaned toward him. "Do you know a man named Vaverek?"

He shook his head, his gaze lasered on mine.

Time to go for broke. "Do you know a man named Van?"

"I might. It's an unusual name but not unknown. Does this Van have a surname?"

"Noziak." The word tasted cardboard dry in my mouth. "Van Noziak."

His head tilted before he spoke in a very calm and measured tone. "He is related to you?"

"My brother."

The intensity in his gaze deepened. "You expect me to know your brother?"

I tried to use a quick sensing spell to determine if he spoke the truth but his warlock defenses were locked into place.

In for a penny, in for a pound. "My brother is being held by a man named Vaverek. Held and tortured."

"And you think I'm involved in this?" He leaned forward, his voice pitched low and intense.

"I don't know." I knew the truth damned me. Around me the air stilled, sounds quieted into unnatural stillness, but I didn't care. I wanted to know what Bran knew and I wanted to know now. "I know your cousin is involved. Since you two are so close. . ."

The temperature in the room dropped twenty degrees. I glanced around, realizing that the silence was not because people had stopped talking, but because they were frozen, caught in time. Bran was spell casting even if he didn't realize it.

What kind of power did he possess to silence a whole room of people in mid-action? Oh, wait, this is a warlock that brought me back from the dead; why was I surprised?

I sent out a guarding spell. Not for me, but for the innocents who didn't know how deadly an angry warlock could be.

"Last night, Alex? Was that a means to an end?"

"Last night has nothing to do with anything else." Why did my throat ache and my eyes sting?

"You're wrong. I think you're hiding from the truth."

"What truth? You wouldn't know the truth if it bit your backside. Dominique is involved up to her groomed eyebrows, yet you protect her." I slammed my mangled napkin on the table. "You ignore reality, to what? To sell dresses? To keep up an illusion of the great Bran fashionista empire. My brother's life is on the line and yet you keep blocking me."

"Blocking you? You've been using me all along." His voice now sounded like ice–cold, controlled, killer ice. The far windows rattled and a breeze whipped through the still room, fluttering tablecloths, erasing the flicker of candles.

"Our relationship has been one big game to you. With me as a pawn."

I shivered in my chair, feeling his will pressing against me. No way was I going to roll over and let his power flatten me. I called forth my magic and pushed back. Little by little and watched his eyes widen in surprise.

"Think what you want to think." I gritted my teeth to hold against him. "But I'm protecting you by telling you what I have. You don't care about me. About my brother. You don't care about anything except covering for your bitch of a cousin and yourself."

"I don't know anything about your brother. Why should I care about him? Why should I be held accountable for thwarting you when you don't trust me enough to tell me about him?"

Why didn't he understand? I was risking my career, possibly my life and the lives of my teammates trying to prove him innocent?

"Someone once said to me, 'I don't need protection'."

Oh, but he did. And I was trying. I was really trying here.

"I protected you, too." His voice sounded heavy now.

"When?"

"All along."

I wanted to say something, break the tension stretching between us, but I didn't. I held my tongue. As painful as this was it might be for the best. Slice me now, or later, what did it matter?

The roll of power between us roiled and spread.

I bit the inside fold of my lip till I tasted coppery blood and watched him wait for my words. The words I wouldn't say.

He folded his napkin and slid it onto the tablecloth. So freaking powerful to act so calm and controlled while sweat broke out on my skin, my heart kicking into high gear to hold against him.

Warlocks and witches. I should have listened to my first reaction to this man. He could destroy me like a gnat.

He stood. "When you're ready to deal with me as a woman, and not as a chess player, I'll be here. Until then—"

He scorched me with his look but didn't finish his sentence before he walked away.

Once he left the room the pressure popped, noise rushed back into the void, waiters glanced around as if wondering what happened.

I sucked air in ragged gulps, waiting for my nerves to settle, my heart to slow.

"Is there a problem, Miss?" a white jacketed waiter had materialized at my side.

Oh, yeah. A big problem and I'd blown handling it on so many levels.

CHAPTER 50

In the tour home late the next day, I stepped back from Franco, ignoring the clients and models circulating through the formal dining and living rooms. Would he take the bait I so juicily dangled before him? My plan was to roust Dominique while protecting as many people as I could.

Franco looked confused, then skeptical, with pinched lines between his brows. "You? An IRS agent?"

What? I didn't look brainy enough? "That's what I said."

"I didn't know the IRS had field agents." He pressed two fingers to his lips. Leave it to Frankie-O to latch onto the one technical glitch in my plan. The man must have been a flea in a past life; he so unerringly knew how to make me itch.

"That's why we're so effective." I was lying, but he didn't have to know that. By the time he realized he'd been used the tour would be over, Dominique would be arrested, and all would be well with the world again.

Almost.

I leaned closer. "I need your help here, Franco."

"Why my help?" His eyes narrowed.

Crud. The man hadn't backed away from good gossip and being the first-to-know since I'd joined the tour. Why now?

"Because you're closer to Dominique than anyone else on the tour." I lowered my voice to a conspiratorial whisper. "It'd make sense that you'd be the one to tell her what you've discovered."

"Not Bran?" A furrow joined his frown.

I released a huff of air. "I'm trying to keep this simple here, not complicate everything."

"And my telling Dominique that you're an IRS field agent investigating her does what?"

Where was a hot curling iron when I needed one?

"I told you. I can't blow my cover, but the rumor is she's meeting with someone here in D.C. to launder money."

Franco's brows vee'd so deep a slalom skier could have used the trench.

I continued, "I don't know if the rumor is true or not. But if it is true, and she knows she's being watched—"

"Then she won't meet with this person."

"Exactly." Or just the opposite, but Franco didn't need to know how devious undercover work could be. He was a civilian after all. A prick, but a civilian prick.

"And you want to protect Dominique because of—"

"Because of Bran." This part was only a half-lie. Exposing Dominique would save Bran, long term; short-term, it'd destroy the only family he had.

But Franco had to be given a reason that made sense, and if that required me to play caring lover, so be it. Two days ago it would have been bought without question. But now?

"But I thought you and Bran were on the outs?" Franco's face took on the highly expectant look I associated with him whenever gossip was to be consumed.

"We had a small misunderstanding." I avoided Franco's too penetrating gaze, while Bran's words echoed in my mind. *"You're using me."*

Here it was true. Not earlier, but here, yes.

"Look." I forced a shrug. "I came to you because I trusted you." Not as far as I could throw him, but he was a slender guy. "I thought you'd want to help Bran."

Finally, some real truth.

"And." The words gagged in my throat. "Because deep down I know you're a good guy and wouldn't want to see innocent people get hurt."

Something came and went in his gaze, before his usual cynical smile returned. "And what do I get out of this?"

Okay, this Franco I recognized.

I stepped closer. "You get to be right in the middle of all the action."

His grin notched up. The man positively buzzed. "The middle? Will I have to testify, because I don't want—"

"No testifying." This I could reassure him on. "Just between you and me."

"And Bran? Will he know?"

"Maybe later. After all is done and Dominique has been contained. But you know he's protective of his cousin and may want to jump in and save her from herself if he can."

There was that "p" word. Bran should have it made into his legal first name. Later I'd have to ask Fraulein Fassbinder if protectiveness was a trait of certain kinds of warlocks.

Franco nodded his head slowly. "I see. You're so right, Bran would save Dominique, no matter what the cost to him. So I *am* the only one that can help you."

Sad but true. "Yes," I kept my tone sincere even as I laid my next words on a little thickly. "The success of the mission is all up to you. I'm trusting you to get the job done."

"Then, I'll do it." He straightened his shoulders, resembling a banty-cock rooster heading toward the hen house.

"Good." *Take the win, Alex.* "Just let me know when you've shared the news."

"Because?"

I straightened until I towered over him, bringing home my point. "Because I want to know."

"Don't get your feathers ruffled." He shook his head. "I was only asking."

"Then we're clear?"

"Perfectly." He examined his nails. "But you didn't mention if I was to be paid for this or not?"

Good grief, the man was a mercenary prick.

"Think glory, action, power," I hummed, enunciating each word separately. "This is not about money, but about saving a good man—"

"Bran."

"Yes, Bran." I stumbled only a little over his name. "And about making sure Dominique doesn't hurt him anymore."

Franco's face turned hard and serious; the transformation was so dramatic, I stepped back, even as he asked, "Is

Dominique behind Sasha's death? Has your investigation uncovered anything about that?"

"No." Not yet, but we would. Not that Franco would ever be privy to that intel. "Sasha's death is unrelated to the IRS investigation as far as I know."

"Then why was she killed?"

"I don't know." I shook my head. "I really don't know."

"If I find out—"

The man really had taken the model's death personally. Or maybe it was his being framed for the murder that still rankled.

"Look, Franco, let's take this one step at a time. You talk to Dominique. We both protect Bran. Then we find out who killed Sasha. A deal?"

"A deal." Franco raised his chin—a warrior rooster. "I shall go find Dominique now."

Excellent. I smiled.

But Franco wasn't finished. "About Bran," he said.

Should have figured it was too easy.

"What about him?" My words sounded only slightly strained.

"He's hurting. I can see it." I pushed down the bile churning through my stomach as Franco continued. "For what it's worth, I believe he truly cares for you."

Great, more acid on the open wound.

"Thank you, Franco." I offered a weaker smile. "I appreciate that." *Like vinegar in a knife cut.*

"Good. It's important that you know."

"Dominique?"

"Yes." He nodded. "I go now."

I didn't release my breath until he disappeared from view.

Phase one complete. On to Phase two.

CHAPTER 51

"The toss away phone is being used near you," Kelly said.

The tour residence was nearly deserted, which was great timing. Everyone had headed to the Kennedy Center, prepping for the event in a few hours.

"You there Alex?" Kelly asked, still on the phone.

"Yeah."

"Problem?"

"No. Just a feeling." The worms in my gullet kind of feeling when something wasn't going right. I hadn't heard from Franco yet, but it made sense the little man had spoken to Dominique. The use of the throw away phones indicated that much. So what was happening and where?

Dominique most likely was somewhere in the rambling house. I glanced out the nearest window. The driveway area was empty except for a pair of security guards hired to patrol the grounds. Bran's way of making everyone feel safer.

Protector warlock.

Or Dominique's way to keeping control of this location. Which was it?

Since most of the tour needed to catch a taxi to get into town, the lack of vehicles didn't reveal a lot. But the quiet in the house did. I decided I'd do a quick look around. What could it hurt?

Then I heard the gunshot.

CHAPTER 52

At least it sounded like a muffled gunshot from one of the upper rooms. Backfire? Or was it nerves?

No one was moving or reacting. Not that there were a lot of bodies around the place.

I tried to cast a quick sensing spell to find out who was still in the house, but nothing happened. Absolutely nothing. I might not be a great witch, but even a novice could do a sensing spell so what was up?

I left the lower floor room for a quick walk about. It took only a few seconds for me to come upon two security guards at the bottom of the stairway, rough looking brutes who halted me before I showed them my badge as a tour member. My ring heated, alerting me to the fact they weren't human. Weres were my guess, but I didn't have a clue what kind. Since they weren't moving, and no other shots sounded, maybe I was making up things?

So what was going on?

"Hey, guys, hear anything out of the ordinary?" I asked the guards.

Glances zipped between them as scowls increased. That was the one thing you could count on with Weres, they all had anger management issues. Any perceived slight was an excuse to get pissed off or go into battle.

One mumbled. "No one's here. No noise."

Try again. I smiled, hoping it looked like a smile and not a grimace. Obviously these guys had been hired by Dragon Lady which is why they were lying. I glanced again at the stairway. Whatever I'd heard had been upstairs, so that's where I needed to go.

"Then it'll be okay to run upstairs?" Surprised how casual I could sound, but then I'd been raised around shifters. They made Weres seem like pussy cats.

"Why?" One guard growled, another clue he was hiding something.

"I left my hairdresser's tote in one of the upper rooms."

"I don't know if—"

"I'll be needing it later." I deepened my smile—the move worked for the models all the time.

One brute frowned at the other. Obviously quick thinking wasn't high on their employment requirements. Or that feminine smile thing really worked. Go figure.

"Make it fast," the other said.

"No problem." It was the truth. Earlier I'd made sure my silver valise had been brought into the house with the personal luggage, meaning it should be in one of the upper private rooms. One of which Dominique might be in, too, if she was here.

I headed up to the second floor, aware two sets of eyes watched my every move until I disappeared down the upstairs hallway. Weres didn't depend only on visual ability; they also were masters of scent. But around a corner and in a closed room there should be nothing to alert them that I wasn't where I should be.

A quick glance at the rooms indicated they were all empty. What now? Dominique's, Bran's, and the largest of the guest rooms were on the third floor.

Did I have time to keep hunting before the guards got restless? Didn't matter. There had been a sound above and to the rear of the house.

A servant's set of stairs at the end of one hallway ended the debate. A quick scout around and I'd have my answer.

I listened for footsteps as I climbed to the higher level— the goons moving around, or a hint that Dominique might be around, but so far the house had been eerily quiet.

With one foot into the third floor hallway I heard a voice. A muttered oath. A man's voice. Then a hard thump, followed by silence.

The noises came from behind a closed door, halfway down the shadowed hall.

Two options. Assume I could handle it, whatever *it* was, or sneak into one of the empty rooms, call for my team as backup and wait. But the team was at the Watergate looking at security issues and couldn't be here for at least forty minutes.

But if someone was in trouble, waiting wasn't an option. Besides, I was a Noziak. I'd grown up learning how to take care of myself, and that was before the agency training. Pitted against shifters since birth meant I wasn't afraid of much, but then my brothers had usually pulled their punches. Unless I got them angry and then I learned to duck and run. On the other hand, I wasn't stupid.

I decided to give a heads up to the team, in case I was making a big mistake; at least they'd know where to look for my body. Punching in a quick text message to Kelly, who'd be monitoring her phone, I turned off and pocketed my cell, swallowed deeply and headed down the hall as quietly as possible.

A different voice reached me. A woman's voice this time. Dominique.

Crap, that couldn't be good.

I paused, sucking in my breath, hearing the thrum of my heart beating faster.

"Don't do anything foolish," Dominique said, as a door squeaked open. "You'll live if you don't act stupidly."

I pressed against the nearest door jam, reaching for the door handle and turning just as high heels clicked two rooms over.

Nipping into the empty room I waited. The tat-a-tat echo of heels receded.

Dominique had left.

Sticking my head out to make sure, I scurried to the closed door.

It wasn't locked.

A good sign or? I pressed the door open slowly; more guards could be on the other side.

But they weren't. Someone else was.

"Bran?" He lay crumpled on the floor, motionless.

A quick glance registered two impressions. No guards and Franco tied to a chair, blood streaming down his right shoulder.

"Damn." I rushed to Bran first, feeling a pulse along his neck. Alive. Thank the Spirits. I whirled toward Franco whose eyes were rolling back in his head.

"What happened?" I demanded, keeping my voice low as I reached his chair. "Who-"

"Dom." It wasn't Franco answering, but Bran, shaking his head and rolling to his side. "She's coming back."

I was scouting for something to stop Franco's bleeding. I grabbed a sheet from a nearby bed, using my teeth to rip it, keeping one eye on Bran lurching groggily to his feet.

Franco groaned as I applied a wad of cloth to his shoulder and pressed hard.

"Help me," I directed Bran. "We've got to get this stopped. Can you heal him?"

Bran shook his head, which looked like it hurt like all get out. "Can't," he mumbled.

"Why not? You helped me." Did I have to spell it out to him—yacht, foredeck, his bringing me back from the dead, which is what Franco could be if we didn't get help.

"I placed an anti-magic ward around the house. No magic can be used inside or out."

No wonder my casting spell hadn't worked. My hands actually shook I was so angry. "Why'd you do a stupid thing like—"

"He did it for me, my dear," Dominique's voice slapped against me like a wet towel on bare skin.

I kept my fingers pressed against the bleeding wound but shifted my gaze.

Yup, there was Dominique, looking very un-Dominique-like.

CHAPTER 53

So this was what a Grimple looked like; three-headed, two heads looking very reptilian while the third head looked like Dominique's human head only on a stick, a long, sinuous neck that made watching her bobbing heads hard. Her body looked like a cross between a crocodile and a boar. The room reeked of cinnamon and sandalwood as her red-rimmed eyes glared.

Not a good look for her at all.

The only human looking part of her besides that talking head was her left hand, very regal, cool, collected, and deadly with her fingers wrapped around a snub-nosed revolver. A revolver pointed right at me.

Funny, I figured the Dragon Lady for a more elegant weapon. Or a more elegant "otherness." Crap, if I looked like her in my natural state I'd be psycho, too. Which was just my mind babbling as I tried to figure out what to do.

"Dom." Bran stood now, looking as stable as a wheat stalk in a wind storm. "Is that you?"

Okay, good news. Bran wasn't used to seeing his cousin in her Grimple form, which meant he was probably unaware of how dangerous she really was.

"Poor Bran," Dominique cooed. "Having a really bad day."

Ouch. The woman did vicious very well.

I ignored Dominique; not necessarily a wise move, but a necessary one if I was going to get Franco's wound stabilized.

"Bran, I need your help." His moving to my side took care of two issues, creating distance between him and Dominique and helping me save Franco's life. If I could. "Tie this cloth tight while I keep the pressure on."

"Don't bother, he'll be dead before you can get help," Dominique said from the doorway, her form morphing back into her human-like persona, which was easier on the eyes, but no less deadly. Especially with the smug smirk to her lips. She waved in one of the goons from the stairwell. He was half-changed, a natural reaction to the fear or fight response. I swore I could see long fangs erupting from his mouth.

What was he? A warthog Were?

And why could these guys shift but magic not be employed?

"I'm impressed, hairdresser," Dominique purred, "You don't seem surprised."

Would keeping her engaged buy me some time to create a survival plan? Or cause her to lash out—kill simply for the sake of killing? Why didn't we have more information on Grimples?

"Elmer, search her for a weapon," Dominique ordered as if she were ordering take out. "Take any phones or electronics."

Elmer? Who called a thug Elmer? Man must have compensation issues. A warthog Were named Elmer.

He also had hands that belonged on a blacksmith. His pat down was brief but thorough, and rough, especially since I kept my own hands tight against Franco's shoulder.

In seconds my cell phone was pocketed, as well as my ring and my ankle anathema. What damage did they think I could do with a ring? Plenty, with the way I was feeling right then.

Bran stepped closer to me, replacing my hands with his; a good idea as he could apply pressure over a broader area. Up close I could see the bruise darkening his temple. He'd been hit with a vengeance.

"You won't get away with this," I said as I slid behind Franco, pulling my makeshift tourniquet tight.

"Why? Because you're IRS?" The woman laughed, a sound echoing through the empty mansion. "Don't be so naive. By the time anyone finds you, I'll be long gone, enjoying the fruits of my labors."

"You mean the synthetic drug?"

That little tidbit deflated the other woman's sails and for a second I thought she was going to morph again as her eyes reddened and her face elongated. I swore I could hear her hiss as she demanded, "What do you know about the drug?" The gun quivered in the manicured hand.

"I know everything."

"What drug?" Bran cast glances between his cousin and me, as if he didn't know who was scarier. I wanted to tell him, welcome to my world, but I needed all my focus to keep Franco alive and Dominique engaged.

"The drug that enabled your dear cousin here to stage the thefts." I answered his question even as I hated slamming Bran with the news this way, but then again, I wasn't the one setting the scene. "A drug that forced unsuspecting victims to act against their will."

I turned to Dominique, going for broke. "Weren't you powerful enough as you are? Or are you compensating for being such a butt ugly creature?"

"My, my, my, what a busy little IRS agent you've been, if that's what you really are." She wasn't acting the way I expected, but maybe Grimples thrived on confrontation. "And here I thought only our Franco was a government mole."

Franco?

I glanced at Bran, but it was Dominique who answered my unspoken question. "Oh, how droll. Secrets between lovers. You mean Bran didn't share the scintillating fact that Franco here is a British agent?"

I looked Bran in the eye as he said, "MI-6."

The prick was British Intelligence? No way. No freaking way.

I grappled with the news. Bran knew. Two undercover agents. Two government investigations. No wonder this whole mission had been like waltzing through landmines. And I'll-protect-you-Bran knew all along.

Served me right for trusting a warlock.

I glanced at Dominique, my brain scrambling, my words lethally cold. "You know what this means?"

"That it'll bring me immense pleasure to silence you both?"

"No. That not one, but two governments will be on your tail if anything happens to either of us. And at least one of those agencies will know to look for you as human and Grimple."

"And that's supposed to worry me?" The woman smiled her snake-smile. "Humans can be so droll. And foolish. Even human witches who get in way over their heads."

She knew? Then I caught where her gaze landed. On Bran.

Dominique laughed, a short barking sound etched by acid. "You really did not think my cousin could hide anything from me, now did you?"

I refused to look at Bran, refused to feel the disappointment welling up deep inside. All the time he'd been sharing with his cousin what I shared with him. Could I have been a bigger fool?"

That laugh came again. "Oh, don't be too hard on him, darling; he had little choice. Did you Bran?"

What the—?

"Enough, Dominique. You've won." Bran kept his hands pressed against Franco's shoulder but turned his head to pin his cousin with a look so lethal I was surprised it didn't singe her. "You've destroyed my world. Used me. Used my powers. Now leave."

Dominique shrugged.

"No, wait!" I shouted, pushing aside Bran's words to deal with later. Right now I needed some answers.

"You wish to beg for your life, puny witch?"

Maybe it was a good thing Bran had been forced to ward the house against magic because right then I would have ignored the promise to my father and pulverized the bitch.

But if she was gone, so was the chance to find Van.

I straightened. "Tell me about Vaverek," I demanded, catching Bran's stilling beside me. So he did know something and had kept that hidden from me, too. Had there been anything honest between us?

"So you know about Vaverek," Dominique purred, the low rumble of a tiger ready to pounce.

Time to go for broke. "Yes. And the Seekers, too."

Her eyes widened, just a fraction, but enough for me to notice. "If you know about them then you know you are doomed."

And that meant what?

As if reading my thoughts she continued. "All humans are doomed." Her smiled ratcheted up in a gloating, smug way.

"Does Vaverek have my brother?" I asked, holding my breath, knowing I was pushing things but it wasn't like I had a lot to lose.

"You mean your shifter brother?" she said, all deadly sweet.

And my heart plummeted. All this time she'd known. Here I'd been pussy footing around playing agent for the IR team. I'd failed my brother.

"You promised you would not hurt him," Bran interjected, keeping his gaze averted, stomping on what was left of my emotions. He'd lied to me, even as he threw it in my face that I was using him.

I sucked at being an agent. At being a witch. At being a sister.

"I said what you needed to hear, dear cousin," Dominique's tone was dry and droll. "If I hadn't promised, would you have created the non-magic zone around the house?"

At Bran's dark look, she added, "No, I didn't think so. Needs must, darling." She paused and then continued. "Without the non-magic zone your little witch here might have been a problem, but as is, she's as powerless as you."

Dragon Lady had it all figured out and wrapped up tight.

"Tell me about Van?" I heard the begging in my voice and didn't really give a rat's ass. "Is he alive?"

"Oh, yes, darling." Dominique's smile deepened. "He's too useful to kill. For now."

Truth? Or more cruelty? I bet on the later.

"Where is he then?" I prodded. "There's no way I'm a threat to you. I'm trapped. You have all the cards." Maybe, just maybe, she'd let something slip that I could use to find Van. And if I survived, I could do something.

"That would make things too easy for you," she laughed. I so was going to take her down if for no other reason than to stop that laugh. "But I will give you an itsy bitsy clue. Just to show you I'm not without a heart."

Too late for me to believe that. "Where?" I growled the single word.

"Why, in Paris. The city of love and light and soon to be darkness." She turned to Bran. "Now I must leave, my poppets. Things to do, lives to take, a world to conquer."

"You can run, but you can't hide." But Dominique wasn't buying the threat. That's okay, neither was I. She'd gotten away with so much over the last year, why should she be worried now? Whatever she was going to do was about to happen and there wasn't a damn thing I could do about it unless I found a way to stop her.

Dominique nodded to her hired guard. The one who showed no signs of changing into his Were persona though I sensed he could if he wanted or needed to. This one had more control than pig-guy Elmer. "Tie them up."

"No, wait." I stepped away from Franco; tied up the man would die, but if I could remain free we stood a chance. A slim one. "What kind of threat are we here?" I glanced around, goading Dominique with my tone. "You've got armed guards. We'll be in a locked room. What possible threat could we be unless—"

"Unless what?"

"You're afraid of us." I leveled a big, cat-eating grin in her direction. Human to predator. Some species would take the taunt as a reason to attack, but who knew with a Grimple. "Afraid of me in particular? Which I can understand since I'm—"

"Nothing." Dominique's tone could have frozen nose hairs. She glanced at her Rolex. "I'm late." She eyed me, then Bran still busy with Franco. "Elmer, leave them; they aren't worth tying up and I'll be back shortly."

She glanced at me, inhaled a deep breath and then blew it out, fanning a thick, dark fog.

Before I could pat myself on the back for giving us a chance Dominique's breath hit me; like deadly swamp gas the smell came first.

Then the darkness.

CHAPTER 54

Stygian shadows surrounded me, thick, inky, cold darkness. I rocked within it, tossing, struggling against a force pressing me down. Where was I? Bran? Where was he? A scream scrambled out of my raw throat.

"Wake up, Alex," a voice growled next to me. A violent voice.

My eye lids peeled open. I was flat on my back, with Bran looming over me. Warlock Bran, face taunt, eyes wild, his hair looking like he'd been dragging fingers through it. He shook me again, his hands gripping my shoulders so tight they bruised.

I pushed against him, rolling to my side, retching. Nothing came up, but still I gagged, until Bran's hand appeared beside me, holding a glass of water.

The first sip gave me hope that I'd live. The second made me wonder if living was a good idea. Every muscle in my body ached as if sucked dry. I croaked, "She gone?"

"Yes."

"What happened?" I shook my head to clear the fog in it, then wished I hadn't. Holy mother of sinners, whatever Dominique blew, it was near-lethal.

"Hydrogen sulfide," Bran said.

I searched for lessons from my first witch instructor. "So it was sewer gas."

Bran's voice deepened. "Yes. Toxic with long-term exposure, but in concentrated doses even a short term exposure can cause unconsciousness."

Like I didn't know that now.

"I don't think she really wanted to kill us," he added, "Or she'd have just shot us."

When was he going to get a clue his cousin did not need his protection? Dollars to donuts I bet she expected her breath to kill us. But we weren't dead. Not yet.

I rolled to my knees, shaking off Bran's helping hand as I pulled myself to a wobbly half-standing position, my palms braced against my legs until I was sure I didn't topple. "How much time—"

"Ten minutes. Not much more," Bran finished, standing next to me.

Good. She hadn't had much of a lead. I turned to Franco, his head lolling on his chest, his color pale, but he was breathing. "Looks like the bullet went clear through, with no arteries hit."

"This is good news?" Frustration coated Bran's every syllable.

"Yeah. An artery would mean death in minutes."

"So now the man gets to bleed to death slowly?"

"Not if I can help it." We weren't arguing about Franco, but about Dom, and we both knew it.

Bran broke the impasse first. "I never meant this to go this far . . ."

That had me straightening my spine. "How far did you expect then?" My voice sounded raw and hoarse. The gas, or the anger, or both roughening it. "You've lied to me all along. You knew what she was and protected her."

"She's my cousin, Alex. The only family I have. She protected me a child and I protected her. It's what families do."

And just like that the light bulb went off. No wonder he and I were on opposite sides. It wasn't because he was a warlock and I was a witch, though that didn't help. Or he a suspect and me an investigator. No, it was because we both wanted the same thing, to protect someone we loved, to protect our blood family. But his protecting Dom put Van at risk and my finding Van put Dom at risk. No wonder there was no middle ground.

Damn, I should have seen this earlier. Too bad knowing didn't lessen the pain of his betrayal.

Arrogance coated his words as he spoke again, "I've been trying to save you from Dom by getting you out of the away."

I snorted. "Yeah, right."

"Believe what you will, Dom has not always acted this way."

"You mean stealing, kidnapping, killing?" Yeah, I sounded bitter because I was. He'd been protecting a monster who had my brother and now that monster was loose on the world. That was pissing me off.

"Forget your cousin, for a second." I staggered toward Franco. "Help me with him."

"I don't have my ability to heal." His tone sounded as bitter as mine.

"Got that, the whole no magic thing. Help me untie him."

"Why?"

"He's a shifter." I was tugging at the ropes around Franco's hands, tied tighter than a piggin' string in a calf roping rodeo. "The Were started to shift, which means some kinds of magic are immune to your ward. To shift is normal to those born to it, so might avoid the definition of magic." I pointed out. "Maybe if we get Franco loose he can shift and heal himself."

Bran didn't ask any more questions as he hip-pushed me away and went to work on the wrist knots. He was right, I was making a mash of it. I moved to Franco's side, noting the sweat beading his skin. We didn't have much time.

"He's an MI-6 agent. Why didn't you tell me?" I said, mostly to focus on something other than the blood saturating Franco's shirt.

"It was his secret to share, not mine."

"Yet you told your cousin I was a witch."

"She figured it out on her own." Bran's attention was one hundred percent focused on what he was doing, until he speared me a dark-eyed glance and added, "I never told her you were an agent. Nor did I tell Franco."

So he drew the line somewhere. Bully for him.

He gave a last tug, probably not aware he was mumbling a useless release spell aloud, but the ropes parted and Franco slumped forward. I caught him as he slid from the chair to a heap on the floor.

"Franco." I shook him, not hard, but enough to break through to him. "You need to shift."

"Not sa..." he whispered.

"You're among friends," I lied, counting myself and not so sure anymore about Bran. "You have to shift or you'll die."

Seconds ticked past as he looked paler and paler.

I cut a glance toward Bran. "If he dies, it will be your fault."

"And you didn't tell him you were an IRS agent and to share that tidbit with Dom?"

Damn and double damn. He was right. I sent Franco in to deal with a Grimple. Worse, I'd thought he was a civilian, which made him as vulnerable as anyone could be. "I screwed up." I mumbled, holding Franco tighter.

"Both of us made unwise choices."

Only Bran could sound like a French BBC announcer when offering a flag of truce.

I turned my attention back to Franco. "Come on, Frank, do your thing. Show me what kind of shifter you are."

Nothing.

"How did you know he was a shifter?" Bran asked, standing over my shoulder.

"A good guess."

"Because you have one in the family?"

"No." I glanced over my shoulder at him. "Because my father and all my brothers are shifters."

That had his brow quirking. "And you're not?"

"I took after my mother." And father, but no need to bring the shaman element into the mix, I was a more inept shaman than I was a witch. Unless?

"What is it?" Bran asked, as if sensing a change in me.

"You've blocked magic, but I might have something else."

"What?"

"Just wait. Can you find a drum or something to drum?"

Bless his black warlock soul he didn't hesitate. Instead he looked around, disappeared for a few seconds and returned with a thick book and a full toothpaste tube from the bathroom. "Rough, but they'll do."

I sat flat legged on the floor, Franco's head resting in my lap. I smeared some blood from his wound over my fingers and drew a crude pentacle on my left palm. Then I closed my eyes. I had no idea if what I was about to do would work or not, but I did know that if I didn't try something, Franco would surely die.

"Beat the drum in slow measured beats," I directed Bran, otherwise trying to ignore him. He and his jagged energy messed with me on so many levels and I couldn't afford that now.

Stilling myself, I raised my hands above Franco and murmured the first ritual words.

"Come death, advise me."

Bran gripped my shoulder, startling me.

"Stop, I have to do this."

"Do what exactly?"

"I'm seeking the return of Franco's soul."

"I'm not a fool, Alex, even though I've acted the part. How are you going to claim Franco's soul?"

I closed my eyes before answering. "I'll travel to the soulless void."

That was the theory. I'd never done this but had heard it could be done.

Bran tightened his grip until I could feel his fingers meet bone, his voice deepened. "I won't let you die."

"I don't plan to die. But I must travel to death's side to convince Franco that his time has not yet come."

"And if you can't come back?"

I swallowed. Deeply. "Then I die."

CHAPTER 55

Breathe by breath. Word by word. Beat by beat, my present world faded as my heart slowed, my breathing matching its pace.

Earth be found
Power be bound
Stall Nature's course
Earth, dust, bone
Bind to me
Spirits Realm welcome me
Spirits Realm call me forth

The cold came first. Bone rattling, skin dimpling, breath-lanced cold. If I opened my eyes I'd expect to see frost coating me.

Instead I waited, listening to the breeze stirring around me. Like an arctic gale it started small then gained in strength. A banshee's blood call, seeking spirits, isolating souls.

Only when the wind whipped against me did I dare open my eyes to a half-lit emptiness. The Spirits' waiting grounds. The resting point between the newly dead, those dying, and those trapped between worlds. Spend more than a few moments here and you became one of the In-Between ones.

The clock was ticking.

But where was Franco?

The emptiness seemed a blank canvas until I looked closer, so close a headache started thrumming behind my eyeballs. What looked like fog was in fact thousands if not hundreds of thousands of churning wraiths, some almost human looking, others mere wisps.

I could hear Bran's faint drumming, replacing my heartbeat. If he stopped, or faltered, I was gone.

How was I going to find Franco in this mess?

I stumbled to my feet, loathe to break the eerie silence, except for the wind. But the seconds ticked by and I had to do something.

"Franco. I seek the spirit of Franco."

Damn, I didn't think to find out his last name, or even if Franco was his real name. And Ling Mai trusted me to come into my powers. If she could only see me now.

"Franco? Come to me Franco?"

After my mother abandoned me I learned about loneliness. I felt it to my core now.

"Franco, I'm not leaving without you," I shouted as loud as I could, stirring the spirits nearest me like wind churning smoke. "Come out, you half-pint bastard. You'll not die on my watch."

"Who do you seek, sister?" A dark spirit floated near me, more voice than shape. A coldness, chilling me. Ally or enemy?

"Who are you?" I didn't have time to sweat the small stuff, but something about the voice sounded familiar.

"I served your master, witch."

So the wraith knew of me. A scary thought. The drum echoed in my awareness.

"I'm looking for a man named Franco. Not tall." I raised my hand to just above my head. "A recent arrival, hovering between the worlds. You've seen him?"

"I can find him."

I heard a but in the voice. There was always a catch. "For a price?" I asked, wondering how far I'd go to save Franco's life. It was because of my actions that Franco was even here; I guess my answer was clear. As far as it took.

"You are wise beyond your years," the voice murmured, not taking the sting out of my cynicism.

"Tell me what you want?" Tick. Tock.

"A favor."

What kind of candy-assed price was that? Talk about your open-ended sinkhole. "What kind of favor we talking here?" My Noziak skepticism was on high-alert.

"Nothing you will not be able to do," came the response.

The guy must have been a politician in his past life, a master of saying nothing while asking for everything in return. Criminy.

"Do you agree?"

"I don't have much choice."

"As I said, wise beyond your years."

I didn't like it, but I needed to get Franco and get out of here. "I'll owe you a favor, something that I will be able to do. Now bring Franco to me."

"My pleasure."

Damn if the wraith wasn't true to his word. Within seventeen seconds, I counted every one of them, a shell-shocked Franco appeared. He was a tamped down version of his usually cocky, in-your-face self, but it was Franco. If he wasn't so insubstantial I'd have hugged him, probably sending both of us straight to hell from the shock.

"Thank you." I nodded to the spirit. Last thing I wanted was a pissed off spirit.

"Remember, you owe me."

Now why did that sound like a threat? Probably because it was.

"Noziaks don't forget our promises."

"Till later then, sister." The wraith dissipated, which should have made me feel better. There wasn't time for that as I could hear the rough drum Bran was hitting grow fainter and fainter.

"Follow me," I said to Franco, "and do exactly what I tell you to do."

"Why?"

Seriously? I risk dying for this guy and he was copping an attitude. "Because if you don't I'll dress your corpse in a pink tutu, have it embalmed, and have it made into a freestanding light in my living room."

I knew I got through to him when he crinkled up his nose in disgust.

"Ready?" It was now or never. "Dad, if you can hear me, please help me." I meant every word. Slowing time and dying was one thing. Reversing the process was a whole different problem.

I started the chant, my voice a lot calmer than my thoughts.

Bound, found, and binding
Let us see the sight
Let us hear the sound
Spirit lost, now is found
Return us hence.
To our earthly realm.

Nothing happened.

CHAPTER 56

I swallowed the fear choking me and repeated the spell. The third time I knew it wasn't working.

I glanced at Franco, seeing in the whites of his eyes the same terror racing through me. We were going to be trapped between worlds. Neither alive, nor ever dead.

What now?

Think. If reversing a seeking for someone lost summons didn't work, what would?

My heart sped up, pounding against my chest, echoing the drum growing quieter and quieter. I wanted to call Bran. I didn't want things to end between us like this: angry, untrusting, unresolved.

That was it. Call to Bran. A soulmate seeking a warlock spell.

I was desperate.

Closing my eyes again I inhaled slowly, framing an image of Bran behind my closed lids. His darkness, the quirk of his brows, the flash of those Celtic blue eyes, the protection he spread over those around me. Over me. My body warmed, a rush of security, of knowingness. Our relationship was complicated and screwed up, but there was something there. Something that deserved a chance. Only then did I start the chant.

Light to darkness. Spirit to earth.
Witch to warlock.
I seek thee. I summon thee.
Bring me to your side.

A bolt of lightning slashed. I chanted louder.

Bound together dark and day.
Time forward meet time reversed.
I seek thee. I summon thee. Bring
me. Bring us to your side.

A whirlpool started, the sucking sound reaching me before the motion.

"Hang on," I screamed, which was pointless. There was nothing to hang onto as Franco and I spun faster and faster. Freefalling through whiteness until we slammed into something solid.

"Damn it, Alex, don't ever do that again," Bran shouted at me.

We'd made it.

Now what?

CHAPTER 57

Peeling my eyes open I wasn't surprised to see Bran scowling; it was a look he wore well and often around me; but I was surprised to see a poodle sitting across from me and staring, as if waiting for me to get with the program. The same poodle I'd seen on the yacht and earlier at the chateau.

"Franco? Is that you?"

A yelp answered me.

"You're a poodle?"

That earned a classic Franco sniff of disdain, sounding the same from the poodle as it did the man, and an upturned nose.

The good news? The bloody area around the poodle's shoulder was already receding, so both man and dog were healing.

Thank the Spirits.

I felt like I'd been tumbled in an industrial dryer and spat out, but my aches and pains would have to wait. We had work to do.

"We have to get out of here. Stop Dominique before she goes any further."

"I don't know if I'll regain enough magic for a bit to stop her. Can you?" Bran asked, a very legitimate question. "Given what she is?"

"I don't know, but she's not my first worry. Getting out of here is."

"Why could you use magic to retrieve Franco?" Bran eyed me.

"Shamanism isn't the same magic as witches and warlocks use," I said, getting my bearings. "I framed my travel as a spell but that was just a formality. Shamanism is communication with the spirits. The best shamans can travel between realms as easily as you and I travel in a car."

"So how shall we leave here with Weres guarding the hallway and no magic?" Bran asked.

That was why I dug hanging around with guys. Focus on the solution to the problem and no whining.

I glanced around the room. It was the largest on the floor with a set of French doors leading to a small balcony. I crossed over and looked out. "Too high to climb down. Nothing to break a fall if we jumped. Not even Franco could do it. And I count three more goons patrolling the driveway." Five to two. Not great but not fatal. Maybe.

I also noticed that Dominique's car was gone. I so wasn't ready to face her again, especially with no magic abilities, but I also knew that meant she was free to wreak havoc.

I looked at Bran. Really looked and asked, "Did your cousin's breath cause you to black out?"

"Yes." His face was creased in confusion. "But not for long. Maybe five minutes. It seemed to hit you harder."

Yeah, but why? Then the light bulb went off. Bran's genetic makeup, his warlock elements, probably negated what Dominique could do to him, or at least what her breath could do. If we got out of here, and confronted his cousin again, I might need to use Bran.

One battle at a time.

"No landline in here." I shifted the conversation from who or what Dominique was to how we could escape.

Bran followed my thought process. "Dom took my cell as well as Franco's."

"Figured that." The IR team might be on their way based on my text message to Kelly, but they might not arrive in enough time. They'd also be walking into trouble they weren't expecting if all the goon guards were Weres or shifters, which I guessed they would be.

I stepped closer to the door. It looked like it had been built in the middle ages to withstand a castle siege. Thick wood, reinforced fittings, and the lock was solid. No ramming this puppy with a well-placed shoulder or kick.

"If I only had—" I glanced around the room again, smiling when I spied a familiar tote.

Bran asked. "What are you—"

"This." I grabbed my hairdresser's case.

"What does—"

"Watch." I opened the top latch and rummaged through the contents. "Here." I held out a jar of styling gel. "You'll need to spread this on the floor in front of the door. About a four foot arc from where the door would be standing half open, to three feet into the room."

"But—"

"Trust me." We both paused, eyeing each other. How many times had we shared that same phrase? And how many times had we failed?

"So be it." Bran grabbed the jar.

Good. We didn't have a lot of time. Franco barked as if to reinforce the urgency.

I dove back into the tote, coming up with two cans of hairspray, some hair dye, styling mud, and cotton batting used to keep dye off a client's skin. Not the traditional battle strategy when fighting preternaturals, but then I wasn't your traditional preternatural warrior without my magic. I had to use what I had.

"What is this stuff?" Bran was spreading the gel in a thin layer across the hard wood floor. "And how much do I use?"

"Use it all. The more the better." I focused on reading the labels on the goods in my hands. "The gel's used to spike hair, but it's also slicker than snot on a glass door knob."

He glanced over his shoulder at me. "It's—never mind."

Different worlds.

I eyed the adjacent bathroom. If what I needed was in there I was in luck. If not—a quick look at Bran spurred me to action.

"Yes," I gave a quiet shout as I dug beneath the fancy marble sink. "Gotcha."

Bran appeared in the doorway, holding up his goo-rimmed hands. "Done. What now?"

"Wash your hands." I brushed past him. "You won't want the gel to get in the way of grabbing a bad guy or his weapon." I didn't mention that the bad guy would be hard enough to catch as it was, given they'd most likely shift as soon as I set off my little surprise. "And stay off that section of floor." I headed to the far side of the room. "And stay as far away from me as possible."

"I've been trying."

His bitter words broke my concentration. I sucked in the regret before giving him a level glance and turning my back to him and Franco. "I mean it. I'm making a bomb. A very unstable, very volatile bomb that stands just as large a chance of blowing us up as blowing up the door."

"Then don't—"

"We have no choice." I kept my attention on the glass hair dye beaker, the hydrogen peroxide, and the nail polish remover spread on the bedside table before me. "Now be silent. I have to get the chemical ratios figured as close as possible since I'm not using them in their pure form."

"Which means?"

"Which means nail polish remover has additives which make it impure. It's not a hundred percent acetone, which works best."

"They teach you this at spy school?"

I looked up. "Nah. My brothers taught me this at home when they found out about the cool chemicals I got to work with in the salon."

"Dangerous siblings."

"Yeah." I grinned. He didn't know the half of it. Then I sobered as I realized I might never see my brothers again. And Van would die. Regret damned near choked me before I shifted my focus back to my task.

"Anything for me to be doing?" Bran asked as I was calculating the percent of sulfuric acid in the drain opener I'd found in the bathroom. "Find some matches."

My hand trembled as I slowly poured the acetone into the peroxide. "Five times more peroxide than acetone." I inhaled once the two ingredients were mixed, but not deep breaths.

This mixture made Dom's swamp breath a fresh breeze in comparison.

The conditions were not optimal. Nor were the time frames. Cooling the mixture made for a better explosive, but I didn't have a refrigerator, a Celsius thermometer, or the time. It was lucky the guards hadn't heard us moving around and investigated. The doors and walls were thick but not that thick for Were ears. So maybe they were just lazy, thinking lowly humans were a non-threat. Their first mistake, but not their last.

"How's Frank doing?" I asked as I grabbed the drain cleaner and the beaker and moved toward the door.

Franco barked in response. I guess that meant okay in doggy-speak.

I carefully stepped in the area Bran had not gelled. Last thing I needed to do was slip and blow us all to smithereens.

"Bran, grab Frank and haul him as far from the door as possible."

"It's not worth your getting killed," Bran's tone razored across me.

"Saving a life is worth it." I set the beaker down, placing the drain cleaner nearby as I spun a length of cotton through my fingers. When it resembled a long, thick fuse I grabbed a plastic stir stick and pushed the cotton into the combination mixture. The stick started to dissolve immediately, but I only needed it to last long enough to fish the cotton out, leaving a tail in the mixture, and a tail over the side of the beaker.

"We're ready." Bran announced quietly from his side of the room over Franco's low growls. "What now?"

"Check the guards out front of the house. See if more are there or if they've moved."

He crossed to the window without comment. The next part was tricky. The drain cleaner was only one element of the final combination, the other part, the booster charge, was plain old ammonium nitrate, an everyday hair dye ingredient.

A three to one mixture of the acetone peroxide to the ammonium nitrate would work best, but desperate times called for risks.

"You all right there?" Bran asked. For a few seconds I'd actually forgotten about him. Maybe dangerous explosives use had good side benefits.

Sick woman.

"I'm okay. What's the status on the guards?"

"Only two in sight. Front door and the far eastern edge of the driveway."

Which might mean there were at least three guards inside. Or more.

Lord, I did love a challenge. Rising from my crouched position I gingerly stepped back, not breathing until I was several feet from the door.

Bran joined me, his shoulder brushing mine. Enough to feel like I wasn't alone. "What now?" he asked.

I shook my head. "Now we pray." I pushed him toward Franco. "I want you there. With this." I grabbed an aerosol can and shoved it in his hands.

"Hairspray?"

"Think of it as mace." He needed to trust me to make the next few minutes work. "When I blow the door there's going to be a lot of smoke and possible flames."

"If you don't blow yourself up."

"There is that. But it's not on my agenda."

"So the door blows. What next?"

"Depending on how close the goons are to the door, one or both may be disabled when it blows." Depending on what the guards were. All Weres? Or something else? Demons would be a bitch, they'd love a little smoke and flames.

"And if not?"

"More likely scenario is that they'll be surprised, then come rushing in with guns drawn."

Bran grinned, a look that had my breath hitching. If I died in the next few moments it was the image of him I'd want to take with me.

His grin deepened as did the crack in my heart. "When they rush inside they'll hit the gel slick."

"Ass over teakettle." Even a Were could stumble and fall. Problem was they wouldn't stay down for long.

"Another family lesson?"

"Yup." I gave him a grin. No need to spell out the risks: the bomb going haywire, smoke being produced but no damage, the gel not working. The list went on and on.

"So let's say one, possibly two come sliding through the door?" Bran was playing devil's advocate now; he wasn't a successful entrepreneur without thinking through all angles of a plan. "What then?"

"I'll be stationed over there." I nodded toward the door's far side. "You'll be on this side. One or both of us will disable anyone not taken down by the bomb or gel."

"With hairspray?"

"Think mace. We don't need to kill the guards." I lied, which was becoming very habit forming. Weres or shifters needed to be killed to be neutralized. One step at a time.

I continued, "We just disarm them long enough to get Franco out of here and one of us to a phone to dial for help."

"Got it. It's one hell of a plan." He shook his head, his features stark. "What are our chances?"

Rather than answer him directly, I grabbed my own hairspray and the matches Bran had found. His can would serve as mace. Mine as a flamethrower.

"Let's not calculate the odds," I said, the pump of adrenaline zipping through my system. "Let's just do it."

"That bad." He shrugged. "But all three of us are coming out of this alive. Got it?"

"Got it."

I moved to a strategic location to create a pincher movement once the door blew. If my homemade explosive worked.

A big if.

CHAPTER 58

The room still and quiet, I squeezed my eyes half-closed as I lit the match and threw it toward the cotton fuse.

It missed, sputtered, and went dead.

I'd have to get closer.

"Get back," Bran rumbled as I stepped nearer the door.

No choice.

I lit another match, holding my breath as the flame hissed. I tossed it gently, thinking of horseshoes as the small wooden stick arced then dropped short.

My brothers would have been hooting and hollering at my missed aim.

"Of all the—" I lit a third match, leaning forward until I was less than an arm's length from the glass beaker.

"Damn it, Alex, don't—"

I ignored him, sucking in a breath as I edged the small flaming torch forward.

"No—" The last of Bran's words evaporated in a cloud of smoke and heat, blowing me backwards and slamming me on my butt, my ears ringing.

Now this my brothers would have approved of. As the smoke cleared the door hung drunkenly on its hinges, a glimpse of the hallway visible in the gaping hole, a groan escaping from the other side.

No time to admire my handiwork. One quick glance at Bran reassured me he was still on his feet as I scrambled to mine. My hairspray in one hand I aimed it toward the fire sprinkler in the ceiling above me, pressed the nozzle, and when a stream of fine mist shot forward, lit my last match.

A ball of flame danced toward the ceiling. A mist of water spray erupted as alarm bells jangled.

Between the fire alarm screaming and my ears still buzzing from the blast I couldn't hear Bran until he stepped next to me.

"Notifying the local fire station?" he shouted close enough his shoulder brushed mine, water darkening his hair and plastering his shirt to his skin. Damn, he looked yum-yum sexy even in a crisis.

"That's the plan." I wiped water from my eyes and stepped back, counting aloud.

"One."

The groan on the far side of the door had been joined by oaths.

"Two."

A booted foot pounded against the remainder of the door.

"Three."

Two armed brutes kicked through what was left of the door, their soles hitting the gel at the same time. One was warthog Elmer. The other morphing into an ape form.

Feet went flying as did guns. Pop. Pop. Pop.

Plaster from the ceiling rained down on us.

Heavy bodies smashed against the floor. Bam.

"Get the—" I didn't have to say more as Bran grabbed the nearest ape-guard by the front of what was left of his shirt and delivered a sweet blow to the jaw. Ape man slumped, having never fully shifted. Thank heavens, or we'd be in deep trouble. Bran seized the goon's fallen Glock.

One had to love a resourceful man when the chips were down.

The third guard jumped over his fallen comrades, landing him within inches of me, gun hand extended, rage coating his face. A face morphing into a hyena. Ugh!

I thrust my palm out, catching him full in his half-human, half-animal face and crushing soft nose cartilage. My knee followed in an upward arc, catching him square in the family jewels.

The man caved, blood spattering from his nose, his groans muffled beneath hands clutching both head and mid-body.

Bran shook his head and arched a brow. "Remind me not to get on your wrong side."

"Too late."

I grabbed the guard's gun. Human or not I drew a line at shooting unconscious beings, hoping that decision didn't come back to bite me. "We've got to get out of here."

"Go ahead. Get to a phone." Alpha male Bran was back. Always the protector. Franco already had jumped through the doorway and was pattering down the hall. No doubt once he returned to his human form we'd hear all about how he led the charge.

I checked the gun for ammo. Full. "Take the second gun with you and don't hesitate to use it."

Bran didn't answer as he slipped the second weapon into his hand, holding it like he knew how to use it.

I jumped over the third guard rolling on the floor, the other two were out; one by Bran's blow, the other by the force of his head hitting the floor. There wasn't time to bind them, not with magic but with rope, as Dominique should have done to Bran and me. Besides, even if we did tie them up, once they shifted the binds would no longer hold.

Second mistake of the day, lady. First mistake was shooting Franco.

Sliding into the hallway I ignored the main staircase. The outside guards should be appearing any second. The back staircase was safest.

Gun drawn, safety off, I heard Bran breathing behind me.

Good. If he followed in my wake, I could clear a path ahead of him. His safety mattered to me, for reasons I didn't have time to explore.

His footsteps echoing mine as I cat-walked down the stairs, I paused at the second floor landing to check that all was clear.

It was, but no telling how long that would last.

Just as we crossed the last flight of stairs, the heavy pounding of boots thundered from above and behind us, though staying in their human form. That worked in our favor even if they were still a threat.

"Get into one of the empty rooms," I whispered to Bran. "I'll continue downstairs, making noise as I go. They'll follow me."

"No—"

"Don't argue. Go."

He did, his last look thunderous.

I stamped my feet hard against the treads, forsaking silence for speed now. The steps behind me slowed, now aware their target was dead ahead.

Rounding toward the first floor opening I ran. A bullet whizzed past my right shoulder, splintering into the wall behind me. I ducked, tumbled to make a harder target, and came up at crouched behind a wingback chair.

Another shot puffed into the chair's side arm, blowing white batting like snowflakes. Defensively my position sucked. The shooter was directly ahead, near the open doorway, probably one of the outside guards. He couldn't hold guns in paws and hooves, so as long as the guards were shooting I wasn't dealing with a rampaging wild animal that'd be damned near impossible to take down.

Front door exit was blocked until that guard moved, shifted, or was taken out. The guy from upstairs would be behind me at any moment. Places to hide were minimal as all the furniture looked fragile and useless.

Just my luck.

The Glock 19 I carried weighed almost nothing. I scanned for options. A quick dart to the right led to a study with windows to the outside. The kitchen lay somewhere to my left. Too far away and I didn't know if it had an exit to outside, or to an enclosed garage.

Another bullet bit into the chair. This time from behind me. The guard from the stairs had arrived.

Study it was.

I lay down a series of quick focused shots as I scrambled to the right. The gunman positioned in the doorway shot wide, the guy behind me either was a better aim, was able to control his shifting better, or had better sighting.

The first bullet hissed past my ear. The second burned a channel of heat across my upper arm.

Hellfire and damnation that stung.

I hit the ajar study door slamming into the room like a runner hitting home base on a slide. My arm screamed. My ears rang. Adrenaline pounded through me.

Yiyhah! It felt good to be alive.

Scampering out of the doorway, I held returning fire until I could get a bead on my target. Either one of them. My ammo wouldn't last forever, but I could already hear the sweet, sweet sound of fire engines in route. The shooters had two options; make a final supreme effort to silence me, Bran, and Franco, if they knew Franco was no longer a man, and hope to hell they escaped before the cavalry arrived. Or cut and run now.

"Run, you suckers," I breathed through my arm pain. "Run fast and run far."

A bullet hit the door jamb near my head.

He wouldn't be the first guy who didn't listen to good advice.

I returned the shot, aiming for the stair guy who'd now taken my former position behind the mangled chair. I was pinned down in a triangle, about equal distance between the outside doorway guard and the one who'd come from upstairs.

At least Bran was safe. But where the hell was Franco? With hope, he was running outside for a potty break or something equally benign. One of us deserved to get out of here unscarred.

I checked the ammo remaining in my magazine. Five shots plus one in the chamber. "If you guys won't oblige." I rose to my knees, crouched for a Butch Cassidy and the Sundance Kid last ditch effort, gun blazing as I charged instead of remaining cowered and whipped. It wasn't the smartest plan but neither was waiting for the shifters to charge.

"On the count of three."

Two bullets struck the door beside me. I ducked but held my position, every muscle tensed, nerves wire thin.

"One."

The sirens screamed closer now. But not close enough.

"Two."

I braced, gun hand tucked close, heart pounding triple time. *Please don't shift, please don't shift.* In a contest between pistols without silver bullets and shifters, a pistol was as effective as a pea-shooter.

Fear clogged my throat.

"Three."

I rose just as a series of shots rang out from the back stairway toward the chair.

Bran.

I shot toward the chair. A man screamed, his voice a half-squeal. Warthog guy. He crumpled to the floor behind the chair.

I focused on the front door. The threat there was greatest against Bran, exposed to that shooter. I had to take the guard out.

Advancing. I aimed and shot. One at a time. Relentless.

"Take that."

A step forward.

"And that." The gun vibrated in my hand. Two shots left. Damn, Bran, he should've stayed upstairs.

"And that—"

"Alex." Bran's voice reached me. "Stop!"

Then I saw the front door shooter, standing now, his gun pointed straight at me.

CHAPTER 59

I twisted, turning toward Bran. The gun in his hand pointed in my direction. The gunman directly behind me.

Time slowed. Sound compressed. Actions became elongated.

Bran's mouth opened. The report of his gun as bullets zapped out, shooting past me. So close I could feel their wake in the air.

A scream. Mine? His? Sirens drawing closer. A voice shouting. Jaylene's?

Sounds and sights merged, a grotesque MTV video snapping out of frame.

Then everything crashed into near silence, broken only by the sound of fire engine sirens.

"Are you stupid or what?" Jaylene, materialized beside me now, a weapon in her hand, anger distorting her face. "You have to be the dumbest cowgirl that ever was, you know that? Two more seconds, or your man slower on the draw, and you'd be the one in a puddle of blood instead of this yahoo. You want to die?"

"Me?" I heard the fear in my own voice, but it wasn't the fear of getting killed, it was the fear of what could have happened. I looked directly at Bran, my voice raised. "I said stay upstairs and what did you do—"

"I saved your life. Again."

I stepped closer to him, anger, and fear punching through me. "These were real bullets here, not some TV show imitations."

"I know—"

"No, you don't know anything. I'm the professional, you're not. Stick to your dresses."

It was a cheap, tacky shot but all I had with the shaking in my whole body—the aftereffect of too much adrenaline. That and the awareness of how bloody close Bran had come to getting killed.

He wasn't a freaking immortal. Hell, he didn't have enough warlock magic operating to save his hide.

"So be it." The muscles in his face were held in check, the pulse point in his temple pounding in contrast. "I'll go back to my dresses. And you're welcome. Next time I worry you might be in danger I'll look the other way."

"Fine by me."

Jaylene grabbed my arm or I'd have stepped closer and slugged the guy. How dare he scare me like that. "And there won't be a next time. We're out of here."

"Best news I've heard for weeks."

So two could do cheap shots.

"Why, you—"

Jaylene grabbed me tighter.

"Alex, the battle's over."

That's what she thought.

"Jaylene, back off, she's been hit," Kelly's voice spoke from near the doorway; a doorway already filling with yellow suited firefighters.

But my attention wasn't on any of them. It was on Bran. Standing near one crumpled body, his focus now one hundred percent on the gun in his hand as if wondering where it had come from.

"He dead for sure?" Jaylene shouted to the paramedics bending over the guard's body in the doorway. Thankfully a human body. Most of the time Jaylene could be a PIA, but right then she was my PIA. Maybe Stone was right, team mattered, as much as family mattered. Damned if I'd ever tell him though.

"He's dead," came the dark reply.

The shot had been fatal, taking out the shooter aiming at me. Bran had killed a man.

My stomach plummeted, air leeched from my lungs. Killing someone wasn't easy. Taking another's life had ramifications, like using powerful magic, any magic for that matter. There was always a price to pay. Bran hadn't had even my little training and now must live with the cost of taking a life. He'd saved me and looked sick about it.

He dropped his gun, letting it land with a loud thunk on the floor.

"You all right, Miss?" a masked firefighter spoke to me, his voice oddly calm and gentle, as if he feared me splintering. "Miss, let me take a look at that arm."

"Arm?" Oh, yeah, I'd been shot. Grazed really, it wasn't anything in spite of the burning, searing sensation.

I shrugged, the movement tangoing more pain across my nerve endings.

I was supposed to be the professional and Bran had saved the day. Not that he looked like a winner. He looked shell-shocked, especially when his gaze lifted and locked with mine. A thousand hells darkened his eyes. Tormented.

Damn, why hadn't he stayed upstairs?

I stepped toward him, but he raised his chin and shook his head, warning me off. He'd just saved my life. Couldn't that weigh against death? A life saved for one taken.

"Bran?" His name emerged raw from my throat. "I—"

"Not now, Alex." Kelly snagged an arm around my good shoulder. Kind-hearted, kindergarten teacher Kelly. "He needs some time."

As if a thousand years could erase the revulsion in his eyes looking at me.

"Your world," he said, the words guttural.

Oh, that was ripe. He was the one with the non-human cousin who had Sasha brutally killed, accusing me of existing in a dark world.

I shook my head, not denying what he said as much as what he wasn't saying. I killed and now he had. He'd been brought into the darkest, ugliest part of my world and was rejecting it. Was rejecting me, even knowing that he had been the one protecting his cousin.

Well, that wasn't news. I bit back unfamiliar emotions: regret, hurt, remorse.

Firefighters shouted around me; pulsating red lights flashed through all the windows. An ambulance crew double-timed past and yet I stood there, caught in a time warp, rewinding the last minutes in my head.

Should haves, could haves—none of them made any difference. Two shifters dead, one at Bran's hand, though everyone except Bran and my team thought the dead men human. Franco's whereabouts unknown. Dominique at large.

That shook me. I glanced at Kelly. "Dominique. Stop her. She's armed and dangerous."

"Where's she headed?"

"Don't know."

"I do." Bran stepped forward, his gaze averted from mine, truly making me an invisible agent.

Ling Mai would be proud.

CHAPTER 60

I scanned the Kennedy Center's video monitors over Mandy's shoulder, the low level whisper of technology humming around us. Bran was standing in the Center's lobby, visible on the screen, ignoring me as intently as I was ignoring him.

Hundreds of milling guests visible, lots of air kissing, enlarged smiles, see-and-be-seen people. Designer dresses. Surgically enhanced bodies. Sparkling jewels blinging everywhere. Bran's world.

I was lucky I was out of it.

My eyes cut toward Bran's image. I caught myself and glanced away.

"There he is." Mandy pointed to the upper left screen as if I'd spoken aloud. Her good hand gesturing, the other still in a sling from the echo-demon drill.

"Who?" Jaylene asked from near the door.

"Bran."

A tense silence permeated the room. Everyone knew the details of what had happened at the house just an hour ago. Bad enough I'd made a fool of myself over a guy; worse was they also knew I hadn't stopped Dominique.

Our team was all behind the scenes, leaving the actual security measures to the Big Boy agencies. Let them have it.

It'd been too late to call off the big gala as it'd already started, though the President's wife had been alerted not to attend as a few other key guests, one at a time, were being asked to leave quietly.

But what about the others? The innocents. We had no idea what Dominique planned, but I held no doubt something was about to go down. Something bad.

Mandy whistled, "Hey witchy girl, you got any plans on how to stop that Grimple?"

My fingers clenched until I released them, one at a time, slowly and carefully, not bothering to rise to Mandy's bait.

"I'm hoping she'll retain her human shape and . . .I'll stop her." I had meant to say neutralize her, but she was still Bran's cousin and he had a blind spot for her.

"That's priceless," the other woman continued, adding an additional whistle. "You going to call up a few echo-demons to help you cuz that worked so well—"

"Cut it out, Mandy," Vaughn spoke from near the console furthest from me, her gaze skimming the crowd shots. "Keep your focus on the event and guests."

Kelly voiced aloud my own fears. "Wasn't finding the drugs in the wall safe at the house enough?"

"No telling if what we found was all there was. Better to be safe than sorry." Vaughn adjusted a dial. "We may have enough material to indict Alex's Dragon Lady, but there was someone on the other end of that throwaway phone she spoke to and until we get them, this mission isn't truly over."

And until we found Van, I wasn't going to stop.

My stomach burned, each word echoing like a residual scream though my system. Something was wrong. But I couldn't put my finger on what or why. Or maybe it was simply Bran-damage eating away my sanity.

Damn.

"I still say that missing Franco dude is the key." Jaylene pushed away from the wall, casting me a wary glance. "I mean he's the one I'd like to strap a bomb to and take out."

I shook my head, aware of a glimmer of a smile. The team hadn't heard about Franco's role yet, only that he was missing.

I straightened. "Let's set the record straight, once and for all. Dominique is a sadistic, manipulative bitch and that's in her human form. As a Grimple she makes taking out a dragon look easy." I could still smell the stench of her breath when I inhaled. "But if I could have stopped her, I would have. You want to fight a Grimple single-handed, go right ahead."

Jaylene nodded as if thinking through something. "You and—" She nodded toward Bran's image on the screen, his hands tight against his sides. "—him make a good team, in spite of all that warlock-witch crap. You don't trust your magic. Maybe if you did, Dominique would be taken out by now."

"I can't believe—" I glanced at Vaughn for support, but the other woman simply raised one shoulder. "Not you, too?"

"It's an interesting theory and could explain a lot."

"It's a bunch of crap and you all know it."

Vaughn looked straight at me. "When you learn to trust your abilities, you're going to stop avoiding magic. You're a powerful woman, Alex, and the only one who doesn't know it is you."

"That's the dumbest crap I've ever heard." I'd been practicing spells. Yeah, behind closed doors but only a fool would go around flashing magic in the crowded venues I'd been in for the last two weeks.

Besides they had no idea, no idea whatsoever how badly using magic could bite. To them it was a parlor trick, handy to make some flash, and open a few locks, but the real stuff, the powerful stuff, that was dangerous and they didn't have a clue.

Vaughn kept her gaze level. "Aren't you afraid that if you become more a witch that you'll turn into your mother who ended up destroying the man that loved her most, your father?"

Insert knife, push deep, and twist. Damn her anyway for knowing too much about my background. And hands off my dad. No one took a poke at him. No one.

As if all the air in the room disappeared, I stood there, my heart squeezed, my focus burning into Vaughn. "My mother has nothing to do with this. I'm not her." Every word ached as it slipped from my mouth. "And you don't know squat diddly about my father."

"You're right, Alex." Vaughn stood up and crossed to me, sliding one arm around my shoulder though I didn't unbend. "I was trying to help."

I shook my head, then took the plunge as I stepped away from the circle of Vaughn's arm, needing the space to breathe. Baring one's sordid past required one's total focus. "Not that the news means anything to any of you, but my mom ran away from my father when I was five." There, I'd spilled my guts. "She ran away from all of us and it was the best thing she could have done. She was a witch, a powerful one, and while that sounds all cool and fun, it's too easy to slide from white to dark magic. And she did. A downhill skid that left only casualties in her wake."

My voice and my heart ached. It'd been twenty years and the hurt still flared.

"Damn," Jaylene whistled, glancing at the other team members. "We didn't know."

"That's because my childhood has nothing to do with the team, with any of you, or with my using or not using my abilities."

"Sure it does." Kelly looked at me eye-to-eye. "Our pasts shape our present, but it doesn't have to shape our futures if we choose to acknowledge and learn from it. If your mother betrayed her gifts that was her choice. You're different."

That was it. That was the missing piece. I didn't have time for this other personal crap, but Kelly's words set off a ripple effect.

"What did you say?" I stepped back to the screens, my whole body tensed, my eyes clearing.

"About being different?" Kelly mimicked my move, both of us now facing the screens.

Vaughn and Jaylene flanked us.

I scanned one screen after the other before I saw what I wanted. Not Bran this time, but Suzette.

"There." I pointed to the screen. "What do you see?"

"People," Jaylene said. "Lots and lots of—oh, not what but who." Jaylene leaned closer. "That's Suzette."

"Suzette," I said, adrenaline humming through me. Adrenaline and fear.

"What's the assistant got to do with anything?" Mandy asked.

I kept my gaze glued to the screen. "Anyone have the date when Suzette joined the tour?"

Kelly slipped back into her chair, clicked the keyboard, but it was Vaughn who answered. "Just after the tour started. Dominique brought her on."

"Which makes perfect sense, Dom would need help within the tour to do what she wouldn't or couldn't do." Like kill a model who knew too much. "When was the first theft reported?" I asked.

"Three weeks after Suzette was hired."

"Three weeks, that makes sense."

"But there were people who've been with the tour that long." Jaylene eyed me.

"There are. But that's why Suzette was used. She was invisible."

"Explain," Vaughn as team leader spoke now.

"Suzette was one of the few on the yacht the night of the murder and had access to all the rooms, including the staterooms. She could have been the victim of the drug as much as anybody else, keeping Dominique's hands clean."

"So she could hide the murder weapon in Franco's room," Mandy said. "But why would Dominique want that?"

"To cast suspicion and doubt. If she suspected Sasha was an undercover agent it could explain the poor girl's death. If Franco was arrested, the whole tour would have been in an uproar, causing confusion and doubt."

"Dominique using this Suzette sounds plausible," Jaylene whistled.

"She's a perfect patsy." My gaze remained riveted on the screen. "Because she's as invisible as we are, only working for a different agenda. Dominique's agenda."

"So what now?" Kelly asked.

"Now we have to remove Suzette from the Center without Dominique knowing. The only way to keep Suzette safe."

"But we still don't know where Dominique is," Vaughn pointed out the fact that was bothering me most.

"Somewhere close to Suzette." I weighed the options and came to the worst case scenario. "Close enough to whisper an order when needed. What if Suzette's already been drugged?" I glanced at the clock. "When are they making the announcement that the First Lady won't be arriving?"

"Less than fifteen minutes."

Which meant once that news was known, nothing could hold back an attack on the remaining guests. "Damn." I sprang to attention. "We've got to do something!"

Vaughn as tactician spoke, "We can alert the Secret Service to keep an eye on Suzette, but if she hasn't done anything we can't break in there and haul her off—her or one of the guests of honor on a hunch just for being present, and Dominique's a guest of honor along with Bran. That's all we've got so far, a scenario that may be way out of line."

Jaylene broke in. "Couldn't the SS folks ask her to step outside? Nice like?"

"But if they did, Suzette could be programmed to react." I couldn't get past my gut feeling. "I know she's in trouble."

"Is that experience or abilities speaking?" Sometimes Vaughn didn't hold her punches. "We have no probable cause to remove anyone without creating an incident."

"And no way to stop Dominique if she's planning to use Suzette. If Suzette's under the influence of the drug she could be primed with anything, a bomb, magic, who knows," Jaylene said. "It's brilliant."

"Brilliant and deadly." I straightened, glancing around the room.

"What are you doing?" Jaylene eyed me warily.

"I'm making a plan."

"And the plan is?"

"The plan's simple." I took a deep breath. "Stop Dominique. Save Suzette. Save the world."

"Oh, good." Jaylene grinned. "And here I thought it was going to be too easy."

CHAPTER 61

I raced from the control room, hearing every second's tick of the clock. Bran was in that room, but more than him there was a room full of innocents who could be hurt simply for being at the wrong place at the wrong time. I adjusted the ear mike I'd grabbed and hustled my way down the hallway.

Vaughn and Jaylene were notifying the Secret Service detail, those remaining now that the First Lady wasn't on site, letting their call determine if they acted. But there were not enough to do a lot. We were on our own.

Kelly would remain with Mandy to scan the monitors, last thing we needed was for Kelly to panic, go invisible, then pop back on scene minutes later blind.

My gut told me the announcement of the First Lady not arriving would change what was about to go down. Suzette being used to kill the President's wife would cause greater headlines, but Dominique killing a senator or general, or any number of the other guests would work, too. It would prove the designer drug effective. That's what Dominique wanted—one last test to prove to the eventual buyers. We may have found a stash of the drug, but she could easily still have the formula. It was sheer brilliance.

I had to stop her.

First step—get into the gathering. Not in the jeans I was wearing though.

I reached a door, guarded by two Rent-a-Cops.

"Halt."

I panted as I held up my security badge. "I work here and am late for the show."

The first cop scanned my badge then me, as if expecting me to bite her. "Looks good," she said to her partner, a tall black man. "What do you want here?"

"I'm meant to wear one of Bran's creations. It's stored with the model's dresses behind that door." I didn't even miss a beat with my lie. "Can I go now?"

"Yeah," the woman waved me on. "You have five minutes."

What woman could get dressed in five minutes? Heck, it took me that long to find the hidden buttons and zippers.

I slammed through the door as I scanned the frenzied back stage activity. What now?

I plunged into the thickest knot of models, sidestepping swaths of silk and organza with experience learned over the last weeks. Franco would have been proud. "Collette?"

The willowy model looked up and smiled. "Didn't expect to see you here, ducky. Tell me you came to do hair? The twit they have nearly torched me with a curling wand."

"Sorry, no can do." I reached the other woman, my breath coming faster now. "Look, I need a huge favor. Will you help?"

"If I can." Collette looked confused then flashed a million dollar smile. "What'd you need?"

"I need a dress. Something simple to get into and I needed it ten minutes ago."

"The fuchsia ostrich one," she murmured, as if it were a secret code. "Where is it?"

"Follow me," she chatted as she headed to the dressing rooms. "Guy who replaced Franco isn't half as anal retentive about the frocks. There should be a couple hanging—there we are." She stopped at a deserted room.

"Thanks, Collette. I owe you." I brushed past her, never so happy to see dresses in my life.

Jade stepped forward and grabbed an orange and yellow column dress sporting a side silver clasp. The fact that I recognized the details had me silently groaning. "You'll tell me what's going on, won't you?" she asked, leaning against the doorway.

"Not that one." Collette joined us, reaching for a strapless feathered confection in fuchsia and thrusting it at me as if my life depended on how swiftly I could dress. My life didn't depend on it—Suzette's did.

"Don't forget the shoes!" Collette called, a pair of kill-me-stilettos dangling from her fingers.

Some days saving the world was harder than it looked. I slipped on the shoes.

Collette gave me a big thumbs up as I finished and rushed to the door, every thought screaming, 'It's too late, it's too late."

I entered the grand hallway, ignoring the gigantic chandeliers overhead, the tide of voices washing against me, the throng of people packed tighter than the holding pens come slaughter time back in Idaho.

Where was she? I pressed my ear mike and murmured loud enough for Mandy or Kelly to hear. "Any sight of them?"

Mandy's voice sounded in my ear. "Ten o'clock. Between the woman with the watermelon chest and the walking anorexia victim."

I scanned the direction but couldn't—

There. Suzette stood there, looking very much her normal self. Quiet. Constrained. Waiting to be summoned, her hands at her side.

Maybe I was wrong. She looked fine.

Then I spotted Dominique, a good foot taller than Suzette, wearing fuck-me red with some fabric tie crossing her chest, her hair scraped back from her face. A very animated face. Smiling. And right next to her stood Bran.

Damn the man. His cousin almost killed him; wouldn't that be enough to cut familial ties?

I touched my ear piece. "Got them."

I weaved between the crowds. Fifteen feet away and gaining.

I'd go after Dominique first, cull her from Bran and Suzette.

I still didn't trust Bran to do what was necessary to bring her down.

Ten feet. Dominique was turning my way.

"You sure you're going to be able to stop Dom? " Kelly spoke in my ear piece.

Five feet.

"There's no wards against magic here. If I have to drop an elephant on her, I will."

Dominique spotted me. Her gaze packed a weighted punch as she stilled, her body tensed, her facial muscles tightening.

Watch out, Dragon Lady, this witch was on the prowl.

"You sure?" Kelly murmured as only a few strangers separated me from my quarry.

"Oh, yeah, I'm sure." My gaze never wavered from hers. People nearby noticed something was up. A few heads angled in my direction. A camera flashed.

I ignored everything, except her.

This close I could see the differences in her; the strain bracketing her eyes, the stiffness of her body. She angled her head but kept her look locked with mine. Her eyes were slightly wild, slightly unfocused, not Dominique's eyes at all.

I stumbled, glancing between Dominique and Bran, who was just now spotting me. Then Dominique and Suzette. What now?

Improvise. I had to get close to Dominique. Get her out of here with none the wiser. But how? Attack? If she were one of my brothers the approach might work, but not in this crowd. Get close enough to pinch a nerve, render her temporarily incapable of anything but basic muscle group movement? Wouldn't last long enough.

So what?

Voices swirled around me; the echo of Vaughn's words joined them. "Don't be afraid of your power. As a witch."

What power? I couldn't run in this dress. Or deliver a roundhouse kick. No weapons on me. What good was—

Wait. Stop confusing agent and witch. I was both. Use both. What better way to contain a threat than to approach with a containment spell? Did I know any strong enough?

Out of the corner of my eye I caught the flash of Bran looking at me, a frown darkening his expression. A few feet from him, meek, mild, invisible Suzette had just now noticed me.

Bran stepped forward. I ignored him. I had to keep Suzette safe and the only way to do that was to stop Dominique.

I raised my head, chewed my bottom lip, and kept Dom's gaze one hundred percent focused on me as I started muttering the only spell I knew that might help.

"Protector, I call upon you. Make me a barrier between man and monsters. I am willing to pay the cost."

Black magic.

How true that was, especially with Dragon Lady in Grimple form as I noted the green rim of her eyes, inhaled the scent of sandalwood and cinnamon even in a room choked with thousand dollar perfumes.

"From head to toe. From ancient times so must it be."

Using one of the few dangerous spells my first and only witch mentor taught me was still with me in time of need. And man, did I need it.

More light flashes went off. Gnats to be brushed away.

I was here to stop Dominique. Only Dragon Lady. Just me and her.

Bran was suddenly at my side. "I've got to contain her," I said, not looking at him. "Get her outside."

"It's not her," he said.

I ignored him.

The skin of Dominique's face tightened, nostrils flared, cheekbones in high relief.

I stepped in front of her, making my actions look natural and easy to all the people standing around. I had to contain her but not here, not where innocents could die if she did something to Suzette.

"Dominique?" My greeting came out husky, not planned but all the better, one woman friend to another.

She said nothing.

I stepped closer. "Dominique, we need to talk." Then added in a lower tone, just between the two of us. "*Deep calleth unto deep.*"

Bran grabbed my arm. I shook him off.

"*To the light, better things and to death. To struggle and emerge, advance as I follow.*"

Her eyes grew wider but I didn't stop.

"*Going on forever, light shines in the darkness.*"

Her whole body vibrated. Her eyes pleaded, her shoulders and arms held rigid, her nostrils tightened like a wild stallion struggling against restraints.

"What are—" It was Suzette's voice, but not sounding like a victim's voice.

What was going on? Could I be wrong? Who was victim and who was threat? If I tackled the wrong one we all could die.

"It's not Dom," Bran repeated, only this time I heard him. Heard him and the protection spell he was mumbling low and intense. So intense sweat had broken out on his brow.

He was protecting Dom? From whom?

Was I totally, one hundred percent wrong?

I cast Bran a quick, desperate glance. If what my gut was screaming was right, he was standing next to Suzette. The real killer. And what was I standing next to?

I whispered for Dominique's hearing alone. "I understand. I know what you're going through, but you can fight it." I stepped closer because of the viewers nearby, repeating in her ear. "Fight it. You're stronger than the drug. Fight it."

I needed her to use whatever powers her Grimple genes could give her without morphing.

She shook her head, an almost imperceptible movement. The drug was winning. The drug and whatever order had been programmed into her. Her pupils were saucer dark discs, sweat dampened her brow.

Then I saw it and tensed. A small square shape. A bomb, beneath the fold of her sin-red dress, next to her heart.

Alpha-3 would be my best guess: dough-like and malleable, odorless, a small amount could cause extensive damage in a closely packed space and without the metallic bond Semtex contained. Semtex couldn't get through the metal detectors into the Center, but its older and less stable cousin Alpha-3 could, especially if sneaked in the back door by a determined someone.

"Bran?"

"I'm here."

I didn't dare glance over my shoulder to verify his nearness. Time for trust. "Remember that stop time spell you did at the restaurant?"

"I didn't—"

"Can you do it or not?"

"Slow maybe."

"Slow will help. Do it. Don't need the whole room, just around the four of us."

"Four?"

"Include Suzette."

Please make it be enough. I stepped closer to Dominique. "I'm here, Dominique. Right here."

Now I had a choice. Save the woman who held Van hostage and tried to have me killed, at the risk of my own life. Or back away.

"Go." I muttered to Bran, the one word wrenched from my soul. "Now."

"Dom?"

Choice made.

"I've got her."

Unless she killed me first.

CHAPTER 62

"We have to go outside," I said to Dominique, interspersing every order with the makeshift containment spell, but I needed to get her and the bomb outside where I could create a true containment spell around her. "I'm here." I leaned closer. "You go down, I go down. I won't let you die but I can't do this without you."

I hoped Dom wouldn't take this as an opportunity to get rid of me and dozens of others standing near us once and for all. That she valued her own skin enough not to do something stupid, even as I noted how badly she was shaking, her skin pale beneath a sheen of sweat.

Was Bran's spell taking effect? It had to be as I felt the weight in my arms and legs, the effort to breathe, the space around me shimmered. Not enough so others could see and understand but enough that it felt like wading through very, very thick air.

I spoke again. "Save yourself."

She closed her eyes, a tormented woman. If the bomb was plastique, it needed a fuse or electrical pulse detonator to set it off. But which one? I guessed the latter. More control but was Dom programmed to explode the bomb herself or would Suzette?

A shift in the crowd as sounds broke through to me. A rise in volume. Some mucky-muck had arrived, squeezing people closer together. Making it harder for Bran to hold his spell.

Crap.

I kept my gaze locked with hers. I'd meant what I'd said. She'd kill us both if she gave into the drug.

Maybe she had no choice.

But I did.

"Dominique." It was Suzette, shouting from a dozen feet away, restrained by Bran grabbing her arms. "Dominique."

Dominique shifted. Stepped toward Suzette.

I blocked her. Good thing I had several inches on her, enough to block her visually from Suzette. "I mean it. You'll have to kill me before I'll let you do anything."

"Get away," her whispered words tore at me, but I didn't budge an inch. I couldn't afford to, for all of our sakes.

"Come with me, Dominique," I said, aware of the pleading tone in my voice. "Take my hand and walk out of here with me."

I grabbed both of her hands to keep control of her and to prevent her reaching for a trigger. They trembled beneath my touch.

"That's right. Fight it. Not me." I nudged against her, but she didn't budge. "Come with me. We'll walk the other way." Away from whomever just arrived. "Let's do this together." I nudged again.

This time she moved. A granite boulder inching uphill, but she moved in the direction I needed her to move. Toward a side door.

My head pounded. I had to fight against Bran's spell while holding one of my own. I'd be lucky if I didn't black out.

I gave Dominique a smile wavy around the edges but a smile. She was moving toward safety.

Shouts sounded nearby. Dominique's gaze faltered and shifted. Mine followed.

Suzette.

Bran had both arms around the woman, bucking and shaking against him like a cornered calf. Security guards were converging on the pair. They'd almost reached them when Suzette reared back, head-butting Bran and breaking free.

Free and rushing straight at Dominique and me, whipping open a cell phone in the process.

The detonator.

CHAPTER 63

I froze mid-breath, aware what I was about to do betrayed my vow to my father and to myself. All magic had a price.

If I didn't act, though, we all died. If I did act, I'd pay the price with no idea of the cost.

"Bran." It felt like I was shouting, but everyone was focused on the hoopla at the main doors. I never thought I'd be thankful for the entrance of a celebrity. "I'm linking with you."

He didn't have a chance to reply as I pulled deep within my core and breathed out.

My mentor witch asked what it felt like when I did what many thought was impossible. I'd told her it felt like being on top of the highest cliff, looking at the world still and far below, and then stepping off.

"*Hemma, hanna, druia.*" The old words, in a tongue I didn't understand, mumbled forth. "*Hemma, druia, sanctum.*"

I pulled forth Bran's magic and made it my own, amplifying like a tornado funnel amplified wind. I pulled not only his but any other non-human abilities within a twenty-foot radius until I was still in the center and oh so powerful and dangerous to everyone around.

Time didn't still, it slammed to a halt. Suzette caught mid-scream, Dominique with a bead of sweat dripping from forehead to chin. Everyone within my radius frozen, except for Bran and me.

I could hear him fighting his own spell engulfing him. He had a little immunity, same as me, but at a cost. My head roared, blood pounded behind my eyes, nerve endings jangled. Fighting against time was a bitch.

"Get them outside," I whispered, focusing everything I had to hold the spell. Stepping inside Bran's power and lashing it with mine merged the two of us. I felt the thud of his heart, his labored breathing, the churn of his emotions: awe, anger, fear.

But I couldn't stop; it took too much to hold time in place.

Bran moved, snagging Suzette as if she were a stiff doll and slogging to the nearest door. I couldn't carry Dominique but held my ground, pushing the spell further out to make sure Suzette wasn't released.

"Hurry," I whispered, not even sure he could hear me.

"I'm coming."

By the time he returned to my side only seconds later, my body quivered, sweat destroying my lovely dress, my head screaming with the mother of all headaches.

He half-lifted, half-dragged Dominique along as I followed closely—each step heavy, painful. I didn't know how Bran was moving and carrying at the same time.

"How are you?" he grunted, the last five feet in sight with Suzette frozen just beyond the open door way.

"Holding." It was all I could manage.

"Later. You tell me what. . ."

I nodded. Explaining to another who wove magic that I was a witch magnifier, an amplifier who could use others' powers, channeling them through me, with or without their permission, was not an easy conversation.

I was a freaking vampire weapon, but not blood driven, magic driven. My father warned me that others would fear and despise me if they knew. Those who didn't would want to use me.

Later, I'd deal with the fallout. Now Bran was wrestling Dominique through the door and setting her down beside Suzette. We were along the outer promenade facing Rock Creek Parkway and the Potomac, the city and National Cathedral lights winking in the distance. A blast of cool air bit my skin, a welcome relief.

"Now what?" Bran bent slightly like a runner catching his breath, staring at me as if I had sprouted horns. Which in his view, and in mine, too, I had.

It was easier holding the spell here, in a smaller area, as I focused only on Suzette and Dominique. The pressure lessened a little on Bran and me, though I could only speak in small bursts. If my attention cracked or wavered in the slightest, the spell would go down and Suzette would be free to activate the bomb.

"Need containment circle," I breathed, my eyes on my captives. Even in the darkness broken by the lights of the Center behind us, I could see the fury in Suzette's gaze. She might be frozen but only biding her time, waiting for the second she was free. "Need blood."

"I don't have any way to draw blood." He came up beside me.

Damn. Never thought of that. Anything that could possibly be used as a threat was rigidly removed from anyone entering the Center.

"Wait." He stepped toward Suzette, spying what I had just noticed. A brooch and brooches had pins. Leave it to the dress designer to spot that detail.

He wrestled the pin off, not easy as the closer he got to Suzette the harder it was to move, but the second the brooch was clear he twisted toward me.

He raised his cuff to slash his wrist.

"No. Mine." I shook my fingers, the only thing I could still move. "Take over spell?"

He nodded, shouldering beside me as I freed myself from him, staggering back as I stepped back into time.

I sucked in deep breaths of air, reaching for the pin clutched in his hand. No telling how much longer he could hold the time spell, but not long by the subtle shifting of Dominique and Suzette.

My head would bleed the most but not with a pin prick. First I had to change the pin to something larger, sharper.

"As thou be, so now change. Thought to image. Image to bind. Bind to blood let."

Now I clutched a small dagger. It wouldn't remain in dagger form for long, but it had to do.

Like a diabetic I started stabbing the ends of my fingers, over and over, dribbling blood in a rough circle around the two women. I closed the circle, murmuring the whole time,

"Continere. Continere. Continere."

My fingers screamed as I straightened, pushing my hair back, aware of the sweat cooling on my skin.

"You can release the time spell," I said, wondering what was taking the team so long to arrive.

Bran raised his head, then bowed, as a man releasing a heavy weight. This time it was Dominique and Suzette who staggered, as if dashed awake. They looked at Bran and me, then at each other.

Suzette acted first. Hurling herself toward me then slamming backwards when she hit the edge of the circle. It held. Thank the Spirits, it held.

It'd taken everything I had, scoured all the magic resources I possessed and then some to get us this far. Now it was time for the team and the authorities to stop these two.

As if in slow motion, Suzette sitting on her backside on the ground, glanced from me to Bran and then to Dominique.

Too late I realized her intention.

Dominique must have grasped the danger quicker as she was already morphing, shifting into her Grimple form.

"No," Bran shouted, lunging toward the circle, but the containment worked both ways. It kept them in and us out.

If Dominique morphed fully the circle would be too small for the two of them. But that wasn't the biggest issue.

Suzette still had her phone.

Four things happened at once, as if choreographed.

Bran screamed, "Dom, no."

Dominique shifted.

Suzette punched a number.

And I . . .I thrust my hands forward and pushed. Pushed with every ounce I had. Pushed with fear and terror pulsing through me. Pushed as if there would be no tomorrow.

Then the bomb exploded.

CHAPTER 64

The blast blew Bran and I backwards but did little more than rattle the Center's windows.

Damn that was one good containment spell. That and the fact I'd tossed Suzette and Dominique over the roadway below the Center and far out over the Potomac. Between the spell, the force of the explosion, and their location I doubted any retrieval team would find even ashes. If there was a retrieval team.

But those thoughts came later. Thrown against a concrete planter it took a moment to shake my hair out of my eyes and look for Bran. He'd recovered sooner and was already leaning across the nearest rail, staring at the Potomac. The cold moving water. The tomb of his cousin.

I crawled to my feet, hearing Jaylene and Vaughn scrambling toward me. "What happened?" Vaughn demanded as she reached my side, helping Jaylene pull me to my feet.

"Problem eliminated." I shrugged off their hands. "I'll report the rest later."

I stumbled toward Bran. Kelly hovered beside him then backed away as I neared.

"I'm sorry Bran." I meant it, too, on so many levels. "I know you cared for her."

He turned. Not fully facing me but enough I could read the anguish and the anger in the shadows of his face. "You killed her."

As if I hadn't been hit hard enough with the first blast, his words sliced me. "I stopped her."

"A witch as powerful as you could have created two circles. Kept her safe. But you didn't."

I didn't know if I wanted to laugh or cry. Me? Powerful? I could barely stand and he'd expected more. Monday morning quarterbacking was so much easier than in the heat of the moment, but truth coated his words.

Dominique and Suzette were both dead. Now we'd never know who was working with them other than Dominique's cryptic words at the house. My only lead to Van was gone. And Bran was alone.

And yes, I'd done that. I'd do it again in a heartbeat if it meant keeping Bran alive.

He didn't want to hear that. Not from me. Not now, and maybe not ever.

I'd killed his beloved cousin, the cousin of his childhood, not the manipulative, dangerous woman she'd become.

Magic always had a price. The cost to me?

Losing Bran for good.

CHAPTER 65

The knock on the Washington D.C. coffee house window startled me until I looked up and spied Franco, if that was his real name. My smile was automatic even though he looked different. The shrieking look-at-me hair color gone, his hair was cropped short and close to the head, blending into the top length which was swept back. He looked different, very sexy different, which had the breath backing up in my lungs.

Franco I could deal with; this edgy, wary stranger was new territory. It was like I'd been expecting something light and fluffy and instead found something dangerous and very, very much a male. The tight lines radiating from his eyes clued me in to the pain he'd been in since I'd last seen him.

"How did you find me?" I asked, as he joined me at the small window table in the nearly empty room.

"I have my sources." His accent sounded more British, more clipped and formal—not sounding like the old Franco at all, until a small grin broke through at my puzzled expression and he added, "Yes, I know. I'm having the same problem reconciling you as a hairdresser and an agent."

I allowed a slight ripple of my shoulders. "But I *am* a hairdresser."

"And a mighty good one," he said. "Though making a peroxide bomb does boggle the imagination."

"You remember that?"

"Heard the details that I missed as well as that little dust up exhibition you put on at the Kennedy Center. The tabloids have been full of nothing else since."

He didn't have to tell *me* about that. But the tabloids didn't have all the details. They knew nothing about what happened to Dominique and Suzette, only that two women had left the crowded room with me and Bran, and even those reports were conflicting.

Bran fielded the press and put his own spin on things. Theft of fashion designs. As if. And the rattle of the windows? Sonic burst from a passing military jet. Ling Mai covered that.

Franco continued in all seriousness. "You saved Bran. Nice piece of work there, too."

I looked away, not ready to deal with emotions that refused to be tamed. One more week or so without seeing him and maybe then I could hear his name without reacting. Okay, maybe a little longer, like a year.

"Just part of my job."

He gave me a shrewd glance and a droll tone, "Really?"

Time to deflect the man. "Is your real name Franco?"

"It's one of my names." He extended his right hand for a shake. "It'll do for now." I could hear what wasn't being said. It was dangerous to expose the real you in our line of work. In a year, when my contract with the agency expired, I could go back to being a civilian, but Franco had chosen this world, and its shadow side for life.

"Frank Harrington at your service."

I shook his hand and scrutinized him closely. Frank fit him, old world solid, and intense. But then so did Franco. I steadied nerves by wrapping my hands around my mug. "Do you mind if I ask a question or two?"

"Shoot." Then held up his hands. "Just an expression."

He earned the smile I gave him. "I understand that your people were involved because of the theft of some British government papers."

"Just as your agency became involved on behalf of your government's concerns about the thefts."

I nodded. "But why didn't MI-6 tell Interpol they had a man undercover?"

"You mean why didn't we share with your agency? Combine our resources?"

"Yeah." I looked at him straight on. "Interpol knew we were going in."

"Need to know basis, dahling." He shrugged, then grimaced. "Always the old need to bloody well know, and now a decent woman is dead."

"Sasha."

Franco's face tightened. "Yes, a new recruit that should never have been brought in."

"Then why was she?"

"We suspected Dominique, but knew she wasn't working alone. We thought along the same lines as your agency." He gave me a shrewd look. "That Dominique might be more than she seemed."

Interesting. "So MI-6 has a—"

He raised his hand. "A branch we don't speak about publically? Yes. More hush-hush and very need-to-know."

I sighed, already wondering if the Brits had better documentation on non-humans than Fraulein Fassbinder. Heck, they had to, even Wikipedia had more intel. Maybe there could be a little tit-for-tat sharing to be arranged.

Franco, or Frank, continued, "Our fellows decided to send in someone to infiltrate the women's world that I couldn't access. That and the fact that when you arrived there was a rumor you were Dominique's contact for the next phase of whatever she had planned."

"Me?"

"It wasn't like Bran to bring on a new staff member without his cousin's prior approval. Dominique, for all her faults, and they were legion, did run a tight ship. Even *I* had to come to Dominique's attention before being hired. Which Bran very nicely set up as we'd known each other from attending Oxford together, but your coming in was the first break in the pattern. Then things changed."

Oxford? Another piece of Bran I didn't know. I looked at Frank. "What things?"

It was Franco's old laugh as he said, "Do not be dense. Anyone with eyes in their heads could see the sparks between you and Bran. Since you knew your job as a hairdresser, it was easy to dismiss you as a fling on his part."

Fling it was. Fast, furious, and not meant to be. Ignoring the tightening in my stomach, I let him continue.

"The home folks didn't trust my intel that you were just as you appeared to be—a hairdresser. My word, I'll never live that one down when I get back to the home office."

"I'm sorry about Sasha." I meant it, too. The poor woman was in way over her head almost from the start, a sensation I could relate to even if my own mission was deemed mostly successful with both Dominique and Suzette neutralized and the drug confiscated.

Franco's jaw tightened. "It appears that Suzette was the one who killed Sasha."

Not new news here as I'd put two and two together. Several official agencies jockeyed for information as to the ramifications of the drug, who had created it, who it had been administered to, who else knew about it. The model's death was just one piece of a larger puzzle, and those agencies didn't even guess at the non-human elements.

Who were the Seekers? And what did they want? And why? Ling Mai had reassured the IR team that we'd know the details in due time. Probably the same amount of time it took me to forget Bran. Another cheery thought.

"So your people know that Suzette murdered Sasha for sure?" I asked.

"Yes. It appears Dominique had no idea Suzette was the puppet master pulling the strings. From what we've been able to piece together, Dominique most likely recruited her assistance in the drug scheme and promised the woman a sizable monetary reward when the drug proved effective. On Dominique's orders, Suzette drugged and killed Sasha. Orders that Suzette fed to Dominique anonymously."

"And the knife?"

"While you and I were finding Sasha, Suzette stashed the knife in my room to add confusion."

"So Suzette was actually the one behind everything." On one level I could accept it. The woman was thorough. On another level, I marveled at how invisible the young woman really had been, slipping beneath everyone's radar. But who was Vaverek? And when would I find him?

I was already making plans to slip beneath the IR radar and head to Paris. I'd done what Ling Mai and Stone wanted on this last mission. Two weeks where Van had remained in the hands of his captors. They wouldn't hold him forever, only until he told them what they wanted to know or broke him. Day after tomorrow I was gone. Team be dammed.

"Diabolical wasn't it?" Frank continued, as if I were paying attention. "Suzette was the one who came across the drug initially when her uncle, who was a French research scientist, described it to her. Originally the drug was designed to help women in therapy but instead could be used against them. Suzette saw its larger and darker potential but needed to be able to test it before buyers would fork over the kind of money she wanted for it. Only drawback to the drug seemed to be that mostly women were susceptible to it."

Including Dominique.

As if I'd spoken aloud, Frank said, "Yes, I caught the irony that Dominique was caught in her own web."

Too bad Bran saw me as solely responsible for killing her. Another thing I refused to think about. Instead I asked, "What happened to the uncle?"

"He died from a hit and run accident."

"How convenient."

"Wasn't it?" He rolled his eyes ala the old Franco. "Suzette no doubt went to work for Dominique with one goal in mind, to use the tour, and its access to women all over the world—"

"Women who in turn had access to anything from art to government intel."

"Precisely. It was the perfect staging ground. Different victims. Different thefts. Different locales so law enforcement wouldn't add up all the pieces until it was too late. Which it almost was."

"So what alerted Interpol?"

"Suzette got greedy, using more and more of the thefts to create a cash flow while she waited for the big break. We couldn't link them to her because the money she was making was channeled through her uncle's accounts. Accounts she could use because she was the executor of his estate."

"So Suzette's cash flow didn't alert anyone," I said.

Frank nodded. "A few less jobs, or a few less valuable pieces stolen and Suzette might have realized her ultimate plan. As it was she created a strong body of evidence that the drug worked."

And to think the woman was only human. Who knew what she might have done if she'd been involved with the non-humans.

"And Dominique?"

"Suzette saw all too quickly that Dominique could also be manipulated, so she used Dominique's need to be a true power-player, coming out from Bran's shadow. Suzette brought Dominique into the scheme in small stages until the woman was truly committed."

I leaned closer. "And the non-human element? Did Suzette know what she was getting involved in?"

"I don't think it mattered, but by bringing in Dominique, Suzette alerted others who saw the potential in the drug, too."

"Against humans."

"If humans were the enemy, then yes. Dominique won't have cared so much if humans were casualties. She was willing to do anything, including destroy Bran."

My heart twisted. He hadn't deserved more betrayal from his family.

"That part I don't understand." I let my anger slip into my words. "Bran had made her successful."

"Successful in some ways, yes, but it was always his name on everyone's tongue. He was the one with the ultimate power. She wanted what he had only more." He lowered his voice as he asked, "Did you figure out what she was? I never did."

"She was a Grimple. More demon than human. Very nasty."

"I so agree." Frank shuddered, not that I blamed him.

"So possessing and selling the drug was going to set Dominique up in a different league than Bran," I mused aloud.

"While destroying him at the same time."

For that alone I could hate the woman. My tone didn't hide my disgust. "Nice lady."

"Not very." Frank's frown agreeing with mine. "But then 'nice' was never a word one associated with Dominique."

True. "So what happens now?" I asked. "To you?"

"Me? Why I go back to work. I do such a fabulous job."

I couldn't help the grin. The first one in days. My Franco was not gone all together.

"And you?" He asked, his brows angled. "What happens with you and Bran?"

"Nothing." The word sputtered out. "There is no Bran and me."

"Come, come, dahling, this is Franco here. There is no need to prevaricate with me."

"I'm not—"

"Of course you are." He moued his lips, which looked odd on him now. "This will never do. I owe Bran. You know he stepped in front of me when Dominique simply wanted to kill me. He earned a nasty blow for his efforts and Dominique's shot landed in my shoulder instead of somewhere more vital."

"I didn't know he'd interceded." The move sounded like something he'd do, heroic and foolish at the same time. "By the way, what happened then? Had she discovered who you were?"

"Sadly, yes. It seems Suzette forced Sasha to tell everything she knew before she was killed. Sasha didn't know anything about you and a little too much about me."

"So Dominique knew you were MI-6 since the yacht?"

"Yes, which was another reason Suzette placed the knife in my room, as an attempt to remove me from the scene. But when that didn't work, thanks to you, Dominique had to bide her time until she could eliminate me. But enough about me, we're discussing you and Bran."

Time to nip this in the bud. "Listen closely, Frank, as I'm only going to say this once. There is no Bran and me. End of story."

"That's not what he said."

That quick my emotions slammed to the fore. Which was ridiculous. The mission was over, the man was out of my life. He had his world, I had mine.

Franco leaned closer, his eyes gleaming. "I know for a fact he wondered where you went."

"Why?"

"Pshhh." It was a classic Franco sound. "Don't tell me you're afraid to talk with him?"

"Course, I'm not." I clamped both hands around my mug, glad it was sturdy stoneware and not porcelain. "There's nothing to say. Job's over."

"Job might be." He made to rise. "But the relationship isn't." Looking out the window as he added, "And since I owe not only Bran, but you, too, for saving my life, I've decided to help you."

"Help me what?"

He slid a piece of paper onto the tabletop.

I eyed it as I would a poisoned rattler. "What's that?"

"It's where Bran is now. His corporate offices are here in D.C."

Another thing I didn't know about Bran. I shifted clenched shoulders. "I told you—"

"You do not strike me as a woman who fears much. And yet you fear intimacy."

"You know nothing about me." I kept my voice low, hard as it was.

He leaned over the table, his eyes serious, more the seasoned agent than the Franco I'd known. "You're right, I don't know a lot about you, about your background, about what drives you, but there is one thing I do know."

He paused until I bit the bullet, strangled my coffee cup instead of him, and asked, "So *what* do you know?"

He whispered. "I know that even folks like us deserve a life." Then he straightened, adjusting the sleeves of his jacket just so. "Think about it. Bran's there now. Don't be afraid."

Afraid my hiney. Noziaks didn't do fear.

I so was not afraid.

Liar.

Okay, maybe I was, just a little, but not about intimacy.

Liar.

I'd had sex with the man, and more than that I'd shared magic with him; what was more intimate than that?

I didn't even wait for my answer as I slammed to my feet. I'd show Frank, and myself, that I wasn't afraid. I could at least talk to Bran. Say my official goodbyes, if that's what I chose to do. What was the harm in a final farewell?

Besides, if I didn't say goodbye in person, my team would never let me live it down.

Yup, I'd do this for the team.

But before I left I turned to Frank and asked, "Do you know anything about my brother Van? Dominique mentioned Paris."

"Sorry, kiddo. I've been out of the loop."

He must have noticed the slump to my shoulders as he leaned forward. "But if I do hear anything, I'll be in touch."

It was enough for now. I waved him away, catching the other women in the coffee shop checking him out as he walked away. Franco the stud-muffin. Who knew.

But there was another stud-muffin I needed to see. No time like the present.

CHAPTER 66

Vaverek feared no man, but the one who sat behind the Eames desk, so casual, so controlled, made the blood in him freeze.

"Is he still alive?" the cultured voice asked, his face in shadows though afternoon sun streamed through the window behind him. Parisian sun, unlike anything else on earth. Vaverek was a pragmatist more than anything and yet he still enjoyed the light of Montmartre.

But for how long?

"I asked—"

"I know what you asked." Vaverek stepped forward, aware of the sweat dampening upon his skin, aware the other could smell his fear, but knowing this one only respected arrogance. "I also know my job. He's alive."

For now.

"Good." The man picked up a letter opener. A very old, very sharp instrument but then the way Vaverek had heard it, this man could make an ice cube into a weapon.

Not an individual a smart person wanted to cross and Vaverek prided himself on his brains. More brains than most of his kind.

"If the shifter dies, you die," the other spoke again, voice husky and low.

"I am aware of this."

"Good. We don't want any mistakes."

Then they should have told him earlier not to be so rough. First they wanted only information, all of it, and the quicker the better. Then they changed their minds.

Vaverek cleared his throat, aware asking too many questions could be lethal, but being kept in the dark could be, too. "I can't promise how long—"

The hand holding the instrument stilled. "A few more days."

He nodded. "That I can do." He inhaled the first breath he'd taken since reaching this office with its view of the Eiffel Tower beyond the bank of windows. "But I can't promise much longer. Even shifters can die."

"As can we all." It wasn't the words but the tone that had Vaverek stepping back.

But the man wasn't looking at him, those ice eyes watching the opener slide through his fingers. It was as if Vaverek didn't exist.

Vaverek cleared his throat. "I'll be going then."

The other raised one manicured hand and waved him off. Only after Vaverek had left did he lift his landline and punch in the single digit number. He spoke before the other said hello. "Is she coming?"

The woman answered. "We expect confirmation at any moment."

"Alone?"

"No." A pause. "But we've taken that into account."

"I want her."

"Patience. A few more days, then she's yours."

"And the brother is yours."

"It's good to work with a professional." A click.

He returned the phone to its cradle. At last, the pieces were coming together. Alex Noziak would be his.

The next stage would begin.

CHAPTER 67

I found him at the address Franco had given me. Sexy, difficult, out-of-my-reach Bran. He was bent over a worktable, Collette at his side, gesturing over a set of drawings when I arrived and was shown into the house by a silent butler who asked no questions once I gave my name.

And now I was here and Bran was there, just across the room. I jammed my hands in my jean pockets as I cleared my throat and he glanced up. His gaze lasered in on mine as the room shrank in size. He looked tired, strain bracketing his eyes, his lips pressed in a flat line, even as he straightened and stilled.

"Alex."

The single word had my mouth going dry.

"Bran."

"Well." Collette cleared her throat and glanced between us. "Since I've become a third wheel, I'll take that as my clue to leave. Nice to see you, Alex."

She left in a flurry of motion. Not that I really noticed. Not while Bran continued to drill me with his gaze. Why didn't he say anything?

Damn him anyway.

"You disappeared."

At last he broke the impasse, though it sounded more like an accusation than a hello.

"My job was finished."

"It always comes down to that, doesn't it?" His tone was harsh, his gaze bleak. "A job?"

"Yes."

"Did you have to kill her?" How like a warlock, a jab to the jugular, no slow finesse.

I answered with the truth. "I don't know."

"Have it your way." He glanced away and shut me out.

But I hadn't come this far to get dismissed. I swallowed hard and stepped deeper into the room. Hearing my own fears. *Parasitic witch. Killer. Murderer.*

Well, phooey on all of the words. They weren't true.

"That's it then?" My voice sounded strained as I stepped toward him. "I saved your life. The least I deserve is a thank you."

He raised his eyes and narrowed them on mine like a hawk sighting a prize. "Is that what you came for? A thank you?"

"It's a start."

"And then what, Alex?" He straightened and threw the pencil he'd been gripping onto the table. "I say thanks. You say goodbye?"

I hadn't worked out all the details yet.

Before I could find the right words he leaned forward, splaying his hands on the table as if bracing himself for a fight.

"Listen," he said, eyes fierce, his voice low and intense. "It may have been a job for you, but it wasn't for me. Never." He glanced away as if battling his own demons. "They showed me a photo of you before you ever arrived and I ached."

That knocked all the wind out of me. "You did?"

He ignored my breathless response. "I told myself it was fear of losing my reputation—merde; I told myself a thousand different reasons and then you arrived."

I couldn't turn away. Not with the lump in my throat, the shaking in my hands.

"I work with women every day. Beautiful women. Accomplished women. Famous and infamous women. And yes, I've worked with my share of witches."

I bet buttons to bluebells he didn't work with many pig farmer's daughters. And if he was buttering me up he was doing a hell of a poor job of it.

He shook his head as if trying to understand his own jerky words. "And then you came into my life and changed everything."

That was better.

"I didn't want you around. Not as an agent." I could read the bleakness in his eyes. "Yet every time I dealt with you your job was thrown in my face. You were a witch. I was a warlock. I knew the lines and if I didn't you drew them between us."

"Not every time." I was drowning here. Out of my depth. Crud, give me something to fight.

His eyes darkened. "You wouldn't let me protect you. I fumbled around like a damn schoolboy at a loss at how to make you mine."

"Bran..." Words escaped me. Reason escaped me. This was not cool, controlled, aloof Bran. This was a man in torment. As I had been in torment. "I—"

"Don't." He raised a hand to stop my words. "Don't tell me again that what was between us is the job."

"You'll never forgive me." There, I inserted the truth into the conversation even as my heart splintered.

"You're right. I won't." Knife to heart.

"What do you want from me?" Stepping off a precipice, an emotional one, one I'd feared my whole life, I unclenched my shoulders and spoke around the huge lump in my throat. "Do you want us together?"

"I thought I did, at one time."

There, that was it, the death knell. Somewhere I found my voice and my backbone. "I'll be leaving then."

"Wait." His voice stopped me. That and the chill etching the word.

I straightened my spine. I wasn't going to be anybody's punching bag. He'd made his opinions of me clear. What was left? To make me bleed a little more? Not possible, the wounds of his words went deep. Not lethal but close. Damn close.

"What do you want?" I bit the words out. Witch speaking to arrogant warlock, the only barrier I could erect right then.

"I need your help." He sounded as happy saying the words as I was hearing them.

"To do what?"

"I can find Vaverek."

The second death knell. The man I wanted and needed to find Van. The carrot to dangle before the IR agency to get them on board with helping me. The sole clue to find out who or what the Seekers were.

In the hands of a man who made no bones over the fact he now hated me.

"That a guess or a certainty?" I asked, ignoring the increase in my heart rate, the sweating of my palms.

"A certainty." His Celtic blue eyes sliced me. Daring and taunting at the same time. "I know where he is."

"And what do you need my help for? You're a powerful warlock." I threw the gauntlet down.

"*Acies acendo adamo,*" he said, each word, slow, measured, and certain. That damn Latin portent he'd used before.

I shrugged, though my shoulders were so stiff they wanted to break. "Spell it out."

"The time of loss. When a powerful warlock and an even more powerful witch join forces, the time of change starts."

"Not clear enough." I wanted to be crystal clear about what I was getting into. I had no doubt I'd go along, it was my only chance to find Van, but like using magic, it was always better to go into a deal with the devil with my eyes open.

"I need your ability to combine powers with mine to find and crush Vaverek. He's also behind Dom's death and I won't stop until I make him pay."

First time I'd laid eyes on Bran I'd thought he'd be a ruthless man to have as an enemy. It seemed I was about to find out how ruthless.

"And what do I get out of this arrangement?" I asked, my throat dry.

"I won't kill you for your part in her death."

The End

FROM THE AUTHOR

Thank you for reading my books! I hope you enjoyed this novel and, if so, will post a review for me. ~Mary B

INVISIBLE RECRUIT URBAN FANTASY NOVELS COMING SOON FROM MARY BUCKHAM

Invisible Power: Book 2-Alex Noziak (May 2013)
Invisible Fate: Book 3-Alex Noziak (September 2013)

PLEASE ENJOY THE FOLLOWING
SNEAK PEEK FROM

INVISIBLE POWER
ALEX NOZIAK – BOOK TWO

CHAPTER 1

"Team report." I spoke the words calmly, coolly even, nothing like my insides felt jumping a mile a minute. The nerves were part anticipation, part terror.

The next minutes would change everything.

I'm Alex Noziak, a witch/shaman in the temporary employment of the IR Agency. I for invisible, R for recruit, and calling any of my five-member team employed was a load of crock. I was here as an alternative to prison. Long story boiled down to a year's agreement to be a member of a small, highly secret organization meant to combat a rising tide of preternatural agitation against humans. Fancy words for saying five of us stood against who knew how many species that, until lately, were mostly content to stay hidden from human eyes.

So here I was, in the exotic city of Paris, lounging in a doorway, a baby buggy in front of me, dressed like a down-on-her-luck Parisian mother.

Sounds charming, but it wasn't.

About two months ago someone or something was no longer happy with the status quo of humans being blithely unaware that were more than themselves populating the planet. Preternaturals had their reasons for flying under the radar, for many of them survival being the biggest reason. Humans tended to kill first and ask questions later when they dealt with anything they perceived as a threat, consider the poor cockroach. As if a bug was really going to do something to them. Non-humans fell squarely under the category of dead must be better.

But someone wanted to change all that and my job, along with my five teammates was to stop that.

Team leader Vaughn, who was sitting at a nearby café table, sipping espresso and looking more French than the locals was also fully human. She also was socialite, pampered money, and stunning looks; more than that though, she was willing to put her life on the line for a cause, protecting those who didn't know they needed protection.

Then there was Kelly, a former kindergarten teacher who was so nice I kept waiting for the catch. Her gift was the ability to turn invisible for short bursts of time. Drawback was she was still learning how to get a handle on not popping away when stressed or scared. Right now though she was playing tourist, complete with a crumpled map, a camera, and a vacuous expression on her face as she looked around the seedy neighborhood. She fit the role so well even I believed she was lost.

Jaylene Smart and Mandy Reyes, with a broken arm and cracked leg, were the two other team members, lounging against a far wall, looking like hookers trolling for johns among a few other women doing the same thing. Jaylene, tall, gorgeous and African American was a psychic, which meant she saw the future. Not always in technicolor or clearly, but that was the challenge with gifts, you had to take the bad with the good.

Mandy, a Latina, was a soulless spirit walker; someone who, like me, could pass over to the spirit world. Difference was I remained a shaman when I traveled between realms. She might as well have worn a neon sign that said corporeal-body-ready-to-be-inhabited to any spirit with chutzpah enough to try.

I figured the reason some spirit hadn't succeeded yet was only because they were wary of Mandy's abrasive personality. Smart spirits.

M.T. Stone was our team instructor and since we had yet to finish our training, was with us here for support. He was dressed as a Parisian workman in a one-piece paint-splattered coverall, poking at a chip in a stucco wall. He should have looked harmless, but there was nothing harmless about him.

One close look and most people's first reaction was to step back, those that hadn't already taken off running.

"Team, report," I repeated, getting antsy. I had the most at stake on this mission. Our primary goal was to catch a man named Vaverek and all we had was a faint description: broad shouldered, stocky, possibly blond, and supposedly living in the first floor, front right flat in the building across the street—a building that was so old that if Stone kept picking at it, it might crumble.

Vaverek was the man behind a dangerous synthetic drug used on people to get them to commit crimes without their knowledge. Four days ago we'd stopped two of the women involved in testing the drug on unsuspecting victims. We also managed to seize a sizeable amount of the drug, which should have been a high-five moment for the team, and for me.

The moment lasted a lot less than sixty seconds when a containment spell I'd cast backfired and killed our two chief suspects before they could give us any leads back to their power brokers, the individuals who financially had backed the scheme and who might still have enough of the drug to pose a threat, or worse, the actual formula.

But there was more. Vaverek was also our only link to the increasing agitation among the world's non-human population. We needed to know who Vaverek was working with and for as well as free the man Vaverek held hostage.

My brother.

CHAPTER 2

"You sure you got your intel straight?" Mandy snarled into her comm link. "These shoes are killing me."

Poor baby. Last mission I'd had to wear designer shoes on more than one occasion and while I could empathize and was glad I was wearing comfortable if butt-ugly footwear this time around, I didn't appreciate being second guessed. Especially by someone who sat most of the last mission out.

"Can it," I cut her off. "Intel's good."

Or I hoped like hell it was. Given the source was a man who threatened to kill me a few days ago, there was a definite degree of doubt riding me. The same man had been my lover the week before that. Oh, and did I mention the man's beloved cousin was one of the two women I killed?

It'd been a busy week.

"We'll move in five. Copy?" Stone's voice washed over the comm.

Finally. It wasn't his brother being held and tortured by Vaverek. On the other hand, standing around wasn't getting us any closer to our quarry. Time to kick this op into fast forward.

I straightened my shoulders, stretched to touch the Glock 9mm in a shoulder harness behind my nubby sweater, and prepared to walk across the cobbled street, march up the stairs I could see from where I stood, and confront Vaverek.

I'd figure out the rest of the plan at that point. Noziaks were more kick down doors and ask forgiveness afterwards.

A quick glance up and down the street revealed about a dozen civilians milling about, in the café with Vaughn, a few hookers around Jaylene and Mandy, even a nice looking couple using hand gestures to explain directions to Kelly.

If I crossed quickly, kept Vaverek contained in his own apartment, and Jaylene, Stone and Kelly managed the street, a frontal assault could contain Vaverek.

I was about to step forward when a hand on my shoulder stopped me.

No Frenchman would be so bold, no team member was close enough, and no bad guy would use this kind of approach. That left one person. Bran. Warlock, former lover, current nemesis.

I snarled as I glanced at him over my shoulder. "You weren't supposed to be here."

"I have as much at stake as you do."

I understood he was still grieving his cousin Dominique's death, even if she was a sadistic, psycho-killer, and that he blamed Vaverek for involving Dominique in the high-stake world of designer drugs and death. But that didn't give him a right to insert himself into this op.

I kept turned toward Vaverek's apartment building. Never lose sight of the primary target, even if it meant having the biggest known threat at my back. "If you kill Vaverek," I said between clenched teeth. "I lose my only lead to my brother."

"If I get a shot I'm taking it." I was ready to pull my Glock on Bran, until he added. "But I won't kill him before I get from him what I want. Vaverek is the head of an organization, but they're not working alone. I want to know who Vaverek reports to before I kill him."

Finally, we could agree on something.

"Then stay put. I'm going in," I said, not loud enough anyone else could hear me, but loud enough to let Bran know I meant business.

I expected him to release his hold. Instead he gripped tighter.

"You have no idea what you're about to unleash here."

Bran was a warlock with an overprotective streak a mile wide. It was that need to protect that had him shielding his cousin far too long, and trying to keep me from harm, even though he knew what my job was and that I was perfectly capable of protecting myself.

I glanced at him over my shoulder. Tall, dark, and dangerous basically summed him up as I ignored the flip flop of my insides just looking at the man. Focus on the job at hand.

"What the hell are you talking about?" I asked. "You're the one who indicated the target is inside that building."

His fingers bit so hard into my shoulder I was going to have bruises. "Stop looking with your eyes, witch. Look around you."

I had. I was.

"Close your eyes and look within your inner sense."

My inner sense told me he was playing his own deadly game, but he was also a powerful warlock, strong enough to pull people back from the dead, and he had a lot more experience than I did in using magic.

I'd give him a minute. That was it.

So I closed my eyes, aware of my pounding pulse, the kiss of a breeze picking up bringing the scent of fresh baked beignets, the peal of bells echoing through stone and stucco streets.

"There's nothing—"

And that's when it hit. The wash of otherness seeping through my awareness. Several Weres, strong enough to hide their scent. At least one vamp, maybe two. I couldn't quite identify the others, not from this far away. Fae, maybe. A demon, and something else.

Too many of them for this to be a coincidence. They were waiting for us.

My eyes snapped open. Why hadn't I sensed them until now? I glanced at my silver ring, specially crafted to alert me to non-humans. Nothing. No heat, no humming, nothing.

But they were there. Infiltrating the street. Surrounding my teammates.

"Abort. Abort," I spoke into my comm set. "Get the hell out of here. Now!"

But it was too late.

THE END

Invisible Power – May, 2013 –

www.MaryBuckham.com
www.InvisibleRecruits.com

About the Author

Award-winning author **Mary Buckham** credits her years of international travel and curiosity about different cultures that resulted in creating high-concept urban fantasy and romantic suspense stories. Her newest Invisible Recruit series has been touted for the unique voice, high action and rich emotion. A prolific writer, Mary also co-authors the young adult sci-fi/fantasy Red Moon series with NYT bestseller Dianna Love. Mary lives in Washington State with her husband and, when not crafting a new adventure, she travels the country researching settings and teaching other writers. Don't miss her latest reference book Writing Active Setting.

Please visit www.MaryBuckham.com for more information.